MICHELLE M. PILLOW

Maiden
AND THE
Monster

ELLORA'S CAVE
ROMANTICA PUBLISHING

What the critics are saying...

ℜ

THE 2006 RT REVIEWER CHOICE AWARD

Top Pick! 4 1/2 Stars! "This is a perfect blend of history, emotion, tension, hot sex and fascinating and sympathetic characters, and the writing is superb." ~ *RT Bookclub Magazine*

Recommended Read! 5 Stars! "Maiden and the Monster is one of the best medieval romances I have ever read...a keeper for me, and I predict it will be for many, many other readers as well." ~ *Fallen Angel Reviews*

4 1/2 Angels! "Michelle Pillow takes her readers on a journey back to Saxon times and delivers. You can just close your eyes and see everything before you." ~ *Fallen Angel Reviews*

4 1/2 Stars! "...This book is a classic love story. It is the kind of story a reader enjoys getting lost in." ~ *Ecataromance Reviews*

"I was so entranced by Maiden and the Monster I couldn't put it down. It's intense, and full of emotion ... powerful and moving...a keeper!" ~ *Joyfully Reviewed*

An Ellora's Cave Romantica Publication

www.ellorascave.com

Maiden and the Monster

ISBN 9781419955242
ALL RIGHTS RESERVED.
Maiden and the Monster Copyright © 2005 Michelle M. Pillow
Edited by Briana St. James
Cover art by Syneca

Electronic book Publication November 2005
Trade paperback Publication April 2007

Content Advisory:

S – ENSUOUS
E – ROTIC
X – TREME

Ellora's Cave Publishing offers three levels of Romantica™ reading entertainment: S (S-ensuous), E (E-rotic), and X (X-treme).

The following material contains graphic sexual content meant for mature readers. This story has been rated S-ensuous.

S-*ensuous* love scenes are explicit and leave nothing to the imagination.

E-*rotic* love scenes are explicit, leave nothing to the imagination, and are high in volume per the overall word count. E-rated titles might contain material that some readers find objectionable — in other words, almost anything goes, sexually. E-rated titles are the most graphic titles we carry in terms of both sexual language and descriptiveness in these works of literature.

X-*treme* titles differ from E-rated titles only in plot premise and storyline execution. Stories designated with the letter X tend to contain difficult or controversial subject matter not for the faint of heart.

Also by Michelle Pillow

ଔ

Call of the Sea
Call of the Untamed
Scorched Destiny
Taming Him

By Michelle M. Pillow & Mandy M. Roth

ଔ

Pleasure Cruise
Red Light Specialists
Stop Dragon My Heart Around

About the Author

৪১

Michelle M Pillow has always had an active imagination. Ever since she can remember, she's had a strange fascination with anything supernatural—ghosts, magical powers, and oh…vampires. What could be more alluring than being immortal, all-powerful, and eternally beautiful? After discovering historical romance novels in high school, it was only natural that the supernatural and romance elements should someday meet in her wonderland of a brain. She's glad they did, for their children have been pouring onto the computer screen ever since.

She is married (madly in love) and has a wonderful family.

Michelle would love to hear from you and tries to answer her emails in a timely fashion. That is if the current hero will let her go long enough to check the computer.

Michelle welcomes comments from readers. You can find her websites and email addresses on their author bio page at www.ellorascave.com.

Tell Us What You Think

We appreciate hearing reader opinions about our books. You can email us at Comments@EllorasCave.com

MAIDEN AND THE MONSTER

ॐ

Author Note

In 878, King Guthrum and his vast nation of pagan Vikings (also known as Norsemen or Danes) had rule over half of Briton. Though initially they came to the shores to raid and pillage, they eventually settled in their newly conquered land. A powerful race, the Vikings were said to be nigh unstoppable. And before the Christian King Alfred of Wessex, known as Alfred the Great, they had gone relatively unopposed.

During this time, the Danish king was at war with King Alfred, which culminated at Wiltshire in what is known as the Battle of Edington. This was the last significant battle between the two kingdoms and Alfred won. Now the tides of power were turning. Guthrum and his Vikings were on the losing side.

After experiencing decisive losses, the Danish king signed the Treaty of Wedmore. The treaty allowed Guthrum to leave with the provision that he never return. Furthermore, the land was divided in two parts — Wessex and what later became known as the Danelaw (Northumbria, East Anglia and Essex).

In accordance with the treaty's demands, King Guthrum had to leave several men from his army in Wessex. These soldiers resided as political hostages — an insurance of peace between the two kingdoms. If Guthrum broke his promise never to return, the hostages would be killed. As part of the treaty, the pagan men were also made to convert to Christianity.

Often noblemen and knights held as prisoners were given leave to move freely, held only by their word of honor. It is in this rocky political climate that our hero finds himself — a prisoner of a foreign king, surrounded by the very people he'd been at war against.

Though the events surrounding the story are fact, the characters, titles of nobility, circumstances and the story itself are a complete work of fiction. The intent is not to be wrapped up in historical detail, but in the characters themselves.

Happy Reading!

Michelle

Chapter One
Lakeshire Castle, Wessex, 879 AD

∞

"*God's bones*, Ulric! Methinks this land of Wessex is making you soft!"

Vladamir of Kessen, the Duke of Lakeshire's, voice was hard due to his exasperation. He knew his tone had a gravelly quality, which reflected a Baltic culture far to the northeast of the Saxon manor of Lakeshire. The heritage gave his softened words a hard bite as the harsh press of his lips gave his features an merciless appearance. Vladamir did it on purpose.

"'Tis irrational, foolish old man, for you to insist I stand downwind of that rotting pile of animal carcasses for nary an instant more. I don't know why you thought I'd be interested!"

His accent frightened the people under his rule. In fact, everything about him scared these people. He wanted the Saxons afraid of him. If they were afraid, they would follow his orders and leave him alone. He'd been in Wessex for a year and the plan had worked so far. It wasn't like he'd been sent to make friends.

Vladamir was the very first Duke of Lakeshire. It was a position he didn't relish. If he had his say, he'd live out his miserable days—alone in a castle far away from everyone and everything. Either that or he'd gladly ride into another war.

Frowning sternly, he narrowed his eyes in annoyance and made no move to leave for his training exercises, though his fingers itched to grip his sword. Instead, he swept the fur lining of his cloak off his shoulder. The breeze lifted the weight of his unfashionably long, straight black hair off his shoulders and he absently watched the strands trailing away from him. He purposely wore the heathenish attire of those who lived in the Danelaw rather than to adapt to the more "civilized" dress of the nation of Wessex. He did it to irritate the Christian sensibilities of his Saxon neighbors and to drive fear into those men who were made to unwillingly serve under his rule.

Yea, everything about me is different than this accursed land. I'm a man without a country. I hate Wessex and I hate the land of my father. And I hate the peace between them both.

Tense, Vladamir raised his arm, motioning to the guard who stood above him on the dark stone of the bailey wall. A black onyx ring glinted on his finger, shining like a beacon the guard would be able to see. With a deft flick of his wrist, the duke silently commanded the knight to raise the outer gate.

The young, fair-haired Saxon didn't hesitate to follow his barbaric lord's order. Like all his subjects, Vladamir knew the guard watched him intensely for any sign of movement, no matter how small. It wasn't out of respect for him that the man instantly obeyed. It was out of fear. Fear was the reason all the Saxon warriors residing at Lakeshire Castle followed his command. They'd all heard the sinister rumors that followed him from his homeland and he'd never tried to earn their respect or change their opinion of him.

Angrily, he jerked his arm, letting his irritation show. Vladamir knew what he was, knew what he looked like and it was his intent to appear monstrous in both mannerisms and appearance. His linen undertunic was dyed to the pitchest of blacks. Although the material was of obviously rich quality, it lacked the perfected embellishments that frivolous nobles prided themselves on.

The sleeves of his tunic hung over his wrists and settled over the backs of his hands in long rolls. The undertunic fell loose over his tightly fitted black braes, the long slit down the side showing a hint of his thighs. He fastened the material of the braes into place with laces that joined at the side and wore a plain, thick leather belt over them. From this belt hung an imposingly sharp knife and a modest leather pouch, which contained small pieces of flint for starting a fire and an iron key that fit a door the servants didn't even know existed.

"Clear it away at once! Methinks you have interrupted my morning training for naught more than fetid garbage!" The duke ordered Ulric, only to growl in anger when the gate didn't rise fast enough to suit his impatience. He rested his hand on the hilt of his sword in warning. The action wasn't missed. Another knight disappeared off the wall, obviously going to hurry the man lifting the gate. Vladamir relished his ill humor, wallowing in it. "*Argh!*"

He sighed as the gate finally squeaked on its iron hinges, making the slow trip up. Gripping his sword, his scowl deepened. Instead of watching the gate, he stared at the hilt. The monstrous broadsword at his waist was in a leather scabbard, hanging from a leather shoulder baldric. The strap crossed over his chest so he could easily draw the weapon at the slightest provocation.

Still irritated, he glanced back at Ulric as the man tried to get a good view of the rotting animals through the gate's crosshatching. The servant turned to the duke, eyeing the nobleman's attire. Vladamir glanced down at his clothes, again thinking of how different he was from the Saxon men.

Over his tunic he wore a woven cloth belt of black and silver. It wrapped about his waist and knotted on the front right. He left the unadorned ends to drape freely about his thighs. The undertunic's oval neckline was laced high and tight against his thick neck, hiding the entirety of his chest from view. It was only on the rarest of political occasions that Vladamir was obligated to don an overtunic. He didn't feel the need of such formalities in his life when it came to dress. But, on those rare occasions, the overtunic was also black with very little silver embroidery.

The only relief to the investigating eye that Vladamir allowed was the lighter colored *rocc*, his fur cloak that was constructed of the skinned hide of several gray wolves. He would've dyed the fur black as well, if not for the ample waste of time and resources the project would consume. He wore the fur side inward for warmth as was customary among his fellow pagans.

"By all that is hallowed!" Vladamir growled, not caring who heard his cry. Many of the servants milling about the yard skidded to a stop at the sound. A small smile of devious pleasure automatically curled the sides of his mouth. It took a few seconds, but soon the servants were hurrying away in relief when they realized they weren't the cause of his present anger.

It was a well-known and accepted fact to the people of Lakeshire Castle that Vladamir had converted to Christianity solely to please King Alfred of Wessex in accordance with the Treaty of Wedmore. The duke did nothing to dissuade their beliefs or make them think that he was sincere in his conversion. Let them believe he was a devilish monster sent by King Guthrum to torment them.

In truth, Vladamir didn't much care for the Christian God, nor had he cared for the many gods of his ancestors. He lost faith when his wife died six years before. As he thought of it, it was quite possible he'd lost his faith before then.

Lowering his chin to glower down from his towering height, he curled his nose in disgust as another gust of wind assaulted him. The air carried a stench so severe that even with his war-hardened training Vladamir couldn't ignore the putrid smell. His slight smile turned quickly into a snarl. For all his rough appearance Vladamir was a clean person, having been influenced by the peculiar bathing rituals of his father's people, the Vikings. He even insisted his household followed suit and bathed at least twice a sennight. It was a completely pagan routine little heard of in the dwellings of the Saxons. He'd received some protest over the decree, but it was necessary to keep such smells as these rotted animals out of his home.

He wrinkled his forehead in irritation and tried unsuccessfully to determine what exactly emitted the foul odor. "What is it, Ulric? It smells of decaying flesh. Who would dare to lay carcasses afore my gate to rot?"

"Mayhap, 'tis a sacrifice in honor of the castle," Ulric offered with a grave shake of his head. The manservant's expression said he highly doubted it.

Ulric had traveled with the duke to Wessex the year before. A short man with a balding head, he had a pleasing face hidden under his trim beard. His jaunty nature was a direct contrast to that of his dark, forbidding lord—just as his rounded frame was opposite Vladamir's sinewy one. He wasn't only the duke's seneschal, but was also the closest thing Vladamir could call friend.

"Nay, 'tis not the season for sacrifice," Vladamir answered as he looked up to the changing sky. It was early morning, yet the sky darkened to purple. He pulled the broadsword from his waist in one smooth motion and flexed the muscles of his sword arm in distraction, scuffing the tip across the dirt in a lazy stroke. Smirking, he said, "Besides, the prelate has forbidden such practices. 'Tis too barbaric a custom according to the church."

He sighed, fisting his hands as he pressed his lips tightly together. Upon closer examination, he discovered that the rotting bundle was actually an oddly shaped mound of pelts. Resting his fingers firmly upon his hips, he was mindful of the tip of the broadsword that still rested on the ground.

The stronghold's gate stopped above him, but he didn't bother to move. The gate was constructed of thick English oak and bound together with iron strips. The pointed ends at the bottom of the gate were wood reinforced with iron, causing them to act like metal teeth if lowered too quickly. Eyeing the spikes, he morbidly though of how effectively they could sever a man in two.

Ulric rushed forward to the pile as soon as the spikes were out of his way. The seneschal's wider frame lumbered with the effort it took him to kneel and he grunted under the strain. Swiping the sleeve of his brown tunic across his forehead, Ulric placed his arm before his nose as he leaned closer to the pelts.

Impatient, Vladamir watched Ulric pick through the skins. He followed silently behind, refusing to sheath his sword. The seneschal sat straight up in surprise.

"M'lord, it would appear to be a maiden amongst these pelts. Methinks I see the entrails of a rabbit in her hair," Ulric yelled through the sleeve of his tunic.

The servant again wiped his sleeve across his brow before returning it to his nose. His small brown eyes shone with concern. With a grumble of disdain, Ulric lifted entrails from the maiden's hair and flung them aside, only to gingerly remove a rabbit carcass the same way to reveal the bloodied lines of her swollen face. It was impossible to see whether she breathed.

In the distance, the sounds of fighting men and clashing swords filled the air as the practicing knights competed in mock battle. A flock of wild birds flew high above to seek shelter from the changing sky. Their song softly drifted downward. None of the sounds pleased the duke as his eyes stayed trained on Ulric.

"A maiden? Out here? And scented with festering carcasses?" Vladamir searched the forest that surrounded his castle. The hum of insects was quite clear on the morning air and he noticed that the red bristled pigs grazing just beyond his walls were undisturbed. Nor could he detect movement within the barren limbs of the trees. Finally satisfied that the girl was alone, he turned his attention back to Ulric. He refused to show any interest in the maiden.

"Wake her and send her on her way." He kept his voice passionless and made no effort to help the woman. "If she is dead burn her, for I won't tolerate that wretched smell in my bailey."

"Should we not try to find out who she is first? Mayhap there are those who search fer her even now. Would you deny her kinsmen a proper burial?" Ulric protested quietly.

"Do as I command!" Vladamir insisted in a low growl. Even as he did so, he saw the knights that manned the wall looked over the girl with curious stares. He heard their whispering as it drifted down, though he couldn't make out their hasty words. He didn't need to. The woman was more than likely a Saxon wench and they would wish to know whom, for none in the manor were missing. If she was dead, there was nothing he could do for her. He didn't need this headache. His life was stressed enough.

Through his irritation, Vladamir saw hesitation on the older man's face and quieted his tone to a logical murmur. "Is she dead?"

"I know not, m'lord." Ulric leaned to touch the girl and then turned back to his lordship. "She is not responding."

Vladamir tried to control his exasperation and repeated his original command, intentionally raising his voice to quiet the knights on the wall. His harsh accent made his words all the more lethal as he ground out, "Then she is dead. Burn her. I won't have her corpse carrying disease to the manor."

Ulric looked to him, searching the duke's face for a sign of compassion. Vladamir didn't give him one, refusing to be stirred to pity. It was easier to be feared than loved. It was easier to be dead inside than to feel.

Sighing heavily, the servant crouched over the girl. The duke stepped to the side, getting a better look at her. She was young and it was clear she'd been beaten. Her clothes were torn and her hair was matted with dirt and possibly blood.

Ulric yelled over his shoulder, loud enough to make sure the watching knights also heard his reply, "Nay, methinks she takes breath. She is not dead, merely insensible."

The duke frowned, knowing the servant hoped he wouldn't dare to leave a Saxon girl for dead, especially with so many soldiers to bear witness. If it had been a decade earlier, Vladamir would've carried the injured maiden into the castle to care for her. He'd have tended to her wounds, oversaw the physicians, stayed by her side until she was better. But the time was now and the duke would never allow himself to care like that again. Life had taught him some hard lessons.

Rubbing his brow, he then ran his fingers through the long locks of his tangled hair to brush it from his eyes. He shifted his weight from one leg to the other and didn't answer the servant. Scowling, he willed the maiden to disappear. He didn't want her in his home.

"Would you like me to leave her afore yer gate to rot? Or would you like to bring her in?" Ulric stood up and boldly matched his lord's stare, his thick jowls quivering in irritation.

Vladamir didn't like his servant's impudent tone and the man's sarcasm didn't go unobserved. He gritted his teeth as he asked with a sullen glimmer of hope, "Is she near death?"

"I know not." The servant once again turned from his overlord back to the pitiful girl. Thunder stuck in the horizon, beating its violent rhythm across the purple sky. The man pulled another carcass from her and tossed it aside.

"Check her." Vladamir purposefully sounded bored as he sheathed his sword. Anger was the easiest of all emotions and he clung to it. His gut tightened and he raised his eyes briefly to the heavens as a droplet of rain fell across his nose. "Be quick, Ulric."

Ulric felt the girl's pulse. "She has a good chance to recover if we move her indoors now."

Suspecting that the man might be lying, the duke paced in a frustrated circle, his hands fitted firmly at his waist. He rolled his neck until it cracked, debating the fate of the girl.

Those who moved about the bailey made their way toward shelter. A small page ran close to Vladamir, a pack of mongrel dogs quick on his heels. The boy laughed as a particularly ugly gray dog tripped him about the legs and sent him sprawling to the ground at the duke's feet. The page's face became wrought with fear as he looked up from the ground. The duke growled at him and the boy scurried away from him as the rain fell harder, hammering the ground with its loud music.

"It would appear she has been badly beaten," Ulric said. "Methinks it would be wise to move her inside, out of the rain, lest she is not like to live through the night. I can have a chamber readied for her abovestairs if you wish."

No matter how badly he wanted to give the order to leave her outside, Vladamir couldn't do it. He silently cursed himself for a fool and gave a self-depreciating laugh.

So much for being a complete monster.

"Yea," Vladamir conceded reluctantly. He stopped his pacing and turned to go, intent on leaving Ulric to tend to the woman.

"M'lord, wait," Ulric's urgent voice stopped him.

"Yea?" Vladamir gripped the hilt of his sword.

"M'lord, it would seem the maiden is a lady."

* * * * *

"Who is she, Ulric? Why has she come? Methinks 'tis a bad omen." Vladamir paced over a quarter length of his main hall only to turn about and walk back in agitation. He always paced when he was unnerved. His arms held strong to his sides and he moved with circular purpose, his feet not stopping in any one place.

Who would leave a lady afore my door to die? Who would dare to conspire against me?

Narrowing his eyes into slits, the duke impatiently brushed back his hair only to slash his hand through the air, striking his palm with a hard crack.

"M'lord doesn't believe in omens," Ulric said logically. The duke growled. Only after Vladamir had finished his small tirade, did the man continue, "So, 'tis impossible fer her to be a bad one."

Vladamir grumbled in response and continued to pace. His feet crushed the matted rushes into the stone floor and he touched the knife at his waist.

"I had Haldana look to her ladyship. It would appear she was badly beaten and may take many days fer the wounds to heal. But Haldana is most hopeful in the recovery." Ulric's bemused statement wasn't the one the duke sought. Sardonically, the man added, "With yer present generosity, m'lord, she should mend quite well."

Ladyship? This woman is no more a noble than you are, Ulric.

Vladamir turned to glare at the impudent man. Sliding the knife swiftly from his belt, he flung it through the air, embedding the blade into a small knot of wood in a nearby table.

Ulric looked unimpressed as he reached for the weapon. With a jerk, he pulled it from the wood and handed it back to his lordship. Vladamir took it without comment and sheathed it at his waist. If he hadn't been in his service for so long, the duke might have considered turning Ulric out of the castle. But, instead, he tolerated the man's careless smirk and paced once more.

"It would also appear that m'lady has either fallen or has been carted in dung. Methinks it would be wise to question the peasants who work with the pigs," Ulric advised. "I instructed that her ladyship should be bathed at once and a new garment sewn fer her."

"Nay, don't waste time sewing for the intruder. Only mend the clothes she has brought with her," Vladamir commanded with another aggravated slash of the hand.

The duke thought of the odorous cloak she wore. As she was carted inside, he could tell the fine cut of the garment, though it was matted. He hadn't wanted to get too close to her and so had refrained from intimate inspection—for not only had she fallen in pig dung, but she'd been covered with the rotted carcasses of gutted rabbits. The rabbits were set ablaze as soon as she was free of them. He imagined that he still detected her awful smell in the keep from when the knights carried her abovestairs.

His voice was abnormally loud in the empty hall and he turned to glare at the servant. "'Tis not my place, nor my desire, to care for her. As soon as she awakens, I want her gone. She has already outstayed her welcome!"

"M'lord." Ulric nodded, not liking the decision to turn the maiden out, but he wisely refused to press the issue.

The servant was unimpressed by the great show of fury coming from the duke. He was well used to the nobleman's moods by now. None who saw the nobleman would know he was unsettled as he paced the floor, for Vladamir appeared to be and was accepted as, a ranting monster. But Ulric knew better. The nobleman might appear to be brooding in his ruthlessness, but really he was just scared of anything disrupting his angry world.

"*Argh!*" the duke yelled in anger.

Just then, Ulric noticed one of the Saxon maids entered the hall carrying a tray laden with goblets. Lizbeth was a beautiful child and so full of life, though she was very demure in her carriage. Her willowy frame swayed and she halted to a nervous stop. She diverted her round eyes from the tempest of straw and dust that his lordship kicked up from the floor in his frenzy. Taking a hurried step back, she disappeared into the kitchen clearly unaware that Ulric seen her hastened retreat.

Ulric shook his head in pity, hating the way the people of Lakeshire feared the duke. Most of the time, the servants tiptoed around him, endeavoring to accomplish their duties when he wasn't present. Like Lizbeth, trying to set the high table for the morning meal while the duke was supposed to be out of the castle.

Ulric knew all the whispers, knew that Vladamir earned those whispers because he had an exalted temperament. Just as he realized that if the duke would stop in his self-pity, he would grow to be an even greater leader. Ulric had become used to his overlord's ways in his many years of loyal service. Just as Vladamir was now feared, Ulric also knew that it hadn't always been so. There had been a time when the duke had been quite charming in his ways, but those times were gone forever, and in the charming man's wake was a self-proclaimed monster.

Ulric shook his head, drawing his eyes away from where the maid retreated into the shadowed kitchen. He returned his attention to the discussion at hand.

"Who is she?" the duke demanded. "Do you not recognize the crest on her cloak?"

Ulric was happy Lord Kessen conceded to letting the woman stay long enough to recover, knowing he could deal with Vladamir's desire to banish her from the castle when the time arrived. Instead, he was more alarmed that the duke acted so merciless in public view, though none were there to witness the tirade. Seeing his lordship desired an answer, Ulric sighed.

"I know not, m'lord. The crest has been torn from her cloak. I cannot see what family she is from." Hiding the mischievous glint in his expression, the servant added, "It would appear m'lady is quite beautiful."

"With welts on her bloodied face?" Vladamir asked, his brow rising to a severe arch, before he waved a dismissing hand. Then, stopping in his restless pacing, the duke took several steps forward so he could face the manservant. "I care not what the lady looks like. I would that she was dead so I could burn her and the offending smell she brings with her."

"M'lord." Ulric nodded again in understanding. He easily dismissed the scathing look directed him and concealed his smile.

"Mayhap her garments are torn because she is a thief. She stole the cloak from a noblewoman she did to death. Ealdorman Baudoin, the incompetent goat, will no doubt commission the Witan and blame us for giving her aid. No doubt Alfred's fyrd will hang us next to her in the gallows." Vladamir's look scathed in its intensity as he narrowed his eyes, appearing to contemplate his actions. "I have changed my mind, take her to the countryside and leave her. We have done our best by her."

"That would be murder. She couldn't survive unattended in the country," Ulric protested in the reasonable tone he knew aggravated his lord. He wouldn't be bullied to anger or driven into fear and had no intention of following the cruel decree given him.

"Very well," Vladamir conceded with an aggravated sound of contempt. He gave Ulric a vicious growl, his mouth curled in a mischievous grimace. "Give her food and water. Then take her to the country and drop her off at some cotter's hut. Let someone else take care of her. I won't have a murderous thief in this keep. I have no wish to be involved!"

"Have you thought that, perchance, m'lady is the victimized noblewoman? Would you have her point the king's gauntlet at you fer not helping her? Would you dare to bring the wrath of Alfred on our heads? And fer what? The paltry cost of a little meat and ale? The insignificant time it takes Haldana to look in on her? 'Tis not as if you need to be bothered with her care. You have no need of even seeing her." Ulric smiled as he saw he had his lord's attention. He scratched his balding head before turning an audacious look to the taller man. "Mayhap, m'lady is innocent."

The comment received the wrathful snarl Ulric expected. He flinched at the pain that flickered over the duke's face. However, the emotion was so brief that Ulric wondered if he'd witnessed it at all. Over the years, Vladamir's emotions had shown less and less, until the servant was left with only an impression of the deeply seated pain he knew to reside within the duke.

"No woman is innocent, especially not one of noble breeding. 'Tis not in their devious natures. Methinks the treachery they are capable of must far surpass that of a man," Vladamir stated. His eyes appeared to turn a supernatural black in his rage and his voice crackled in its low tonality. As his chest heaved, he continued under his breath, "If she is not guilty of murder she is guilty of something. All women are. Mayhap, 'tis why she was banished to die."

"Perchance this one is innocent," Ulric persisted, softening his tone. "Besides, would you dare to anger King Alfred while we are living in his land on his good graces? You should at least find out who she is afore you sentence her to death. Mayhap the king will reward you fer yer chivalrous deeds."

"More reward than this?" Vladamir snorted as he lifted his hand to encompass the main hall of Lakeshire Castle. He swept his fingers past the line of his vision to move over the dusty black stone of the wall and the dirty straw rushes of the floor. The hall was undusted and unkempt, just like Vladamir ordered it to remain. "Methinks I don't wish for more reward from the king. The empty title and foreign land, 'tis enough while I reside peaceably in Wessex and await the war that is sure to come."

Ulric gave a wry laugh and tried to hide his disappointment in the duke's attitude, but the man's disposition was getting harder and harder to put up with. "These times of rest cannot last forever. The killing will soon start again. And then, perchance, you can find yer own peace as you bloody yer sword with the Anglo-Saxons' fluids. Never mind that you have lived amongst them fer a year."

"Yea, soon we will be fighting our way back to the border or dying in the try." Vladamir smiled at the prospect. Ulric grimaced. The duke didn't notice. "Though, I don't care much for going back. What says you? Shall we head south instead and join the Franks or even the Moors? Do you think Guthrum will notice if we were to leave tonight?"

"Yea, if his peace treaty is broken because King Alfred's most prestigious hostage disappears, methinks he might take note." Ulric shook his head in denial. "I won't be the cause of war."

"Yea, but I must be the peace of it," Vladamir grumbled in anger. The duke had said on many occasions that anything would be better then wasting away in a place he had no liking for. Pointing his finger at Ulric, Vladamir asked, "Do you think it would matter if one of the other hostages disappeared? Methinks the kings wouldn't even take notice. By hell's fire, the others are probably returned home as we speak."

"'Tis no one's fault but yer own that you're here. You asked to be sent as a prisoner. 'Tis a prison of yer own making." Ulric had little sympathy as he reminded the duke of their situation. Vladamir flung his hand with a sound of annoyance. Unlike Ulric and some of the others who felt they had no choice but to come to the foreign land, Vladamir had been given an option. Albeit, a narrow one. "You made yer deal with the king, now 'tis you who must live with it and the responsibility it bears. And if that responsibility means you're to reside here in peace, then 'tis what you'll do."

"*Argh!*" Vladamir fumed with an unearthly growl as he again pointed a long fingernail in the manservant's direction. His eyes darkened and shot out with a vaporous light. Snarling, the duke's face contorted into that of a great beast. For a long moment he didn't move from his pose. Then, whipping his finger back toward his chest, he said, "Fine! She can stay. But you mind after her care and alert me as soon as she awakens or when she is dead. I don't wish to be bothered with her afore that time."

"Yea, m'lord." Ulric hid his smile by scratching his whiskered chin. He took a deep breath, pleased with the small victory.

"And clean her up! I won't have her filling the manor with her stench." Vladamir's voice crackled through the air as he glared at the stairwell.

"Yea, m'lord as you wish." Ulric bowed, wiping his sleeve over his forehead.

"Nay, if 'twas as I wished it, she wouldn't be here at all." Vladamir stormed from the room, only to bark over his shoulder, "I go back to my exercise!"

"But, m'lord, the storm!" Ulric called after him. It was too late. A blanket of rain emerged behind the duke as he passed through the open doorway. Within a blink, Vladamir disappeared into the thundering morning air.

Ulric's smile didn't fade as he turned to the stairwell. His steps were light as he made his way up the narrow stairs to the maiden's chamber. The ring of keys on his belt clanked a merry tune with each bounce. It had been a long time since he'd seen Vladamir unsettled and the old seneschal knew that the duke was well overdue.

* * * * *

"So m'lord is letting the poor child stay?" Haldana asked when Ulric came to the dingy chamber to check on their guest. Graying red hair sprouted about her head in short curls that bounced with her every vigorous movement. "Can we move her from this chamber to a more suitable bed?"

"Yea, Haldana, she can stay." Ulric smiled sadly, ignoring her last question as he leaned to give the woman a brief, affectionate kiss on the cheek. Going to the narrow window slit in the wall, he watched as lightning illuminated the sky. Ulric saw the duke's silhouette clearly. Vladamir slashed his sword through the air as the rain assaulted his clothes. The nobleman viciously fought against an imaginary creature in exercise. With a wry shake of his head, Ulric knew it to be more like a demon from the past that his lordship sparred with. Sadly, he knew in the end the demon would win. "I told you he would let her."

"Nay, I'd almost bet you convinced him. Did he command you first to drop her off in the forest?" Haldana sighed almost wistfully and laid her hand over the kiss she'd received on her plump cheek.

Haldana was a big woman, but she carried her excess weight with such energetic grace that she appeared much smaller. Her limbs were in a constant state of movement—tidying a bit here, straightening a bit there. However, she never seemed to get much cleaning done and her days were filled with a whole lot of little nothings.

"Nay," Ulric laughed, shaking his head at her astuteness.

"Really?" Haldana asked in surprise, taking her hand from her cheek only to wring her hands in her apron. She followed Ulric's gaze to her patient.

"'Tis the countryside, he said," Ulric remarked dryly.

"I knew 'twas something." Haldana shook with a gentle laugh. Her body fidgeted as she moved to tuck the blankets around her motionless charge. "What else did he say? To leave the poor dear naked?"

"Nay, he wishes fer her gown to be mended. He doesn't want to provide fer her any more than he has too." Ulric breathed heavily as he moved forward. "And I didn't dare ask to move her, fer 'twas hard enough to get him to accept her presence here. Methinks he only agreed as not to anger King Alfred and upset the treaty. He claims that he doesn't care fer peace, but methinks 'tis a lie, a lie to himself. Fer as a boy he couldn't stand the fighting that tore through the land. 'Tis why he worked so hard fer peace while under King Guthrum's service."

Haldana nodded sadly.

"But when his lady wife would let no peace reside in his home, he stopped trying and went to war. We must have faith that Lady Lurlina didn't drive all compassion from him.

Methinks I catch a glimpse of his old self every now and then."
Ulric turned to the maiden, shaking his head in pity as he
moved from the window. The girl didn't move, not even to
toss in sleep. He stood over the woman and studied her for
some time before continuing, "M'lord believes that she may be
a murdering thief."

"Nay," Haldana said with a sound of dismay. "Just look
to her and you'll see. She's a lady, of that I'd bet my life. Her
fingers, once they heal, will be as smooth as a pot of cream.
This child is no hardened thief."

"Yea," Ulric agreed with a slow nod. He looked at the
woman's young, battered face in pity. Her skin was bruised,
her eyes were swollen completely shut and her features were
so dark and distorted that one couldn't even make out the
lines at the sides of her nose. What's worse, he'd seen the way
her gown was ripped from her breasts. He didn't want to think
of what most likely happened to her. "Will she survive it? I
told his lordship she would. I didn't want to give him an
excuse not to help her. Methinks that if he suspected she was
near death, he would turn her out."

"I don't know. Methinks it depends on her will to live. If
she doesn't want life, she'll die." Haldana sighed. "I'll stay
with her and watch over her. Please, direct the girls to take
over my duties."

"Yea. 'Tis already done." Ulric narrowed his eyes in
heavy contemplation, drawing back the coverlet at the girl's
bruised throat. His frown deepened. It looked as if she'd been
strangled. "M'lord has put her in my charge until she
awakens. He wishes to speak to her then."

"Methinks that m'lord is more frightened of her being
here because she is a woman and a woman of his class."

"Yea, methought it also. He didn't think much of me
saying she was a beauty." In truth, Ulric only saw the line of
the lady's slender body outlined by the coverlet and the
fullness of her lips, but he'd mainly called her beautiful just to
aggravate his lordship. He let go of the coverlet, letting the old

material fall once more to cover the noblewoman's neck. He moved his fingers to stroke the wiry hairs of his mustache.

"Wouldn't it be nice if she was sent here to melt the curse from his lordship's heart?" Haldana sighed, wistful. "Yea, even the curse from this castle. Then the Monster of Lakeshire would leave us be once and fer all."

"You're a romantic dreamer, dear girl." Ulric kissed Haldana briefly on her forehead and turned to leave. "Let me know at once when she awakens."

"Yea, Ulric, I will." Haldana let her girlish giggle echo in the chamber as he shut the door. From outside the chamber, he heard her say, "Poor child. You don't know what you have gotten yerself into coming here."

Chapter Two

ഌ

The gigantic training broadsword slashed through the air with a bloodthirsty force. As the blunted metal blade heaved over his head, Vladamir growled with a fierce barbaric intensity that echoed the length of the bailey. He advanced against the Saxon knight using the long slashing movements of the Viking attack, something he hadn't done for some time.

The exercise yard echoed with the grunts of the two combatants, their exersion-laden cries only to be outdone by the rowdy cheers of the onlookers. Vladamir was on the field thoroughly enjoying the freedom of his morning exercise. The watching soldiers pushed at each other, jockeying to get a better view of the action and the young pages and squires observed the battling foreigner with open-mouthed awe.

The sun was unseasonably hot, but the duke still wore his tunic. It stuck to his sweat-dampened back as he moved his hand above his head, twirling the weapon around in crazed circles. The motion was meant to drive fear into the opponent—a simple Norseman's trick but it worked to perfection almost every time.

Guthrum bid him not to teach the Saxon soldiers too much, lest it prove to be an advantage in battle against his army of Vikings—if there was to be another battle—but it wasn't proving to be an issue. The Saxons favored fighting in their manner and with their own weaponry, preferring the use of a smaller sword in battle to thrust toward their opponents, rather than slash.

The unseasoned knight Vladamir sparred didn't stand a chance against the more experienced lord. Nevertheless, Raulf handled himself bravely in the light of imminent defeat. The thinner Saxon sword the man carried was built to be of a lighter weight so as to be easier to maneuver, but was no match for the sweeping heft of the broadsword as Vladamir brutally slashed his weapon once again through the air. The weaker sword cracked in two, the blade falling uselessly to the ground.

The soldiers mumbled with appreciation as the Viking weapon returned unscathed. The duke's opponent looked to his sword in shock before tossing the useless hilt to the ground. Holding up his shield, he awaited the next devastating blow.

Vladamir knew the Saxon knights hid their fear as they watched the cryptic way he moved. The broadsword became part of his arm and he wielded it with practiced ease. Even blunted, a sword was lethal if used right. The duke harbored no thought of death as he surged forward. In the heat of battle most knights aspired to fight courageously, but Vladamir laughed in the face of death, daring it to come and get him. In a way, he wanted it to take him.

The duke growled with open hostility as his adversary fell to the ground beneath him. If Raulf was ever to be in battle, he needed to learn to survive. Taking it easy on him would do the man no good. Vladamir wasn't sure why he cared, but if he was going to train a man, he would do it right. Besides, though loath to admit it, he liked Raulf.

The duke swung down hard across the defeated knight's shield, breaking through the thick wood. The blow sent Raulf's arm jarring into the ground. The man grunted in fear as the two objects of his defense lay broken and he was left without protection.

"Hold!" the defeated man hollered in panic. Raulf rolled away from the duke's sword. His sweaty, naked back coated immediately with dirt and his brown eyes rounded in fear. "Hold!"

Vladamir shook his head, coming out of a daze as the cloud of battle left him. Momentarily puzzled, he dropped the sword to his side. Reaching his hand out to the fallen man, he hoisted Raulf up off the ground. The duke flashed him a rare smile, although it was stiff and harsh and was more painful than pleasant. He'd been close to killing the man.

"Methought you were like to kill me. What manner of fighting has come across you, m'lord?" the man exclaimed. He swiped his forearm across his sweaty brow and dusted off his bared chest. "'Tis fairly possessed you were! I have never seen the like."

"Raulf," Vladamir answered with a forced laugh. The low tone rang clear over the men, though inside the duke was shaken. "'Tis the peace that makes you say such things. You've been too long from battle."

"Perchance you're right, though I have nary a quarrel with peace, m'lord. I much prefer it to fighting against you on the field of combat." Raulf laughed and scratched the back of his shortly cropped hair. Rubbing his shoulder, he shot Vladamir a sheepish smile. "But methinks 'tis more like the lovely Lizbeth who is making me soft."

"Lizbeth?" Vladamir frowned. Perspiration drenched his brow and made his black linen undertunic stick to his skin as the color drew the heat of the sun to him.

The duke pulled the tunic from his back and lifted it over his head in one sweeping gesture. Raulf turned his eyes downward at the movement. He gave a nervous swallow and leaned to pick up the pieces of his discarded weapons, only to busy himself by taking them to a squire.

Vladamir rarely disrobed for exercise, though many of the men fought in such an unclothed state. It wasn't out of modesty that the duke hid himself beneath clothing, it was because of the stares he received when he didn't. He watched with practiced indifference as Raulf turned his eyes back to him. The younger man was careful not to look at his lordship's chest.

"Lizbeth?" Vladamir prompted, when the man didn't answer his first inquiry. He nodded for the rest of his men to continue with their practice. Waving at a boy, he waited for the squire to bring him his sharper broadsword, gripping it tight as he gave the blunted blade to the child. He didn't like being too far from his sword at any given time. "From the kitchen?"

"Yea, 'tis the same," Raulf admitted with a telltale gleam of anticipation and fear in his eyes. He swallowed nervously. "I wish to speak to you about her."

Vladamir eyed the knight before him. Raulf was young and hadn't seen many days in battle, but he showed promise and he came as part of the arrangement made with King Alfred. He was a trusted man of the Saxon king and was to serve as one of the highest-ranking knights in Vladamir's regiment. The duke found he didn't mind the arrangement, for he liked the man. Raulf had proven himself loyal, a hard worker and an astute student. However, he was also a handsome lad who would easily win much feminine attention. A scheming maid would find him a well-fought-for prize of a husband. It was why Vladamir hated to see the knight wedded at such a tender age, for he knew that it was Lizbeth's hand the young man was going to ask for next.

Over the past fortnights, Vladamir watched Raulf and Lizbeth's flirtations with little interest. What did he care if his servants took lovers? However, he hadn't realized the man's intentions developed so boldly. He could well imagine that is why the lad had been so eager to fight against him in mock battle, despite the duke's forbiddingly black mood.

Yea, for there is naught more distressing to a man then to find himself locked to a woman – especially a woman a man feels tenderly for. 'Tis why marriages should be arranged. 'Tis the only safe way to form an alliance of such magnitude.

"Nay, Raulf. Not now." Vladamir said, turning to leave. A pain flickered in his stomach and he ignored the guilt he felt in denying the man. "I have much to do. I cannot give you counsel today."

"But?" Raulf beseeched, but his plea was ignored.

Vladamir moved from him in dismissal. "Continue your exercise. I wish to see your skill much improved the next time we fight."

The duke growled as the young man tried once more to stop him. He moved from the exercise yard, his feet hitting hard upon the rock-lined earth as he went sullenly to the main hall for a drink of ale. His insides shook with a mighty force as he entered the castle. He'd nearly slain the man and for nothing.

Vladamir hesitated at the archway leading into the great hall, taking a calming breath as he thought of the lack of control he'd just shown on the practice field. Entering the shade of the hall, he gripped his moist tunic in a fist and wiped his brow before moving the shirt to the nape of his neck. He lifted the heavy, hot length of his hair sticking to his back.

The hall was cooler than the bailey. There were two corner fireplaces on opposite ends of the hall that had no fire in them. Because of this, only the candles and the thin ribbons of sunlight peeking through the narrowed slits in the ceiling lightened the dimmed hall.

The main hall was in need of a cleaning. The duke hadn't ordered it done since he was given the property nearly a year before. Vladamir knew it was a strange contradiction that the servants were kept so clean and yet he allowed his home to rot. Cobwebs hung from the high rafters. The once proud and spiraling patterns had dissolved into thin threads that fluttered in the draft. The matted straw rushes lining the stone floor, even though they didn't smell, were old and filled with dust.

A raised platform was fixed into the side of the hall. It too was made of the same black stone of the castle. It held atop it four majestic wooden chairs for himself and any honored guest he might deem worthy enough to grace the high table. Usually he dined there alone. The dining table of the raised platform was the only permanent table in the hall. The lower tables and benches, where the servants and soldiers dined, were portable and had to be dismantled between meals by the kitchen maids and scullions.

At the far end of the hall hung the curtains, behind which soldiers slept on straw pallets. The servants who didn't have use of a pallet slept in the rushes. Usually, it was customary for the lady and lord of the house to also sleep in the main hall, on a large bed in the center, hidden from view by curtains. But, since King Alfred originally refurbished Lakeshire as a military base for himself on the easternmost edge of Wessex, there was a chamber abovestairs for the lord of the castle to reside privately.

Though as long as I'm lord here, there will be no Duchess of Lakeshire! Vladamir swore vehemently.

The duke found he much preferred a private bedchamber. He didn't wish to spend his nights listening to the sexual fulfillments of the soldiers with their giggling servant wenches. It had been hard enough in the past not to invite the company of the fairer sex to his bed too often, though in the long run he thought it a wise decision. And he never invited maids from his own keep.

The guest chambers near his own were not taken advantage of—except by some of those seeking adulterous privacy away from the hall as not to get caught frolicking by their spouses—and for all purposes had been shut up and abandoned. That was until the mysterious maiden arrived. It was within one of these abandoned bedchambers that the lady now resided. He placed her in one of the tower rooms, far away from his bed.

Vladamir glanced briefly up the stairs leading to his mysterious guest. The woman had been there for over a sennight with no sign of movement, only being kept alive by Haldana's caring attentions. Not for the first time Vladamir wondered why he allowed Haldana to bother with the woman. If Haldana were to stop tending her charge, the maiden would assuredly starve. Something kept the duke from ordering her to give up. He purposefully didn't command her bedchamber cleaned, not wanting to give her special attention because of her station—just as he allowed no tunic gown to be sewn for her.

Vladamir hated to admit that part of his restraint was due to his curiosity to see who the lady really was. He knew his life would be better off if she died and he could be rid of the body. A noblewoman only brought trouble.

Let m'lady rise to a dreary domain, for if she is displeased she'll be all that more anxious to leave!

The duke hadn't seen the woman since Ulric directed the knights to carry her to the chamber. Though tempted to see if the claims on her beauty were true, he hadn't gone to investigate. He only briefly acquired of her status and Ulric, following his orders, didn't bother him with the details of the maiden's recovery.

Nonetheless, since the woman arrived in her disheveled state, Vladamir hadn't been able to get her from his mind. He thought of her during the day and dreamt about her at night, which was preposterous since he hadn't even been afforded a good view of her features. What he'd seen was covered in rotting entrails. The fact didn't stop him from fantasizing. The thoughts tormented his sanity as his arousal tormented his body. Too many times as of late he'd been tempted to grab the nearest maid and ravish her against the castle wall, taking her soft body in hard, unforgiving thrusts until he'd taken his fill. He hadn't as of yet, but it didn't stop him from yearning for release.

The duke found himself feeling oddly protective of the maiden left for dead. It was apparent that she was more than likely a lady. He thoroughly examined her cloak before having it burned. The cloak had been beyond repair and was imbedded with the smell of her previous rotted bed.

Vladamir was a thorough man and had made sure there was nothing amiss by sending Raulf and some of the others to inquire within the small villages. There had been no rumors of murder in the villages contained within his small duchy. If a person were to disappear in his dukedom, by law he would be the first to hear of it. Being a lawmaker was one of his more monotonous duties he carried as duke—even though his decision could be overridden by the Saxon king.

What was even stranger than no report of a missing peasant was that there were no reports of a missing lady. Ladies of gentry weren't something one could easily misplace. Vladamir doubted he would be the first informed if a Saxon noble was to go missing, though he might very well be the first accused.

"Lizbeth!" Vladamir yelled as he spied the woman peeking at him from the kitchen doorway. He fumed to think of the spell she wove about his man, Raulf. The reminder made him bark at her more harshly than usual. The slender maid jumped at the call and moved tentatively forward. Keeping her distance, she stopped several feet away from him.

"Yea, m'lord?" Lizbeth's lips parted and her breath came out in trembling pants. Her green eyes rounded in dread.

With cutting gratification, the duke saw her hand shake. Most of the servants, save a few who arrived in Wessex with him, were deathly afraid of him though he'd done nothing to harm them. But the fear they carried was more from what Vladamir hadn't done. He hadn't shown any compassion. He hadn't shown any kindness, save the fact that he hadn't brought harm upon them—*yet*.

"Ale," he ordered. The duke glowered at her.

The maid was comely and that was no doubt why Raulf was so foolish as to fall for her charms. Her eyes reflected the softest of pale greens and her long blonde hair looked almost translucent in the sunlight. Across the bridge of her nose were little dots of freckles. He imagined her pulse beat erratically against the flesh of her creamy white throat. His body stirred, growing heavy beneath his braes, much to his displeasure. Being lord of the manor, no one would stop him should he bend Lizbeth over right there in the hall, lift up her skirts and sample her feminine wares. His stomach tightened at the idea of warm, wet flesh wrapping around his shaft, accepting him as he plundered and took.

The maid visibly swallowed as she stared at the muscles of his naked chest and her look quickly killed his desire for her. Vladamir didn't want fear in his bed. When the maid didn't move to obey immediately, he yelled, "Now!"

Lizbeth's eyes turned to his before finding their way to the floor. The duke growled again, loud and monstrous. The maidservant scurried away from him. He let out a deep breath before slowly climbing the platform stairs that led up to the head dining table. Placing his sweaty tunic and sword on the table, he sat at his chair. He leaned his head back, closing his eyes to think of anything that would take his mind from the needs of his body.

His hall was small in comparison to some he'd seen in his travels, even though he'd been given the title of duke. The title and properties were gifts bestowed upon him for his part in the Treaty of Wedmore. King Guthrum named him duke, so that Alfred would have a high-ranking nobleman as a hostage. None of the other nobles under Guthrum protested the honor given him, glad that it wasn't they who were to be banished. King Alfred granted him the small dukedom for his troubles.

Lakeshire Castle was a small fortress, having been rebuilt by King Alfred as an outpost for his campaigns. Though Alfred thought the outpost put to better use as Vladamir's property, for it was much more prestigious to have a duke with land holdings as a political prisoner than it was to have a mere nobleman. Vladamir was required to work the land and he was allowed to train his own men as part of the bargain.

King Alfred's reasoning wasn't all that unsound. Vladamir knew the king hoped he would form an attachment to his new home and the power afforded him with his rank. He automatically had an honorary seat in the Witenagemot, though he didn't assume the rest of the Witan would listen to his suggestions when it came to the true politics of Wessex.

And, in fact, Vladamir didn't bother to meet with the other nobles.

Only a few of his servants traveled with him from his small property in the northern regions of Northumbria. Many had been too afraid to go to the foreign soil. Though he didn't mind it for they only served as a reminder of all that happened back home.

Hearing a noise, Vladamir opened his eyes and watched as Lizbeth came forward with the ale. She set the goblet and pitcher gingerly in front of him. His gaze dipped unbidden to the soft globes of her breasts.

So much for distracting himself from his physical needs.

The servant girl came with the castle along with most of the other servants. King Alfred admitted quite confidentially that he'd chosen the comely maid to see to the more personal needs of the duke. Vladamir banished the most relieved woman from his chamber the first night. He couldn't force himself to bed an unwilling woman. Shifting uncomfortably in his seat, he scowled. The mass between his thighs wanted to protest the fact.

"M'lord?" the maidservant faltered when he didn't dismiss her. Her delicate voice wavered like a trembling fall leaf about to jump from its branch. She didn't make the mistake of staring again, but turned her eyes demurely downward. Vladamir watched her, sickened by her fear.

"Go!" he bellowed, only to smile in grim satisfaction as the girl ran from the main hall in fright. He lifted his goblet to take a drink.

The smile faded from his lips as his eyes gazed over the rim of his goblet. He once again looked toward the stairwell, wanting to see the mysterious woman who lay there. No doubt it was his thoughts' preoccupation with her that made him so eager to attack Raulf, so eager he almost slew the young knight. With a thud, he slammed the goblet on the table and swallowed over the lump in his throat.

'Tis decided then. Healed or no, the noblewoman must go!

* * * * *

Blackness surrounded her. Eden's mind swam in it, dreamless. It consumed her, urging her to fall completely within it, but her will was too strong. She fought the darkness and the anguish it brought. By small degrees, a light invaded her inky prison until she was compelled to awaken and face the full force of the pain that had driven her into the blackness to begin with.

Slowly she tried to open her eyes, but only one of her swollen lids allowed her to see. The bright light came through the narrow slit, blurring her vision so that everything danced around her in an unfamiliar slash of color. The heavy fall of her breath came in uneven pants and her chest felt as if a weight pressed upon her. Gradually, the pounding of her heart subsided and she tried to listen to the sounds of the ominous chamber. The room was quiet, too quiet by her measure—like a tomb.

Have they found me? Am I caught away in his castle? Blessed saints, please no. Am I to be his bride? Am I his bride already?

Eden shook her head against her pillow as she tried to focus her mind. A moan of confusion escaped her, sounding odd as it left her parched lips. She couldn't remember where she was or how she'd gotten there. All she knew is that she hurt.

"M'lady?" a strange voice cut through her wondering thoughts. She didn't recognize the accent.

Eden gasped and forced herself to sit up only to grab her head as it throbbed at the sudden motion. She didn't move. Her body ached. It felt like she'd been in bed for years, only now to awaken in a different, strange land.

What is wrong with me? My thoughts, they make no sense and yet they are mine.

Eden didn't know whether her vision was blurred from the beating dealt to her head, or from the fearful tears that crept into her eyes. Turning to the place where she thought to hear the woman's voice, she tried to speak but couldn't force any words.

"I'll tell him yer awake." The woman's cheerful tone seemed oddly out of place for a tomb.

Eden made out the blurry vision of a maid's apron as the servant opened the door to the chamber and left her alone. She lifted an unsteady hand to try and touch the phantom, but it was gone. Had she imagined the woman?

Tell him? Who? By all the saints, where am I? Father, why did you do this! Luther?

Eden's head swam. Nausea rose to stick in her throat and she covered her lips to keep it from coming out. She was sure she didn't know the chamber, even though she was unable to focus her sight long enough to see it. The bed smelled old and dusty. It wasn't a smell she was familiar with. Her home carried the scent of fresh herbs this time of year.

What time of year is it? Where am I?

Through her blurred vision detected fire burning in what had to be a small fireplace. She couldn't make out details but she could see the orange light well enough. The flames were too low to adequately heat the chamber. Holes were worn into the matted fur of the bed's coverlet. A chill racked her and she touched her limbs to ensure they were attached. She winced, groaning in pain as she lifted her left arm. Her shoulder ached as if it had nearly been ripped from its socket.

Then, to Eden's horror, she realized she was naked under the coverlet. Her heart beat wildly in her chest. It pounded as if it wanted to escape her as she wanted to escape her pain. Propelled into action, she tried to find clothes on the bed, but there was only the holey coverlet.

Pulling the fur over her breasts to cover her nudity from whomever the "he" was that the maidservant went to get, she didn't move. She stared at the door, waiting. Finally, a quiet knock sounded.

Luther? Please don't be Luther.

Her grip tightened on the fur and she trembled violently in fear, squeezing her thighs together in silent protest of what might come. The door cracked open and for a moment the light from the hallway torches was darkened by the movement of a figure.

"M'lady?"

Eden nodded, unable to answer the kind voice. An odd relief came over her as she didn't hear Luther or her father speak. Although she didn't recognize the gentle voice she did hear, she could tell it was an older man.

"M'lady, can you speak?" the voice continued. His words held the same foreign accent that the maid's had.

"You...? Yea," she answered at length. She forced a ragged breath of air and she tried her best to appear calm and forced her words to come more firmly. "Are you the lord here?"

"Nay, m'lady." He seemed confused by the question. "M'lady can you see me?"

"Who are you?" she refused to answer as she jutted her chin into the air. She hoped that they believed her to be composed. Hoping to look haughty, she squinted to bring the man more into focus. The action didn't help. "What have you done with me? Why do you keep me here? Where is my gown?"

"My name is Ulric, m'lady. I'm seneschal here. Yer gown is being mended. Haldana thought it best to leave it off you so she could tend yer wounds. I'm sure she has gone to fetch it."

Eden nodded in understanding as she tucked the coverlet more firmly over her shoulders so that the fur fell over her back and covered her completely, except for her head. She pulled at material behind her with her hand, holding it tight against her shoulders.

"If m'lady wouldn't mind," Ulric continued. "I had a few questions of my own. Mayhap then I'd be better able to answer yers."

Eden again nodded, this time with more severity. What else could she do? She was trapped on the bed by her nakedness. Even if she was to brave an escape, she couldn't see where to go.

"Who are you?" he asked. "Why were you in the forest alone outside this castle? Fer 'tis obvious you're a lady by yer dress. Did you separate from yer traveling party?"

Eden's eyes teared. She felt like a scared child, locked inside a dark room. "Yea."

"You were separated?" Ulric persisted.

"Yea."

"You're a lady of gentry?" She felt him move closer as if inspecting her.

"Yea." Eden focused her eyes forward, intent on convincing him that she was a lady and above him.

"Who are you? Where were you heading?"

"I'm Lady Eden. I was on my way to a nunnery in East Anglia." As she spoke her hands shook. She forced herself to swallow the lump that kept rising into her throat to crack her voice. "I'm to live there."

"Which nunnery?" Ulric asked smoothly.

"The one to the south," Eden weakly offered her lie. In truth she didn't know the name of any nunneries in East Anglia. Surely, with the pagan king newly converted there would be something. She only hoped that whichever lord lived in the castle would see fit to send her there. "I don't believe that they have named it, for 'tis new."

"Hmm." Ulric's voice pondered her answers. "So you have already taken yer orders? You're a nun?"

"Nay, I'm to take them there." Eden turned her face away from him. She couldn't lie about such a thing as already being ordained. It would be too blasphemous. The fact she said she was going to be was bad enough. "I'm sure they expect me. If you would see fit to send —"

"I see," Ulric broke in, thoughtful.

Eden wondered at the delighted tone in his words. His blurry figure shifted away from her, only to come back. She leaned away the best she could on the uncomfortable bed.

"Please, good sir." Eden sighed and tried to relax, feeling no immediate threat from the old man. "Where am I?"

"You don't know?" Ulric laughed lightly in surprise. "You're at Lakeshire Castle. We found you near death in front of the castle gates. Methought you might be able to tell us how you came to be here and most importantly why."

"Lakeshire?" Eden gasped in horror, looking down as she mumbled in shock, "He left me here? How could he have left me here?"

"Who left you?"

Eden stiffened. The irritated voice wasn't that of Ulric. It instead came from her left, near the fireplace. Her skin tingled and she noticed that the fire burned hotter than before. The man's tone sounded wicked, spoken in a strange accent. The word "who" was murmured with a softened "v".

"Are you...?" she began, but had to take a calming breath. It didn't help.

She was frazzled. Her heart already beat in fear only to pound in time with her head, resounding in her ears like a battle drum. She shook with fear, her body so hot it was surely on fire. The way the flames spread through her she wondered if she was in the company of the devil himself. Rubbing her chin on the fur to make sure it still covered her body, she asked weakly, "Are you the Monster of Lakeshire?"

Vladamir eyed the trembling creature before him with unconcealed disdain. The way his nickname came from her lips irritated him to no end and he was all too aware that she refused to answer his question. By her own admission it was obvious someone planted her in front of his castle, perhaps thinking she was already dead.

It was clear from the first moment that she didn't know he was in the chamber. The way she kept squinting at Ulric belied the fact that she couldn't make out the figure before her. Was her impaired eyesight due to her natural vision or a result of her beating? He told himself he didn't care and didn't wish to be in her company long enough to find out. In fact, he didn't want her in his home longer than necessary.

The maiden's hair was dirtily matted to her head, so much so that he was unable to make out its true color. From what he saw of her frame under the thin fur, she seemed slender in stature, probably more so due to her prolonged illness. Her skin pulled tautly against her cheekbones, bones that were high and proud. Beyond that simple observation he couldn't make out her features.

"Are you the monster?" Her breath continued to come out in audible pants and her one good eye searched for him. "Am I to be your sacrifice?"

Vladamir watched her lips tremble at the question. Her mouth was in the best condition of her whole face with a fine arch of the upper lip and the full pout of the lower. If the rest of her face healed to displeasure, he would be contented to look only at her delicate mouth. His body hummed to life, reminding him how long it had been since he'd taken a woman to his bed. The painful mass between his thighs only annoyed him. He didn't want to feel desire—not for her, not for any woman.

Who could ever willingly accept a monster into their bed?

The duke felt a glimmer of regret at the timid way she searched for him with her troubled, swollen gaze. The faint white of her eye was a bloody red as if she'd been strangled near death. He suddenly frowned as he realized that someone indeed had tried to kill her. Did they think to have succeeded? Who would want her dead? What exactly had she done?

He saw the fear in her and didn't believe for an instant that the woman planned on joining a nunnery. There was something in the proud way she lifted her chin and the aristocratic tilt of her head. He saw her breeding, even through her marred expression.

Yea, m'lady, there are those who would think me a monster.

"I have been called that," he answered at last, afraid if he didn't respond, she would continue to grow pale until she passed out once more on the bed. He needed too many answers from her to let her rest quite yet.

Eden licked her beautiful lips, much to his carnal delight. He felt another twinge in his lower stomach as he eyed her unsightly face. It was a feeling that brought him no satisfaction. He longed to kiss her — his aroused blood stirring his body to new heights with a disarming suddenness. Narrowing his eyes, he frowned as his need for her became almost painful.

Glancing over the fur coverlet, he forgot his resolve against women. The more terrified she became, the more she tugged at the bedding, causing the matted fur to pull across her generous breasts and cling to her tiny waist. There was a hole worn into the fur just below her navel, revealing her smooth, white flesh and what appeared to be a small bruise. The duke was sure that she didn't know the hole was there, or she would've covered herself better.

He looked lower, to the long line of her thin legs as they sprawled out on the bed underneath the flimsy barrier of fur. They'd be easy to part. He could order Ulric from the room and have his cock buried to the hilt with little effort.

"What is your family name?" Vladamir asked, his voice a rough murmur. He momentarily forgot that Ulric was in the chamber with them, forgot that he planned on being quiet. Without thinking to stop, he took a step toward her, his breath deepening. It would be so easy to take her. His body wanted to act the part of the monster and tear the fur from her hands.

Only by the strength of his resolve against women did he refrain.

"I'm Lady Eden..." Eden paused and swallowed hard. Vladamir smiled as she mustered up her courage to continue. "...of Hawks' Nest. My lord father is Clifton, Earl of Hawks' Nest."

Vladamir heard Ulric's breath catch in his throat. His rising passions drained instantly from his limbs to be replaced by a sudden rage as he ignored the older man. For a moment he wasn't sure he'd understood her.

"*You* are the earl's daughter?" Vladamir kept his voice deadly calm, but the harsh tone was unmistakable, even to him. The woman jumped in alarm and edged away from him. Her one good eye rounded and darted about the chamber in confusion. It would be easy for her to detect the hatred in him. He didn't try to hide it.

"Yea," she whispered. "I am."

"Then 'twas your father that brought you here," he concluded with a vicious growl. Only the fact that her face was already so violated stopped him from striking out. "To what purpose?"

"Nay, not my father. He doesn't know where I am."

Vladamir scowled at her, a grim light of determination unraveling inside him. A long moment of silence passed, marked by the heavy panting of the frightened woman. The confusion on her face was evident as her naked arm came out from under the coverlet. Her long, delicate fingers twitched in the air as she searched for him with the tips of her broken fingernails. Suddenly, the duke grinned, causing Ulric to tremble in response.

"Ulric, Lady Eden is now my prisoner. She is not to leave this chamber until I give her permission." Vladamir stalked toward the bed, letting her hear his steps. Another bruise blackened her arm and led over her shoulder to disappear beneath the fur. The sight didn't affect him. He had no pity in his heart for Clifton's seed. "Ulric, leave us."

"But, m'lord," Ulric began, distraught, even as his tone held a bit of warning in it. The duke held up a dismissive hand to ward off anything the manservant might say in the maiden's defense. The servant nodded and hurried from the chamber.

The door slammed shut and Eden jumped in alarm, fairly screaming. "Please, don't. Whatever you're about, stop. I've done nothing to you."

Vladamir ignored her entreaty as he drew near. Her legs twitched under the coverlet, pressing tightly together. A wry smile of amusement lit his face at the defensive act. It would take more than her will to stop him once his mind was set.

He sat next to her on the bed, his weight causing her to lean toward him. The fire crackled loudly, marking the time that passed in silence. The bare, black stone walls of the small chamber reflected the eerie orange light. The room was musty with the smell of dust and old straw. Vladamir paid the chamber little heed. His attention focused on the slender woman before him as he struggled to contain his fury. A faint trace of lilies wafted up to him. Haldana must have used the costly soap to clean the woman. Seeing the caking of blood in her dark locks, he wondered why the servant didn't also wash the noblewoman's hair.

"I don't understand," Eden said. "Why would you keep me here? Why would you not send me back to my father's keep? And if not there, then on to the nunnery—any nunnery. Surely even a monster would be kind enough to let me live my days out as a nun. I'll cause no harm. If you please, I'll never see my father again. You have my word on it."

Vladamir didn't answer. He got the impression from her hasty plea that it was her wish to never see the earl again. If it was her father that beat her, he couldn't blame her. But, through his blind hatred, he couldn't feel pity for the seed of his enemy. He drew closer to her and realized that she was sick. Her eye still held the feverish light of the ill in it. That is why her body radiated with such drawing heat. She held herself well considering. Why he hadn't realized it before?

"Do you understand m'lady? You're not to leave here. This is your new home." Vladamir licked his lips, seeing the texture of her flesh. She was so close, so warm. Would her thighs be soft? Wet? Would they part willingly for him if her were to coax them apart? The duke liked that she couldn't see him, liked that she was ugly from the beating. Lowering his tone to a deadly, guttural whisper, until it cracked with the darkness of his words, he said, "And I'm your new master."

"Yea-nay," Eden stammered, shaking her head. The blood drained completely from her face and she swayed on the bed. Her hand dropped to the straw mattress, but she didn't pull it under the covers. "Would you eat me? I heard you must dine on the flesh of your victims or you'll die. I always thought it quite sad."

"Sad for whom? The victims?" Vladamir chuckled despite himself at her innocent superstition, though he was intrigued by the thought of dining on her flesh, but not in the morbid way she suspected. His body hummed with a wealth of mixed passions and he couldn't stop thinking of the ways he would take her. He'd denied his baser needs for far too long. What better revenge on his old enemy than that? But, no, he would bide his time before deciding how best to use her.

"Yea and for you. You must be so lonely. Methinks..." Her swollen lid shut briefly. "Please—"

"Please?" he taunted against her throat, feeling her to shiver as he brushed his lips along her earlobe. His cock throbbed, urging him on. It would be so easy to end the suffering he felt. "You wish to be my sacrifice? You want that I should dine on your body? You feel sorry for me and wish to feed me?"

"Nay." The protest wasn't as strong as it should've been. "I wish to be let go."

"Nay, you're my prisoner. Resolve yourself to it." Forming his words carefully, so she couldn't mistake him, he added, "For you won't be released and you won't be saved. You'll never escape me and I'll never let you go."

"Why?" Eden moved to sit up straighter, but fell backward when her cheek brushed up against his. Biting her swollen lip, she lifted her hand to touch his jaw. The action caught his attention, adding fuel to the already dangerous fire inside him. Her hand missed and instead found itself on his neck, her fingers instantly grazing the bumpy texture of his skin. He waited for her scream of fear as she touched his neck, running her fingers up to his jawline. Instead, she calmly asked, "Why would you keep me here? I have done naught to deserve this."

She searched his skin in light feathery caresses, but didn't pull away. Not knowing why, he let her touch him. He leaned forward, knowing she didn't understand him, knowing she wasn't well. Closing his eyes, he held still and waited. Finally, her hand fell to his shoulder to rest on his undertunic, nestling into the material. The rise and fall of his chest appeared to give her some comfort.

"Would you like to be a feast for a monster?" He touched the tip of his tongue to her hot flesh, making her shiver. A frail groan of surprise came from her and she leaned closer to him as if she might rest upon his arm. He grabbed her by her dirty hair and drew her head sharply to the side, away from any such tender action. She gave a slight moan but didn't push him away. Her fingers clutched nervously on his tunic, twining into the laces.

The rapidly beating pulse at her neck pounded fiercely under the dark marring of her skin. A fading bruise started at the base of her throat, only to taper into five very notable finger marks. It was as he guessed. She'd been strangled. Was it all a ruse? Was Clifton trying to confuse him? Trying to make him feel pity for the woman? It wouldn't work. He'd lost all pity long ago.

Hadn't he?

Vladamir frowned as he studied her. His rage and desire mixed with concern. Leaning his head against her temple to keep her from pulling away, he took his free hand and gently touched the line of her cheek.

The duke twisted his hand, thoughtfully drawing the backs of his fingers over her cheek and throat. The black onyx ring glided over her skin, contrasting the paleness of her flesh. Her breath caught in her throat. He continued downward, waiting for her to yell, to pull away in fear. She never did. As he looped his finger over the top edge of the fur coverlet, he kept his face close to her neck, letting his breath fall on her skin. Since her grip on the coverlet lay behind the small of her back, it was easy for him to tug the material over her breasts. She gasped as the air hit her flesh.

The duke loosened his grip on her hair and his touch became gentle, caressing. He tugged the fur down slowly, not looking at her chest, merely feeling the scorching heat that radiated off it. Her hand fell from his chest to squeeze the tight muscle of his exploring arm and yet she still didn't push him away.

Vladamir couldn't resist. Her breasts lured his hand downward. It was too much. He needed release, needed to bury himself into something soft. The woman seemed willing—more willing than many in a long time. At least she wasn't fighting him off.

He looked over the soft skin of her throat to her shoulder and then lower to the perfect breasts, aching to take them into his palm, to feel her nipples hardening against his flesh. His body lurched. Blood pumped heavily into his loins, burning his flesh with a passionate fire. His cock grew taller, harder, as it strained to be set free.

He knew she couldn't see him, but that was part of the appeal. What was it about this maiden that drew such a response from him? He didn't want to feel, not now, not after the years of blessed numbness.

She appeared unafraid of him and didn't try to resist. Her eyes didn't boldly stare, or look away with pointed dismissal. She didn't cringe with disgust. He detected her confusion, sensed her apprehension and saw the fevered light of her eyes. The desire for human contact that came from the basest and most primal of human needs welled within him. He wanted to touch her, wanted to feel the closeness of flesh along his own. He refrained and instead contented himself to look at her creamy flesh, ignoring the bruises that littered her body.

And then she moaned, a soft plea—the sound a woman made when she wanted to be touched. Vladamir couldn't resist the spell of her. He leaned in, gently kissing her throat, brushing his lips softly against each of the finger bruises. She moaned again. The sound would be his undoing.

He drew his hand to her breast, lifting it in his palm. Her skin was soft against his calloused fingers. Again she made the soft, accepting noise. It had been so long since he'd bedded a woman.

So long, so long…

Vladamir flicked his tongue over her neck, deepening his kisses and he worked his mouth against her skin. Her breath caught and held. Emboldened, he couldn't stop. She didn't touch him, didn't fight him off.

He massaged her breast in kneading circles, drawing his thumb over the erect nipple. Adjusting his body on the bed, he became more forceful. He took a nipple between his lips, sucking at it, biting it. But, when he moved his hand lower to test the wet resolve between her thighs, she stiffened and her moan of pleasure became one of fear.

Vladamir instantly drew back, breathing hard. What was he doing? This could very well be Clifton's trap. He looked down at his hand. The roughness of it contrasted her softness. Emotions warred within him when he would rather not feel a thing. Taking a controlled hand, he pulled the fur upward, purposefully grazing the back of his hand over a nipple on the way. He stifled a groan, wanting his numbness back. He didn't want to be awakened — not with passion, not with anything — and he especially didn't want to be awakened by Clifton's daughter.

The duke doubted he could control himself if he were to stay in the chamber with her. Already his body pulsed with desire for the soiled maiden. His lips ached with the need to pull her erect nipple back between his teeth and his fingers itched to dip into the sweetness of her wet slit. His arousal pulsed to thrust within her most sacred of places, as if knowing her pussy would cling to him, tight and hot. He could have her and no one would ever know. Angry with himself and with her for tempting him, he howled a loud and monstrous sound.

Eden gasped as pleasure shot through her. Her mouth gaped open in wonder at the new sensation and her stomach throbbed with the rest of her body. The emotion made her weak in her illness, until she was sure she might swoon.

The duke was so near. The sound of his voice vibrated through her, sparking her body to life. His weight shifted on the bed. She couldn't move, hearing well the commanding tone in him when he spoke. This wasn't a man she would want to disobey.

Her flesh tingled to the point that she felt herself losing awareness. Only his hand on her hair holding her up and his deadly sounding admission stopped her from collapsing. She was all too aware of his presence and how vulnerable she was in it. His breath hit her skin, smelling of mint. Transfixed by his nearness, she breathed deeply. He smelled of the earth.

How could she fight that which she couldn't see? How could she fight a beast of fire? Eden sensed that he drew nearer still. Her flesh tingled in anticipation of his touch, until her nipples ached and her thighs tightened, waiting more.

When she'd touched him, the texture of his skin intrigued her, even as it terrified her. His wasn't the smooth face of a man. Her throat worked in confusion, as the blood stirred violently in her veins. His accent, his words excited her as no man ever had. She didn't understand that excitement. It both mystified and terrified her. She was helpless against it.

That is because he is not a man. He is a monster. He is a demon who sets my blood on fire.

It might be foolish, but she felt no fear of him. He entranced her senses with his nearness, wove a spell about her with his dark words. She waited for the feel of his lips to come back to her with innocent anticipation. Her head throbbed. She closed her eyes and quit trying to see about her. The light only made her headache worse.

The fur caressed her injured skin in a gliding stroke as he pulled it back over her chest. Time was suspended in the heat of his nearness. Eden was nervous and afraid. Never before had a man, let alone a monster she couldn't see, looked at her naked, touched her naked flesh. All too aware of where his breath touched her, of where his hand had glided on her flesh, she wanted more. But more of what?

"Please." She moved her hand from his arm and tried to pull the fur more fully around her body. "Let me go. You don't want me as your prisoner. I have done nothing to you. You have no reason to keep me."

"You'll pay for the sins of your father. 'Tis all you need to know." He laughed, low and cruel.

"Will you kill me?" Clutching the dirty coverlet to her chest, she tried to wipe off the feel of him. "Will you ravish me?"

"What I do to you will depend on part by your actions."

Eden opened her mouth to speak, but the door opened and she heard him leave. Her lids grew heavy and black. She lay on her side and curled in a ball, unable to get the feel of the quick brush of his hand off the skin of her chest.

Who are you? What do you want from me?

Chapter Three

ಐ

"M'lord, please reconsidered yer decision. She had naught to do with what transpired between you and the earl. She would've been no older than a child when it happened. *By hell's fire!* She is no more than a child now." Ulric had been waiting for his master to come from the maiden's chambers and now hastened to keep up with the duke's faster pace. Wiping the sleeve of his tunic across his bald forehead, he said, "You punish the wrong person!"

"Nay! I shall use her to punish the right person. She is a means to an end. Her life is mine. I saved her from death." Vladamir growled, slashing his hand for silence. The belt at his waist twisted erratically in the air as he walked faster. "Besides, she has the ignorant tongue of her father."

"Because she called you a monster?" Ulric shook his head, trying to follow his lordship's irrational reasoning. "'Tis yer own fault you're known as such. Since when do you care what the people of Wessex call you? Methinks you feel sorry fer her. Methinks you like her! That is why you make her yer prisoner. You have grown lonely and don't want her to go. You want the maiden fer yer bed."

"Nay," Vladamir denied. "Enough of your blathering nonsense. I'll have none of your illogical sentiments. Lady Eden of Hawks' Nest means only revenge to me, naught else. She is my prisoner — *my slave*. I own her. I just have to decide how to best use her."

"She is just a young woman — an innocent young woman already treated more cruelly by her father than you ever were. Just look at her face!" Ulric tried in vain to hide the censure in his voice and failed. He struggled to keep up with his master's stride, lumbering down the stairwell. "You couldn't think to harm her. She has been through enough. If anything, you should be protecting her. Did you not look at her poor face? What has happened to you? Where is yer honor, m'lord?"

"Nay, she is his child." Vladamir glanced back, his face hard. "She is his heathen seed so don't speak to me about honor. 'Tis not in her bloodline."

"And would you say the same fer Lady Gwendolyn, yer daughter?" Ulric returned, unabashed. The duke's temper was always quick to rise as though it seemed to bubble just below his surface at all times. "Would you see her persecuted fer the sins of her father?"

"That is different," Vladamir retorted with a growl. "Gwendolyn has naught to do with this."

"Nay, m'lord, 'tis very much the same. Mayhap you had better think afore you condemn Lady Eden to whatever dark thoughts are swimming about in yer head." They reached the bottom of the steps leading from the above chambers. Ulric lowered his voice. "M'lady is innocent in this. You cannot harm her. If you just let yer anger cool, you'll see it also."

Rage warred with hatred in Vladamir's eyes—a dangerous combination. *Ulric had always* known there was a bitter hatred boiling within the duke, but he hadn't suspected the hard depths of it.

The servant took a deep breath. "I'll send one of the maids to her with food. Methinks it wouldn't do to have her starve afore you could extract yer revenge."

The duke growled, glaring at the manservant. Grabbing a fistful of Ulric's tunic, he gave him a rough shake, desperately wanting to quiet his tongue. His fingers flexed, releasing the man just as quickly. He shook his head in torment, unable to harm the man—no matter what he said.

Swallowing hard, he endeavored to remain calm. Ulric stalked away from him. Even in his anger, the duke was reluctant to punish the aging servant for the disobedience. He still valued his seneschal's opinions, no matter how ungratefully they were delivered. Even in his outrage, he was loath to give up such loyalty as Ulric showed.

Curse your logic, Ulric! And damn your accused, meddling ways!

Vladamir watched after the servant until he disappeared into the kitchen. Grumbling, he slashed his long fingernails like claws through the air to erase the image of the defiant man. The man usually spoke his piece, but Vladamir couldn't remember ever seeing Ulric so defiant.

Over the years, every time Vladamir thought of Clifton his rage would return tenfold until he couldn't even see clearly. It was that rage that kept him alive during some of the hardest times of his life. It was that rage that fed his soul and kept him from giving up. Vladamir clenched his hands as they shook with barely contained fury.

Vladamir growled, thinking of Gwendolyn's sweet face. The child was the only bright spot in his life and he missed her dearly. It wasn't easy leaving her in Northumbria to be looked after by nuns, but he had nowhere else to keep the child. Thinking of the woman, he cursed. He couldn't stop the rush of hatred when he thought of her father.

Haldana poked her head from the kitchen doorway. Her hair was covered in soot and he saw her blackened fingers from across the main hall. The woman walked toward him, her defiant expression evident by the hardness of her round face. He could only guess Ulric had quickly told the woman of his plans for Lady Eden.

Turning abruptly on his heels, he stalked to the archway leading to the bailey, ignoring Haldana's gasp of dismay as he left her behind. He gripped a blunted Saxon sword that lay by the main hall's entrance and swung the weapon into the air, catching it easily on its way down with his opposite hand. The duke didn't wish to face the meddling servant woman, already able to hear her reprimanding words in his head, and he certainly didn't wish to be reminded about what transpired with Lady Eden.

* * * * *

A prisoner? The Monster of Lakeshire Castle has made me his prisoner? By all the saints, it cannot be true!

Eden tried not to cry as she pulled the coverlet closer to her chest and pressed her arm over her breast to stop it from aching. She still felt the brush of the monster's fingers on the erect nipple—could feel the heated burn where his breath touched her skin. The monster seared her body with a fire she couldn't name or fight.

After he left her, she fell into a troubled sleep—a sleep full of demons and fire and slain human carcasses. The skies turned as dark as night with a flood of crimson clouds, until blood poured from the heavens to soak the thirsty earth, running over her naked flesh as the shadowed figure of the monster loomed near. She didn't know how long her nightmares lasted, only that when she did finally awake she was drenched in sweat.

Eden sat on the bed, straining her ears against the deafening silence. The fire crackled in the fireplace only to grow louder the harder she tried to listen past it. She tilted her head toward the place where the monster first appeared in the chamber. It was only logical that a demon would travel by hell's own fire. Was he with her even now? Had he taken her sight from her? Had he already taken something else from her? Her innocence, mayhap? Or had that been taken before by Luther?

Eden cursed her eyes for not seeing the monster, though she was somewhat glad she couldn't for she could well imagine what he looked like.

No doubt his is a demon with bulging horns and sharpened fangs. His skin is likely to be the scarlet staining of blood and his teeth would be marred with the fluids of his many victims, with eyes as black as the moonless night and as devoid of life as...as a... By all the saints, cease!

Trembling, she fought the image her mind produced of him. She'd heard well the stories that were whispered about the Monster of Lakeshire. He was said to be half human, half devil—his ugly face contorted into that of an evil spirit as a reminder of his life in the nether world. His voice was thick with a demon's black tongue. That is how she'd known it was he who spoke, for his voice was unlike any she'd ever heard. It sent shivers over her spine. His touch had been hot against her flesh and when his breath fanned against her neck he'd controlled her completely.

"M'lady?"

Eden jumped as the voice invaded her thoughts. She'd been so wrapped up in her own feverish mind that she hadn't heard the maidservant at the door. She turned to the sound. It was the voice of the earlier maid. Squinting, she tried to focus her eyes. "Please, don't go get him again."

"M'lady?" the woman questioned, her puzzlement evident by her tone.

"Who are you? I cannot see you. My vision swims in my head. My eyes don't rest and I cannot think clearly."

"I'm Haldana. A servant here in the duke's home," the woman responded. "Has yer vision always done that?"

"Nay." Eden paused, confused. "The duke's home?"

"M'lady, yer clothes!" Haldana gasped. "I forgot that you weren't dressed proper fer visitors. 'Twas that I was so relieved that you finally awoke that I forgot!"

"'Tis done." Eden waved her naked arm in frustration and then winced at the pain it caused. She tried to remember what she asked through the haze in her brain. It was getting harder to concentrate and she closed her eyes, leaning her head back. Remembering what she wanted to know, she snapped her face around. "You said this is the duke's home? What duke?"

"Yea, this is Lord Kessen, Duke of Lakeshire's castle. Methought I saw his lordship come in here and introduce himself."

"Of course, the monster has a human name," said Eden under her breath as her fists tightened on the fur. She kept her attention on the serving woman as Haldana moved throughout the chamber. "Please, tell me, is he still here in the chamber? Did he come back? How can you tell when he is about?"

"Nay, m'lady. The door didn't open." Haldana came to the bed and lifted her hand to feel Eden's forehead. Eden jerked from her touch.

"But, he—the fire…" Eden pointed toward the heat, only stopping when she realized she heard the frown in the other woman's words. "But, how did he get in last time? I didn't see him come through the door."

"M'lady, please calm yerself. M'lord is not a monster." The servant patted her arm before urging her to lie down. "You're sick with the fever. Methinks that is why you say such things. When you feel better, you'll see you're mistaken. There are no monsters at Lakeshire."

Of course! The monster would have his loyal minions. But this minion pretends to be friendly. I must be on my guard lest the beast lures me into his trap. Oh, how I wish I could see!

Eden groaned dramatically and raised a hand to her head. "I don't feel well. Perchance my thoughts are still muddled."

The woman gave a nervous laugh. "Naturally! You have been asleep for nigh a whole sennight and three days."

"Please, leave me be. Methinks all I need is rest." Eden sighed as she turned her face from the maid. "I'm just so tired."

"I'll have someone come with food," Haldana said. "Mayhap you should try to stay awake long enough to get something warm in yer belly. It will help you to heal faster."

Eden's only answer was a long, weary sigh.

"Yea, you rest." The woman tenderly pattered her back. Eden moaned in response, too tired to speak. "Yea, rest child. I'll check on you in the morning hours."

"Thank you, Haldana," Eden breathed. She didn't reopen her eyes. For the moment she didn't care that she was in the monster's lair or that the monster wanted to feast upon her. She was happy just to be away from her father's home and her fiancé's lecherous grasp.

* * * * *

Eden trembled under his strong hands, her slender shoulders no match against the monster's exceptional strength. She'd wanted to confirm he was a solid man built of flesh and bone and not the mythical demon come to haunt her. The man who touched her could be either creature or man. His grip tightened fiercely. She moaned in pain at the pressure along her arms as she wasn't yet completely healed.

The hardened fiber of the monster's body forged daringly against hers. His immense thigh worked indecently between her legs to flatten itself against her sex. The heat of his body wove around her. She smelled his very masculine scent and it only heightened the feeling of need inside her. Moisture gathered between her thighs—an odd reaction to be sure. Closing her eyes, she breathed him in.

She squeezed her legs together to try and push him away, but he was too strong. His leg pushed up into her sex, making her body respond the only way it could—by building with hot cream. Although she again tried to pull away, she curiously wanted to explore the sensations his indecently massaging movements arose in her stomach.

The heat from his hands was making her dizzy with confusion. Although she knew she should want to leave him, she found that she was oddly drawn to stay with him to see what he would do next.

She pressed into herself, wanting to stop the fluttering he caused inside of her. Her heart raced in a violent rhythm and eyes rounded in astonishment as they sought him in the darkness. She licked the warm taste of him on her lips and shivered. Her sex throbbed like never before, angry at being neglected of his touch.

They were wet with blood as it rained from the heavens. She didn't care. Drawing her nearer, he sucked her bottom lip between his teeth and bit lightly into it. She gasped in surprise. He took advantage of her opened mouth. Delving his tongue just over the border of her lips he licked at her gently. She moaned louder. The sound wasn't one of pain, but of confusion.

M'lord, yea, take me….

Eden gasped in surprise, opening her eyes. It was just a dream. No, not just a dream. It was the dream—the same dream she'd had every time she closed her eyes. Two very long days had passed since she first awoke and the monster didn't visit her again. She shivered every time she remembered his strange accent, of the increasingly erotic dreams she had of him. Surely his kiss was a dream, wasn't it? The blood falling on her from a devilish sky? His lips wrapped around her breasts, suckling her, touching her? Nothing in real life could make her feel so *excited*.

Could it?

Outside the walls of her dreary prison, the rain continued to fall. The sound pounded relentlessly from the outside, her only visitor for much of the time. Her eyesight had slowly returned over the course of those first days. Except for the occasional blurring it was as good as new. Sighing, she looked about the chamber once more. The improved vision only dampened her spirits more for now she saw the hellish prison the monster kept her in.

Vladamir. His name is Vladamir of Kessen and perchance he is not really a monster, but a man and men can be persuaded. I must really have been out of my head with fever to say such things. I'm a grown woman and don't believe in the silly superstitions of the peasants. I don't believe in monsters!

She'd already explored every corner of the dingy room and discovered nothing of interest. Withered cobwebs hung from the ceiling, although it appeared the spiders had abandoned their musty homes long ago. There was the bed, a rough-hewn chair and the beautiful stone fireplace. It was as if she was the first one in the room since it was built. The bed was dusty, small and emanated a musty odor of decay. At least it was a bed and not a pallet on the floor, even if it was as if the mattress had been stuffed of dampened wool and not straw, though the firmness belied its little use.

The only rare visitor to the chamber, which she now thought of as her own, was Haldana. The servant woman was kind to her, though she did have a talent for interrupting when Eden talked. The woman's compassion only convinced Eden that she'd been out of her head when she heard the monstrous voice and Haldana graciously refused to speak of her sick rantings again.

For assuredly, monsters cannot exist!

When Eden was able to sit without her head feeling like it spun in circles, the servant had ordered a bath brought to her chamber. None of the curious maids who carted the steaming buckets were allowed in the chamber with her. Haldana poured the bath herself, only to have the maidservants haul the buckets away. Eden didn't mind, appreciating the privacy. She wouldn't have been able to concentrate well enough to counter the maidservants' inquisitive stares. The steamy water had felt good as she'd washed her grimy skin and she was relieved to brush the tangles from her hair.

Eden knew she might have gone insane with fear if not for Haldana's periodic visits. She hoped that Vladamir would change his mind and let her out of her imprisonment or at least her prison. When she slept the whole day, it wasn't bad in the chamber, but now that she found herself alert more hours at a time, the boredom was beginning to bother her. So far she had yet to be treated like a prisoner, though they didn't let her leave the room, and she'd been cared for and fed.

Eden smiled as a soft knock sounded on the chamber door. Haldana was ever courteous. Only as she watched the door open, it wasn't a woman who stood there.

She glanced down, thankful to be wearing her old gown no matter how shabbily the repairs caused it to fit. The gown had been ripped down the front, so when it was sewn back together, the bodice pulled tightly against her chest, binding her bosom uncomfortably close. The material pulled down at the neck, so when she looked down she saw her cleavage peeking up at her.

"M'lady?" the elderly man questioned, patting his bald head with his sleeve as he smiled kindly at her, his face pleasant. He wore a brownish-red tunic and baggy brown braes that were both fitted together at the waist with a festively red belt. Garters wrapped up around his legs. His attire was that of a pagan, though she could guess by his carriage that he held much authority in the castle. As if proving her point, she noted the ring of keys that jingled at his waist when he moved.

Running her fingers idly over the matted fur coverlet, she tried to place his name. She recognized his voice but couldn't remember where she might have heard it.

"'Tis Ulric," he prompted when she didn't answer, studying her. Eden lifted her hand to her face, noting that the swelling was gone. When she last looked, the white rings around her brown pupils had lost most of the red. Still, she had to look frightful.

"Yea," Eden answered, forcing a demure look through the thick of her lashes. All of a sudden, she remembered meeting him and looked to the stone fireplace to see if his master mysteriously appeared. She wanted to scold herself for being a fool when she saw the space still empty.

"I trust you have been well cared fer. Methought it best to let you rest afore I paid another visit." Ulric twisted his long sleeve, unrolling it over his hand only to fold it again to his wrist. "Please forgive my coming to yer chamber, but I'm afraid his lordship has not changed his mind about keeping you as his prisoner."

"Then I wasn't dreaming? He's keeping me here?" Eden fell back into the mattress, dejected, and gave a forlorn sigh. Her mind reeled at the injustice.

"Yea. But take heart, m'lady. I have known m'lord fer a long time. He won't let you come to harm. He's a good man."

"He won't hurt me?" Eden looked at the man, pleading with him to understand. "He said he might feast upon my body. He said he was to eat my flesh. Surely those are not the words of a generous man."

"Nay, you angered him is all." Ulric stared past her. "Surely you don't believe that superstitious nonsense about his lordship being a monster, do you?"

"Angered him?" Her heartbeat quickened. "How? I did naught but wake up. I didn't ask him to care for me. He should've let me die out in the forest. I didn't ask to be rescued—and certainly not rescued by the Monster of Lakeshire!"

Eden flung herself back against the stone wall with a pout. She sniffed delicately as a tear came to her eye. Peeking through her lashes at the servant, she wondered if her sorrow was having any effect on him.

"If 'tis that you're upset about, then you must blame me. Fer 'tis I who found you and brought you in from the cold. You would've died if I hadn't." Ulric pulled a chair from the corner of the chamber and set it in front of the bed. He seemed pleased that he could so easily dismiss her misery. "M'lady, do you mind if I sit awhile?"

"Yea, please sit." Eden motioned her hand to the chair in distraction. She bit her lip when she saw her tears were put to waste. This man wouldn't be one to help her to escape.

"Thank you, m'lady." Ulric sat in the chair.

"Why does he keep me? What did my father do? What crime has he committed? What offense?" Eden tried to accept her new role in life as the monster's prisoner for it was here she would have to stay if she couldn't find a way to escape.

"That is fer his lordship to say, m'lady. Why do you wish to be dead? Surely yer family is looking fer you. A husband mayhap?"

"I'm not married." Eden said in disgust of the idea. She crossed her hands over her chest. "I was going to the nunnery to take my orders. I wish to be a nun."

"But, why? Yer so young to take orders. Are you a widow?"

"Nay." Eden hid her emotions behind a solid mask of ice. "My reasons are none of your concern. All I'll say is that my life is my own and I'll do what I wish with it. I wish to live in a nunnery and mayhap care for orphans."

Eden had been afforded time to study the old man. He had compassionate eyes, the kind of eyes that didn't lie, though she got the impression the man lived through a lot and would no doubt be loyal to his master. She sighed, knowing she would find no release through him.

"Child, who beat you? Is he the reason you wish to waste away in a nunnery?" Ulric leaned back in his chair. Eden wasn't fooled. She knew he'd report anything she said to his master. "Though 'tis a noble pursuit to help others, that life is more fer widows and old maids. Not young, beautiful noblewomen with much to offer the world."

Tears overwhelmed her at his interest and she couldn't remain emotionless for long. "I cannot say why I wish it, for it doesn't matter. 'Tis the only choice I have."

Ulric frowned but asked no more, as he stood and moved the chair back to its original place.

"Am I really to be kept in this chamber forever? What does he mean to do to me? If you know him, then you must know his reasons," Eden reached out from the bed as the servant tried to take his leave. "Please, I have a right to know what my father did."

"I honestly cannot tell you. 'Tis not my place." He patted his balding head with his sleeve. "M'lord has a lot of demons in him. I don't know what he'll do with you."

Eden saw the truth in the man's expression, though it was of little reassurance. She nodded, unable to speak. Her nose burned with the force of her unshed tears. Looking away, she was ashamed that she had shown such weakness in front of a servant.

"I'll try to talk to him on yer behalf, but I don't know if it will make much difference." Ulric left her alone in the chamber, closing the door quietly behind him.

A tear slipped down her cheek. Her heart squeezed painfully in her chest. This couldn't be happening! She looked about her dingy chamber—with the dusty stone floor, the rotting tapestry, the decaying straw mattress, the neglected fur coverlet—and she wept.

Eden didn't lament her situation for long. With tears still seeping from her eyes, she fell into a troubled sleep. When she awoke, it was late at night and someone had left a bowl of cold fish porridge on the old chair. Wrinkling her nose, she ate the meager dish without tasting the flavorless meat. It was the same porridge she'd been served for every meal.

Eden sighed audibly and forced herself to be tough as her father raised her to be. She knew the earl wouldn't be coming to rescue her, for he didn't know where she was, and held no false hope of liberation from that front. If by some miracle her father did come, she wasn't sure she wanted to go back with him. The nunnery was her only choice and she would have to take matters into her own hands to get there.

Feeling well enough to stand, Eden walked to the thick wood door of her prison. She was surprised to find that the door wasn't locked and no guard stood outside. A sense of foreboding overcame her, but she swallowed it down into the pit of her stomach.

The dark monster that dwells within these boundaries mustn't care if I'm to escape him. That or he knows there's no escape from these black walls.

Discovering an old torch on the floor outside her prison door, Eden quickly made her way back into her chamber and lit it in the fireplace. She took a deep breath and stepped into the hall, taking halting steps as she reached forward to feel into the darkness. The hall was much like her soiled chamber. Although the torch sputtered with a low flame, she was grateful for the light it afforded her—so little light, however, that she saw no more than a few feet in front of her.

The black stones in the walls were chipped and unfinished and the tapestries that hung along them were rotted so badly that one couldn't see the designs in the faded colors. Spiders had spun their webs freely over the ceiling for years and not one of the servants bothered to sweep them from their home. The blackened walls reflected nothing, only soaking the firelight into their inky depths. The floor was littered with pebbles broken from the walls. They crunched under her feet and were the only noise her ears could pick up. There was no sound of insects drifting in from the outside world and no sign of life, save her trembling movements.

Does the monster watch me even now? Does he lurk just beyond the edge of the torchlight? For he has to be a monster to keep me prisoner without my having committed offense.

From the narrow window slit in the chamber she knew that she was high above the ground. So even if she found an opening big enough to squeeze through, she couldn't jump. She wondered if the monster only came out at night and if she would be better off trying to leave during the day. But she reasoned that in daylight the loyal servants to the beast would be awake and she couldn't fight them all. Perhaps in the darkness the beast wouldn't see her and she could make good her escape. Or, in the very least, she could learn her way around his castle.

Along the wall, imbedded into the stones, were little carved inlets constructed to hold torches into place, but there were no torches to light. Eden shivered as she continued past. It was as if no one lived in this part of the castle. Her feet moved by slow degrees over the hard floor. She was about to quicken her pace when she heard a deadly voice whispering over her from the darkness.

"What are you doing out of your chamber, m'lady?"

Eden gasped and dropped her light. The torch's straw embers slashed across the floor and sputtered out until only one small flame remained at the base. Her heart raced and she backed away from the low voice. She forced her feet to move and her breath sounded odd as it came out in rough pants. The figure stood just outside the realm of faltering light. Silver flashed on a black sleeve before it too disappeared into darkness.

"Are you still...there?" Eden tried to force her body to bend, reaching to pick up the discarded torch. Her waist wouldn't submit to the movement.

"You didn't answer my question." The duke's voice grew louder and softer as if he paced the length of the corridor in an instant. It was as if he was all around her at once. His tone was behind her, in front of her, under her. She looked up as if to see him there, along the spiders' ceiling. All that greeted her was inky blackness.

"Please, don't hurt me. I meant no harm." Eden held out her hand as an offering of peace. Hoping to feel him, she only touched air. She took a step back. "You have kept me in that prison for days. I wish only to walk about. Would you have me grow mad with idleness? Is there not something I can do?"

He chuckled. "You still think me a monster?"

"I don't know." She lowered her hand to her waist. Eden begged the darkness to part with her eyes, but it didn't change. "Are you?"

He didn't answer her.

Eden took another step from him, moving away from the ever-dimming light. When he talked to her, her legs weakened as if they were suspended off the dark floor into nothingness. As he said nothing, the only sound to her ears was her own panicked breaths. She touched the solid stone of the passageway wall and her fingertips tangled in a spiderweb. Snapping her hand to her side, she brushed it clean. Then, she again reached to the stones to guide her way.

Eden took another step back and then another. The heel of her worn shoes caught on a loosened stone. Screaming, she fell onto the hard floor.

Vladamir lunged forward, his hand outstretched as if to help her. Eden gasped, scurrying away from him. His fingers glowed pale in the torchlight, contrasting the darkness of his nobleman's ring. The skin of his hand crinkled with the marks of a scar. His manicured fingernails were overly long, much more so than an ordinary nobleman.

His clothes were all in black, except for the glinting of silver thread along the high collar of his wool tunic. A strand of dark brown leather was wrapped about a lock of his raven black hair at his temple, winding down the whole length past his shoulder, nearly to his waist. A few of his forelocks were cut shorter, falling just below his eyebrows.

But it was neither his clothes nor his hair that frightened Eden. Nor was it the sight of his once-burnt hand. It was his eyes. They were as cryptic and luminous as the rest of him, yet they glowed with an eerie light, the like of which she'd never perceived. They were as dark as a moonless night, just as they had been in her dreams.

She forced herself to look away from the mystical orbs and instead drew her gaze along his face to the side of his neck. A fiery scar led from his lower chin to disappear into the neckline of his tunic.

That is where I touched him.

Her palm blazed at the memory and itched to do so again. She held back, refusing to fall under his devilish spell. If that memory was real, then perhaps the rest was real as well? Had he kissed her neck? Her body heated at the thought. Had he touched her breast, massaging it in his palm, sucking it between his teeth? Her nipple instantly puckered in response. Her thighs tightened and to her shame, she wanted him to touch her again.

Vladamir didn't move from the light. Forcing himself to stand still, he let her study him, waiting breathlessly for the contempt and loathing to enter her eyes. He wasn't disappointed. She still thought him a monster and now looking at him she would have her proof of it.

As he eyed her pink, delicate lips, he thought of many sordid things he wanted her to do. His cock was full, throbbing painfully as it urged him to act the beast and take her right there on the dirty floor, to demand she suck the turgid shaft between her lips and suck him until he found his release. It was a reaction he thought to have subdued after seeing her last time. Obviously it would take more than self-pleasure to work her from his system. Flexing his hand, he longed to touch her breast. He refrained, determined to act the gentleman in part—at least for the moment. Besides, last time he'd touched her he'd nearly gone mad with lust. He didn't wish to go there again.

"You wear the marks of the fires of hell." She crouched lower, her husky tone oddly erotic. "'Tis true what they say."

Vladamir saw her walk down the hall, saw her apprehension as she braved the darkness. She was beautiful, more so than he could've imagined, despite the fact her features held glimpses of her father. For a moment, her beauty took him by surprise and he was unable to move. He'd just stood and watched her, like a fool, until she'd drawn too close and he was forced to say something to stop her from stumbling into him.

She'd done much healing, though the bridge of her nose was still darkened with a black and blue mark. Brown hair fell over her shoulders, the exact color of her eyes. Her tunic gown was ragged, but it was now cleaned. It appeared to be mended in a few places. The bodice of her overtunic hung low, mended as if ripped while her assailant tried to defile her.

Was he successful? Vladamir pondered in regret. His eye dipped over her thin frame, unable to determine an answer.

He knew he frightened her for it had been his intent, but the moment her eyes fell upon his scars he knew. He saw the panic in her and was sorry for it. An intense sadness haunted him and for a brief moment he longed to be whom he once was — devilishly handsome, charming, irresistible to fairer sex. A decade ago he would've lured her to his bed without thought. A decade ago, she would've come willingly. A decade ago, she'd have already been on her knees before him — her lips working over his shaft and her fingernails imbedded firmly into the cheeks of his ass.

"Argh!" He whipped his dark wool cloak around his shoulder to hide his face from her accusing gaze. Turning away, he was intent on storming down the passageway. He wanted, *needed*, to get away from her damned eyes. He was already losing himself to them. With those eyes she could control him and with her lips she could command him.

"Wait! Please don't go. Come back."

He cursed himself as he obeyed.

Already she commands me. Her woman's spell captures me.

"Are you still there, m'lord? I cannot see you." Her voice was gentle, like a cooling summer breeze. "Please, come back.

Forgive me. I didn't mean to say such things. I don't know why I have such a wicked tongue."

Vladamir turned and slowly made his way back to her. He stopped as the light from the torch sputtered out completely. His eyes were accustomed to the night and he saw her panicked features clearly.

"I'm sorry." Eden paused as she moved to stand. "'Tis wrong of me to call you a monster. I have no right to say such horrible things. Please forgive my senselessness."

Vladamir didn't move. She took a hesitant step toward him and bit her lip as she reached her hand forward. It swung though the air in sweeping searches, missing him each time.

"Are you there?" Eden inched slowly closer. "I cannot hear you. Have you disappeared? Have I driven you away?"

"I'm here," the duke answered, unsure as to why he did. He stayed back from her reach.

"You're Vladamir of Kessen, Duke of Lakeshire?"

"I am," he answered. His lips tightened as he denied himself the taste of her mouth.

"Why do you keep me here? What is your grievance with my father? For whatever has happened I'm sorry for it. I should like to help make it right."

Vladamir stiffened as he remembered whose seed she was. Growling at the reminder, he stalked forward in the darkness to grab her about the upper arms. "You're my prisoner. Give me your pledge that you won't try to escape again." He was angry, but loosened his grip when she groaned in pain.

"I cannot give my word on that, m'lord. Without better reason, I cannot agree to stay here with you. Without knowing the crime I'm being punished for, I cannot say I'm guilty."

"Give your word," he ordered as he leaned into her. She was so close, under his complete control. His nose almost touched hers as she swayed under his brute strength.

Take her! his body urged. *It is your right to do so!*

"Give it," he said instead of following his natural instinct to release his built-up desires, "or I'll send my armies to march against your father's home. I'll have all who reside within Hawks' Nest killed."

"I give you my word of honor," she complied. "Please don't harm my father's people. They are innocent. They don't deserve your wrath."

Vladamir was surprised at how easily she surrendered her freedom. Why didn't she struggle more? Why did she give in?

Mayhap, 'tis because your words aren't worth the air used to speak them. Ladies have no honor.

"Why are you like this?" Her arms fell listlessly to her sides. "Why are you so cruel? What has happened to you to make you so — ?"

"You think this cruel?" He laughed hard as he gave her another shake. "Why don't you ask your father about cruel?"

"I would if you'd but let me go," she snapped. Closing her eyes tightly, her head turned to the side as if bracing herself for his strike.

Vladamir's stomach tightened at her gesture. She thought he would beat her for that? What had happened to her? And why did he suddenly care? His hands loosened until his fingers moved on her arm, almost a caress but not quite.

"Please," she pleaded, not fighting him, "just let me go. I'm of no consequence to you. You cannot really want me here. Surely I'm more of a burden to you than anything."

"Nay, don't ask for your freedom again. It's a useless plea. I won't release you." He watched her lips as she flicked her tongue over the edge. The scent of lilies came to him from her hair as she moved her head to the side. He wondered if Haldana had purposefully used the scent. It had been one of his favorites long ago. He breathed in the enticing perfume of her. For a moment, he was lost in her spell. "Tomorrow you'll be given new quarters."

"The tower? You wish to put me in a real prison? Or mayhap even the dungeon? I have sworn to you I won't leave. At least give me a chance to prove my honor afore you doubt it. If I prove my honor false then you shall imprison me with my blessing, for I won't deny that then I'll be most deserving of it."

"Nay, m'lady, not the tower and most definitely not the dungeon," he answered softly, the sound a vast contrast to his usual hard tone. He wanted to laugh, for he didn't have a tower save for the chamber she was already in. "Prove your honor."

"Then, you're to make me your...?" Again she tried to pull from his arms. "I'm to be put in your chamber, m'lord? With you? Won't your Duchess be upset?"

"There is no Duchess of Lakeshire." Vladamir couldn't draw his gaze from her delightfully full lips as they quivered enchantingly under his watchful eyes. He thought of chaining her to his bed, forcing her to be his bed slave until he took his fill of her. "M'lady's prison shall be of gilded bars. You'll be afforded full use of the castle. You'll be fed. The servants will treat you with the respect due your station, unless you prove you deserve otherwise."

"Thank you."

"But," he warned, squeezing her shoulders once more and causing her to wince. "You won't be permitted outside the bailey walls. I don't care if the castle is burning to the ground. If you don't have my permission, you shall stay and burn with it. If I find you trying to leave, I'll lock you in the dungeon for all your days and I'll besiege your father's keep until all those who live within starve. I'll burn his crops, slaughter his peasants and his cattle and leave them to rot where they lay. And you, m'lady, will know the full meaning of hell afore you die."

"I understand," she said softly. "I won't try to escape. My only wish is that you'll reconsider and let me go."

"I won't do that," he answered, his voice harsh. His chest heaved with rapid breaths, but his growling tone turned soft. "M'lady will do well to wish for other things for I'll never let you go."

"Then I'll stay here true to my word and I'll only leave with your permission." Eden conceded, taking a deep breath. "I will swear it on mine own blood, but only if I may have one demand. Methinks it fair."

Anything.

Vladamir nodded his head and then realized she couldn't see him well enough through the darkness to make the gesture out. "What?"

"Don't harm my father's people. They don't deserve your wrath. I don't know what plans you may have, but keep your quarrel with my father only. If it is he who has spurred your anger, then he shall have to face it." She pulled away from him and he let her go. Her chin lifted proudly before him, even in her fear of him. "If you don't harm them, I'll stay here. But, if I find out that you hurt them in any way that wasn't self-defense, I'll break my vow and will do whatever is in my power to escape you. I'll spend the rest of my days if needs be bringing you to justice and I won't stop until 'tis done. Do we have a deal?"

"Yea, m'lady." He smiled at her courage. It puzzled him that she showed no concern for her father's safety, yet cared so openly for the lives of peasants. "I won't harm your father's people."

"Good." She held out her hand, her fingers shaking, but she didn't back down. "Hand me your dagger, m'lord, so that I may keep my word and pledge my honor with my blood. Let us seal the bargain so it shall be done."

"I won't demand your blood just yet," he said softly, denying her his dagger. Instead, Vladamir clasped her outstretched hand and pulled it to his chest over the beating of his heart. Not stopping to think of the consequences of his actions, he swung her into his arms. Shifting her off balance so she fell to the side, he encased her within his embrace. She was so small and fragile to him as she trembled in surprise. His body lurched, wanting this. He bent down and pressed his mouth against her parted lips, unable to resist her temptation a moment more. He needed to feel her heat, her soft lips.

The duke ran the fingers of his free hand into her hair and pressed her to him. The sweet petals of her mouth parted as she sought her breath. She moaned lightly. His tongue daringly traced the line of her lips and her slender body molded into his as if it had been carved for him to hold.

Vladamir had been a long time without the comforts of a woman's embrace and was a man long used to taking what he wanted. Eden clutched his tunic as he held her to his chest, feeling her intimate heat along his thigh, burning him. He pushed his leg against her, eliciting a soft moan. Innocent, she backed her hips away from his searching. Unable to resist, he grew bolder, forcing his thigh between hers. He massaged her slit through her clothing, smiling slightly when her breath deepened in surprise.

His cock brushed her side, eager to be set free. He rubbed harder and her legs wavered, loosening their grip on him. She copied the gentle rocking of his body and her sudden show of desire fueled his own as she became soft and pliant under his hands. Pressing his hips into her, he undulated his body along hers, mimicking the thrusts he desperately wanted to give her.

"Ah," she moaned softly. The sound was music to his ears.

Vladamir pushed her up against the wall, trapping her as he reached to grab her breast in his palm as his free hand worked down over her hip to pull up her skirt. Unable to stop, he thrust his hard cock against her stomach. He started to deepen the kiss but she moaned, her back arching.

The sound was his undoing. His cock surged from the pressure of rocking against her. Hot cum filled his braes as he climaxed inside them. His lips stopped moving on hers. The kiss was never deepened. Without warning her, he let her go, jerking back.

Eden stumbled and fell against the wall. One hand fluttered to her stomach and the other to her throat in a protective gesture as her breasts lifted with deep breaths.

"'Tis sealed," he stated harshly, embarrassed by how he'd lost control. He stopped her protest with the delicate press of his fingers. Her lips were moist and swollen from his kiss. He drew his hand away, needing to get away from her.

Chapter Four

ॐ

"M'lord, she cannot be found. 'Tis as if she disappeared." The knight tried to stand his ground against the fury of his master, but lowered his head slightly when he witnessed the man's building wrath. "We searched everywhere."

"Obviously not everywhere if she is still missing, you dimwitted fool," came the harsh reply. "Look again. Look harder!"

"It won't do any good, m'lord. There's no a trace of Lady Eden. We have searched the forest to the south, the marshes to the north. There's no evidence that she has passed. None of the villagers have seen her, or they aren't talking if they have." The knight rested his hand lightly on the narrow sword at his waist. He scratched the shortly cropped blond hair behind his ear with his gloved hand before suggesting timidly, "Methinks we should wait fer notice of a ransom."

"I don't care to hear your opinion!" The Earl of Hawks' Nest stalked up to the soldier who dared to defy his order. He backhanded the man across the face with a beefy arm and sent him sprawling to the dirt. Then, turning around in circles, he spied a dog lying nearby in some straw. The animal gnawed absently on an old bone. Storming to the animal, the earl kicked the dog in the gut. The mongrel yelped and scurried off across the bailey.

For a moment, the earl didn't move, finding no pleasure in watching the dog run off. No one moved to help the fallen man as he gathered himself to his feet. The knight stood, not daring to fight back. Lifting his head proudly, he remained silent.

Clifton glared briefly at his castle wall in need of repairs. The uncovered stone was beginning to crumble. Inside, the great hall's floors were lined with straw rushes, but were constructed of dirt and not stone. His castle was falling apart around him. He needed money — and quickly.

With his daughter missing, the servants grew lazier in their duties because she wasn't there to direct them. Dust settled in every crevice, litter lined the bailey floor and the garderobes omitted a foul odor he could no longer ignore.

The earl wore an undertunic of fine cream-colored linen with tightly fitting sleeves at the wrists, over which he wore a crimson overtunic of fine wool with sleeves that reached only to his elbows. The elaborate gold trim of large florid design was frayed a bit at the cuffs of his sleeve, exposing the fact that the tunic was old. His brown braes were faded at the knees and buttocks, which he tried to hide with the length of the overtunics. However, when he walked the worn spots showed through the slit in the side.

Sighing at the thought, the earl rubbed his forehead before saying, "I won't hear what you cannot do! Find my daughter! She couldn't have gotten far without help! If needs be, make example of a few villagers. Then see if they will talk. If they don't — *take their children and imprison them!*"

"You heard your master's order." Lord Luther came up to stand beside Clifton. "Find my fiancée!"

The earl swung around to glare at Luther. He frowned before clenching his fists and baring his teeth. He didn't appreciate the interference though he'd grown used to Luther's meddling.

Luther was a tall man, towering over many of his peers, and was an odd match to Clifton's coarse nature and shorter stature. But with his height he hadn't gained width. He was overly slender with cheekbones that were sunken into his face, making him undesirable to women. Spoiled dreadfully by his late mother who raised him while his father had been away at war, he had a nasty temperament.

But their appearances weren't all that contrasted the two men. Clifton was a titled man and a great landholder. He was respected amongst his peers as a fearless leader, though he mostly sent men in his stead to the battlefront, choosing instead to handle the more civilized politics of war as an ambassador does. The late King Aethelred of Wessex respected him as a loyal ambassador and the earl liked to think that Aethelred's successor, King Alfred, felt the same reverence for him. He'd spent years traveling to foreign countries, meeting with dignitaries. He was a noble member of the Witan often being called to lead them in their decision making. And he was poor.

Luther had wealth and lots of it, but he didn't have a castle or a large contingency of fighting men. He had no land to speak of—save a small manor made of wood. Due to his great fortune and the luck of familial connections he was considered a noble, although he wasn't officially titled. He wasn't on the Witan and he was only well-known by the knights he fought with as being a type of man who would do anything to get what he wanted. Luther wanted power.

Clifton had no male heirs of his own, his wife having died after delivering twelve stillborn boys and Eden. The earl needed Luther's fortune to keep his line and Hawks' Nest together. Luther wanted the power and prestige that came with marrying the earl's only living child and thus inheriting his title and land.

"Go!" the earl hollered unnecessarily with an exasperated dash of his fist. After the soldiers departed to do as they were told, Clifton turned to his daughter's intended. "We must find her, lest there can be no alliance."

"We will find her and the man who did this." Luther narrowed his eyes to watch the men ride through the castle gate. His sunken eyes were blank as he glanced back at the earl.

"Eden wouldn't have left on her own," the earl returned with a dark frown. "She knows her duty by you. She wouldn't run from it."

Luther didn't speak. He nodded his head in slow agreement.

"Any news of the handmaiden, Lynne?" Clifton inquired.

"One of the villagers reported seeing her pass through afore Eden even disappeared. The servant girl merely ran off with a lover," Luther responded bleakly. He shielded his eyes as he looked over the yard in distraction. "Methinks 'twas a cotter from the marsh settlement."

"Stinking lot of peasants the marsh cotters are," the earl grumbled. He dismissed the missing servant girl with a wave of his hand. "That Lynne was always strange."

Luther's lips curled into a snarl. "I'll ride out myself with your men and find m'lady. She couldn't have gotten far. I cannot sit aside and watch their ineptness a moment more."

"Yea, Luther, you do that," the earl grumbled in mounting irritation. He kicked at a loosened stone by the gate. "For 'tis your future you ride after. No marriage, no title."

Luther frowned. "With no Eden, there will be no other choice for you, Clifton, but to give me the title."

* * * * *

Eden scrunched up her nose and pulled her skirt closer to her waist, trying in vain to keep it out of the black soot. The kitchen hearth looked as if it hadn't been cleaned since its making. The stone was marred with the burned remains of past meals.

Her tunic gown was of poor quality, but constructed of very thick wool. It was a servant's garment and was less glamorous than that she was used to but under the circumstances she didn't care. She was just glad to get anything so long as it was laundered.

Sighing, she thought of the many colored wimples and veils she'd owned at her father's home. The earl saw to it that she was well clothed as to befit her station. So much so that sometimes Eden felt that what her father lacked in love he tried to make up for with gifts. The last gift he'd given her was a beautiful cream-colored tunic made of fine linen. It was to soften her disposition so he told her the news of her betrothal to Lord Luther. It was to have been her wedding tunic.

Those days are over. Now I'm less than a servant. I'm a prisoner.

Eden scolded herself for the whimsy and focused her attentions on the task at hand—cleaning Lakeshire Castle. The old black cauldron which hung within the fireplace reeked of fish porridge—the only meal she'd been served. Feeling the eyes of the kitchen servants boring into the back of her head, she ran her hand over the brim of the cauldron, knowing her fingers would be covered with grime before she even looked to them.

The fireplace was but one example of the disrepair and neglect of Lakeshire Castle. It began with the cobwebs in Eden's new and old chambers and grew steadily worse from there. Eden had optimistically thought that the poor condition of her first prison was because it was a prison and the chamber hadn't been in use before her arrival there. But she grew disheartened as she saw the abovestairs passageways and the condition of her new, larger chamber—a chamber that had been set aside for her as the duke promised.

Abovestairs, the stone walls were dusty and chipped. The tapestries were rotted, the straw mattresses were musty and the gauze hanging from the canopied beds was decayed. Belowstairs, the main hall fared little better. At first glance it appeared cleaner than the bedchambers.

But that is only because people live belowstairs. 'Tis hard for things to compile refuse and dust if they are being utilized.

Turning around in disdain, she sighed and looked coolly at the gathered servants. Eden eyed each separately before speaking. "I ordered this cauldron and fireplace cleaned afore I came back. 'Twas nearly two hours past and it hasn't been attended to."

None of the servants answered and none moved to touch the offending cauldron. Eden wiped her fingers on the borrowed apron only to push her hair from her face with the back of her hand. She'd strapped the locks with a piece of leather so that it wouldn't fall into her face while she helped to clean.

"The duke bid me to act in stead of the lady of the manor. Do you wish to answer to his wrath? For 'tis not only I who will suffer if this keep is not brought up to his approval." Eden hadn't wanted to resort to fear, but the servants refused to listen to her. She'd been struggling against their laziness all morning.

At first she tried to get them to replace the rushes in the main hall with fresh scented straw, but they wouldn't. Then she tried to get them to sweep the cobwebs from the rafters above the dining hall, yet still they resisted. It was the same when she tried to have the bailey cleared of debris and refuse. When she asked about the resident stonemason, she'd been laughed at.

"I know not how many days his lordship will be gone. But I do know that if he doesn't see a vast improvement in his keep..." Eden looked to her wringing hands in horror, purposefully leaving the apprehensive servants to their own imaginations. The effort wasn't lost as the women gasped and mumbled amongst themselves. Gradually, one of the taller girls came forward.

"M'lady." The maid gave a small curtsy. "We don't know how."

"You don't know how to clean a cauldron?" Eden asked in disbelief. "How is that possible? 'Tis a simple enough chore."

"What I mean, m'lady, is that we have not been instructed as to what our duties are. Which one of us shall clean the cauldron? Which one of us should replace the rushes?" The servant shrugged delicately in helplessness and glanced at her dirty feet to kick at a loosened stone. "All of us were sent here to work by King Alfred. Our village was ravaged by the wars and we had no home to go back to. The Vikings burnt our cottages to the ground. The king gave us the opportunity to work as servants to m'lord while he was here as his prisoner."

"What is your name?" Eden asked.

No wonder this keep is falling apart! The master has had little to do with it.

"Lizbeth." The servant looked up briefly and then back to her feet. Taking the edge of her apron in hand, she tugged at a thread.

"Does anyone know about cleaning the rushes?" Eden inquired of the group at large. One of the maids raised her tentative hand, glancing around nervously to see if she was the only one. "Excellent. You'll be in charge of the task. Start a fire in the bailey and pick six to help you. The others will dust the cobwebs from the rafters. We shall begin our cleaning in the main hall and kitchen before we work our way abovestairs. I want this keep to sparkle afore his lordship comes home. I should think we would want him pleased with us."

Eden bit her lip in thought as she pointed to a pixie-looking maid, "Go find the stonemason. Tell him we need these loosened stones repaired at once. As you clear the rushes inform him of any others you might find in the hall floor. It won't do for the guests of his lordship to trip."

The maids giggled as they turned to the girl who had been instructed to get the mason. The woman's face paled and she looked miserably at the castle's new mistress.

"Harold won't take kindly—" the pixie began in dread of her task.

"Tell Harold that he'll be the first thrown to the monster upon the master's return. Methinks he'll do it fast enough!" Lizbeth put in before Eden could answer. The maids giggled. The pixie gulped but nodded her head in understanding.

Eden tried not to frown at the way they viewed their master, but she didn't wish to encourage them. Every time she thought of Vladamir, she didn't think of him as a monster as she'd been wont to do at first. All she remembered was the feel of his hands on her body, the press of his lips on her mouth. Something had sparked between them—hot and potent. But then he stopped, pulling away from her before the final explosion in her body. Maybe it was for the best that she didn't explode. Eden blushed as she realized the maids watched expectantly. With a wave of her hand she commanded, "See to it."

The maids complied and filed out of the kitchen. A few whispered to each other in wonderment of the noblewoman's blush. Eden pretended not to hear. Lizbeth shyly hung back and Eden turned to her with interest.

"M'lady, his lordship will return two days hence," the servant offered. "'Tis all the time he ever stays away from the castle."

"Oh." Eden wondered where he'd gone. "Then that should be plenty of time to whip this keep into shape, if we work hard at it."

"Would m'lady like me to tend to the cauldron?" Lizbeth hesitated. She kicked at the loose stone and stopped herself with a guilty glance up.

"You may help me with it," Eden directed with a firm nod. She struggled to pull the weighty cauldron off the hook and set it on the floor. "We will need water and lye if we are to do it right."

"There is a well in the bailey," Lizbeth offered with a growing smile, "and plenty of lye in the larder."

"In the larder?" Eden shook her head in dismay. "By the food?"

"We didn't know where else to put it." Lizbeth shrugged.

Eden got the feeling that the maid stayed behind to do more than help her clean. Was this comely woman the duke's mistress? Lizbeth was one of the more pleasantly featured servants. It would make sense if she was intimate with the duke. A pang of jealousy unfurled in her chest at the thought.

'Tis not like I want the position.

Eden forced a pleasant smile on her tight face, afraid that it would crack her skin with the effort.

"Help me carry this to the bailey well," Eden ordered. Suddenly, she found she wanted the girl's company. She grabbed one side and looked expectantly at the servant.

Lizbeth nodded and grabbed the handle, obviously surprised to see a lady of gentry dirty her hands with the household chores. As the women struggled out of the side door in silence, Lizbeth nodded her head past the small vegetable and herb garden.

The scent of sage, parsley and chamomile was strong on the breeze as the two women hurried past it. The garden was small with a rough stone long-seat. Someone had left a basket by the base of the bench full of fresh vegetables—celery, onions, cabbage. Beyond the garden by the black stone wall was a large oak tree. The tree seemed somewhat out of place growing by the garden, but Eden assumed it was there because, like everything else, its master neglected it.

They took several hurried steps under the pot's massive weight as they drew closer to the bailey well. Their slender arms strained more with each step. Mangy dogs came running toward them as they walked, trying to sniff at what they carried. Lizbeth tried to kick several away from her skirts, almost tumbling over in the process. Eden watched in displeasure as a mongrel ran into the kitchen.

As the women steadied the cauldron on the ground with a few grunts of excursion, a brawny knight came forward. He tossed his damp brown hair as it fell just below his eye. His young lips curled with a mischievous grin, though the action seemed completely unintentional.

"Here, let me help you with that," the knight put forth gallantly. He looked as if he was just back from his morning exercise for his naked tanned back glistened with sweat. Giving a boyish smile at Lizbeth, he turned to bow to Eden. "M'lady, I'm Raulf. If ever you have need of my services—"

"Thank you, Sir Raulf," Eden broke in pleasantly. She nodded at the handsome man and hid her smile as she watched Lizbeth through the corner of her eye. A light blush stained the servant's cheeks a comely rose. The woman sighed prettily as Raulf lifted the cauldron from their hands with one swift movement. Raulf held the black pot with little effort and grinned shyly at the serving girl.

Eden saw the look of longing between the couple and tried not to laugh, feeling somewhat relieved. For even if Lizbeth was Vladamir's mistress, it didn't seem that the young maid liked the duke very much. Eden gently drew their attention by saying to Raulf, "Your assistance is most welcome, sir."

"Where would m'lady like this?" he asked with a tilt of his boyish head.

"By the well," Lizbeth answered for Eden. The serving girl jumped onto her toes to point in the obvious direction of the water. Licking her lips, she looked bashfully away.

Raulf moved in front of them with a nod of his head and then proceeded to carry the heavy pot to the well with little trouble. Eden turned her attention to Lizbeth, but found that the girl was lost in her own daydreams of the handsome brown-eyed knight. Turning back to follow slowly behind Raulf, she gave an exasperated sigh as a hen ran by pursued by a hungry dog and made a mental note to have a separate pen built for the fowl at once. She didn't like the prospect of being accosted by livestock every time she tried to walk across the bailey.

Eden wasn't too impressed with Lakeshire Castle thus far. Though it appeared to have much potential, it wasn't taken advantage of. The servants had been lazy in the care, though now she knew it was more like the master who had been lazy in instructing the servants.

She knew little about the castle and surrounding property. What she did know came from eavesdropping on political conversations at her father's table, though one could hardly call it eavesdropping when they talked right next to her. It wasn't her fault they forgot she was there.

Lakeshire was one of the smallest dukedoms in Wessex and had only been made into a duchy the year past. The castle was small, especially for a duke. Her father, who was only an earl, had a larger home with much more property. She remembered her father thinking it quite a scandal to put a foreign monster in a position of such great power, when loyal men like himself didn't advance in title.

"Tell me, Lizbeth." Eden stopped walking and motioned to the servant to do the same. She only continued when Raulf was out of earshot. "Why would you say m'lord is a prisoner?"

"Because he is, m'lady." Lizbeth looked over in surprise, dusting the soot from her hands onto her apron and leaving a black streak across the gray wool. She gave Raulf one last glance of longing before giving her attention to Eden.

"But, how? He holds all of this. How is that a prison?" Eden asked in wonder. "True, 'tis a dirty keep but still he is titled with land. In my travels I have seen much worse than this. For at least the castle is built of stone and not wood, which can burn. So how can such a privileged duke be a prisoner?"

"He is King Alfred's prisoner, m'lady. Lakeshire is really King Alfred's land. At least that is what most of us think. Once the Vikings start another war, the duke will be banished by the king." Lizbeth's sprightly green eyes became round with awe. She appeared amazed that Lady Eden hadn't been told the story. The women slowly walked toward the well. "The King of the Danelaw bestowed him the title of duke only after he came to Wessex to be a hostage. He was sent by his King Guthrum to ensure peace between the Vikings and us. 'Tis whispered that King Guthrum made a pact with the devil and was given the duke in return. Then the king sent the demon lord here to bide his time until he's to tear all of Wessex apart."

"Nonsense," Eden lifted a skeptical brow but didn't order the maid to stop her tale. It shamed her to remember she'd also thought that of the duke. She'd heard her father talk of a treaty between Wessex and the Vikings, but hadn't thought much of it at the time, for men were always making and breaking treaties. "A demon?"

"Yea, m'lady," Lizbeth said softly. The maid put her hand on Eden's arm to stop her. She glanced about before hurrying in a rushed whisper, "Have you not seen his fiery scars? They are the marks of hell. I have seen them, up close. They are truly frightening."

"Yea, once," Eden answered in distraction. She'd only seen him briefly the one time in the darkened hallway and even then most of the seeing hadn't been done with her eyes but with her hands. Touching her lips, she blushed. Vladamir had been gone the morning following their shared kiss. Haldana wouldn't tell her where he went and she wondered if the servants even knew where the duke was.

The morning after the kiss, Eden had been promptly moved to the new chamber as was promised. The different accommodations were delightful compared to that of her first prison. The bed was thick, covered with new fur. Even though her first order of business had been to clean the dusty chamber, she was pleased with the change.

"Then you know 'tis true. He's marked by hell." Lizbeth nodded. "I've seen him bare, m'lady. 'Tis an awful sight."

Eden shivered at the admission and tried not to be disappointed. She was well aware that it was natural for noblemen to sleep with many of the fairer servants. Her father had conquered the questionable virtue of all in his castle. Why wouldn't the duke do the same?

Eden remembered her own hasty words when she saw the duke's scarred hand. Hadn't she said close to the same thing about him? But when she saw the flicker of pain that crossed his enchanting dark eyes, she'd been sorry for it. In that short-lived moment she saw a man who wasn't at all a monster. That one memory could make her forget all the threats he uttered against her.

"He's marked by fire, not hell." Eden corrected, quickening her steps. "There is a difference."

"Nay, 'tis the fire of hell," Lizbeth persisted, moving to keep up.

"Has he harmed any here?" Eden wiped her fingers on her apron, pretending to examine the material. Her hands shook as she awaited the answer.

"Nay, not yet, but he has only been here a year." Lizbeth smiled at Raulf, who nodded from the distance. He'd dropped the cauldron by the well and was slowly making his way back to the exercise yard. Lizbeth blushed as the man winked at her. "I told you, he bides his time."

"How did he get those scars? Do any here know the truth?" Eden reminded herself not to be too sensitive where Vladamir's reputation was concerned. The servants would believe of him what they wished, regardless of her intervention.

And who am I to intervene?

"Nay. None, except mayhap Ulric. He and Haldana came here with his lordship. Some others came too, but Ulric and Haldana are the only ones under his complete spell." Lizbeth leaned over the well and lifted the bucket. "They scold us if they hear us talking."

They worked in silence for a moment, dumping the water into the pot. They rinsed it several times, pouring the contents to the ground. Several of the castle's dogs came to lick up the old food. Eden gently nudged one shaggy animal away as the mongrel came close to her foot in its frenzy.

"M'lord may not have brought harm upon us, but he is a demon make no doubt—a demon that is biding his time." Lizbeth nodded her head in confirmation of her decree. Her eyes seemed to shout, *heed my words!*

"What have you heard? Tell me what you know and I'll see if 'tis reasonable."

"His voice," Lizbeth began.

"Nay, I have traveled and have heard many different ways of speaking. His accent is not so rare."

Well, 'tis not entirely a lie.

"His scars," Lizbeth continued with a dubious nod. "'Tis whispered he held his wife down in fire while she burned. He tried to hold down his baby daughter next to her and he would have killed her too fer his wife. She wouldn't have it. She threw the baby from the flames and took them all into herself to save the child. After the wife died, he saw the child and allowed her to live fer now the child also wore the mark of the devil."

Eden frowned.

"He hides the child away somewhere. 'Tis said she is being schooled in the black arts." Lizbeth shuddered and made the sign of the cross over her breast. "He waits fer her. The day they are rejoined they will tear apart Wessex. The land will be covered in rivers of blood, the—"

"Enough." Eden broke in as she turned back to her work with a dismal shake of her head. She remembered her dreams. The skies had rained blood. Maybe there was something to the story. She lifted the rinsed cauldron to take it back to the kitchen.

"But...?" Lizbeth protested. She helped to hoist the pot. It was much lighter now that the food was out of it. "I was about to get to the best part of the tale."

"What of you and Sir Raulf?" Eden dismissed the serving girl's persistence. She was desperate to change the subject, not wishing to hear any more of the girl's alarming tale. Surely the man Lizbeth described was not the same man who'd kissed her so intimately.

Lizbeth began to cry, her thin shoulders trembling with the gut-wrenching sobs. "We wish to be married, but the duke refuses to speak of it with Raulf. We cannot be wed without his consent. Raulf is one of his men and I'm his servant."

Eden set the cauldron down and tenderly patted the dramatic, emotional girl on the shoulder. She didn't know what to say to her. In light of her life, Eden couldn't think favorably of marriage. She didn't know what the duke's reasons were for not hearing the knight's counsel.

"We were sort of hoping that you'd talk to him fer us. Perchance ask him to say 'tis all right." Lizbeth smiled at Eden, her eyes glimmering with girlish hope.

"'Tis not my place to interfere." Eden dropped her hand. "I'm as much a prisoner here as his lordship—mayhap more so for I cannot leave Lakeshire."

"Nay, you're a noble lady. You're of his class. 'Tis you he would listen to, if he were to listen at all," Lizbeth persisted. She refused to let her hope die. "If he told you to look after his keep..."

Eden peered into Lizbeth's hopeful gaze as her words trailed off unspoken. When she saw that the girl was about to cry anew, she said, "If the subject ever comes up I'll try. But I don't think my words will have any great effect in influencing his decisions."

"Oh, m'lady, thank you!" Lizbeth exclaimed in pleasure. She wrapped her arms around the noblewoman's neck. "I knew you would be the one to convince him!"

Eden ignored the impropriety and let the girl hug her briefly before prying her arms away. She was a little uncomfortable with the closeness. Straightening her shoulders, she turned to pick up the cauldron. "Let us get to the keep, lest the duke won't be in a mood to hear aught but his own wrath."

Lizbeth nodded. A soft smile of assurance clouded her pretty face as if she just knew Lady Eden would make her dreams of a life with Raulf come true. Eden wished she could be as sure.

* * * * *

Eden was pleased with how well the manor came along under her care. The servants labored quite hard, once they knew what was expected of them. Lakeshire Castle was in want of minor repairs and there wasn't much to be done for the black color that the stone of the walls were built from. She tried to brighten the color with lye and only succeeded in darkening them into an even more dismal black.

She had Ulric direct the men to help with some of the harder chores that she was too weak to do and enlisted Haldana to take charge of the women, at least until Vladamir came home and approved of the arrangements she'd made. Eden doubted that he would mind what she'd done for he hadn't taken much care with the organization of the castle himself. It was as if he didn't care about his home.

She even ordered the servants to freshen the duke's sleeping chamber, though not much was to be done for it. His coverlet was of an interesting blend of material, like none she'd ever felt. Her hand had glided over the smooth, silky cloth with ease until getting caught in a strand of dark hair. Lifting the abnormally long strand from its silken resting place, she sighed, only to wrap it around her fingers.

When no servants looked, she tentatively put her nose to his pillow. It smelled as he had when he held her. The memory made her tremble anew and she almost didn't move her face from his linens for the smell intoxicated her so. Just thinking of his smell made her body wet with anticipation. She damned herself for her attraction, even as it baffled her.

The linens were laundered and the stone swept and scrubbed clean. The cobwebs were dusted from the rafters. Eden thought she might learn more of the man by seeing his private chambers, but the large room was sparse. He had an immense bed with a canopy, which had curtains that could be drawn to keep out the draft and a large stone fireplace. There was a stool set before the fire. His personal trunk rested at the end of the bed, but it was locked shut. It was if he had no real personal belongings. She was severely disappointed.

When she was finished with the abovestairs chambers, even the ones not in use gleamed with freshness. Although the beds needed new coverlets and the stone floors needed fur rugs, Eden laundered and left what she found in them. She didn't dare order things made, not knowing what Vladamir's resources truly were. By the look of his castle, he wasn't a rich man and might not take kindly to her wasting his money. His poverty didn't bother her though. The cleaning took care of the most predominant of the problems.

Eden didn't go into the section of the castle where she'd been kept prisoner. She merely had the maids scrub the part of the dirty passageways that could be seen from the lower level.

She also held true to her promise and didn't try to escape. Notwithstanding, it didn't stop the thought from entering her mind upon occasion. It would've been easy. The gate was often left open for the peasants to go through and Ulric had even offered to let her borrow one of the horses in Vladamir's stables to go for a ride. Although the thought had merit, she didn't dare venture outside the walls of Lakeshire Castle. The duke might misconstrue such an act as betrayal and she'd given her word.

She prayed nightly that her preparations would please Vladamir. For the more she stayed out of his company, the more she doubted the pain she felt from him that night in the darkened hallway. She didn't know the man, beyond the impressions she got from the servants. None of the impressions were good, save for Ulric and Haldana. Even their loyalty was somewhat discouraging.

But there was something to the duke—to his voice that haunted her. It was in an accent so hard and virile. His presence sent a shiver through her body. It wasn't quite unpleasant but a tremble mixed with both excitement and fear. He'd kissed her mouth until it had been willing for his touch. Men had tried, but none had succeeded in kissing her before now. The kiss had been mostly tender, unlike his harsh reputation. So many things about him were contradictions.

Eden sighed as her lips throbbed anew. She rubbed her shoulder as she spread out the rest of the fresh rushes with her foot and turned to Lizbeth. "Did you hear that?"

"The front gate, m'lady." The girl looked to her in fright. Her eyes grew round with her exclamation and her voice squeaked out in an ominous whisper, "The monster returns."

"Lizbeth, don't call him such in my presence again." Eden had begot a strange sort of friendship with the girl and smiled to ease the reprimand. "The duke is not a monster."

"Yea, m'lady." Lizbeth nodded, though her eyes still glowed with doubt.

Eden felt as if a dark cloud suddenly dropped over the manor. Lines of stress edged the faces of servants where just a moment before there had been smiles and laughter. They stopped in their duties to look about in anxiety. She saw a few of them kneel to the rushes to straighten them needlessly in hurriedly frantic motions. Still others ran into the kitchen to hide.

She ignored the distraught servants as she went to the bailey. Despite all her fear of him, she couldn't wait to finally see Vladamir in the daylight. Maybe then he wouldn't appear to be such a mythical creature. As she moved, she felt a gentle hand on her elbow. She turned and nodded to Ulric, who escorted her out to the bailey.

"Ulric," she said as they passed through the door leading outside. The sun shone brightly in the sky making the keep once again unseasonably warm. Nevertheless, she shivered in anticipation. Focusing her eyes on the raised gate she continued, "Do you think he'll be angered at what I have done?"

"And what is it you have done, m'lady?"

Eden froze as the accented voice came from her side. A cooling breeze washed over her, whipping strands of her hair loose across her face. She hadn't thought Vladamir would already be well within the bailey walls. She didn't like the way he addressed her as m'lady. The word sounded contemptuous coming from him.

Ulric gave her a reassuring squeeze before dropping his hand from her arm. He backed away without comment.

Eden hesitated, suddenly afraid to see the man who kept her a prisoner. She waited in turmoil for him to come to her, to command her. The wind grew stronger, pushing her gown tight against her body. The gentle scent of him, of horse and man, softly enfolded her. She didn't know whether it was truly from him or a figment of her imagination. Nonetheless the smell stirred her body. When he didn't answer, she cautiously turned.

The sun was bright as it fell into her eyes. She squinted and raised her hand to her brow. Pushing the hair from her face, so that it would blow back away from her forehead, she shaded her vision from the brilliant light. Her breath caught in her throat as she saw him clearly for the first time.

She watched him push lazily away from the black stone wall. It was as if he'd been lounging there for quite some time. The bright light haloed his head, bringing orange relief to the long black strands of his hair. His hair was so dark it almost looked blue and it fell nearly to his waist in barbaric length.

The man towered well above her, just as she suspected he would. She leaned her head back to look up at him. She felt her gaze first go to and get trapped by the depth of his disquiet eyes, eyes that were much lighter than she recalled from the darkened passageway. His skin was only slightly tanned and gave his features a pale masculine beauty. His nose was strong and straight, his lips firm and alluring. He had a strong jaw, whose perfection was only marred by the scar that lined its edge. Eden didn't care about the scar, she couldn't see past the swarthy perfection of his eyes.

She licked her lips as her chest rose with pants of air. Vladamir's gaze darkened intently as if to silently growl at her. A wave of longing accosted her senses. She forgot what answer he required of her. Her body trembled, growing wet and hot under his probing attention.

He took a step toward her, confident in the fear he bestowed around him. His gaze held her steadfast in its grip. His body loomed over her, its muscles clearly defined under his black clothing. A cold smile curled his lips but didn't reach his eyes.

"You haven't answered." Lowering his chin, he leaned to the side to form a barrier between the sun and her face.

Eden quickly nodded her head. As his shadow fell over her, she cautiously lowered her hand to her waist and entwined her fingers together.

The sides of his hair were constrained back, so she was afforded ample view of his features. The wind blew from behind him, pushing a piece of his bound hair over his shoulder to hit him across the face. Eden glanced at the dark wave and moved to gently push it back. His presence caused her heart to beat irregularly fast, however the blood in her veins seemed to thicken and slow. His skin was warm. She let her hand languidly caress his cheek. The movement made the nerves in her finger jump alive to jolt down her arm in a pleasingly new sensation. When he looked at her, she felt as if they were the only ones in the world.

She tried to swallow to relieve the sudden dryness of her mouth. It didn't help. His harsh eyes were watching her, studying her, judging her. He radiated a fiery heat. His eyes glittered with an untamed anger. She wanted to touch him more, but stopped herself.

Confused, she was all too aware of the power the duke had over her. Not only was he her self-proclaimed master, but he also ruled her senses and caused her to speak too freely. She would have to be more careful in the future lest she draw his physical wrath down on her head.

"Well?" Vladamir demanded as he stepped closer, regretting that the action caused her to withdraw from him with a blush. She dropped her hand to her side and looked away, apologizing silently for the unwarranted boldness of touching him without permission. Her hair picked up reddish tints from the sun, an odd but beautiful contrast to her pale skin.

By all the gods! She was beautiful, more so than he remembered. He'd thought of her often, stroking his cock to the image in his head. While he was gone he'd spilled his seed on the ground so many times he couldn't count. In the sun, there were streaks of red in the brown. He'd been stunned momentarily by her true beauty. Her skin was smooth and flawless, except for a dark shading of an almost completely faded bruise. The swelling was gone from her eyes. Her lips remained full and pleasing and a dimple hit her cheek when she smiled. But she wasn't smiling at the moment.

"I forgot." She shook her head as if to clear her thinking. "What did you ask of me?"

"You wondered if I'd be angered at what you had done and I asked, what you have done," he reminded her. A lazy smile curled on his lips as he studied her, but he didn't let the smirk reach his passionless eyes.

"Yea, naturally," she sighed. Biting her lip, she took a deep breath, "I..."

"You?" he prompted her to proceed when she hesitated. His watchful gaze darted to her lips and then back. He wondered at her puzzled expression. She didn't appear fearful of him, yet she struggled to speak.

"I cleaned, m'lord," she answered flatly with a shake of her head. Her tongue flicked over the corner of her lip.

"Cleaned?" he asked, confused. Her answer threw him off guard. He thought that she'd tried to escape.

"Yea." She nodded her head in confirmation. Clearing her throat, she put forth boldly, "I cleaned. You bid me to have free run of the castle. So I directed the servants to clean."

"I see. The Monster of Lakeshire's lair wasn't to your liking. 'Twas too foul for you, m'lady?"

"Nay, you bid me to act a lady here." She frowned. "I was following your order. Methought that since the manor was in need of a scrubbing, that you'd want me to," she paused, gesturing helplessly, "well, you're a man and men don't know, don't care about—"

"Nay, I said you were to have freedom to go in the castle where you will," the duke corrected. He was somewhat pleased that she didn't back away from his menacing tone. The fact surprised him. He hid his pleasure under an icy mask. "And that the servants would treat you as a lady. I said naught about scrubbing."

"I know, but methought you meant to imply...well, you said there was no duchess and methought..."

"I'll always say what I mean. There's no need for implications." He narrowed his eyes and watched her pulse quicken in her throat. Her fear slowly trickled into her rounded eyes. A lock of her waist-length hair brushed across her forehead.

"I didn't mean to offend," she offered weakly as she let her gaze fall momentarily to his lips then back to his eyes.

"Then why do you stare?" he countered as he raised his eyebrow in censure. It was the first time in a very long time he'd called anyone on their rudeness over his scars.

Eden quickly looked away, turning piously to the ground. Nervously, she twisted her heel in to the dirt. "You're not pleased with me."

Vladamir watched her through a veiled expression. He saw her shoulders tremble slightly under his steady gaze. Finally, she raised her head and looked past his shoulder. Her eyes were moist, though no tears fell. He felt a foreign sense of remorse deep in his gut.

"I didn't mean aught by it. Methought I was doing as you bid me, for 'tis how my father raised me to be a lady. He said 'twas my duty to see to the comfort of first him and then to the comforts of my husband." Eden's words were said with such an earnest candor that Vladamir was hard-pressed to believe her. She glanced at him and then away again.

"But I'm not your husband," he reminded her. Leaning in, he whispered, "And this is not your keep."

"I know, 'tis my prison," Eden spat. Her shoulders shook with the effort it took not to shout at him. "I have no need of the reminder, m'lord. Methought only to make the best of the situation. 'Twas how I was raised. And I didn't mean to insinuate that methought of you as husband. I only meant that—"

"Quite your father's daughter, aren't you?" He took a menacing step forward, forcing her to step back toward the castle entrance.

Vladamir wanted to touch her. His body longed for her, though his mind protested. He was almost sorry for scolding her, for now she refused to look at him. Her lush lips haunted him while he was away and now he stared at them. They were parted with her even breathing and were moist from the nervous licks of her pink tongue.

"Nay, m'lord, I'm afraid if you were to ask him you'd find I'm a disappointment to him." Her jaw hardened and her eyes dried at the statement. Still, she averted her gaze.

His eyes roamed over the length of her body only to come back to study the lightening bruises of her nose. She wore her hair long and loose, only the locks near her ear were gathered in a plait that ran over her back. The waves crashed over her shoulders to seductively outline her figure. A wayward strand curled around her succulent breast. Her chestnut eyes gleamed with a vulnerable light.

Vladamir's grimace of displeasure deepened. The overtunic she wore belonged to one of the servants, but Eden carried herself like a lady and the gown didn't belittle her station. The bodice was too small and pulled tightly at her breasts. He found his gaze lingering and it wasn't revenge he thought of when he looked at her.

Vladamir had tried to purge the temptation Lady Eden presented from his body. He sought out a peasant who could easily assuage the fire in his gut for a few coins. But to his extreme disappointment he couldn't find a woman to light his desires like this noblewoman did. He'd gone without female company and stroking his own cock no longer held any appeal. He wanted more—much more. He wanted to feel her soft, wet pussy gripping him, taking all of him.

"M'lord?" When he didn't answer, she pulled further away from him.

"Yea, m'lady?" Vladamir despised the fact that he was attracted to her. His lust only darkened his mood until he mercilessly scowled at her.

"May I take my leave? I'll stop the servants in their duties as you wish."

"Nay." Glancing over the line of her creamy neck to the place where her throat met her ear, he really didn't listen to her words or the responses he gave to them. His body took over his mind, taunting him with his unsated desires and beastly lust. His tongue ached to lick the rapid beat of her pulse to see if he could make it quicken. He used to hold such power over women — well, most anyway. "Let them work. I'll inspect that which you have done. If I'm pleased, you'll be rewarded."

Vladamir lifted his callused hand to touch her neck. Her eyes fluttered closed briefly and her pulse drummed against his hand. She stiffened, but to his surprise she didn't run. He cupped her chin gently before letting his hand fall to the side. His mind once again gained its control, but at a devious cost.

What would you, m'lady, want with a monster? You, a maiden of great beauty.

"Begone," he ordered under his breath. He watched her slender hips as she darted inside, disappointed that she obeyed. Then, sighing, he turned to the exercise yard. "Yea, what would you want indeed?"

Chapter Five

മ

"M'lord, I trust the ride went well," Ulric called from the side yard. His smug grin revealed the fact that he'd watched the interplay between the prisoner and her keeper with interest. He wasn't the only one. Many of the servants and knights in the yard had stopped in their duties to watch. "Are you to train straight away?"

"The ride was as to be expected," the duke answered tersely. He naturally slowed his steps so the older man could catch up. "And, yea."

Vladamir had been to see King Alfred. As part of his hostage agreement he rode to where the king or an appointed ambassador was and made known his presence. It was a way for Alfred to keep an eye on him. He'd also ridden the length of his small dukedom in hopes that he would hear something from the peasants about Lady Eden. They told him nothing. For the most part they trembled at his presence, hiding their children from view.

"Did you learn aught about m'lady?" Ulric inquired as if reading his master's thoughts.

Vladamir grunted in response and scratched his jaw as he quickened his pace. They made their way across the bailey. The pathways looked swept and the weeds, which normally grew wild in the corners of the dirt yard, had been cut back. He also noted that the fowl were gathered and put into a pen and not running about underfoot.

"She would say naught to me about herself. I still don't know how she came to be here," Ulric offered.

The Duke listened with interest, though on the outside he remained devoid of emotion. It had been his order to question her.

"You did tell King Alfred about her, did you not? Surely he would have heard if a noblewoman was missing. He would be able to locate the earl more readily than us," Ulric persisted. The duke said nothing. "M'lord, you cannot keep her as yer prisoner! You risk much. If King Alfred found out that you held a maiden, nay a *noble* maiden from his land as yer prisoner, he would petition King Guthrum fer yer head. You would be banished by both countries. Yea and mayhap start a war between them."

Vladamir stopped and turned his cold gaze to stare at Ulric. He gave her his most lethal of smiles, a look that showed no pleasure, only cruel intentions. "I told the king's ambassador nothing and I have decided how to best extract my revenge. So fret no more old man. Soon Lady Eden of Hawks' Nest will be of no concern."

"Nay, m'lord. You cannot mean to kill her," Ulric said in horror. He shook his head violently, watching his lordship's emotionless face. Vladamir kept his expression blank, giving nothing away. "I have prayed that you have not become so heartless. Lady Lurlina, she was never worth—"

Ulric bit his tongue at the black look Vladamir shot him. Rage poured from the duke and he couldn't help the hatred and anger that seeped out of every pore. Lady Lurlina, his late wife, was a forbidden topic. She had been since the night of her death.

"I won't let you," the servant said, but his words lacked conviction.

"You cannot know what I mean to do," Vladamir answered with a malevolent snarl. "And you would do well to stay out of my way. Lady Eden is mine. If I wish for her head to roll, then roll it will. Don't think I won't do the same to you if you get in my way again. I granted the woman life and I can take it away just as easily."

Ulric gasped, growing pale. Vladamir twisted his face, contorting it into a bloodthirsty sneer. Then, turning abruptly, he stalked away to the exercise yard, leaving the seneschal gawking fearfully behind him.

* * * * *

The hall smelled fresh and the black stones shone with inky perfection. Even the tapestries that hung on the walls had been mended and cleaned. Though they were still old, they looked a lot better now that the dust had been beaten from them. The portable dining tables and benches had all been carted to the bailey and cleansed before being set up in the hall. Eden heard several of the knights murmur in pleasure at the change. Some even smiled in newfound pride.

She sat alone at the high table, overlooking the gathering soldiers of the main hall. A cheerful playfulness had alighted over the keep. One that even Vladamir's dark presence couldn't completely thwart. The air crackled with life like the anticipated day of a great banquet celebration. Near the head table a man-at-arms told a ribald joke about a serving wench and her flying skirts. She blushed as the knight announced the shameless outcome of his tale and tried to look away. Too late, the soldier saw her eavesdropping and snapped his mouth shut. Looking apologetically at his fellow companions, who roared unashamedly with laughter, he helped himself to some mead that had been set on the tables.

Eden felt isolated by herself at the head table. Being the only one who was set high on display, she grew nervous. It was the first time some of the men had leave to study her and they did so with open curiosity. A few of their faces even showed her pity. She'd been directed to sit in the seat of honor by Haldana, whom Eden came to discover only carried out the order of Vladamir. Eden wondered momentarily if this was the "reward" the duke promised. Did it mean he was pleased with her work? Did he really think putting her on display was a reward?

Eden knew that she was very fortunate, for in ways of a prison it could've been much worse. Her captor stayed away from her all day and it would appear Vladamir was to keep to his word to treat her as a lady. It was really more than she'd dared hope for.

Eden shivered. There was something odd with the way the servants kept eyeing her. None dared to come near her. It was if they all tried to communicate something dire with their eyes, but their message was lost. She saw Lizbeth and smiled at the woman, hoping she would come forward. The servant shook her head and backed through the door to the kitchen. Maybe the mood was because of Vladamir's arrival. No doubt the servants waited anxiously for his approval of their work.

She took a nervous breath and looked to her right. The seat was empty. Vladamir had yet to show. Spying Ulric across the hall, she hesitantly smiled at him. The old man appeared shaken, as he wrung his hands. A look of foreboding crossed his features. Eden stood up in alarm, intent on finding what was wrong with the man and for that matter the rest of the keep.

"Where do you think you're going, m'lady? Didn't I order you to remain here?" Vladamir's tone was sharp as he stepped up the dining platform. His body moved with lethal purpose as he neared and he narrowed his dark eyes to study her.

A wave of pleasure came over her at the familiar sound of his voice, even though his tone was harsh. She turned deliberately to him, allowing herself only a moment to indulge in the depths of his eyes before looking away. She forced her gaze downward in a demure pose.

"Something ails Ulric. Methought to attend him to make sure all was well," she answered meekly, although on the inside she trembled. "Methinks I may have requested that he work too hard for an older man."

"Hmm," Vladamir acknowledged as he seated himself beside her. When she didn't move, he ordered, "Sit."

Eden immediately obeyed his command, instantly feeling the warmth of his body next to her. It was as if he purposefully leaned too close. She was all too aware of the watchful eyes of the servants as they studied the high table. A chill shot through her and she was glad that she had her own chair, instead of the benches that graced many manors. If the duke's body was to touch hers she might scream. Whether that scream would be of fright or something else entirely remained to be seen.

"Does m'lady feel a draft?" Vladamir asked politely when she shivered. The hall was warm, too warm for a breeze.

"N-nay," she said softly, the word broken. Sitting forward, she wiped imaginary crumbs from the clean table.

"Then mayhap 'tis my company you find repulsive?" He probed with a sharp, unapologetic bite to his words. Leaning back in his chair, he rested his elbow on the wooden arm.

"Nay, m'lord." Eden rested her hand in her lap, pressing her lips tightly together.

"You're upset with me?" Vladamir chuckled. The sound took her by surprise. It was a mixture of pleasure and amusement, not like the evil laughter she had so recently heard from him.

She shivered because the question was more of a statement. "M'lord, I'd request some semblance of etiquette from you. 'Tis not proper for you to speak so—"

"Honestly?" He asked with an amused tilt of his head.

"Nay, I was going to say vulgarly." Eden swiped the back of her hand over her lap in an effort to hide her nervousness. "Candid honesty is fine when 'tis amongst friends, but we—"

"I have no use for the games of etiquette. If one doesn't say what one means, 'tis useless for one to talk." He shot her a smug look of superiority, his gaze daring her to disagree.

Eden snapped her mouth shut at his words. Doing her best to contain her irritation, she looked carefully about at the seated men. Laughter broke over the hall from the back. She tried to see to what started it, but couldn't tell what was going on, but she did hear someone make comment about the lack of food.

Eden took a deep breath and forgot herself as she studied the duke. The blood ran thick in her veins and kept her throat from swallowing. Every time she was near him her body ran so hot and cold she couldn't think straight. Her thighs tightened and her stomach tingled. Maybe he was a demon casting a spell over her.

"M'lord?" she asked after the laughter died down. Eden was all too aware that they were still being watched. She refused to look at him too long, lest he again accuse her of staring.

Yea, wouldn't do to be reprimanded once more in public hearing.

Vladamir rested his temple against his knuckles, leaning on the arm of his chair and he awaited her next scolding in anticipation.

Eden flicked her fingernails nervously. The plain brown tunic she wore was drab in comparison to her hair. He wondered if she regretted being at his manor for surely she was used to rich, embellished gowns. She acted like a lady and he was pleased with what she'd done in his hall. He'd already noted the mead that had been laid on all the tables. The men had been livelier upon his entrance, but now they quieted to a low murmur.

"M'lord?" she repeated, a little more forceful. He liked her courage as well.

"Yea?" he answered, busy staring at her delicate ear. It would be so easy to lean over and suck it between his teeth. He considered ordering everyone to leave so he could draw her onto his lap and take her right there in the hall.

"Would you like me to call the servants in?" she asked. "Those in the hall are waiting to dine."

109

"Please," Vladamir commanded, surprised by the observation, even as he was a little disappointed in her restraint. Amazed, he watched as she lifted her arm and made a single gesture. As soon as her arm was again at her side the door to the kitchen burst open. Servants carried trays of food forward and laid them on the table. The trays were laden with roasted mutton and herbed potatoes and fresh loaves of bread that still steamed from baking. There were boiled turnips and even freshly churned butter in crocks.

He'd also noticed, to no small surprise, the cleanliness of his keep. The spiderwebs, which he'd grown oddly fond of, were dusted from the rafters. The rushes on the floor were cleaned and scented. The stone walls and tapestries were scrubbed. To Vladamir the cleanliness appeared out of place in his home. It took away from the somber atmosphere he tried to cultivate around himself.

His stonemason, Harold, even complained of Lady Eden's bullying orders. That was until Vladamir told the drunkard that he bid her to command him in his absence. The fat man had cringed and went straight back to work, harshly ordering the servants about in his indignation.

The Duke eyed a servant who passed and saw that her short hair was wet as if she'd just recently bathed. The locks were freshly trimmed and were combed behind her ears. The maid's clothing had been recently washed and mended. Suddenly turning, the maid slowly made her way to the head table and set her tray before them.

"I hope that m'lord doesn't mind the mutton in place of fish porridge. Some of the lambs were past their season and the herd was overrun," Eden stated as she nodded to the timid servant. The girl nearly tripped as she rushed away from the main table. "Besides, I thought it would be a nice reward for all the hard work your people have—"

"Not at all," he interrupted.

"M'lord, would you like me to pour your drink for you?" Eden asked, her eyes giving away her uncertainty as she turned them down under her dark lashes. Her lips pulled down into an unintentional pout.

Vladamir felt a piece of his hardened core chip away. His insides shook with an unfamiliar force. He couldn't tell if it was mercy or pity that welled within him. Where had this come from? Where was the willful woman who so definitely stood up to him? Vladamir had hid his smile at her sharp tone. He drew much pleasure from her willfulness. Seeing her fear of him, he wanted to wipe the pain away, wanted to tell her it was all right. But he couldn't show weakness. He wouldn't fall into her womanly trap.

Vladamir nodded his head and leaned back in his chair to study her small waist, as she turned from him. He liked the round curve of her ass. Wicked thoughts danced in his head when he looked at it. He thought of grabbing her, lifting her skirts and pulled her down on his lap right there in the hall. Swallowing, he briefly closed his eyes. His fantasies were becoming all too frequent. Just one look and he was trying to calculate ways to get his cock shoved deep into her wet pussy.

Moving his hands to rest easily underneath his chin, he rubbed the back of his fingers over the scar on his jaw. Eden's hands trembled as she filled his goblet and set the pitcher on the table. She raised his cup and held it out to him.

Vladamir took the goblet from her unsteady hand, purposely brushing his palm against hers. She visibly swallowed and avoided looking at him as he scrutinized her. Then, frowning, he brusquely grabbed her hand before she could withdraw it. Studying her palm he looked at the raw flesh he found. They weren't as the hands of a noblewoman should be. They were red and sore as if she'd joined the servants in scrubbing his home. Eden curled her fingers and tried to pull back. Vladamir let her go, his face was expressionless.

"M'lord," she sighed as she filled her own goblet. Setting the pitcher down, she thoughtfully bit at her lip and kept her palms turned from view. "I'm afraid..."

"Afraid of me," he inserted when she faltered. His eyes didn't budge from her face, as he slowly moved his goblet to take a drink.

"Nay." She glanced scornfully at him and set her goblet on the table. It was clear she didn't think much of his constant interrupting. "I was going to say that I'm afraid I don't know clearly what 'tis you wish my role to be here. For I don't know how to act as a prisoner and you seem displeased when I tried to act as the lady my father raised me to be. Methought that you could better explain how 'tis you wish me to conduct myself, so that I may not be a disappointment to you in the future. I want my life here to be as inconspicuous as possible, so you won't have to give me more than a moment's thought."

Vladamir frowned at her admission. He wasn't at all displeased with her actions thus far. Ulric informed him—in a desperate act of exploiting her honor in hopes of changing his mind—that he gave Eden ample opportunity to escape as he'd been instructed. The man had even gone so far as to suggest a ride or a walk outside the castle walls, unescorted. Eden refused the offer, saying she wasn't permitted beyond the gate without the duke's company or permission.

It would seem you're truly held here by your own honor.

The duke found little pleasure in the thought. It meant all his preconceived notions of the opposite sex weren't altogether true. He wasn't so vain as to believe Clifton sent her to his home to murder him. Once his anger cooled enough to think logically, he doubted the earl thought of him at all.

"M'lady, now I'd like for you to dine." He set the goblet on the table, tracing his fingernail over the rim of the cup where his lips had touched.

Vladamir carefully trained his gaze on her movements. He had a feeling she wasn't being openly herself, that she was hiding a wealth of opinions and feeling within her. His stomach tightened with an unknown emotion. It ate at his gut, filling him with guilt. The emotion didn't set well on him. For years he'd dreamed of nothing but revenge and now that he had it he was sorry for it.

The Duke ignored his self-reproach and instead turned to his meal. He tried to ignore the astounding woman at his side as she fluttered about filling their trencher and then pretended to eat. Shaking his head, he realized that it wasn't so easily done.

The gathered throng steadily grew louder during the meal until the jesting laughter of the men and servants could be heard outside the hall. Vladamir dined quietly. He watched the change brought about in stunned albeit hidden amusement. Although they laughed, he saw many of the knights' eyes stray to Lady Eden at his side. He knew well the glints of manly appreciation that grew there. Eden paid the men little heed, keeping her eyes downcast and her attention on her lap. Vladamir noted the noblewoman's modesty with grim approval.

Now you, m'lady, are a mystery.

Shaking his head, he turned back to his meal, doing his best to remember whose daughter she was.

* * * * *

Eden couldn't force herself to eat the salted mutton and boiled potatoes in their shared trencher. She didn't have the appetite for it. However, despite that she tried to put on a decent enough show for her captor. Though she mainly rearranged the food laid out on her side of the trencher, pushing it over for the duke to eat when his attention got caught elsewhere. Finally as the meal was drawing to a close she turned to Vladamir and asked without preamble, "May I go now, m'lord captor? I should like to retire if no more performance is required of me."

Eden didn't mean her words to come out as sarcastic as they sounded. Nevertheless, she didn't bother to look apologetic. Vladamir hadn't spoken during the meal and he certainly hadn't answered her question as to her place in his keep. In fact he told her nothing of her future and Eden found herself growing tired of her necessary performance.

Mayhap, that is because I'm to have no future here! Panic rose in her chest as she looked at Vladamir. *He is displeased with me. Mayhap, I'm to have no future at all!*

"Nay, I wish you to speak with me."

"But I have naught of import to say to you, m'lord." Eden matched his harsh tone with one of her own. She glared slightly when she looked at him, exasperated. "And one shouldn't talk if there is naught on one's mind to talk about. Is that not right, m'lord?"

Murmuring, so only she heard his whisper, he boldly admitted, "But there are things I'd have you say."

"Oh," Eden gasped in surprise, shooting him a quick sidelong glance as heat washed over her face. She hated that he could make her blush.

"There are things I wish to know."

"Here? You wish to talk here?" She was tired of the prying eyes of the household. She felt as if she were on display being set so high before them. Yet somehow she was afraid of being alone with the duke and the public scrutiny became welcomed. For although she knew none would come to her aid if she were of such a need, their distanced observation gave her small comfort.

"Nay."

Eden's eyes flew to the stairwell and she wondered why she was excited. "Then? You'd have us go where?"

Vladamir followed her gaze. It led to his bedchamber. He suppressed a frown, but not before she saw it.

"Let us walk." Vladamir stood and waited for her to do the same. He didn't offer her his arm and he didn't escort her from the high table. Instead he walked before her, expecting her to follow like a servant.

Eden frowned silently at his back as she stepped soundlessly behind him. A few of the knights noticed her defiant look and grinned to themselves. The hall hastily quieted, watching the nobles in curiosity. She was all too aware of their gazes as she moved away.

"Does he go to kill her now?" she thought to hear someone whisper.

"Nay, 'tis not yet the witching hour," she perceived another to respond.

Eden wasn't sure how much was her imagination and how much of it was true.

Vladamir didn't turn about once to make sure she obeyed him. Somehow, the fact angered her. He treated her as if she were a trained mongrel. Glancing to the stairwell, she wondered if she had the courage to run and hide from him. It would serve him right. The thought soon fled. She didn't dare to openly disobey him and continued to follow behind him.

As they made their way outdoors, the evening sky was just beginning to turn. The air had cooled some, thanks to a pleasant breeze. Orange streaked across the heavens, only enhanced by the dotting of a few white clouds. The black castle stood out magically, touching the sky. Eden was glad she ordered that the bailey to be raked. It had smelled of dog manure and stale earth. Now the sweet herbs and flowers wafted on the breeze as they neared the gardens. Sage, chamomile and mint teased her senses. Eden took in a deep breath and smiled to herself, feeling a momentary, fleeting moment of freedom.

"There is a bench," the duke broke into her thoughts roughly. The smile fell from her lips at the sound to be replaced by a grimace. He nodded toward the long stone seat in the shade of the big oak tree. "Sit."

"I'm not a trained dog," Eden snapped, his words reminding her all too clearly of her position. She gasped and

115

covered her mouth with her hand, waiting for his wrath. Never had she been so outspoken. What was he doing to her?

He turned at her yell and smiled. The cold stare of his eyes wavered and softened, but the moment was so brief she believed to have imagined it. Eden was surprised that he hadn't instantly lashed out at her. Her father would've had her whipped for such a contrary tone.

"Please, sit," he amended his previous command. The sky behind his head turned deeper with the oncoming darkness. He waved his fingers gallantly through the air to encompass the bench, appearing very much like a graceful and noble gentleman. Eden was taken aback at the practiced ease of his fluid movement. However, the expression he carried made no doubt that it was still an order that she must obey.

Eden took a hesitant step forward and then paused, unsure. The wind drew her eyes to his chest. His hair floated delicately on the breeze and his black tunic ruffled slightly to reveal a knife hidden at his waist.

Eden nodded weakly, intentionally keeping her back from him, mindful not to try and anger him further. Seeing the weapon reminded her of the servant's glances of warning and hushed whispers as they'd left the hall. Her heart squeezed tightly in her chest as a grim understanding came over her. Fear gripped her and she would've run if she hadn't seen that the gates were barred.

The duke motioned to the bench and Eden followed his silent command to take a seat. Her arms pulled stiffly at her sides and round eyes kept him in her sidelines. Coming to the edge, she sat along the end of the stone, allowing for room if he wished to join her. To her relief, he didn't.

Vladamir instead towered over her. His dark locks reflected the purpling of the setting sun and haloed around his head in unrefined waves. When she looked to him she didn't see scars, she saw a handsome man with a hard, impassible face. His nearness made her stomach quake with excitement.

She looked away, trying not to forget her fear, trying not to forget the easy access of his deadly knife.

"'Tis time you told me how you have come to be here," he stated without the pleasantness of idle discourse.

Eden shivered at his unrefined manners. "Nay, 'tis none of your concern."

"Tell me." Vladamir loomed over her at the order. She shivered and lifted her chin higher in defiance. "Everything in this manor is my concern."

"If that is true," she began with a matching frown, "name all the servants who work your kitchen. Prove to me you're concerned with this manor."

Vladamir's mouth dropped open and his eyes narrowed into dangerous slits. "I'm tired of playing games. You'll answer me."

"Nay," she returned just as stiffly. She stood and hurried to go, only to stop when she felt his hand wrap her arm like a striking snake. He held her in a deathlike grip, his fingers clasping her in warning.

"I didn't dismiss you."

"And I won't answer your questions. I'm your prisoner, but that doesn't give you leave to pry into my private thoughts." She heard well the whispers of him, saw his callous ways and yet when he was near she was unafraid. "If you persist in questioning me, I'll bid you good eve, m'lord captor and leave this manor at once."

"What do you hide? Who are you protecting?" He pulled her back until she stood before him, not releasing her arm. He ignored her threat. They both knew it to be idle. She couldn't escape him or Lakeshire Castle. "Why will you not answer me?"

"Because I won't be sent back to him!" she yelled before she could stop herself. She quickly covered her mouth, stunned by her own admission.

"Back to whom? Your father?" Vladamir asked with a growl. He shook her violently when she didn't answer. His eyes bore piercingly into her, demanding to know everything. Her hand fell from her mouth at his rough handling.

"Nay, 'tis no one." Eden looked at his tunic where she knew his knife lay hidden. Tears brimmed in her eyes. She wanted to plead with him, but knew it would do no good. "Please, free me. Let me go to the nunnery to take my orders. I'll tell no one you tried to keep me here. In fact I'll be most grateful to you for your kindness in the deed. I shall remember you every eve in my prayers until I die, if 'tis your wish."

"You don't appear to be of such a temperament. Somehow I cannot conceive you kneeling piously in prayer every day of your life, m'lady captive," Vladamir observed coolly. "How is it you're off to a nunnery? Does your father so readily give away his only daughter to such a higher purpose? Methinks not. I have met your father. He isn't so generous a man."

"I haven't told him I'm going," she admitted with a nervous look. "He doesn't know where I am."

"Ah, then he has other plans for you. Is that why you're here?"

"Promise me that you'll kill me instead of sending me back. 'Tis your plan anyway, is it not? I saw how the servants whispered. 'Tis why you didn't want me speaking to Ulric. He was going to warn me, wasn't he?" Eden swallowed as she licked her lips. With a muffled sound of despair, she sniffed back her tears, feeling the sting of defeat. Pain rolled over her body. "Please, not by the knife. I don't wish to die that way. Give me that. Mayhap, give me a draught of poison so that I may drink it—but not the knife."

She tried to be nonchalant, but her eyes strayed to the knife at his waist. Her stomach knotted and her limbs grew numb as she continued her entreaty.

"I don't know what my father has done to offend you. But, if 'tis revenge you wish to have with my death, then take it gently. For 'twas my father not I who committed the offense." Tears steamed down her face and her lips trembled as she begged for an easy death. His heart tightened and squeezed. "Please, m'lord."

"Why should you care how you die?" Vladamir asked sharply. "'Tis all the same in the end."

Eden forced down a sob, trying her best to appear brave. "Please, if 'tis the same to you in the end, why not give me what I want. It would be less for the servants to clean after."

"Why do you not beg for your life?" Vladamir scowled with a violent shake of her arm. He leaned into her and his voice had lowered to a hoarse whisper, but she didn't shrink away from his anger. Then, glancing at his tight hold on her arm, he instantly loosened his grip. "Why do you just give up without a fight? What happened to the insolent woman who tries to defy me?"

"I know well that the life of a woman is of little worth to you. I have seen how you look at me. You don't like me. I'm worth nothing to you but revenge." The sun had fallen completely out of sight and now the sky turned a royal blue in the twilight. Eden turned her gaze to the chamomile in the garden. She took a deep breath before continuing. "Would you hear my entreaty with an open ear? Would it affect your decision after 'twas made?"

"You're right," he conceded easily. "After a decision has been made I'd be hard-pressed to change my mind. It would contradict the reason for the making in the first place. A man cannot be counted upon if he questions his own resolve."

"Then you have made your judgment. I'm to die." Eden shivered and again looked to the chamomile. Her breath became shallow and she stopped shivering. Her arm became limp in his hand. A tear fell from her wide silent eyes.

He placed a tentative hand under her chin to bring her face around so he could study her gaze and gently swiped the tears from her cheeks with the pads of his thumbs, grimacing even as he did so. "I've made no decision as of yet."

Eden nodded as sweet relief flooded her. She had a chance. She'd known that to beg for life would be pointless with a man like Vladamir. If he'd made up his mind, there would be no changing it. If she were to try and run, he would catch her. She would be no match against his strength. But if he hadn't decided she still had a chance. "Then you're considering sending me on to the nunnery?"

"Nay."

"Then to my father?"

"Let us begin again," Vladamir stated, ignoring her question. He dropped his hand back to her shoulder and she shook under the steady weight of it. "Why are you here?"

"If you give me your word that I'll die afore being sent back, I'll tell you all that you wish to know." She shook her arm free of his devilish grasp.

For anything is better than being under the yoke of my intended.

"You'd rely on the word of a monster?" The idea seemed to amuse him greatly.

"Nay, I'd rely on the word of a man." She dared a glance at him. Her eyes strayed briefly to his smirking mouth. He had great lips, lips that felt so good kissing her. Would he kiss her again? Would he press his body to hers as he had in the hall? Each night she ached for him to do that and more. "I'll take your word as one of honor for I have yet to find any reason to believe that it would be otherwise."

The twisted smile faded from his lips and he nodded. "You have it. I'll see you dead afore sending you back to your father."

Eden consented to the morbid pact on her life with a nod. She moved to once more be seated in front of him on the bench. "What would you like to know?"

"Who battered you?" The shadows of the night hid his face.

"My fiancé." Suddenly, she gasped and shook her head. "Nay, I'm afraid I must insist that you promise not to give me to him either. I know I said my father —"

Vladamir held up his hand to stop her flow of words. "I give you the same bargain. You'll die afore going to either of them."

"He is rich and might try to offer you money for me," Eden persisted.

"I give you my word."

Eden nodded in gloomy relief and looked at her hands as she spoke. "My father arranged for me to marry Lord Luther of Drakeshore. Lord Luther is very rich and my father is titled. To them it was a perfect arrangement. Foolish as I was I agreed, thinking that finally I'd have some freedom as a married lady."

"Hmm."

Eden ignored his interruption. "I was going to do my duty by my father and wed with Luther about two sennights hence, but Lord Luther wished for an alternate arrangement afore the marriage. He planned a rendezvous with me and some of his male friends, only he forgot to tell me about it aforehand."

"I know Drakeshore," Vladamir frowned. "He's an old man."

"Nay, not too old to beget his heirs for my father's purposes," Eden interjected bitterly. "Methought that he wanted to learn more about me, at least that is what I was led to believe. He took me riding outside the castle in the forest. ''Tis to be a hunt', he said. 'Your sire is waiting for us', he said. The only thing waiting for us was a used, dirty coverlet thrown on the ground and a hunting party that didn't hunt for meat, but for carnal pleasures with my body. He sought to fulfill his marital rights early and with ample witnesses. When I refused him and tried to run off to a nunnery, he followed me."

"And his friends were to watch?" Vladamir asked in disgust.

"Nay, his friends were to join," Eden put forth resentfully. She shivered in revulsion at the memory. Her stomach lurched as she pictured the lustful men avidly in her mind's eye. Shaking her head, she tried not to cry anew.

"Continue." His tone wasn't as cold as before.

"Luther would have ravished me then if not for my handmaiden, Lynne. She didn't trust Luther's intentions and even tried to warn me against them. When I didn't listen to her, she followed us. He killed her for her interference, ran her clean through her stomach with his sword. It took her a long time to die and her eyes kept pleading with me to help her. There was blood running from her mouth over her chin and some of the men...they..." Eden moved her hand to brush a strand of her loose hair behind her ear. She touched her lips softly as she thought of her friend. Lynne's screams echoed in her ears. The maidservant had been ravished repeatedly as she lay dying. "I couldn't help her for I had yet to untie myself."

"And once untied, you escaped." Vladamir stated logically.

"I don't know. I remember Lynne being run through and I remember trying to run away from him—*them*." A tear slipped from her eye and she dashed it nervously away. "Someone or mayhap something hit me over the head afore I got too far. When I awoke 'twas raining. I ran for the shelter of the forest. I don't remember falling upon your castle gate, but that is where I ended up or so Ulric tells me."

Vladamir turned from her and paced, clearly mulling over her words.

"So you see," she continued, "now I have no alternative but to take the vows of the church. I cannot wed a man who would share me with others for who knows what other unnatural games he has in mind for me. After the vows are spoken, there will be no one to naysay his right. As a nun I'll be under the protection of the church. My father wouldn't dare go against God, no matter how angry he is with me."

Vladamir nodded.

Her tears echoed in her soft voice as she said in dejection, "I don't even know if I'm pure. I don't know what sport they have taken with me, if any. I cannot wed with another with such questions about me. No respectable nobleman would have me and I couldn't blame him."

"'Tis the belief amongst my people that the maiden is never to blame in such an event. That the man is at fault when he ravishes a woman." Vladamir stopped several paces from her and turned. The gentleness in his gaze was swiftly hidden away.

"'Tis not the way of it here. It would be my fault for seducing him. At least that is what they would say of it. And that is if they even believed me." Eden shook her head in firm denial. "Nay, I would that no one knew the truth of it. For how can I prove that which I cannot even remember?"

"I know of a nobleman named Blackwell. When his bride's maidenhead had to be established he ordered her checked. You could do the same. I'd order the checking and then you'd know the truth. It would be private," Vladamir offered quietly. His face held little compassion under the icy mask of disdain, but she had the feeling that his anger wasn't directed at her.

"Nay, I know that 'tis foolish, but I don't wish to know." Eden sighed as she peeked through her lashes. "I fear the worst. My stomach...it hurt when I awoke."

Vladamir's whole body was tense. "You do have another solution. You might not have to wish so readily for death or church."

Eden observed the gentle savagery of his motions before turning once more to her hands. The movements of his body were untamed and barbarous. She felt the stealthy magnetism that radiated off of him like a wild beast. A tear rolled over her cheek. Lifting her gaze, she implored his understanding. She didn't know why she trusted him with such intimate details, but she couldn't seem to keep quiet. The truth had spilled forth from her with the force of a breaking dam.

"What? To live here as your prisoner so that you may seek your revenge?" Eden snorted in disgust. "What kind of life is that? I'm no better than a slave, only my future is more uncertain. Besides, being here there is always the chance my father or Luther will come for me. What is to happen if your king calls you home or the peace is broken and you're off to war? I'll be left at their mercy. I don't wish to risk it."

"Nay, not as my prisoner." Vladamir's low voice drifted on the wind. His piercing gaze bored into her and she shivered at the low tone of his words. "And most definitely not as a slave."

"As a servant? Would you have me change my name and become your servant woman?" Eden fumed, growing angry with him. "Too many here know the truth of my identity and I could run away and become a servant! Oh, I see. You decided you liked your keep cleaned and your food prepared in a washed cauldron."

"Yea, I find I like it very much," he admitted without penitence. A smile curved his firm mouth, breaking the spell of doom that wove about them in the night air. Leisurely, he strolled over the garden and picked a stem of chamomile from the plant that had so held her attention before.

"Well, then direct the servants you have to do it. You don't need me." Eden once again stood up, only this time she was enraged by his persistence. She glared at his back. "They work well if the master is not lazy in the directing."

"I don't mean as a servant." The Duke's words stopped her from leaving. He turned to her with a lowered chin and tilted his head to the side. His tongue flicked over the corner edge of his mouth and traced his lower lip. Sparks filled her at the motion, making her body all too aware of him. The coldness of his gaze softened. He slowly let his eyes roam over the lushness of her form.

"Concubine?" Eden shot incredulously, before laughing at the thought. She shook her head in dismissal.

"Nay." Vladamir spun the stem in his large, strong fingers.

"Then what? A wife?" Eden laughed again and looked at him. Her chuckle ended when she saw the seriousness of his eyes. Her face paled. He wanted her to marry him. She stumbled back in breathless awe. Her legs weakened and she sat once more on the bench. Nearly out of breath, she asked, "But why?"

"I wish revenge and you're in need of protection." Vladamir held up the herb for her to take. It was a small gesture, which was belittled by the sharpness of his words. "Methinks 'tis a perfect arrangement."

"Arrangement?" She trembled at the odd proposal. It wasn't the enraptured admission of love that she would've wanted at such a moment. However the thought of being protected by such a man did have its merits. And he did stir her blood with fiery sensations whenever he was near. Looking at his mouth, she sighed. Without taking the flower, she asked, "Just what kind of arrangement would this be?"

"I'd provide you with a home. I'll feed you, clothe you, protect you and being thusly wed you won't have to marry Lord Luther." His tone lacked all emotions and he dropped the herb to the ground when she didn't take the gift. Eden numbly watched it fall.

"But you don't know me." She searched his face for any sign of a tender sentiment. He was cold, blank. "Why would you bind yourself to me?"

"I know enough. I know that you're the daughter of my most hated enemy. I know that I seek to revenge myself and others against him. What better way then to deprive him of Luther's money? From what I understand you're his only child and the blow will undoubtedly be devastating." Vladamir's eyes blazed as he stared at her, but he didn't reach for her. Eden desperately wanted him to. "I know you have no wish to go back to your father."

"How do I know you won't harm me after we are wed?" she asked, staring down at the discarded chamomile. "How do I know you'll treat me with kindness?"

"A reasonable question," he admitted with an approving nod. "You don't for sure. But what choice do you have? You were so recently begging me to use poison on you."

"What would you expect of me in return?" Eden inquired, cautious. She shivered as she thought of his unusually cold proposal. Was being married to an emotionless monster better than death?

"You'll care for my home, instruct the servants and keep the manor clean. You'll sew our clothing or have them sewn by the servants. You'll do any number of wifely duties. You'll be a duchess," he answered with a dismissive wave of his hand. It was as if he was bestowing on her a great gift. Eden stood to face him as he spoke. "And mayhap someday we will leave this land of Wessex and go back to the Danelaw to my castle there. That will bring you far from your father's reach."

"I don't care about the title," she stated numbly. Her face tightened with her words and she knew that he wouldn't fully believe her. "There are more important considerations for me than title."

The duke smiled at that, crossing his arms over his chest as he grazed his lip thoughtfully with the tips of his fingers. "Fair enough."

"What else?" Eden wrung her hands nervously in front of her. She was amazed that she even considered it. Yet she knew that if he were just to soften a bit and offer her his embrace she would've flown readily into his arms with a rush of agreement. If he softened she would've done anything he asked, but he didn't.

"You'll help me care for my daughter. I wish to bring her here to be with me." He watched her reaction closely.

"You really have a daughter? Where is her mother? Your first wife, I mean?" Eden turned her eyes to the night sky as if the brightening stars held untold answers. If they did, they didn't give her their secrets.

"If you ask, you must know that she is dead. I won't speak of it with you." He growled, his eyes darkening for a brief moment. "Ever."

"Fair enough," she returned wryly. Turning her back to him, she didn't want him to see the uncertainty in her movements, or the unexpected tingle inside her. Her mind ached for a tender sentiment from him, however untrue it might be. Gladly, she would've taken a kind lie to ease her nervousness. "Is that all?"

"'Tis not enough?" He'd moved closer to her back.

"What I mean is," she swallowed and blushed. Moving to face him, she was startled to find him so near. She sighed into his darkly clad chest and lifted her hand between them only to let it fall before touching. "I suppose what you're saying is that this is to be a marriage of convenience only. That we won't live as man and wife and that you don't think to bed me."

"Nay, I didn't say that. I said that you'll have to perform other wifely duties." He boldly reached as if to touch her heated cheek. Then, when she didn't move to accept his touch, he let his hand drop. "That condition was meant to include the marriage bed. All men have needs…a need of heirs. I should like a son."

"Oh." His latter statement was offered weakly. She took a step back from him and fell upon the bench. He said it so coldly, like it was to be a chore.

He doesn't want me because I'm soiled.

She delicately sniffed back the tears that threatened her eyes.

"You may remain my prisoner for now," he stated with a dead ring in his voice. Eden gasped. When she didn't acknowledge the decree, he turned to leave her.

"Wait," she called lightly to stop him from storming away. "Please, don't be angry with me. Are you always so quick to temper?"

"Your answer is nay. 'Tis fine. You won't be punished for it," he said coldly. His back stiffened to her. "I believe it a most logical decision on your part."

"I didn't say that."

"You didn't say anything," Vladamir breathed.

Eden studied him for a moment. Just like every time she was close to him, her body stayed wet between her thighs and she couldn't stop trembling. She quickly bent down to retrieve the discarded herb from the dirt. Pressing the stem to her breast, she went to him. She lifted her hand to lightly touch the strong contours of his back, hoping to draw him around to her. He stiffened and didn't move. His heat jumped along her fingertips, down her arm to make her insides quake with the desire to hold him. It was an unfamiliar sensation and Eden quickly drew her hand away.

"I was overwhelmed by your proposal, is all. 'Tis not everyday one receives such a generous offer of marriage. 'Tis not an easy decision to make." She closed her eyes and took a deep breath. When again she opened them, she still didn't move to look at him. Instead she looked at the dark stone of Lakeshire Castle.

Vladamir didn't answer.

"Why is this place called Lakeshire, if 'tis not on a lake?" she wondered aloud. Then drawing her thoughts back she moved to stand piously before him. Seeing his hand, she lifted it into hers. He didn't resist her. In fact he didn't move at all. Staring at the black onyx that rested on his finger, she said, "Illogical as you might think it, m'lord, my answer is..."

Vladamir watched her expectantly, not moving his hand in hers. She let go of him, watching his arm drop to his side. It seemed an eternity passed before she could again speak.

"Yea," Eden murmured, lifting the chamomile shyly to her nose. She bit her lip and met his steady gaze with her uncertain one. Her heart lurched in her chest as she quietly answered, "I will marry you, m'lord."

Chapter Six

ဆာ

"M'lady, you cannot bind yerself with the devil!" Lizbeth pulled frantically on Eden's arm, trying to stop the noblewoman from adjusting the white veil on her head. The maidservant stood in Eden's bedchamber and was supposed to be helping her to prepare for her wedding, but the woman was more of a hindrance than help. "Yer soul will be condemned to hell! At least give it some time, m'lady, afore you throw yer life away with the monster. Wait the proper—"

"Lizbeth, I've warned you about saying such things about the duke. I won't warn you again for 'tis my future husband you speak of." Eden rearranged the flimsy veil on her hair and tried not to visibly shiver as she said the word "husband". It was all so new to her.

As soon as they concluded their agreement, Vladamir hastily dragged her about the manor to make the brief announcements of their intentions three times in three different areas. The announcements served, albeit loosely, to replace the posting of the banns as recently ordained by the church. She remembered the stunned faces of the stable boys as their master came rushing in, made his speech and just as quickly left, dragging his pale bride behind him. He then led her to the kitchen and then to the main hall. By the third decree to the knights, she realized that he meant to marry her that very night. He'd even dispatched Raulf to rouse a priest from a nearby settlement as one wasn't yet residing at Lakeshire.

For her dowry she'd given the duke the promise of what little money she'd inherited from her mother's estate. She wasn't sure of the exact amount, but Vladamir didn't seem to care. It was more of a formality really. Her father would no doubt keep her inheritance after news of her nuptials reached him. She had little hope that the earl and the duke would become friends.

Eden had no idea what Vladamir would give her for her *brudhkaup*, her bride price. She sort of assumed that the piece of chamomile would do nicely. Since there was no time or inclination to alert her father to the marriage, Vladamir suggested that when the earl found out he would make arrangement for the *handgeld*, a gift of money to her father for the control of legal guardianship of her. Eden didn't care what Vladamir paid her father. The earl had made plenty from his arrangement with Lord Luther. She smiled as she thought of her father giving the coin back to her former intended.

As far as the *morgen-gifu*, the morning after gift, Eden told Vladamir that it wasn't necessary. Theirs wasn't a conventional marriage after all. She hardly thought it fitting to make him give her anything for her part in it. Freedom from her father and Lord Luther was *morgen-gifu* enough.

She went to the bed and picked up the drying chamomile that Vladamir picked for her from the garden. She smiled, gingerly fingering the plant. It would seem her new fiancé had given the matter of their marriage a lot of thought. She would only be technically engaged to him for about an hour before they wed. Though there had been much debate amongst the prelates with the Witan, luckily secret marriages were still legal according to the church, so long as they were presided over by a priest.

Eden tried to breathe but couldn't. The elaborate tunic gown Vladamir sent to her chamber was too binding along the bodice. The undertunic was constructed of the finest of linen, soft and well sewn. The lightweight cream material had light gold embroidery on the edges, which was rare in an undergarment, for usually such extravagance would never be seen. It only confirmed her conclusion that the tunic gown was expensive. She wondered where he'd gotten it.

The rounded neck of the overtunic pulled high on her chest, with a strip of gold embroidery. It was the same kind of cream-colored linen as the undergarment, only it was a bit thicker. The gown tapered to fit snugly at her waist, showing it off to perfection. A cord of gold braid wrapped about her hips for effect more than function. The cuffs and the hem had matching designs of gold thread and braid and the sleeves of the overtunic were fairly wide and only reached to mid forearm on the top, so that the undertunic's embroidery showed as it hugged her wrists. The underside of the sleeve hung low to about her waist, sweeping around her arms in grand design.

Eden knew that gown wasn't made for her, for the chest proportions were all wrong and it was too long but the constriction of her breasts was only part to blame for her uneasiness. When Vladamir proposed marriage to her, she hadn't imagined that he meant to wed her so quickly.

"Yea, m'lady," Lizbeth said quietly finally consenting to Eden's scolding. She swiped her hand on the back of her mistress' gown, unnecessarily straightening it with the rough gesture.

"Lord Kessen is not a devil. He is a man and men are capable of both good and evil. 'Tis our duty as women to encourage the good," Eden explained, though she didn't completely believe her own words. She looked in the piece of polished metal that Lizbeth brought with her to the chamber and pulled at a few strands of her hair, forcing the tresses into place on the crown of her head. She was nervous and wanted desperately to make her future husband proud of her, though the reason why she wished to please the duke still eluded her. Even though revenge was a powerful emotion, theirs wasn't to be a match of love. As a matter of fact it was far from it.

"Yea, m'lady." Lizbeth nodded, though her tone was disagreeable. She kept her mouth shut as she helped to arrange the last bit of ribbon in her ladyship's upswept hair. Then leaning back she nodded her head in grim approval of her work.

"I'm ready," Eden stated with false bravado. Her hands trembled as she attached the plain cream wimple to her veil. Holding the chamomile tightly in her fist, she took a deep breath and said, "Let us go down afore he changes his mind."

Or lest I change mine.

* * * * *

"What is taking her so long? I told her to be belowstairs in fifteen minutes!" Vladamir raged under his breath. The servants who gathered in the main hall turned their heads at his unpleasant growl and moved to whisper to one another in fright. Vladamir ignored them as he glared over their heads to the stairwell, impatiently waiting for his bride.

"M'lord, these things take time," Ulric answered logically, busying himself by dusting the sleeves of his tunic. "You cannot expect to propose and marry quickly within the same night."

"Can I not?" Vladamir cursed as he turned on the man, his foul temperament hiding the nervous beating of his heart. It was quite possible Eden might have changed her mind and decided she couldn't force herself to wed with him. He narrowed his eyes, glancing back to the stairwell with a sinking feeling in the pit of his stomach. His lips curled into a snarl as he began softly, "I…"

His words trailed off in bewilderment, as Vladamir gazed across the main hall. A murmur rose over the crowd like a wave as curious eyes followed his and then all went silent. Eden stood at the bottom of the steps. At the rapt attention of the hall, her face colored to a becoming shade of maidenly pink. She tried to smile and failed.

The cream linen of her gown paled her face, until the bruising was hardly noticeable. It set off the fire in her hair and added a peculiar gleam to her lovely eyes. Finally taking a step down she managed to tentatively smile.

Eden gazed over the crowd until her eyes found him waiting by the high table and she took a deep breath. Vladamir's chest lurched as she looked at him. His body hummed with life and he couldn't wait for the formality of the nuptials to be done with. Sensing her fear, even from across the hall, he likened her expression to that of a human sacrifice. It was as if he felt her heartbeat quicken with his own in a primal rhythm. He tried to penetrate her with his eyes as he silently bid her to come to him. She jutted her chin into the air and stepped bravely forward, even as her gaze turned down.

Licking his lips, they were suddenly dry. He studied her in silence for a moment, wanting to touch her but not daring to be so bold. Surely his monstrous embrace wouldn't be welcomed. He frowned.

You cannot even bring yourself to look at me can you, pretty maiden? The scars of the monster repulse you, do they not?

The bulk of her heavy locks were swept up on the crown of her head, held first by ribbon and then by the wimple and veil. Wispy tresses fell around her small delicate ears, drawing his eyes to her bare throat. He regretfully had no jewels to give her, yet her beauty held its own without the adornment. As she approached he saw that the overtunic hugged to her bodice tightly, pushing her breasts up and forward for his enjoyment.

His shaft was hard, but that was nothing new. It was always hard—his cock full with desire ever since he met her. The embarrassing release in his braes had done nothing to stem his passions for her. He wanted her, wanted to sink his body deep inside hers and never leave.

It was obvious she didn't know the effect she had on his senses. The way she looked about her with hope and naiveté drove him mad with lust. He had the strangest urge to fold her in his chest and protect her from ever seeing the harsh realities of the world. He'd desired her since the moment he saw her awake. Then he'd been unable to see her full beauty, but only the fullness of her pleasing lips. Vladamir watched her mouth, growing entranced by its erotic movements. How he longed to feel them moving against his body, sucking him, kissing him, licking him.

As the days passed, she recovered quickly, but her healing only revealed his worst fear. She was indeed a maiden with the potential to be a great enchantress. She had the power to be his ruination and he was marrying her willingly.

It would appear I have not finished punishing myself. For in you, beautiful maiden, I have found my demise.

Vladamir scowled, even as his shaft practically lurched from his pants. Thankfully, his tunic covered the almost constant erection. His eyes dipped over her. He longed to run his tongue over the silken prominence of her collarbone, kissing his way to a supple breast. Every fiber in his being wanted to devour her.

Vladamir turned to the priest, motioning him to come forward, and didn't look directly at his bride as she joined him. He couldn't for she was too stunning and her beauty only served to torment him more. His first wife had been beautiful, though she held within her a darker prettiness. He foolishly thought he loved her for her mystic ways, but soon found that the feelings he carried weren't returned.

"M'lady." Ulric bowed gallantly over her hand. He shot the duke a disappointed grimace and lightly kissed her hand. Vladamir's scowl deepened. Ulric ignored him. "You're a most enchanting vision."

Eden blushed at the compliment and turned a timid gaze toward Vladamir. A frown marred her brow.

"Speak," the duke commanded the priest. His breath caught in his throat and he knew his tone was overly harsh, but he couldn't help it. Eden took up his arm in hers, wrapping fingers firmly around him. He tensed. Tension worked its way over his body from her touch. The hall was quiet.

"Yea, m'lord," the priest consented doubtfully refusing to meet the couple's eyes. His words stuttered in fear as he began and it was clear he didn't intend to stop speaking until the couple was quickly wed with little ceremony. It didn't matter. The words fell on deaf ears.

The priest held up a plain silver crucifix that hung about his neck and recited a brief prayer in Latin. The couple dutifully bowed their heads, but Vladamir kept his brooding eyes impiously on the priest, a scowl deeply imbedded on his features.

Just a moment longer and she will be mine.

He cares not that he marries me! What am I doing? I don't know this man! He doesn't love me. I don't know if he can love anyone! Mayhap he is truly a monster!

Eden shook violently and her heart hammered in her chest as she peeked out the sides of her eyes to Vladamir. He didn't pay any attention to her.

"I will," Eden whispered at the priest's prompting, still looking at Vladamir for a sign of tenderness only to be disappointed. He didn't turn to her and his face remained emotionlessly blank. The hard line of his lips pressed together and she thought that he might once again growl at her. Then, in surprise, Eden realized the ceremony was over.

"You may seal-kiss," the priest stuttered and didn't finish. He patted a piece of his robe to his sweat-laden brow and dropped the crucifix from his hand to hang back around his neck. Continuing, he stated his last words like a curse more than a blessing. "You're man and wife. 'Tis done."

The priest hurried from the platform, almost tripping in his haste to get away from them. She looked to the gathered servants and soldiers. Their faces were solemn as if at a funeral. She felt her head spin as the reality of her actions came crashing about her—the reality that reflected in the fearful expressions of the witnesses' faces.

I have made a pact with the devil!

She turned her head sharply back to her new husband. Tears swam in her eyes and she slowly shook her head in denial. Eden wanted to move, but couldn't force herself to. Her lips parted and her breathing became heavy.

She couldn't take her eyes from Vladamir. He was foreboding, from the blackness of his tunic to the dark pits of his hard eyes. In a flash she saw what others did in him. He hadn't dressed up, having chosen to look the same as he always did—nebulously evil. All of a sudden he frightened her.

God save me. What have I done?

Eden clutched at the stem of chamomile in her hands as he leaned toward her. Her eyes fluttered to his lips and then back to his gaze. His eyes never left hers as he lifted his long fingers to her neck. Her heartbeat sounded inside her ears, so loud that she thought he would surely hear it.

Even as her heart stood in fear of him, her mouth longed for the taste of him. Would it be like when he kissed her in the hall? Would he press his rock-hard body to hers? She waited in sweet, breathless anticipation for the feel of his firm mouth. She leaned her head back to receive her husband's kiss. The wistful brush of his long nails worked over her neck and she shivered uncontrollably. Gazing up at him, she knew she would do anything he commanded of her. He owned her.

Vladamir's lips were hot and passionless as they pressed against her mouth. They didn't move and he didn't close his eyes. Instead he stared boldly into her, daring her to scream. She wanted to scream—scream at him for being so distant from her, for trying to scare her—but she held quiet. With a delighted smirk his grip tightened on her and he pulled her from him in a boorish manner. The erratic pulse at her neck beat against his hand. Forcing her to turn with his hand on her neck, they faced the gathered crowd together.

"Your duty is done this night. You can go," Vladamir commanded the crowd. He dropped his hand from her neck as if satisfied that she wouldn't run. There was no place she could hide. She was his — *forever*.

Vladamir held out his hand to her. She glanced at his strong fingers, marred by the scars of a fire. Her own hand quaked with a violent force as she reached out to take it. She heard the shuffling feet of the servants. A path formed before them, growing to the stairwell. There were to be no festivities, no dancing, no formalities of any kind — just the harsh words of the duke as he commanded everyone out of his way. The servants kicked at the rushes in their haste to withdraw from the newlyweds.

The warmth of his fingers worked up her arm, stirring her blood, as he led her in the direction of the stairs. His palm was calloused despite the scarring and she stared at the hard ridges of muscles he'd gotten from fighting. Nearing the stairs, he walked faster and she tripped in an effort to keep up with his longer stride.

"Let go," she pleaded quietly, ripping her fingers out of his grasp. She crushed the dying flower to her breast.

The duke appeared overanxious and his eagerness made her shudder in response. She wondered if he intended on bedding her with the same unemotionally cold fashion. His face was blank with only the slight raising of his eyebrow showing his interest.

"I can walk myself, m'lord," she offered weakly by way of explanation. "This gown is too long and you make me trip on my own feet with your undue haste."

He turned away with a careless lift of his hand to climb the stairs without waiting to see if she followed. The servants watched her expectantly. Taking a deep breath, she hastened after her husband.

Eden caught up to him and slowed her pace. Trailing behind him, she took the opportunity to study his figure in the darkened stairwell. His back was stiff and straight. He carried himself with an arrogant air of strength and his body was well made, moving with great purpose. She doubted anything could penetrate the hard core of his emotions. The thought tore at her heart.

Her eyes lingered on his firm butt as it moved just above her face. She swallowed as she wickedly thought of touching it. Although she knew that she would never dare to try such a wanton thing. Surely, her new husband wouldn't take her curiosity kindly.

When they reached the top of the stairs he turned to her. Eden's body quivered in innocent excitement. She still felt the press of his lips against hers, though they had held none of the passions she did in her chest. Now that they were alone she wondered if he would really kiss her, like he had the first time. Would he press his tight body to hers? Would he move against her, stirring her?

"Yea, m'lord?" she asked, breathless. She looked away from him, choosing instead to fuss with the drying herb she carried. She pulled at it, watching the stem spring back from her finger. She prayed she hadn't angered him again with her staring, but she couldn't seem to keep her eyes off of him.

"Do you regret your rash actions in marrying me?" he asked quietly. The stone composure lifted from his features briefly as he spoke and his eyes softened.

"Nay, m'lord." Eden said, overtaken by the concern that reflected in his eyes. Even though she was now his wife she was held even more so his prisoner. She thought of his revenge. "I wouldn't call them rash. 'Twas the most logical of decisions to marry. You were right. I have no desire to live as a nun. You have proven to me that 'tis not to my temperament for when I'm around you, I speak too boldly and what man beside you'd want me after what was most likely done to me?"

"Come, let us go to bed." His words gave little doubt as to his intent. Back was the cold nature he'd cultivated.

"But...?" Eden faltered. "You mean now?"

"Yea, m'lady. If we don't consummate this marriage your father could have it annulled. You could still be forced to marry Luther and all this would've been for naught."

She didn't answer, save for the shaking of her shoulders. Confused, she pushed the strand of hair he'd abandoned over her shoulder.

"Would you rather spend many nights with Luther and his friends than one night with me?"

"Nay, m'lord."

"Nay, what?"

"Nay, I'd prefer to bed with you than him — them." She again sprung the chamomile stem from her fingertips.

He nodded once and turned once more to go to his bedchamber. As he strode to the room, he took a lit torch out of its holder on the wall of the passageway. Walking into his chamber, he threw the torch into the fireplace to light it with one powerfully swift movement. The flames ignited and sparked only to settle to a more pleasant temperament.

Eden entered the room behind him. All tenderness was gone from him and she was suddenly unsure as to what he'd expect of her. She chastised herself for forgetting why she agreed to marry him in the first place — protection. This wasn't a love match, never would be.

She shivered at the bold power he exuded. Even the stone of the castle seemed to fall beneath his command. If he so ordered it, the stones would most likely crumble away beneath his feet. If anything, this man could protect her.

"Your speech," Eden began, trying to think of anything to say. Coming into the chamber, she lingered just in front of the door, desperate to take his mind from his task. She didn't know what to expect this night, but the thought of finding out brought a strangely erotic sensation to her naïve body. If only he would look at her with affection, with any emotions for that matter. Did he want her as a woman? Was he attracted to her? Did he want to bed her? Or was it only revenge that brought him here before her? As she looked at his blank face, she was afraid she had her answer. It stung, almost as bad as the feeling in her gut, making her thighs damp and her nipples sting.

"What of it?" Vladamir walked to the door and loudly shut it behind her, giving her a start. Going back to the fireplace, he turned, keeping his distance.

"I have not heard it spoken." Eden glanced at him through her lashes. In the firelight the blackness of his hair was haloed by the eerie orange glow. He seemed to be ever changing. She pulled the wimple and veil from her head, suddenly feeling too constrained by the clothing. "Where were you born?"

"Northumbria," he answered shortly. His accent was hard, just like the rest of him. He rested his arm on the stone hearth in a lazy motion. Her eyes followed his every movement. Just looking at him made her knees weak and her lips tingle with need.

Why wouldn't he just kiss her again? Why wouldn't he smile at her? Touch her? Press his body into hers?

"Northumbria?" she gasped, trying to cover the odd silence as she indulged her wicked thoughts. "None from there sound like you. My father was an ambassador there for the late King Aethelred. He brought me with him on his travels to northern Northumbria. In fact he took me on his travels to a lot of places, though he didn't allow me to mingle with the people who lived where we journeyed. Perchance were you raised elsewhere?"

She snapped her mouth shut when he lifted an eyebrow in amusement. It arched handsomely on his forbidding face. With a self-demeaning grimace, she realized that she babbled like a witless maid. Something about this man disarmed her and made every intelligent thought in her head evaporate. She frowned and studied the stone of the black floor.

"My mother and her people were the dark kin to the Vikings. They were a Baltic tribe that came from the east. My sire kidnapped her and enslaved many with her. 'Tis said my mother captured my father's heart with her heathen beauty. She used to dance naked under the stars for him and became his mistress. Eventually they were married. However, my sire was killed afore I was born. My mother freed my father's slaves and they raised me when he died. The accent I learned from them. I didn't know 'twas different until I was much older but by then 'twas too late." His lips curled into a mistrusting frown.

"And your mother? Will she object to this marriage?" Eden asked in fascination. The lines on his face softened at bit when he talked of the woman who gave life to him and in truth her new mother-by-marriage did sound like a fascinating woman. There was hope in her voice as she asked, "Where is she? Will I meet her?"

"Dead," he stated flatly. His expression closed to her once more.

"And the others? What happened to them?"

"Dead also. I have no family, save my daughter. She you will meet in a few sennights' time. I have already sent for her."

"I'm sorry to hear about your mother." Eden gave him a look of compassion. It didn't seem to affect him. "I myself never knew my mother."

Vladamir nodded but didn't inquire. Sitting upon the bed, he shrugged off his shoes and tossed them to the floor. Eden watched the lazy movements of his apt hands with fascination. The dark strands of his hair fell over his eyes as he looked to her. His elbows rested on his knees and his back hunched over them like a waiting beast.

Eden took a deep breath and concentrated on keeping her gaze averted. She resisted the urge to go to him. She wanted to pull his head to her breast and stroke his hair as she held him, she wanted to feel his hands about her waist, wrapping her in his strength.

Assuredly, he wouldn't welcome my attentions.

"What is your daughter's name? How old is she?" Eden wondered aloud, desperate to keep the talk between them. She felt him pulling away again.

"Gwendolyn. She is about six years." His voice softened as he said the girl's name. A cloud formed over his eyes and for a moment he was lost in a memory of his daughter. "It has been a year since I have seen her. I couldn't have brought her here with me for 'twas too uncertain of a journey. But, now with our marriage, I'd have you look to her."

Vladamir frowned and studied her intently.

"What?" Eden was flustered at the deliberate silence. She saw the piercing gaze through the corner of her eyes and trembled.

"Do you like children?" He pushed the waist-length hair from his eyes to better study her.

"Yea, m'lord," she answered in surprise. She fingered the wimple and veil in her hands, turning them nervously. Fixing her most earnest expression on him, she sighed. "I'm most anxious to meet Gwendolyn. I'm sure she is a beautiful—"

Vladamir's frown broke off her words. His eyes narrowed into fine slits as he studied her. "I'd expect you to care for her as your own, to never give her a moment's doubt of her place in my home."

"I wouldn't dare," Eden wondered at the pain in his voice. Were the rumors true? Was the child also marked by fire? Suddenly, she understood his meaning. He was afraid she would reject the child because of her disfigurement. How bad were the child's scars?

"M'lord," Eden paused, nervously licking her lips, "if I may be so bold?"

He nodded. Turning back to his task, he pulled at the wool stockings to also discard them on the floor. He flexed his toes as his bared feet fell against the stone. Eden absently watched his strong feet.

"Methinks I'd love the child, if she'll let me. I'd like to be thought of as her mother, if that is all right with you." Eden blushed as his head snapped up to study her. She bit her lip. Somehow being near him drew the truth from her without regard to propriety. "Though, I don't pretend to replace her own mother and I don't pretend to know all that much about children, but I'm sure I can learn."

"Eden," he drawled out, not looking up, "such an unusual name."

"'Tis derived from the ancient lands to the south." She licked her nervous lips. "My father said he met a young child who was named Eden a month before I was born. He said it was a lucky sign."

Vladamir lifted his foot to his knee and rubbed the arch of it gently. The length of his hair once again fell over his features to hide his face from view. A strange, unfamiliar sensation continued to grow in her stomach at the sound of his voice. Her own name had never sounded so pleasant to her ears as when it rolled from his tongue.

Suddenly, Vladamir stood and stalked over to her. He didn't stop until he was a hairbreadth away from her body. Eden paled at the swift way he stalked her. He took her hand that held the chamomile and pulled it up. Watching her palm with an intensity rarely seen, he took the nail of his smallest finger and ran it across the taut flesh of her wrist. Eden quivered. Her skin was still red from scouring his hall.

Vladamir sighed. "I don't wish for you to scrub my hall. Have the servants tend to it from now on."

Eden gasped as the weightless caress moved over the palm of her hand to lightly pass over each of her fingers. Her palm was sore, but it looked worse than it felt. Their skin glowed orange in the firelight, hers lighter than his naturally tanned fingers. Her hold on the headpiece loosened and the wimple fell to the floor, the veil fluttering behind it.

She glanced up to gaze into his eyes, but he didn't look directly at her face. This time she couldn't look away from him. Her fingers shuddered in his grasp. He was so close. She saw the rise of his broad chest underneath the black linen of his overtunic and could smell the strong fragrance of his masculinity. The heady scent intoxicated her like a poison, making her his slave.

You told me that I wasn't to be a slave, but I am. You said that I wasn't to be a prisoner, but I remain as such. I'm more a prisoner to you now than before for I cannot even think of defying you and I'm a slave for my will belongs to you.

Eden was frightened by her own thoughts. They were so unlike her. It was as if they were put into her head. Never had she felt so strongly for a man. Never had she dreamt of relinquishing her total control over to one. She stared spellbound into his eyes, frightened by the depths of her unreturned feelings.

And then, Eden felt him press something into her palm. She glanced down as he let go of her. It was a vial, the kind often used by alchemists. It rolled in her hand to lie next to the dried flower. Staring at it, she froze, not daring to move her fingers.

"What is it?" she wondered aloud. Her whole body shook. Did he mean to kill her now? "Poison?"

"Blood," he corrected in his low resonant voice. He took another deliberate step back from her. His chin lowered so that he looked at her through the animalistic narrowing of his eyes.

"Blood?" Her hand jolted and she almost dropped the vial.

Blood! What kind of…?

"Tell me," he broke into her thoughts. "Do you know what happens between a man and woman?"

Eden gulped but didn't move. His query demanded an answer she knew not how to voice. She knew her body wanted to be next to his, knew that when he kissed her she couldn't think and afterwards she could think of nothing else but begging him to do it again. He studied her with an enchanting tilt of his head.

The duke blinked slowly. When she didn't move, he smiled, softening his face. "Do you know about consummation?"

"A little." Eden licked her dry lips. "Some of my father's maids used to talk about it when they didn't know I was listening."

"What have you been told?"

"I know that a man goes inside a woman and then the woman loses her maidenhead and that the stomach aches deeply after," Eden answered him with a guileless innocence. It didn't occur to her not to be honest with him. They were married after all and would be consummating very soon. Her body ached, feeling very empty.

"When a woman loses her maidenhead there oft is blood at the loss. That is why I give you this. For if you're not pure none need to know about it. You'll have no explaining to do." Reaching up, he touched a lock of her hair and smiled slightly.

Tears sprung to her eyes at the thoughtful gesture. Vladamir backed away from her.

"I," Eden began as she watched his hasty withdrawal through the corner of her eye. "Thank you."

Vladamir nodded and stopped his movement. His gaze pierced through the air with the concentration of a bird of prey circling its next meal and his face was hard and emotionless. Eden couldn't read the thoughts that swam in his eyes like a turbulent storm.

"You cannot bring yourself to look at me. You think I'm a monster." The statement was simple, although he didn't mean to say the words aloud.

"Nay," she instantly denied. Her wide-eyed expression found him in amazement.

"'Tis all right." He frowned. "Know this for I'll say it only once. You'll never play me false and you'll never lie to me, for those are the two gravest of offenses a wife can commit."

Had your first wife committed such an offense? What happened to her? Did you truly kill her? What happened to your face? How were you scarred? Why won't you smile at me? Why won't you kiss me? Truly kiss me?

Eden blushed but couldn't answer, so instead she nodded in understanding. Questions welled within her. He was such a contradiction, one she couldn't begin to understand. Sometimes, if felt as if he liked her — just a little. Other times, if felt as if he merely tolerated her.

She was touched by his kindness in giving her the vial. Tears crept to her eyes at the thoughtful gesture. He sought to save her the embarrassment of the manor discovering her shame for the shame would be on her head and not her husband's.

"You're scared of me," Vladamir stated with confidence. His stiff mouth and hard stare dared her to deny it.

Eden shivered, feeling as if he was all around her, confronting her, consuming her soul with his closeness. She managed to nod her head in agreement. "Yea, you do frighten me and I'm afraid of what you'd do to me."

"You think me a monster," he continued, taking a single step forward. His eyes held her captive.

"M'lord, I don't know what you are. I don't truly know you." She paused, wondering how best to explain how she felt. "I cannot judge that which I don't understand but I don't feel that you're monstrous. Mayhap you have done things in your past that you're not proud of. Mayhap those acts are considered monstrous by most but that is the past and the future is linked between us. So far, I have no reason to believe that you're a monster. I can only hope that you'll treat me with kindness and perchance a bit of caring in time."

"Mayhap monster wasn't the right word. You don't look at me. You're repulsed by my appearance. You're afraid of my scars."

Eden shivered, unsure how to respond.

"'Tis all right," he put forth when she was silent. "But I'd have the truth of it from you."

How can you think me repulsed? I can hardly keep my eyes from you when you're around and I cannot keep my thoughts from you when you're not.

She said nothing.

"Are you repulsed?" His words were more like a confirmation than a question.

"Nay, m'lord," Eden gasped her denial.

"I said never to lie to me!" Vladamir seethed, his voice rising by degrees with each word. He flew forward and grabbed her about the neck. "I won't tolerate dishonesty."

Eden jumped in surprise at the power with which he moved. He always looked like a stalking beast ready to pounce but to actually see it! It filled her with quivering excitement, made her eager to touch him, to be touched. She clawed frantically at his hand. He didn't squeeze with much force, but still she felt the strength of his grip and for a moment her heels lift from the ground as she stumbled to regain footing.

"We will try again and this time mind your words, m'lady. I'll see the lie in your face." Vladamir's voice echoed with deadly warning, so much that his eyes blazed with an eternal heat. He stated again, his words enunciated and clear, "You're repulsed by me."

Eden looked into his dispassionate gaze and took a deep breath. "Remove your hand. You have no need to restrain me. I won't run away. I have given you my word on that account. You have yet to release me from my promise. I'm bound within these walls."

"Answer," Vladamir commanded with a growl. "You say that you aren't repulsed, so tell me how you feel toward me."

"I don't know how to feel, m'lord! Yea, you do frighten me. That much I have admitted. Yea, I once thought you might be a monster but bear it in mind that I was sick with fever from Lord Luther's beating." Eden stopped pulling at his hand. Her weaker strength had no effect on him anyway.

She saw what he believed in his eyes, but he was wrong. He didn't repulse her. His hand about her throat was powerful and electrifying. It excited her as did the rest of him. She wanted to be touched by him. Her body was so hot, so wet, so alive with the fire of his nearness. Vladamir's eyes bored strangely into her. The man confused her emotions and sent her blood to boiling. She closed her eyes and prayed he would believe her. Her single word came out in a soft gush of air. "Nay."

"What?" Vladamir's grip tightened slightly, but not enough to do damage to her throat. He was a contradiction of gentle roughness.

"I said nay, m'lord. You don't repulse me." Eden opened her eyes and gazed into his intensely dark stare. She didn't know how to act around him. Leaning into his possessive hand, her head fell back. "You confuse me. You confuse my emotions. I don't know how to feel around you but you have never repulsed me. If you think that your scars take away from your beauty you're wrong. They add to it. I don't even see them when I look at you. All I see is your eyes. They haunt me, m'lord. Methinks you have bewitched me."

Beauty?!

The duke tried to hide the tremendous pleasure her modest words caused in his chest, though he couldn't help but wonder at her motivation. Vladamir knew that Eden didn't care for him, had only married him to save herself from a worse fate.

For all Eden's repulsion, he couldn't help himself. She captivated him and having been without a woman for a long time, he desired her more than any other. Smiling to himself at the irony, he kept his face blank. It was the first time in many years that he hadn't purposefully tried to intimidate someone—especially a woman—only now he wasn't sure how not to frighten her.

He didn't trust women in general and hadn't wanted to be involved with them, until now. No matter how much he wanted to hold her at the moment, he couldn't force her. He would never force a woman to his bed. He wasn't that much of a monster, no matter how oft he tried to convince himself he was.

The duke had read well the words she refused to say when she spoke of her virginity. It's why he gave her the vial. With her beauty, it was unlikely Luther let her go without sampling her wares first. The knowledge of it glowed from the hollowed depths of her round, terrified eyes. Despite his distaste for the female gender he never felt they deserved such cruelty. But after such a thing how could he expect her to want him—even without the scars?

It bothered him at one time how people stared, but now he was used to it or at least he thought he was. Mayhap if he turned out the lights his appearance wouldn't repulse her so. That is why he'd grown used to walking in the dark in the first place. But she'd said it herself, she only chose him because no other man would have her after she was ill-used.

What man besides me? Me, a monster with no hope of better.

At least he was better than being ravished by the lot of dirty soldiers he knew Lord Luther to call friends. Drawing from his thoughts, he studied her, trying to see the humor in her eyes. He found none. He tried to find mocking, yet she was devoid of that also. "You say I bewitch you, then why do you look away from me always? You don't meet the eyes you claim to haunt you."

"You told me not to stare, m'lord." She lifted her hands in a helpless gesture. "You bid me look away. Methought 'tis how you wished me to act."

At that Vladamir's lips curled into a half smile. He had said that earlier. How quickly he forgot his own words.

"Must you always be displeased with me?" Eden raised her hands once more and touched the vise-like grip around her throat. Instead of trying to pull it off she ran her hand lightly into his sleeve. Her touch grazed over his forearm, skin that was unscathed. How he wished he was the man he'd once been—handsome, charming, carefree. If he was that man, he'd have something to offer her—something more than the scarred, bitter man he was now. How could she want him? Why would she?

Vladamir felt her pulse quicken under his palm. Her lips parted as she leaned her head back. Unwittingly, she invited his kiss with the downcast draw of her eyes.

Maybe she did want him. Maybe the gods had finally forgiven him for the past.

"I'm not always displeased." He swayed into her, his chest tight.

"Will you kiss me again, m'lord?"

Vladamir couldn't deny her. Gently, he pulled her forward with the hand that restrained her slender neck. He brought his lips down to her and lightly rubbed his mouth against them. Flicking his tongue over her bottom lip, he tested the truthfulness of her response and was rewarded with a slight moan. He still didn't trust her, but he couldn't resist her sweet entreaty either.

Her eyes closed and remained so for a moment. Vladamir kept the caress light. He drew his lips away to watch her face. When his mouth left her, her eyes fluttered open to gaze insecurely at him.

"Now, 'tis you who must answer me. Do I repulse you, m'lord? Am I not to be looked at with kinder eyes?" A red flush crept hotly over her features. "Is that why you don't kiss me as I have seen the soldiers kiss the maids? Or does one not kiss a lady like that?"

Vladamir smiled at the innocence of her question. He felt the artlessness within her. She'd yet to learn the female craft of deceit.

Mayhap I should lock you in a tower so you never will.

"Or perchance you're repulsed by what was done to me," she concluded through lush trembling lips.

Vladamir didn't wish to discuss this, not really. He'd rather put her lips to better use. His body tightened, every muscle rigid with his control. If he didn't find release soon his cock was sure to explode inside his braes again.

"You don't want what is not pure. That is why you gave me the vial. So you wouldn't have to touch me."

Eden tried to pull away from him, but he didn't let her go. Her voice soft, she said, "Please, I understand your reason for the vial. I'll tell no one we didn't finish this night. I cannot blame you for your repulsion. I'll try not to be so revolting in the future and mayhap when you're far into your cups you'll be able to beget your heir. I hear that is when most babes are begot anyway."

"Nay, methought only to save you embarrassment with the vial." Vladamir kept his face passionless. "I care not about your maidenhead for you cannot help how that was taken. You're a maiden in your own mind, 'tis what matters."

Eden nodded. "Then 'tis because I'm not comely that you don't kiss me."

"M'lady searches for compliments," he stated with distaste. Mayhap she had learned the woman's craft after all. "Men have surely told you of your beauty."

"Men?" she asked with a rueful smile. "Nay, my father wouldn't let them near me. He flogged a man once for talking to me. The soldier merely asked for directions to some place called *Paradise Passageway*, 'tis said to be near the *Garden of Eden*."

"Ah," Vladamir sighed as he tried not to laugh at the soldier's wit and his wife's innocent candor. He grudgingly appreciated Clifton's heavy-handed ways in raising his daughter.

"Though I didn't think that the Garden of Eden was truly an existing place." With a delicate shrug, Eden smiled at up at him through the fan of her lashes. "Methought 'twas an ancient village of some sort."

"Nay, m'lady, you don't repulse me," Vladamir broke in, afraid of what he would do to his lady wife if she kept talking of such things at length. Already his mind kept conjuring images of her lips around his shaft as he squirted his seed down her throat.

"Eden." She sighed as she once more tilted her head back. She licked her lips, inviting another kiss. "I liked how my name sounds in your voice. Your accent is so unfamiliar, so unlike that which I know."

"Eden," he obliged before once more bringing his lips to hers. This time he traced the line of her mouth with his tongue. It had been a long time since he'd seduced a woman, but the natural instinct of his former ways rushed back full force. His hand remained seductively forceful around her throat and she gasped into his capturing mouth. Slowly he caressed her, expertly scraping his long nails over her quivering flesh.

Her hands climbed up his biceps to rest on his shoulders. Her breath came to her in long pants as he withdrew to lighten the kiss and tease her lips. She touched the side of his face, running her palm across his jawbone over the hard texture of his scar. Not fully returning his embrace, she just let it happen, leaning fully to him as if instinctually wanting to be closer.

She moaned, a virtuous sound. Vladamir deepened the kiss, moving his tongue deeper into her unresisting mouth. He delved it between her lips with the tender force of his passion for her. Every instinct urged him to throw her down and take his fill of her, but he held back, wanting her willing for his touch. His hand moved from her throat to the back of her head as he compelled her more fully to him. Eden made a small sound of surprise, but soon her hips were rubbing along him, her soft body rocking into his hard cock.

Suddenly, Vladamir stopped. Her movement wantonly thrust her hips—too wantonly for an innocent maiden. He pulled away, a frown marring his brow as he looked to her. Desire warred with prudence. She was his wife and he didn't have to stop. He could do as he willed with her, could conquer her repeatedly until he could come no more and no one would dare deny him it. The urge to toss her onto the bed and take her was strong.

"What?" The sound of her voice combined with her heightened breath begged for him to continue. Her fingers were wound in his hair at the nape of his neck and she let them fall to his shoulders. "Did I do aught wrong?"

Vladamir smiled so that the hard line of his lips pressed together in a cruel, disapproving scowl. He backed away from her and her hands dropped to her sides. He wouldn't fall for her trap. He would discover her motive in coming to his home. "You're good, m'lady. I bow to your true cunning."

"Cunning?" She made a move to go to him, but stopped when he snarled. "Of what do you speak, m'lord?"

"You know well of what I speak, maiden. You think to make a fool of me with your charms, your calculated innocence? I'm not a fool, though I do admit you almost took me in with your words." He frowned as his foot came up against his shoes. He kicked them under the bed with savage intensity and sat down on the mattress. "No innocent maiden acts as you do. You're not as virtuous as you'd have me believe."

"M'lord, you give my actions too much credence," Eden protested. "If I acted wrongly, please just tell me what I did."

"Nay, m'lady, I didn't give you enough credit. You're truly your father's daughter. Did you plan this with him? Did he beat you afore laying you at my gate?" Vladamir grabbed the edge of his tunic and pulled it over his head. The shirt muffled his words. "Did you think to win yourself the title of Duchess? Did you wish to land a rich husband?"

"Nay! My father's holdings are more profitable than yours are m'lord. I should daresay that you're even poor by most noble standards. As to the title, I said that I don't care about that and I certainly don't care for your conceit."

"So you say." Vladamir could consent that she didn't know how rich he truly was, for it wasn't common knowledge in Wessex. "Tell me then. Who beat you?"

"I already told you, 'twas Luther." Eden tried to move toward him. His dark look kept her back.

"So you've said, maiden." Vladamir frowned at her look. This woman was trained well.

Eden was mad that he could even accuse her of such a deceitful thing. Wringing her hands, she tried to remember what she could've possibly done to upset him. He invaded her thoughts, so that all she remembered was the feel of his embrace. She wanted to draw him back to her arms, to make him continue the foreign turmoil he alighted within her body.

He'd pressed his body into hers. His hair had been soft as it fell against her wrist. When he leaned over her in his passion, the long black waves cocooned her. The strength of him made her shiver with excitement as it molded to her length. She longed to rub against him as they had in the hall. Fires burned wet and hot in her sex, throbbing and needy.

She wanted him of that she was certain. But how to ask for it? Her body was tight with frustration, needing him to release her. She wanted to tear at her clothes, free herself from them. Better yet, she wanted him to do it for her. Let him act the monster for it excited her when he tried to dominate her.

She wanted him to throw her down and kiss her roughly. When he was with her, his lips to hers, she felt him holding the beast within him back. How could she tempt the beast to break free of the man and give into his passion? How could she get the man to break free of the beast and find his heart?

For all his frightening appearance, the duke treated her with such tenderness. Aside from the poke of his knife into her side, he'd been gentle. She'd moved her hips to deftly settle next to the blade so that it wouldn't poke at her tender stomach, only to be poked by something much larger. That's when he stopped. Why did he stop?

Her attention was distracted from her thoughts as she watched him take off his overtunic. He threw it to the floor. The flesh of his back was strong and smooth, not at all marred by fire. A divot ran up his back, indenting his spine surrounded by thick, war-hardened muscles. His lean sides tapered into his braes, turning into slender masculine hips. Eden froze in anticipation sure he'd continue to disrobe.

Then he turned to her and the large bulge between his thighs briefly captured her notice. Her eyes traveled upward to his chest, her hand shook and she dropped the vial and flower. The flames had burnt him down his side causing the disfigurement to climb over his neck to cover his shoulder. It traveled down the length of his arm to his elbow and gnarled most of his right side. The dark skin of his chest became discolored as it grew into the variegated flesh of the old injury.

"Look your fill, maiden," Vladamir spat, holding still for her observation.

"What happened to you?" She motioned her hand wanting to touch him, soothe him. "Who did this to you?"

The hard set of his features kept her back as fire burned in the depths of his angry eyes. "Have you not heard? My father, the devil, scarred me to remind me of hell. 'Tis a warning to mortals that I'm a demon."

"I don't believe such things. They cannot be true." Eden shook her head, hearing well the sarcastic ring in his tone. The old pain reflected from his eyes. "I care not what others say about you. I don't believe you're a demon sent from hell."

"M'lady is quite right. She shouldn't speak on matters she knows naught about." Pointing to the bed, he ordered, "Into bed lest I perform yet another monstrous act in my lifetime."

Her blood ran cold as he threw her words back at her. Her lips trembled and she felt like an idiot. Running to the bed at his jarring order, she quickly moved underneath the coverlet. The tight linen of the lavish gown pressed against her breasts and she wanted to ask if he would allow her to disrobe from it and don a more comfortable nightgown but considering his temper she thought better of it.

"I'll think of how to deal with your treachery later." Vladamir didn't bother to pull the privacy curtains that hung from the canopy as he lay down. He rolled toward her and narrowed his eyes. Taking the tip of his nail, he pressed it to the tender divot in her throat and held it against her like he would the point of a knife blade. "You'd be well advised to tell me what it is your father plans. What do you have to gain by marrying me? For, fair maiden, I don't believe you're bewitched by my charms."

Eden didn't dare answer him. She got the feeling that if she said one word he would tear her asunder with his bare hands. Her eyes from strayed to his chest, horrified by what he must have been through. However mortified she was by the look of his scars, she wanted to reach to him and touch him. He mesmerized her and she thought him beautiful except for his nasty temper. For even under the marred flesh she saw that he was well formed. She itched to press her fingers along his skin, wanting to feel him, to run her hands over his unique texture.

He rolled away from her and she felt rejected, alone. Her body throbbed, wet and needy for his touch. Sparks flamed her blood, causing her nipples to reach out against her bodice.

157

Each breath was like a fiery caress, sending jolts of lightning down her stomach to her sex. Reaching out to touch his naked, muscled back, she let her hand hang in midair. She didn't touch his flesh out of fear of his wrath. Instead she lightly patted a piece of heathenish black hair as it sprawled along his pillow. Tears came to her eyes when he paid her no more mind and with a heavy heart, she rolled away from him.

Why do you insist on acting the monster, m'lord? I have done naught to deserve your anger.

Eden tore the ribbons from her hair and flung them to the floor, causing them to flutter in the air before resting on the hard stone. She closed her eyes to the moisture that built within them. Her heart ached for something she couldn't name and her body trembled for his touch. She didn't understand this man she'd married herself to. Stuffing her fist into her mouth, she bit down until her teeth imprinted into her flesh and there she stayed, choking on a sob so he wouldn't know she cried.

Chapter Seven

ဢ

Eden's night was full of restless dreams and she awoke the next morning weary from her sleepless night. The gown she wore pulled uncomfortably at her skin and she suddenly wished she'd gotten up in the middle of the night to don some nightclothes. But she hadn't dared to anger Vladamir more. He slept so quietly that she didn't know if he truly slumbered or if he lay awake waiting for her to defy him.

She turned to find her husband already awake, studying her intently. He once again wore his black tunic. The eve before when he'd thrown the garment on the floor she got the impression that he deliberately tried to shock her. It had worked but not in the way he meant it to. Instead of fearing him her heart went out to him.

Vladamir moved stealthily to tower above her. His hands rested in fists on his lean hips. Black circles smudged under his eyes, belying the fact that he also slept poorly.

"M'lord?" she asked, hesitating. Vladamir was a breathtakingly handsome man. His gaze pierced her and she cowered beneath him. Although his strength excited her, she knew it could very well be deadly. "Are you still angry with me?"

His eyes narrowed even more to soundlessly answer her question. Eden noticed that he was completely dressed for the day, except for his bare feet. She waited for him to speak, wanting to hear the smooth accent tell her that all was right and that he wasn't upset. A knock sounded from outside the chamber. Vladamir sighed and moved to answer the door.

"M'lord?" Eden asked, unsure what she would say if he answered her. Inching her bottom to the edge of the bed, she

159

stood. The pain in her chest grew as she realized he wasn't going to turn 'round to acknowledge her.

"Yea?" Vladamir snarled as he forced open the door. Then with a furious growl, he relaxed one hand on his lean hip. Grabbing the top of the door, he pulled it to his elbow and leaned into the hard wood, blocking Eden from sight.

Eden studied the fierce line of his muscled back. It was so hard, so unforgiving. She knew not what she'd done to deserve his callous treatment of her. Lifting her chin into the air, she waited to see what the intruder wanted.

"M'lord," Ulric answered. The man glanced around Vladamir with a look of panic. When he saw her, he sighed with visible relief. Eden knew her face had to be pale and drawn and she wore her crumpled wedding gown.

"I apologize fer the rude disturbance," Ulric said, "but methought you should be notified. There are fires lit outside the castle. An army gathers even now."

A throaty growl escaped Vladamir. He pushed past the seneschal to assail upon those who would challenge his keep. Eden watched her husband's back in silence. His long hair swayed with his body as he stormed from the chamber, stalking away without bothering to acknowledge her before leaving and she noticed he didn't cover his bare feet.

With a fearful leap of her breast, she felt her heart squeeze tightly in her chest. It was as if he wasn't interested in talking to her at all! She could see it in his expression, even before he learned of the army outside the castle gates. Why was he so displeased with her? Whatever the reason, she knew she'd better find out quickly. Her future depended on his good humor.

"M'lady?" The seneschal made a move to leave, but stopped as he witnessed her wan expression. Wiping his sleeve over his bald forehead, he asked, "Is all well?"

"Besides the fires of a siege?" Her words were thick with sarcasm. Then, realizing that she was taking her frustrations out on the wrong person, she softened her tone, "Yea. All is well."

"Very good, m'lady," Ulric sighed, unwilling to probe too much.

"M'lord forgot his shoes. I should take them to him," Eden mumbled to herself, unwilling to let her husband run away from her so quickly and glad for an excuse to seek him out. The people of the manor seemed to let the duke dwell too often in his ill temper. She was going to make him face it and she intended on pestering him until he did.

Kneeling on the floor she reached under the bed in search for the discarded shoes. She still wore her wedding tunic from the night before and her feet were bare. Sighing in exasperation, she leaned close to the stone floor to peer under the bed. The shoes had made their way far under and she had to lean down close to the stone to reach them. Finally as her fingers touched the rough leather, she pulled them to her. Standing quickly, she brushed off the cream colored tunic and pressed the shoes to her nervous chest.

"The land is at peace, who would lay siege to the castle?"

Ulric had walked so far ahead that he didn't hear her question. With a sigh of exasperation, she moved to the door. Suddenly, she stopped with a slight jolt of alarm, stubbing her toe on the vial of blood Vladamir had given her. It clanked across the stone floor but didn't break.

"Such a lovely *morgen-gifu*," she said as she picked the vial up. Dropping the shoes onto the stone by her dried piece of chamomile, she quickly shut the door to the chamber and went to the bed. Her words held a sarcastic ring as she mumbled, "So thoughtful of my dear, monstrously tempered husband to remember me."

Well, m'lord. What is done shall forever remain done, for I won't go back to my father's keep.

Eden took a deep breath and tore back the fur coverlet they'd used the night before. Pulling at the crude plug in the top of the vial, she was careful not to spill any of the blood on her expensive gown. Holding her breath, she flung the liquid onto the satiny linen.

Eden watched the deep red fluid stain the beautiful beige material with some regret. She hoped that the linen hadn't cost him a fortune and wouldn't permanently stain. The blood stopped spreading and she nodded her head in satisfaction. "'Til death us depart, m'lord."

She turned back to the discarded shoes, picking them up with grim determination. Then grabbing the flower with more gentleness, she found she didn't have the heart to dispose of it. There was no safe place to stow it so she buried it in the tight fitting sleeve of her gown. She would just have to request her own trunk from the servants.

Eden made her own way down the dark corridor, stopping by a door that led to a chamber she knew to be empty. She opened the door and gently rolled the empty vial into the darkness.

"There, m'lord, 'tis done." She frowned, regretting the need for secrecy, but as she continued down the hall a smile played on her features. Hugging his shoes to her chest, she was intent on delivering them to him straightway. The smile widened as she thought of her husband's handsomely angry face.

Let him try to disregard me again! I won't be ignored so easily.

* * * * *

"M'lord," Eden hesitated, shading the morning sun from her eyes to watch Vladamir climb down from the wall. Holding her wedding gown high in her hands, she kept it from the dirt. It was still very early in the morning hours. By her guess the men outside the castle set up camp within the night, mayhap even during her wedding and lit the fires with the dawn. She heard the soldiers on the other side of the wall. Their strong voices shouted unrecognizable commands over the distance. The sound startled her as she naturally moved closer to where her husband would land on the ground.

Looking up with a lump forming in her throat, she watched in breathlessness as the duke jumped the rest of the way down from the wooden ladder. Eden couldn't get over how handsome he was and now having seen firsthand his muscled upper body she found herself staring at it in hopes of catching a glimpse. She knew that his scars caused him much grief, knew also that many would feel the same if they had them. But she found they only added to his dangerous allure, his primal heathen attractiveness.

Eden longed for what he'd started the eve before. It was to have been the night they consummated the marriage. She wasn't sure what took place exactly during this consummation, but she knew that if it felt anything like his lips pressed to hers, she would enjoy it. As she looked him over, she wished he wouldn't wear his collar so high to his neck. Many men showed their chests as was the style, then why not her husband?

The scars, Eden concluded dismally. *But I care not about the damned scars!*

The duke's feet were still bare so she didn't feel so foolish holding his shoes to her chest. Eden could see the tendons working under his skin as they ran up from his masculine toes to the fronts of his ankles. The bottoms were caked with mud and a bloody smudge swept over the callused flesh of one arch. She gasped as she rushed the rest of the way to him.

"You're hurt," she breathed heavily in concern, her eyes narrowed to study his injury.

Vladamir lifted a bemused eyebrow at the statement. He followed her worried gaze downward as he turned his heel to better see the inside of his foot where he'd scraped it. "Nay, 'tis naught but a slight graze. I've had much worse in battle."

Eden licked her lips and held out his shoes. "You forgot these under the bed. Methought you might have need of them and I see that I was right."

Leaning against the stone wall, he swiped the mud from his feet with his hand and quickly slipped into the leather shoes. Then, with more concentration then was necessary, he tied the laces and secured them into place.

"'Tis a siege, m'lord?"

"It would appear so." Vladamir nodded as if it was an everyday occurrence and nothing to be distraught over.

"What have you done?" Eden shivered in fright, swinging back 'round to face him. "The land is at peace. Why would any want to start a war?"

"'Tis hardly a war, m'lady." Vladamir laughed, the sound rang almost sarcastic as it echoed in his accent. He pushed himself away from the wall and took a lazy step toward her. His eyes darkened seductively as he lowered his jaw to argue. "The land is never at peace, only in short periods of rest between wars."

"'Tis a most cold opinion you have of the world. It would imply that the wars of past were fought for naught. That the lives lost in those wars were for naught," she countered as she met his eyes. "It leaves nary a ground for hope."

The duke thoughtfully narrowed his eyes at her sentiment, but didn't answer. It was as if her convictions amused him. Eden's mouth suddenly felt dry at his attention. If not for the look, she would've believed he'd forgotten their kiss the night before. She knew she couldn't forget, for her body heated anew at the reminder. Feeling insecure as a flush darkened her cheeks, she glanced away from his probing eyes. It was a mistake for her eyes went straight to the strange, growing hardness that pressed against his tunic. She no longer felt as if she had to avert her gaze from him, though she still didn't know what she'd done to deserve his wrath in the first place.

Her thoughts turned to the wall as a shouted command came from the distance. She jolted in fear at the harsh reply that the yell received. Never before had she been in a castle while it was besieged by an army. She looked over her shoulder as she took an involuntary step toward the ill-tempered duke. The wall prevented her from seeing anything unusual.

Mayhap, I'm not an accomplished lover. Perchance, 'tis only that I have disappointed him, Eden thought with a worried frown, for she didn't know how to be better. *Or perchance my husband is a man who will never be pleased.*

"Who is it?" she asked, aware of how much time had passed in silence. Not taking her eyes away from his growth. She wondered if the monster was changing shape. A moment's fear overwhelmed her, until she found that she was oddly excited and not at all scared.

"The banner," Vladamir paused and suddenly frowned as if he remembered what was happening outside his castle walls. He shifted his waist so the tunic fell forward and away from his bulging erection. "The banner is that of your father."

Her head jolted up in surprise. Eden shivered at his claim, believing to understand his thoughts. In an effort to change his mind, she leaned forward to plead with him. "You cannot send me back there, no matter what you believe. Remember your promise. I have your word of honor."

A firm press of his mouth was his only answer as Vladamir tilted his head to the side. He folded his arms menacingly over his chest.

"Please, don't think it!" Eden looked over his shoulder as if she saw through the stone of the wall to her father's army. She knew her father commanded many men, men who were loyal to the earl because they believed him to be a man of great power and in many ways the soldiers were right in the assumption. She shook her head in apprehension. "Just make him leave, I beg it of you. If you're skilled at all in the black arts, frighten him and make him leave."

"I cannot force him to go afore he makes the decision himself. All I can offer is incentive."

"You cannot mean to give me to him?" Finally, unable to keep her hands from him a moment longer she flung herself forward to pull at his arm. "You promised you'd kill me first. I won't wed Luther! You weren't there. You cannot know what he is capable of."

"Do you forget your vows so soon, dear wife?" he asked in cynical amusement as he dispassionately untangled her hand from his forearm. "Methinks it speaks poorly of my worth as a husband."

"Nay," Eden faltered under his gaze. Letting his arm go, she took a step away from his preoccupied dark eyes and regained her composure. She tilted her chin proudly in the air. "Methought that is what you meant as incentive. Methought you meant to send me back and deny the marriage, since 'tis not yet truly consummated. It would be the easiest route for you, being that your men aren't matched to my father's army."

"We could rectify the consummation quickly if you're so concerned. Mayhap then you'll remember who your new lord and master is," he offered with a cruel smile. "Should I lift your skirts and take you right here in the bailey? There would be plenty of witnesses to attest to the marriage being done." When she shot him an alarmed look, he chuckled under his breath. "Besides, have you forgotten also my reasons for marrying you? It wouldn't be revenge if I was to send you back to him, unless 'twas dead and I'm not yet sure that is your best purpose."

Eden gasped at the dark look of hatred that overcame his face. She took yet another step back as he stalked her. Her hand trembled and she dropped her gown into the dirt. Hastily, she grabbed it back up but it was too late. The hem was dirty.

"Don't worry about the consummation," he stated, continuing forward with his wicked smile firmly in place. His gaze dipped to the exposed tops of her breast. Her blood heated at the look. "We will tend to that detail soon enough."

Eden shivered at the promise in his words, though in her opinion they didn't seem to bring him much pleasure. He grabbed the arm that held her tunic.

"What?" she questioned in panic. "Do you mean to hurt me? Will you decide to maim me as your revenge? You're not going to consummate...here? Now?"

"M'lady," Vladamir said cruelly, his lips curled in mischievous delight. He leaned forward to whisper darkly into her ear. "What I do to you remains to be seen. Methinks that remains mostly on you. Have you a confession to make?"

"You said never to lie to you, so, nay, I have no confession."

"Very well." He didn't let her go. "Then shall we make your father welcome?"

"What games are you playing at? I don't understand!" Eden raised a shaking hand to plead with him as she pulled in vain to free herself. "You cannot invite him in. He might hurt you."

"M'lady, 'tis you who plays games. Now cease your womanly hysterics, they make my head ache." Vladamir leaned over and grabbed the hem of her wedding gown. He yanked it roughly from her grasp. Eden froze, sure he was going to make good on his threats and take her right there in the bailey as his men watched. He ripped off a large piece of the expensive tunic with three hard jerks. Gripping it in his hand, he turned and waved to a nearby knight.

"Hand this up the wall," he stated to the man as he passed him the cloth.

"How dare you disrobe me out here?" Eden seethed, skirting away from him. Taking a few steps to distance herself, she glared at him openly. She felt a pang of anger at the torn dress.

"I can disrobe you wherever and whenever I like. I can lead you through this bailey naked. You're my wife," he answered with a sneer as he walked to the main gate. Relief flooded her when he didn't move to take her against the wall. He lifted his hand and motioned at a soldier. The man nodded his head and Eden saw him wave her dress in the air, like a battle prize.

Vladamir turned back to her, a gleam of merriment lining his grim eyes, only to say, "Get abovestairs and change. We shall greet your father and tell him the joyous news of our union."

Eden shivered at his cold laughter. It sung out over the yard as she ran from him.

I don't know this man who is my husband. Mayhap, I did truly marry a monster!

Vladamir watched Eden run from him with a sense of shallow victory. Her round gaze had sought him with such naiveté that he was hard-pressed to believe anything she'd ever said to him. But that would be foolish.

He wouldn't be swayed by a pretty face. As he'd pulled on his shoes, he'd leisurely let his gaze travel over the alluring length of her form—from her hair as it floated in the breeze to her small ears then past to the delicate line of her throat and the pulse that beat erratically there. Her face had been calm, but she'd nervously sucked on her lower lip while looking at his erection. It had taken all his willpower not to put her mouth to better use.

Watching her run off now, he felt his braes tighten even more. *By all the gods! What is this woman doing to me?*

Even though the duke knew her deceit as a woman, he couldn't help wanting to touch her. Every time she was near, he had the insane urge to hold her and protect her. Part of him wasn't even mad at her, though he did distrust her and he liked to make her angry, just to see where her heated passions would bring her. He felt a strong urge to make her mad more often.

Vladamir turned to the main gate and waited patiently for Clifton's reply to his call of a truce. The duke didn't know how the earl would gather that his daughter was at Lakeshire Castle, unless she'd been placed there by her father's deceit. Vladamir hadn't told anyone about his captive, not even while checking in with the king. It was unlikely the servants had gossiped outside of the manor, since none had left Lakeshire in a long time.

From the top of the wall, he recognized Lord Luther's banner at the back of the earl's camp. It was possible that his wife's former fiancé tracked her to his castle gate. At least in the alliance between the two men his wife spoke the truth. He was glad for the siege as it was an excuse to not face his treacherous wife so soon. The promise of a good fight always did something to lift a warrior's mood and he was still too enraged to deal with his little scheming duchess.

After many moments his gate was raised and he saw an undersized man ride in. The soldier was poor, his woolen clothes hanging on his thin frame. As the man's horse timidly approached, Vladamir smiled for the man sent to him was actually a boy and a weak one at that. He could hardly keep astride his saddle. The page looked shakily about the manor before settling his eyes on the infamous Monster of Lakeshire.

"You ask fer mercy?" his voice squeaked with his boyhood changing. The page slowly reined the horse in front of Vladamir and swallowed hard.

"Nay, I do not. Tell your lord that I wish to know why he dares to lay siege to my castle. Tell him to face me like a man. I give my word that he'll be escorted safely back, if he acts honorably," Vladamir said in his darkest tone. He hid his laughter as the boy nodded and tore out of the castle. Minutes later, four more horses rode forward.

Vladamir froze, keeping his expression a hard mask to hide his vengeful thoughts as he recognized Clifton. He would've known the man even without the help of the white and blue banner that flew behind him on his soldier's horse. The self-important man by the earl's side could only be Luther.

Vladamir raised his fists to his waist as he stared at the approaching men. To their credit they didn't hesitate as the small boy had as they rode their mounts straight to him. Two soldiers Vladamir didn't know halted their stallions behind their leaders and held back as the nobles rode forward to confront him.

"What is the meaning of this?" Vladamir narrowed his eyes but made no move to arm himself. He hadn't bothered to carry his sword, knowing Clifton well. The earl wouldn't attack an unarmed man, at least not in the presence of so many eyes. The duke smiled coldly as he saw that Clifton noticed his weaponless state.

"Arm yourself. I have come to avenge the death of my daughter." Clifton looked down the length of his nose from his horse, his bulky stature not the least bit intimidating to his opponent. What the earl lacked in height he made up for in width. His broad shoulders were tight with war-hardened muscles, but it wasn't his physique that demanded obedience. It was his bearing.

"Nay," answered Vladamir, his expression giving nothing away as he grinned in pleasure.

"Nay?" Lord Luther injected from the horse at Clifton's side. "Are you a coward? Can you only harm defenseless women?"

"Someday, I may ask you the same thing." Vladamir dismissed the man with a turn of his head. "Come inside, m'lords. Let us discuss this problem in a more civilized fashion. At least in Northumbria that 'tis how 'tis done as you may well remember, Clifton."

Clifton stiffened at the overt reminder of his deeds. He gave a perplexed glance to his cohort before turning his attention once again to the duke. Clearing the phlegm from his throat, he came down from his horse. His feet landed in the dirt with a heavy thud as he nodded at the others to do the same. Two stable lads came forward to collect the reins.

"Leave them saddled," Clifton grumbled harshly to the lads. "We won't be here long."

The towheaded boys nodded and walked the horses to the stables where they could tend them. As Vladamir walked he motioned to Raulf to follow. The man obeyed. Turning his head slightly to the man, the duke said, "Raulf, inform the other men that we have guests. Tell them to make their presence known in the main hall, lest we are considered inhospitable and when they don't care about hospitality, tell them there is mead for all."

Raulf laughed at the implication and did as ordered.

"Mead!" bellowed Vladamir to a passing maid. He strode to the high table and sat down just in time to see Clifton and Luther slowly follow into the hall. The two soldiers with them came in, but hung back by the door to stand in watch of an ambush.

"What is the meaning of this, Vladamir?" Lord Luther roared from the entryway as he stormed into the hall. He looked suspiciously around the black keep. Noting the hall was empty, he continued forward. "We are here to demand justice. If we aren't satisfied we will leave here and lay siege to Lakeshire until you and all within these walls are dead."

Vladamir scowled at the slender man's tone. He'd never met Luther and was instantly thankful he wouldn't be in the offending man's presence long. The man looked arrogantly up at him from his towering height. A smirk lined Vladamir's lips as he turned his eyes slowly away from the objectionable man to stare expectantly at the earl.

Clifton hesitated, once again looking about the inside of the castle. Then, lifting his chin slightly, he smelled the air only to frown. He moved forward to the high table, telling Luther diplomatically as he passed him, "Quiet. We will drink and hear what the duke has to say."

Vladamir nodded to the maid who hesitated when she saw the angered men. She came forth and filled goblets with her wooden pitcher and quickly set the cups before the duke at the high table only to retreat.

"I have killed no daughters," Vladamir said without preamble as the men took their seats. He leaned lazily back in his chair and looked about as if bored. His ring finger tapped lightly on the chair's wooden arm. Then as the men looked to him, he said, "I'd know by what right you lay siege to my castle, for 'tis an act of war to do so. King Alfred and King Guthrum won't be pleased by this."

Clifton threw a torn piece of cloth to the table. The scrap of wool was of fine quality, though it was soiled and ripped. It carried the same blue and white design of the earl's banner. "We found this outside your castle wall. 'Tis a crest from my daughter's cloak."

Vladamir picked up the torn material and pretended to examine it closely. Blood stained it. Waving the piece of cloth in dismissal, he threw it back onto the tabletop. "What of it? The wind could've blown it there."

"'Tis not likely Vladamir and you know it!" Luther interrupted. His large, thin frame shook with indignation. "I'll have justice!"

"Duke," Vladamir stated simply with a frown. When Luther looked in confusion about the hall, he clarified in an irritating tone, "I'm now a duke and I have not given you leave to address me so informally, Lord Luther."

Luther swallowed hard, saying under his breath, "You're a prisoner, naught more. I do not bow to foreign dogs."

"Luther!" Clifton growled. The man shut his mouth.

"Now, my lord." Vladamir turned to the earl. "As I was saying before being so rudely interrupted, I have killed no man's daughter. In truth I have killed no man since arriving in Wessex."

"I know she was here!" Clifton slammed his fist on the arm of his chair. "You cannot deny it!"

Vladamir raised an eyebrow but said nothing. He took up his cup of mead and drank with a great show of leisure. Drawing the goblet away from his mouth, he spun the mead about in the cup to watch the swirl of dark amber liquid.

"*By all the saints!* I can smell her mixture in the rushes. There is no other like it in the Kingdom of Wessex!" Clifton said with purpose. "You have killed my daughter."

"And why would I have done that? For scented rushes?" Vladamir laughed as he set down his goblet, letting his eyes glint with mischievous pleasure. "I care not what smells come from my hall."

"I know not why you would have cause to commit this grievance." Clifton swallowed visibly at the expression Vladamir gave him. The earl was treading on dangerous ground and they both knew it.

"I would be careful if I were you, Clifton," returned Vladamir darkly. He scratched the corner of his lip with his fingernail. Then, pulling his finger into his line of sight, he studied his nail by running his thumb over the tip. "I'm sure there are things you wish never to be said."

The earl gulped at the nebulously spoken words. The color drained from his face.

"Enough of this banter!" Lord Luther crowed. He picked up the scrap of material and flipped it over. Pointing at a bloodstain on the back of the cloth, he raged, "Lady Eden was to be my wife. You have killed her. All the evidence points to it. I'll have my revenge against you for it. I challenge you—"

"Silence!" Clifton yelled with a quieting slash of his hand. He frowned at the man's hasty actions. Trying to talk in a reasonable tone, he said under his breath, "Don't act with such haste, Luther."

Vladamir dropped his hand to the arm on his chair and glared at the men in annoyance. He narrowed his eyes as they quarreled in hushed whispers.

Finally, Luther stood and made a move to leave. "Come, Clifton, let us go. There's no reasoning with the Monster of Lakeshire."

"Wait." Vladamir's tone was nowhere near a plea, but more like a restrained command. A lazy smile curled his lips as he saw the earl's flustered expression.

"What have you done with her, you monster?" Slamming his untouched mead on the table, Clifton stood up as the brown drink splashed over his hand and spilled from the overturned cup to the floor. He hit the table twice with his flattened palm. "Tell me!"

Vladamir didn't know what the earl and his lackey were up to and he still wasn't sure of Eden's involvement in it, but he would watch their game and find out. The duke glanced at the stairwell, a smirk curving his hard mouth. Eden had just rushed down. Her gaze flew about the main hall in search of her father and Lord Luther. She changed her gown to a simpler one. It was of an earthen brown, a few shades deeper than her hair. Vladamir wondered absently where she had gotten it, only to assume it was borrowed from one of the maids.

At the same moment of his wife's timely arrival, the duke's men filed into the hall. Their hushed voices broke into the silence. The tables hadn't been set up for the morning meal, for it was still early in the day for eating and a couple of the men grabbed them as others took up the benches. In no time they were ready for drinking. With lazy yawns and tired eyes they turned their watchful gazes forward to see what warranted mead so early in the day.

Raulf led Lizbeth into the main hall, whispering into her ear. The maid blushed as she gazed across the hall to the angry men at the head table. Seeing the duke, she frowned, but nodded to Raulf in agreement as she did so. Then, scurrying off to the kitchen, she left.

The two unwelcome guests followed the duke's unwavering stare to his wife. Clifton gasped in shock when his daughter walked toward him. Her head was bent piously to her feet, though her walk was too fast to be considered solemn.

"By all the saints!" Clifton made the sign of the cross over his chest. "It cannot be so. I was sure she was dead."

"Father," Eden stated simply, though the shaking in her voice belied her lack of confidence. She moved her hand to pat down her hair, though the tresses didn't need straightening. "How is it you're here?"

Vladamir watched the interplay with practiced indifference, though he noted every detail of the exchange. He leaned back in his seat and crossed his arms over his chest and lifted his injured foot to fall across his knee. The scratch on his arch throbbed in mild irritation.

"I'm here to avenge you." Clifton leapt down from the high table in two big steps. Holding his sword steady at his side, he strode forward to his daughter. Eden cringed slightly at his advance.

"Avenge me?" Eden inquired demurely. She looked overly modest as she eyed the ground at her feet. Trembling, she flexed her fingers slightly at her sides.

"Yea, tell me child. What has this monster done to you?" Clifton demanded loudly, obviously hoping his daughter would denounce the man in front of the Saxon soldiers. He moved his hand to clasp her shoulder and squeezed it hard in warning. Dragging her by her shoulder, he brought her to stand before Vladamir. The earl held his daughter away from him, not showing any fatherly concern for her safety. When she didn't move, he jerked her by the arm as he directed her gaze to the duke. "Speak, Eden. Tell what the monster did."

"Monster?" Eden squeaked. Vladamir hid his amused chuckle. She pretended to look around the silent hall. Patting her hair to her head, she didn't appear to notice the rough handling of her father.

"Don't play daft child, lest I be tempted to beat you," the earl snarled. He raised his hand as a threat and then lowered it slowly back to his side. Stopping in his tirade to study her gown, the man frowned.

"But...?" Eden tried to feign innocence. She once again refused to look directly at the duke. Her body jolted as her father once more shoved her forward.

"You look like a servant," Lord Luther spat as he came up from behind her father. He narrowed his eyes in a display of intimidation so the older man couldn't see. When he spoke his words were low and distinct. "What has he done to you?"

"He has done naught to me, father," Eden stated simply, ignoring Luther. The earl dropped her arm in surprise. She took a step back from the angry men, glancing to her husband for help. Vladamir stood, but he didn't come to her rescue. "Naught that would be construed as dishonorable. He has treated me well."

"Then you're still pure," her father assumed in relief. "Good. We leave at once. You're to wed with Lord Luther tonight. There will be no more waiting. I'll have my alliance."

"Nay." Eden clutched her fingers together as she turned her pleading expression to Vladamir for assistance. He stood unmoving, determined to see this game through.

What are you doing? Tell them! Say something! Say anything!

Eden studied Vladamir in disbelief. Why wasn't he saying anything?

"I said move!" Clifton yelled in outrage. He yanked her arm and threw her toward the door. "You have caused me enough grief, child!"

Eden stumbled but didn't fall, her feet skidding heavily in the rushes. The duke's knights frowned in disapproval but didn't stand to give her aid. One of them took a knife from his boot and laid it on the table. The men watched Vladamir for any signal that they were to fight but Vladamir held still.

The earl turned to glare at the duke, not waiting to see if his daughter obeyed him. "Thank you for looking after her, m'lord. I shall take her and go but if I find you have harmed her I'll be back with the king's armies behind me."

"Nay, father! I cannot marry Lord Luther tonight." Eden moved forward to stand between her father and her husband. With Vladamir near her, she found the confidence to defy her father yet again. Her shoulder ached where he pulled at her and she rubbed the offending muscle gingerly. She glanced around the immobile crowd, pleading silently for assistance. No one moved.

"You insolent wench!" Clifton shouted, not bothering to hide his mounting wrath. "You'll do as you're told. 'Tis not your decision to make. You're lucky Luther would still have you after all that you have done—running away like you did. I raised you to be a lady, *his lady wife*, and that is what you'll be. Tonight."

"Yea, father, 'tis my decision. I won't marry him. You don't know what he has done!" Eden wanted desperately to explain the type of man Luther was, she wanted to make her father understand that it was his choice in suitor who was the true monster. Her mouth opened, ready to explain what type of treachery Luther had been up to, ready to tell him what happened to Lynne.

Luther stepped forward, looking as if he might protest. His mouth opened at the same time Eden's did. They were both silenced when Clifton raised his hand. With a heavy-handed swing, he struck her across the face with the back of his fist. She went sprawling into the rushes, straw flying into the air to land gently atop her. Blood trickled from her nose and pain radiated from her face. Tears entered her eyes as she glanced up to look at the men. Luther's frown turned into a pleased smile as the two men stood over her with their arms crossed over their chests. Her body shook. Luther's face lit in delight and Clifton's fell in grim determination. When she didn't move, Clifton turned to his men.

"Take her to the camp," Clifton ordered as he motioned to fallen daughter. "Come, Luther, let us make an end of this."

Chapter Eight

ඟ

Vladamir was surprised that the man had actually gone so far as to strike his daughter in front of witnesses. Until that moment he thought their interchange was a play put on for his benefit. He watched Eden fall as if in slow motion. Her head snapped back on her neck, the sound of the man's fist against her face was too loud and too real. Blood trickled from her mouth and nose from the impact. The second his wife hit the ground he sprung forward with a lethal force. Leaping down the platform, he drew back his arm and punched the unsuspecting Clifton on the chin.

"You will keep your hands off my wife!" Vladamir fumed. The older man tumbled back but didn't fall. Luther's mouth dropped open in his wide-eyed outrage, but he took a step back. The duke moved to stand in front of his wife, blocking her from their view. "Lest the next time you touch my property it will be your last."

"Your wife?" Luther asked with a toss of his blond hair. "Nay, she is my fiancée! You have no right to make such a claim. Clifton, say something!"

"Nay, she was your fiancée. She is my wife," Vladamir responded in his most reasonable tone. He heard Eden stand up behind him. Taking a deft step to the side, he kept them all within his sight.

"Eden?" Clifton questioned in disbelief. He turned his round eyes to his daughter, willing her to deny the duke's claim. "'Tis true? Did you bind yourself to this monster willingly?"

"Don't call him a monster. You're the monster, father. You and Luther." Eden quickly dusted her skirts, noting a tear on the side where it had scraped against stone. Her nose bled profusely from his blow and she swiped her hand across it with a jerk, getting blood on the sleeve of the tunic. "Yea, I'm his wife and willingly so."

"You're coming with me. We will have it annulled. We ride for King Alfred at once." Clifton moved to grab her, but hesitated as Vladamir stepped in his way. Growling, he looked around for help and found none.

The hall filled with the mumbled protests of the soldiers of Lakeshire. A few of the men even stood from the tables. All let their mead set untouched as they stared at the group. The unwelcome guests looked about the manor with bravado and backed away.

"My place is here. I'm staying with my husband. There is no ground to annul the marriage," Eden said as she took Vladamir's arm. Then, in a show of defiance, she looked demurely at her husband. Finally after a shy smile of adoration came over her face she turned to her father. "The marriage was consummated last night. Check the bed linens if you don't believe me. You're a day too late."

Vladamir tensed at her words. She glanced at him through the thick of her lashes and gave him a hesitant smile, her gaze begging him to trust her. He understood her silent look and nodded his head.

"I don't believe you," Luther stated boldly. "'Tis a trick. Where is your ring? You don't know what consummation is. That is why you say such things."

She shook her head in denial and licked her lips as she looked to Vladamir's mouth. The obviously planned action had the desired affect on Luther. Much to Vladamir's amusement, the man turned white in anger. Eden smiled defiantly at her father.

"You're still pure, are you not?" Luther asked. The dark complexion of his face turned to a ruddy red. He looked about the manor for confirmation. "You said so."

"Nay, my father assumed so!" Eden trembled but didn't let go of his arm. "I'm not pure. In fact I'm far from it! We are man and wife and if you must know, we consummated this union at least fourteen times last night. So there is no disclaiming it!"

By all the saints! Fourteen times in one night!

The duke was amazed that his wife dared to make such an outrageous claim. In his day he prided himself on his virility, but fourteen? His little wife was indeed more naive than he had given her credit for, or more stupid. He struggled and finally succeeded in hiding his smile. His wife really did have high expectations of his performance. Though, but the twitching of his cock, his body was more than willing to try and prove her words true.

The gathered maidservants gasped and murmured in surprise. A few gave the duke looks of feminine appreciation and wonder. The younger girls looked at him in horror and at Eden in pity. The fighting men grunted in admiration of their lord, a few of them snickering at the very idea.

Eden's confused expression turned up to him and he could practically see the question in her eyes. He was hard-pressed not to laugh.

"You wretched whore!" Clifton screamed in outrage, eyeing Vladamir warily. His short body shook with his indignation. "I don't believe it. He's making you say such things."

"Lizbeth," Eden turned to the girl. The servant hovered with a group of maids outside the kitchen door. "Go to his lordship's chamber and produce the bridal linen for all to see, so that none can deny the validity of this marriage."

"Take Lady Eden and one of Clifton's soldiers with you," Vladamir added as he agreed with his wife's command. "So that they know there is no deceit."

"'Tis not necessary, m'lord. I'll stay here, if 'tis your will. I already believe that it happened," Eden said, just loud enough for her father to hear. She gave her husband another demure smile before blushing.

Vladamir nodded to her, granting her request. He didn't want her from his sight at the moment anyway, lest Clifton's man take it upon himself to restore the earl of his daughter. He felt exhilaration at the torment in the older man's face and it wasn't lost on him that Eden's actions were the cause of that torment.

The gathered crowd waited in silence for the maid to return with the linens. Vladamir felt Eden's hand shake as she hugged herself to him. When he glanced down, he saw her bloodied face. Her body trembled against his and he saw her fear. At that moment he knew that he was the lesser of two evils for her and that she was indeed not in league with her father.

Vladamir trained his eyes steadily on the intruders. Their gazes met in silent battle. It seemed an eternity before Lizbeth's steps sounded on the stairwell. The maid emerged carrying the linen and the soldier solemnly trailed behind her.

Clifton's knight appeared as if he saw a spirit flitting about the manor's hall. When he stepped before the throng, he couldn't meet the earl's eye. His face was ashen and he gulped as he looked to the floor. Lizbeth's face was pale and drawn. Without waiting to be commanded, she jerked the satiny material and unrolled it for all to see.

The onlookers gasped at the sight. A light murmur began in the crowd as they all looked to Eden in horror. The noblewoman blushed at the scrutiny, drawing closer to his side. A few of the Saxon soldiers shook their heads in puzzlement. One of the duke's Northumbrian warriors chuckled.

As the red bloodstain stared back at them, Clifton's face turned scarlet with anger. "What have you done to my daughter, you barbarian? You unearthly monster. You demon spawn. You'll pay for this!"

Vladamir hid his amusement at the stain, not caring what damage it might do to his reputation. His wife poured the whole of the vial on the linens, making it look as if he was most barbaric in his treatment of her the eve before. But it wasn't the size of the oblong stain in which he found the most amusement, it was the placement of it. From the look of the linen he'd taken her maidenhead through her throat.

"You have your proof, now draw your soldiers away," Vladamir stated coldly. He had to bit the inside of his lip in the effort it took not to laugh. Pushing Eden behind his back, he put his fists to his hips. "Or I'll petition King Alfred. 'Tis my land you trespass on."

"Lizbeth, you can take that to laundry," Eden commanded in a frantic hush from behind him. He felt her move and could just imagine the hurried wave she gave the woman.

"But—the ceremony! It cannot be binding. It doesn't stand if 'tis done to his pagan gods. It won't be recognized," Clifton protested weakly. His broad chest puffed with rage.

"I'm converted to King Alfred's religion a year past. Mayhap you didn't know. King Alfred himself was at my baptism and one of the king's priests performed the wedding ceremony. 'Tis most binding." Vladamir smiled wickedly at the man's discomfort. "The documents are being finished by the priest today."

"Yea, father," Eden broke in. She came to the duke's side and he saw the taunting amusement that flitted over her features when she looked at her father's irate face. "I have given the duke my dowry on your behalf, though I'm sure you'll want to add to the sum. I promised him only that which I knew could be given—my inheritance from Mother's estate. Please send it along with some of my wardrobe. As Luther pointed out, I'm not able to dress as a duchess without it. 'Tis too inconvenient of a time to have more gowns sewn."

"I don't believe your insolent tongue," Clifton said.

"Believe it father," Eden leaned closer to Vladamir. "There is naught you can do about it. 'Tis done."

"Look behind you. There are your witnesses," Vladamir stated, his temper growing in bounds at the earl's persistence. "Raulf, step forward."

Raulf stood from the quiet table where the knights sat. He smiled graciously and nodded his head. "M'lord."

"Tell them," Vladamir ordered not looking directly at the man he summoned. His eyes bored with victory into the earl's. He silently drank in every sorrowful movement of the older man's face.

"Yea, I bore witness," the man said in a loud steady voice. "'Twas a most binding and proper a ceremony, performed by the same priest the king sent here to man the village church. Not one detail was missed. We all bore witness."

"You won't get away with this!" Luther fumed, tired of waiting for Clifton. "She is to be my wife. I won't stand for it. She is bound to me. We were as good as wed."

"Since honor dictates it, I'll pay you for your inconvenience. Name a fair price." Vladamir smiled as he reached behind his back to grab Eden. Pulling her into his arms, he held her possessively to his chest. Her forehead pressed against the linen of his tunic and her shoulders trembled under his embrace. She didn't fight him as he wrapped his arms completely around her in protection.

"I won't have money—" Luther began.

"Fine, then 'tis settled, for you're not taking the duchess." Vladamir nodded his head to Raulf. "Escort them out."

"Yea, m'lord." Raulf turned to go and waited for the men to follow. Several knights stood unbidden as they moved to help Raulf.

"Luther will stay outside the castle to make sure you don't try to escape. I'll ride at once to the king. I'm a trusted and loyal leader of the Witan. You'll pay for this insult on my name. Ealdorman Baudoin will demand your head afore I'm done!" Clifton stormed angrily from the castle. Lord Luther turned on his heels to follow behind.

Vladamir watched the men leave before easing his hold on his wife's slender form. Leaning his chin on her hair, he smiled viciously over her head. Absently, he ran his hands over her back in a soft caress. She clung to his side long after her father's soldiers followed their lord out of the hall. In a whispering sigh, her breath fanned over his tunic.

Realizing they were being watched, Vladamir cleared his throat. Eden looked up at him from the confines of his chest. Her round eyes stared innocently into his. He tilted his head in question, glancing briefly over the tight hold of her embrace.

"Forgive me," Eden said softly, dropping his arm. Her nose had bled onto his tunic shirt, though it didn't show readily on the black material. Grimacing, she swiped the blood with her hand. The motion didn't help. Finally, unable to wipe away the stain, she sighed and dropped her hands. "Thank you for keeping your word."

Vladamir lifted his finger to lightly touch the end of her nose. He frowned at the swipe of blood that ran across her cheek and down her chin. Already the bridge swelled with a purple bruise.

"I know." Eden tried to hide her nose under her hand and turned from him. "I must look hideous."

Vladamir was about to answer when he looked up. The onlookers were quiet, watching the noble couple in awed silence. He swallowed over the lump in his chest and ignored the low thud of his heart.

"I'll go clean up," Eden said when he didn't answer her. She rushed from him holding her nose, nearly running through the crowd in her haste to be gone.

Vladamir was disappointed at her withdrawal but let her leave. He felt the coolness of her blood on his chest and quietly motioned the gathered throng to depart. The duke wanted to go after his wife, but knew that he couldn't as he walked toward the bailey. He first needed to make sure his uninvited guest left without incident.

"Fourteen times?" a redheaded soldier asked with a knowing nod of his head. He moved to follow Vladamir as the soldiers who heard the jibe laughed with merriment.

Vladamir didn't show his surprise at the comment, nor did he answer when several others added their own jests to the first barb. Never had the Saxon men approached him so freely. The duke found he quite enjoyed their easy banter. As one of the men pounded him on the back, Vladamir smiled and said with much seriousness, "What? Don't you bring a woman pleasure that oft in a single eve?"

The men laughed louder showing a newfound respect for their leader.

* * * * *

Eden trembled with the memory of the warmth of her husband's strong hold. She felt safe in his arms. His chest was hard and lean and his arms were like a pleasurable vise binding her to his manly body. The tips of her breasts ached where her nipples had pressed into his tunic. A curling heat lit in the pit of her stomach. She hadn't wanted to move as she took comfort in his unyielding strength.

Now that she was away from the hall, she didn't know what to do. By the reaction of the witnesses, she had a feeling she'd done something wrong with the linens. However, she couldn't begin to guess what.

What am I to do? The king cannot annul this marriage. I cannot marry that miserable lout of a toad, Luther. I'd rather die the most horrid of deaths. I'd rather be turned alive on the rack, hung in the gallows…

"Cease!" Eden cursed herself as the mental imagery of her thoughts came forth in her mind. Gingerly touching the tender bridge of her nose, she shook her head. "I must not think such dreadful thoughts."

Withdrawing her hand, she fidgeted with the cord at her waist and paced around the small bed in her bedchamber. It was smaller than that of her husband's. She'd thought it nice, despite the sparse belongings, until she saw the luxury of the duke's larger chamber. His room was also sparse in decoration, but his bed was freshly stuffed and more comfortable. Albeit, she'd been too preoccupied the night before to properly appreciate it. She refused to go back to Vladamir's room.

After the way he acted in the hall, she wasn't sure she would be welcomed in the duke's bedchamber anyway. It was true in many noble households that husband and wife slept in different beds.

But that cannot be my household! Not yet. For if my father knew that I was estranged so quickly from my husband after we wed, it would give him further evidence to the king. There is no way Alfred would let the marriage stand. Not if Luther was willing to take me tainted. I must stay married to the duke at any cost. But how does one convince a king? And even more puzzling is how does one convince a husband?

"Yea!" she called to the door in irritation at a soft knock. Eden held her breath, hoping it was Vladamir in search of her and knew that it wasn't.

What could be the most sensible reason for the king to allow this marriage to hold true?

Political alliance? Possible.

Money? The duke has none.

"Heirs," Eden exhaled, smiling with the brilliance of her plan. The king would have to let her remained married if she was with child and her father wouldn't like that big of a scandal attached to the name of Hawks' Nest, no matter how disappointed he was in her choice.

"An heir, m'lady?" Haldana laughed merrily at the door. She shook her head in denial, the short curls bobbed with her energetic excitement. "Nay, 'tis too soon to tell. Takes a full two sennights, I believe, and even then you cannot be certain."

"Wh-what?" Eden spun around, embarrassed that she'd spoken aloud and without censure. "I didn't say heirs. I said *hairs.*"

"Hair, m'lady?" The servant woman carried a basket of herbs in her hands, which she balanced on one plump hip. She turned to close the door, her expression doubtful.

"Yea, I was wondering why the duke didn't choose to cut his *hairs,*" Eden lied shamelessly. In truth she liked Vladamir's long waves. She narrowed her eyes as she spied the basket. Almost remorsefully, Eden touched the bridge of her nose and winced. It still throbbed. She could taste a tinge of blood in her mouth where the blow struck the tender skin of her lips against her teeth.

She tried not to let her eyes spill over with tears as she remembered her husband's cold face when he watched her father's treatment of her. Well, in Vladamir's defense, he had punched her father in the chin. Still, she'd thought her husband would've protected her.

When had she begun to feel so safe with the duke? When had she gotten to feel so unjustly secure? Sure, Vladamir came to her aid, but too late. By that time she'd been facedown in the rushes, her nose bleeding for the entire hall to see. She tried not to feel resentment at Vladamir's indifference, but couldn't help it. Resolving to take a new approach to handling her ill-natured husband, she took a deep breath. If she were to keep the marriage, it would take a lot of planning on her part.

"How did you know I was here?" Eden asked.

Grinning at her mistress, Haldana winked. "Methought you might be hiding here."

Eden smiled halfheartedly at the older woman as the servant bounced about the room. She dropped her hand from her nose and sat on the bed. Edging back on the mattress, she moved to lie on her side and looked up at Haldana. "What have you got there?"

"Herbs," Haldana answered with another wink. Her voice was ever pleasant as if nothing was amiss. "Fer yer nose."

"Oh," Eden sighed at the reminder. Looking around her in embarrassment, she licked her lips. She resisted the urge to feel her face again.

"You heal fast, m'lady, but methinks this will help." The servant went about her business, digging through the contents of the basket to set vials and jars next to Eden on the bed. Watching with interest, she knew she'd never been useful when it came to using herbs. Her father didn't believe in such nonsense as the use of healing poultices. He thought it best to "live out" any ailments.

"'Tis a brave thing you have done, m'lady," Haldana said as she finally set the basket on the bed next to the vials. She lifted a crude, wooden bowl and set it on the small table in the corner. There was a little bit of water at the bottom of the bowl, which Haldana used to mix the herbs.

"Brave?" Eden pushed her hand into the mattress, lifting her tired body slowly up in surprise. "Because I stood up to my father?"

"Nay, because you wed the duke." The woman scratched her whitening hair in thought before picking up a dried herb. Nodding to herself, she dumped it in the bowl.

"But, why — ?"

"Why would I say such a thing?" Haldana lifted several dried herbs from her basket to stroke the seeds off of them and into the water and poured a few contents of the vials into the mixture. After several seconds she was mixing a paste with her fingers. "Because you look as if you need to hear it."

"Haldana," Eden tried to begin and was once again interrupted.

"Nay, m'lady, I know that his lordship is not an easy man to be around. But I believe that 'twas a miracle that sent you here — a true miracle." Haldana rubbed the grainy paste onto her hand and lifted it to Eden's nose only to rub it into the injured skin. "You were sent to tame the monster, so to speak."

Eden winced at Haldana's administrations and then frowned as she recognized the servant's discarded vial. It was the exact same type as the one that held her "maiden" blood.

"Haldana? May I ask you something? In confidence?"

"Yea, m'lady." Haldana wiped her fingers on her apron and loaded her herbs back into her basket. She wiggled her finger at her mistress with pride. "I'm not one of these chattering Saxon girls. They don't know when to keep their mouths shut. Always gossiping they are. Did you hear this? Did you hear that? 'Tis utter nonsense if you be asking me."

"Did you give my husband something afore he came to me last night?" Eden probed, purposefully ignoring the older woman's comment about Saxon women. "A healing draught of some sort?"

Haldana laughed. "Nay, m'lady, 'tis mostly natural what happened but mayhap yer husband should be the one to better explain it to you."

Eden nodded, not completely understanding but pretending to.

"Although fourteen times in a single eve? That is not most natural at least in my experience and all that blood—mayhap his lordship saved himself too long. Mayhap that is why you were hard-pressed to endure..."

Haldana gave the duchess a guilty blush and snapped her mouth shut. Eden swallowed in embarrassment and darted her eyes away.

Clearing her throat, the servant busied herself needlessly with her basket. "But 'tis naught to concern yerself with, m'lady. I'm not all that experienced in the ways of noblemen."

Eden forced a blush as the older woman suggestively wiggled her eyebrows. She sighed in relief, realizing Haldana knew nothing of the blood's origin. Then clearing her throat, she tried to excuse her curiosity by weakly saying, "I just wondered. I have never seen aught like it."

Haldana lowered her voice as she leaned forward in confidence. "His lordship's member is meant to do that, m'lady."

Eden's blush turned real and she couldn't help from asking, "Do what?"

"Methinks the duke best explain the rest. Ask him to go slower. Sometimes men go too fast fer the woman," answered Haldana with a motherly sigh. She gave Eden a gentle pat on the back of her hair. "But, they be men and it cannot be helped."

"Methinks he'll explain naught to me," Eden pouted, moving to stand. Haldana finished placing her herbs in her basket. Reaching over, Eden began picking the herbs up one by one to carefully study them as they talked.

Haldana chuckled but said nothing. She unnecessarily straightened the slightly rumpled coverlet on the bed.

"What happened to the duke? He won't tell me. How was he scarred?" Eden asked, careful to keep her tone light. She knew that Haldana was loyal to her husband. "Methinks if I knew that then I could be a better wife to him. Mayhap, I could understand him."

Haldana smiled and shook her head. She reached to take an herb from her mistress' hand and placed it back in the basket. "'Tis not my place to say, m'lady."

"But," Eden tried to protest. She let her mouth hang open for a moment before resigning herself to the servant's interruption.

"Nay, m'lady," Haldana broke in as she held up her hand. "Now, if you're done in here, I'll direct the girls to move yer personal items to yer new chamber."

"Wait," Eden rushed, unwilling to end the conversation. She picked up a piece of chamomile from the basket. "Do you know a lot about herbs?"

"Yea," Haldana admitted warily. The servant seemed afraid her new mistress was going to keep pressing her about his lordship.

"If for some reason I was to disappoint the duke and not readily produce an heir for him, would there be something I could take to help the process along?" Eden tried to act nonchalant as she placed the chamomile back into the basket. She focused her eyes carefully away from the older woman. "Like a draught to get with child."

Haldana smiled at the innocent question as she gave the young girl a reassuring pat on the shoulder. "Don't worry about such. Yer young and healthy. Methinks you should breed fine. Besides, there is no hurry fer that kind of thing. Get to know the duke. Concern yerself with that and when the time is right the other will happen."

"So there is nothing," Eden concluded.

"There are things, like dead rats underneath the bridal bed. A potion mixed with sheep dung and chicken's blood." Haldana smirked knowingly when Eden wrinkled her nose in disgust. "M'lady won't have to resort to such things, just be patient."

Eden shuddered, wondering exactly what one would do with such a concoction, for surely it couldn't be consumed. She couldn't inquire for Haldana ushered her from the chamber with a gentle shove. Looking about the inky hall in confusion, she heard the chamber door shut behind her. "Wait, Haldana."

Turning, she saw Haldana wasn't with her.

My new chamber? Where is his lordship putting me now?

* * * * *

The bonfires of Luther's encampment burned brightly against the night sky as brilliant lights reflected off the many soldiers who camped around them. Their bodies glowed like orange apparitions as they appeared to float restlessly over the field below Lakeshire's bailey wall. Hundreds of knights wandered about the site, not settling for the night as the eve was still young. Their robust laughter and the loud neighing of their horses filled the air.

Eden squinted, unable to make out the men's faces as she gazed over the land surrounding Lakeshire Castle. She'd climbed to the top of the wall to better see the strength of Luther's and her father's armies. What she saw made her blood run cold. Their combined strength spread over the countryside like the spotting pockmarks of the plague.

She imagined that many of the knights she'd grown up around were there awaiting her father's return. She knew they were loyal and wouldn't attack in his absence, however Luther's men were another tale altogether. Eden shivered as she imagined the very men who attacked Lynne were below her even now and prayed Luther would keep them at bay.

As the night darkened into a deeper blue, she watched several more bonfires alight in the distance, spanning the already impressive army's force further over the countryside. Fire dotted the land until it disappeared in the distance to mingle with the stars. The orange glow outlined the many tents that were still being erected.

"By all the saints," Eden whispered, her hand fluttering to her throat. She took a careless step forward to the side of the wall and heard the laughter of the men in front of her. Her husband's home was quiet in comparison. Leaning over the black stone, she squinted into the besieging army's campsite in search of Luther. It was too dark to see any of the men's faces. Under her breath, she mumbled darkly, "Where are you hiding, you loathsome cur? Mayhap, I could find an arrow —"

"Those are not the words of a would-be nun." Vladamir's laughter broke into her quiet ranting. His accent was low and his words were like a careless whisper drifting on the breeze.

Eden froze, taking a deep breath. Casually, she turned to Vladamir and let a slight, self-possessed smile form on her lips as she met his gaze. He stood on the ladder, having just climbed up onto the nearly empty wall.

Waiting for him to come to her, she leaned her butt against the stone. Defiantly, her back faced the surrounding enemy. Her eyes were empty as she stared at him and she pulled the corner of her lip between her teeth. She dared not let her pleasure in seeing him show.

The duke was breathtakingly handsome. His laughter faded into a slow smile that settled agreeably on his alluring lips. For the first time, Eden noticed that his eyes held a glimmer of humor deep within their depths, but there was a mild approval there also. She felt her cheeks pinken at his attention and forced the heat from her face as she took a deep, steadying breath.

Vladamir easily stepped over the last rung of the ladder and moved forward, searching her face. Eden lifted her chin, willing her mouth not to widen the nervous smile on her lips as her breathing deepened slightly. When she didn't speak, he turned to the camp. Leaning his hands against the wall next to her, he said quietly, "I'm regretful that I allowed your father to strike you. It shouldn't have happened."

Eden nodded her head, unsure what to think of the unexpected apology. "'Tis not your fault. You had no way of knowing that he would do that. Me on the other hand, I should've known I tested my boundaries too defiantly with him. I knew 'twas how my father would react to my defiance."

"It happened oft?" Vladamir asked with a disgusted curl to his lips.

"In the kingdom?" Eden returned with a coy smile. "I should say so. Is it not what is encouraged amongst you men? Could you imagine if you didn't beat us? The kingdom would be overrun with happy, compliant women."

Vladamir gave a soft laugh. One of the bonfires sparked as the soldier threw more wood on it. The floating ashes were quite beautiful in the night breeze as they drifted about, spiraling upwards into the dark heavens. The smell of burning wood filled the air and the corner of Vladamir's mouth twisted up. "It's a great smell, is it not?"

"You favor the smell of bonfires?"

"Yea," he answered softly, closing his eyes. "It reminds me of my mother's people. When I was a child they would have great celebrations out of doors. There would be tremendous fires that would burn all the night."

"And what were you celebrating?"

"Life," Vladamir stated with a growing frown. He lost himself to thought.

Eden turned to him. After giving him some time to think, she drew him back to their conversation with a light touch to his sleeve. "You don't laugh oft. Why?"

"'Tis the way things are," Vladamir sighed.

"Nay, methinks 'tis the way you make them." Eden lifted her chin and stood her ground. "Do you think you'll ever tell me the secret that haunts you so?"

"Nay," Vladamir stated blandly with a straight face. He glanced to her appalled expression and chuckled.

"You, m'lord, are incorrigible," she announced. For a moment the soldiers melted away and she imagined her husband as a young boy, so full of hope. She imagined he would've been a happy child. Looking away from him with a feminine pout, she fought the charm of his easy manner. When he looked at her, she felt her insides tremble and weaken toward him. Her defenses crumbled at his lightest of sincere smiles.

Vladamir pushed away from the wall only to lean over her. Touching her arms tenderly, he ran his strong hands down her shaking limbs. With an obnoxious lift of his brow, he murmured, "Yea, very incorrigible."

His gentle fingers moved firmly over hers. Feeling a rough spot by her knuckle, he took her left hand up and brought it into the surrounding moonlight. A blush filled her face as he inspected her finger. On it was a plain silver band, the metal was old and oddly bent into a circle as if no care had been taken in the making of it.

"M'lord." Eden licked her lips when she saw his hesitation. "Let me explain."

Vladamir turned his expressionless face to her. His mood hadn't changed and his dark, demon-like eyes glistened in the moonlight as they studied her.

"Luther noted earlier that I had no ring and when I found this on the ground near the stables, methought to have the blacksmith smooth it out a bit so I could wear it. Only until this matter with the king is settled. If it bothers you I can remove it. I only thought to—I mean no insult. I care not that you—*we* cannot afford jewels. I don't need such finery." Eden tilted her head to better study his downcast eyes and gave him a hopeful look.

She waited for him to speak, telling by his gaze that he didn't care about the ring. A part of her felt he liked the idea. He kissed her fingers and lowered her hand back to the wall.

"M'lord? You're not angry?"

"Use my name." His eyes narrowed languidly and he studied her with a deep intensity. The tips of his fingers grazed softly over her cheek. His gaze bore into her, captivating her with its brilliance.

"M'lord of Kessen, Duke of Lakeshire." Suddenly, Eden curtsied out of his embrace. Vladamir grimaced. Whirling past him she smiled and danced backward with a lightened step. When the back of her legs came against the wall, she turned to climb down the ladder. Her heart beat within the walls of her chest, pounding an incisively primal rhythm and she wanted to stay with him forever on the wall but she had to force herself to leave before he did. If she was to have any chance at getting through to him, she had to put on a tenacious air. It was time he wondered about her mood for a change.

Realizing she hesitated, Eden felt his hand on her elbow stopping her from touching the ladder. He stepped up next to the back of her body and the heat of his breath fell against the nape of her neck, coursing in shivers to her toes. He stood so close that she couldn't help but tremble at his radiance.

His exhalation of breath came over her shoulder with the words, "Methinks 'tis m'lady that is incorrigible."

"Nay, m'lord, I go to dine for the hour is late and the hall is sure to be famished," Eden answered demurely, forcing herself to be strong against the unfamiliar sensations he awoke within her. In the distance the bonfires and the shining stars swam around her to join them in the embrace. He caressed the length of her, without having moved from her arms. Instinctively, she leaned her back into him and her eyes fluttered shut.

Vladamir nuzzled his mouth against her neck. His hair tickled her chin as it blew about in the breeze and he kissed her pulse lightly to test the response in her. Eden gasped. The duke growled, vibrating her flesh, making her so wet and shaky her knees weakened.

"Why do you bind your hair now?" He ran his hand up her arm to undo the strands of her hair. It was bound in a coiffeur at the nape of her neck as was the fashion for married women. Her long locks fell about them in submissive waves to mingle with his.

"I-I married." It was all she could get out.

"Mm, I wish to dine, m'lady," Vladamir said, his voice hot. He cupped her scalp and pulled her head to the side to allow him better assess to her throat. Hot pants claimed her skin, making her shiver all the way to her toes. Her nipples pebbled against her bodice, begging to be set free.

She let the thrill of his handling overtake her as his teeth grazed her sensitive flesh. Her eyes flitted closed, concentrating on the hardness of him against her lower back. She was helpless when he touched her and couldn't find the will to fight him. "Would you dine on flesh?"

Vladamir chuckled darkly against her skin. "Yea, I would."

His hand glided up her waist, cupping a breast in a heated palm. She gasped, arching as he massaged her. Pushing at her nipple through the material, he teased the sensitive tip. He rocked his hips, pressing his hard heat against her with slow thrusts. Her body moved to push back against his, learning his rhythm. It felt nice, but she wanted more. Her thighs tightened. She wanted him to touch her there, to move his hand between her legs. The lips on her neck became more aggressive as he kissed her. Eden moaned, reaching behind her head to hold him tight. Slowly, his hand dipped down her stomach, moving to press along her skirt.

Her body exploded with urgent need as he grabbed between her thighs. His hips pressed her from behind, forcing her to thrust forward into his hand. The material dampened with her cream and still he made her ride his hand. Eden gasped, weakly grabbing at his hair to keep him close. Vladamir pulled at her skirt, eagerly baring her legs. The night breeze hit her and they were surrounded by the sounds of the surrounding army but the wall was dark and they couldn't be seen.

His fingers found her flesh once more, this time touching her naked flesh. Dancing around her sensitive bud, he worked his hand along her wet slit. Eden gasped at the sensation his movement caused. The duke growled.

"Ah, yea, like that." His words were low, whispered hotly to her neck. He breathed as fast as she, rocking his hips harder as he quickened the pace. Then a finger slipped up inside her and she nearly died at the pleasure she felt. Another digit slipped further back to stroke a tender piece of flesh leading to the cleft of her ass. "You're so hot, so wet. I want to taste your cream. I want to bury my face between your soft thighs. Would you let me dine on you there? Would you let me taste how you come for me?"

It was too much. Gasping, she tensed as a hard spasm racked her body.

"That's it," he urged, "come for me. Get my fingers nice and wet so I can taste you on them."

His words were sinful. Surely she should tell him to stop but she couldn't. Pleasure poured over her from his hand buried inside her sex. He kept moving his hand, milking her body of each shiver. After, he slipped his hand from her and let her skirt fall back to the ground. Eden watched though heavy lids as he lifted his fingers to his mouth. He licked her cream from them, moaning softly.

"Mm, delicious," he whispered, before giving her a wicked grin. "Go see to your table, lady wife."

The low tone washed over her like a heated growl as he released her. He stepped past her and descended the ladder first. Eden watched with a grimace of dismay as he leapt down into darkness.

Damn you, m'lord.

She rubbed the side of her neck gingerly. No matter how hard she tried, she couldn't erase the feel of him. Cursing her weakness, she followed him down.

You were not supposed to rule my defenses so readily. I'll have to be more careful of you in the future, my dear husband.

Vladamir hid in the darkness, waiting until he saw Eden walking to the hall. With the soldiers camped outside the wall, the men of Lakeshire were on the highest alert. The duke had given his men orders to keep an eye on Eden when she was alone about the bailey so that nothing would happen to her. However she wasn't to know about it.

One of the knights standing watch along the wall had seen her walking in the bailey and had sent word that his wife might be trying to escape. Vladamir went after her, though he hadn't been concerned by the report. He was more worried about her standing in harm's way. Somehow, he knew she wouldn't leave him. She'd given her word.

He hadn't meant to get so carried away with her, wanting only to enjoy her company in the cool night air. It was just she was so beautiful, standing in the moonlight. He couldn't stop himself and when she moaned, giving in to his devilish whims it was all he could do not to throw her down and ravish her like a beast. So, instead he'd made her come, letting her sample the pleasure he could give her.

He glanced at his hand, still dewy wet from her cream. The taste of her was in his mouth. Licking his fingers again, he smelled her on him. The duke glanced around, hiding in his shadowed corner, and slowly reached to unlace his braes. Keeping his hand close to his mouth so he could smell her scent, he shoved his hand down the front of his pants and grabbed his full cock.

His erection pulsed as he fisted it hard—almost painfully so. Imagining his wife's tight virgin body on him, he closed his eyes. With one hand he stroked his hard cock, keeping her taste on his lips with the other. *By all the gods*, it was good.

He jerked his fist over his shaft roughly, wishing it was her body he took with such fierce thrusts. If he had his way, he'd pound his cock into her silky flesh, bending her around the turgid shaft until her sweet pussy was shaped to him.

Grunting, he came hard, spilling his seed in one long hot spurt over the ground. His body weak, he slumped against the wall. He had to get control. Each time he released himself, he thought of taking Eden with rough passion. It didn't help that she'd responded so freely to his touch, so willingly. Until he could get his beastly nature under control, he'd have to be careful not to tempt it.

Chapter Nine

ഇ

Vladamir purposefully stalked the darkened hall of his manor, avoiding his wife. Flashes of the night sky passed him, framed by the narrow slit windows of the castle. The full moon gave just enough light to see in the inky depths of the black stone hall. After his self-pleasuring session, his cock was only too eager for more.

I have to get myself under control.

But the more he fought to subdue his desires, the more they fought to be free. There was no avoiding it. He wanted Eden—desperately, wantonly, any sordid way he could have her. Avoiding his bedchamber, he didn't want to face his wife, worried that if he went to her his hands wouldn't be able to keep from touching her supple body and he couldn't stand to see the rejection shining out of her beautiful eyes, for surely now after she had time to think about what they'd done there would be rejection. What else could there be for a monster like him?

But, on the wall, she'd been relaxed. He hadn't expected it from her, for she'd let him touch her without fear. Mayhap since it was dark out she could forget what he was. He could keep her turned from him so she couldn't see his hideous scars.

Even if she saw past his scars, how could she want him— *really, truly want him*—when he'd broken his word? He told her once that he would protect her from her father but he'd failed. A small snort of disapproval came from him, remembering Clifton's treatment of her. He believed that a man who had to use force to rule a woman was indeed less of a man. It was too easy to strike that which was weaker than you. The true test was in outwitting your opponent.

Footsteps echoed over the bare passageway, interrupting his thoughts. She'd found him.

"M'lord is not very good at keeping his word," Eden said from behind him.

"Eden," Vladamir answered, trying not to show his surprise. He let a softened smile fall onto his lips and a teasing light enter his eyes. "You dare question my honor?"

"Yea, m'lord," Eden returned as she took a bold step forward. Her chin lifted proudly in the air. "I do."

"Tell, what is your complaint?" The duke let his hands fall motionless to his waist. Her eyes caught him in their grasp and he smiled, for once not worried about his scars as he looked at her. "Mayhap I have only yet to perform the task. Perchance, 'tis you who has not given me ample time. Pray tell, what promise did I speak to you?"

"'Twas not in words, M'lord Kessen," Eden simpered demurely. She looked up at him through her lashes. Then, with a dreamy line alighting on her lips, she said, "'Twas with those eyes I believe I was promised something."

"Yea?" he asked, moving lithely through the darkness to meet her.

"And with those hands."

"Hmm." Instead of touching her, he paced about her in circles as she held her place. She didn't turn to watch him, instead choosing to stare forward. Secretly, Vladamir was pleased that she'd sought him out, willing to continue what they started on the wall. "And what, pray tell, did my eyes and hands promise? For they didn't confide such developments to me."

"Well, if they don't speak, then neither shall I," came Eden's flippant response. With a pout, she gave a careless toss of her shoulders. "I suppose 'twas I that was mistaken."

"And what would m'lady have me promise her?" Vladamir spoke in hushed tones as his lips whispered past her exposed ear. He couldn't help but wonder what she was about with this game as he moved around her, pretending to be in thought. "Exquisite gowns? Jewels? Shoes carved from gold?"

Eden wrinkled her nose. Vladamir kept his face earnestly blank.

"Nay. Methinks a promise to tell me a secret," she stated before pouting her bold lips, but her eyes shone with a different kind of mischief—a mischief that she herself couldn't be completely sure of.

"What kind of secret?" Vladamir asked, intrigued by her sudden assertiveness. Usually she fluttered about him in a nervous state of excitement. Now, she powerfully held her ground against his stalking. Her bravery excited him but it also excited the beast inside him. His cock was hard, ready for more. The taste of her cream was just a tease to his senses. He wanted to devour her—every last inch.

"A secret about you." She licked her lips as he passed once more by her back. He stopped directly behind her. He could barely see her face. "I find that I don't know much about you and 'tis not as I would have it."

"There is naught to know." He blew over her neck in a light caress. It took all his control not to throw her to the ground to claim her like a wild stallion. Her nearness was driving him past the point of reason.

"I beg to differ, m'lord. There's much I would know about you." Eden breathed deeply. "I don't know what you like best for your eve meal. I don't know what season you prefer. Where you have been, where you'd like to go. What color you prefer me to wear, if you prefer me at all."

Vladamir chuckled at her candor. What harm could it do to indulge her a bit? He stayed behind her, breathing into her ear matter-of-factly. "Pork shoulder, salted. Fall. I have been well over the northern lands and many of the southern. I'd like to go back to my mother's homeland. I like the color you have on just fine, though methinks a red would do nicely and I prefer you to any other wife."

Eden took a heartening breath at his confidence. Although it was only simple things he disclosed, it was the most he ever told her about himself aside from the few anecdotes from his past. She deliberated before trying to discover a bit more about her elusive husband, for he was driving her mad. Tilting her head to allow him access, lest he take it to mind to kiss her there, she sighed, hoping he would.

"I'd have a more daring secret charged me," Eden shivered as his hot breath fanned her skin. Tilting her head a bit more she panted for air and her heart raced in anticipation. Already she felt cream building for his touch. The release of his fingers on her sex had been heavenly and she wanted it again. Her nipples budded. "Methinks those matters would be common knowledge."

Eden waited for him to answer. He didn't.

"However, in the spirit of justness, I'll answer any one of your questions honestly if you tell me something about you, something honest, something no one else knows. It doesn't have to be a tremendous confidence, just a little one, so that I may feel privileged in the knowledge and so you may learn to trust me a bit with the secret you charge me." Eden flushed. Her own words made her nervous but she knew she had to try. She was glad he couldn't see the apprehensive expression on her face. Behind her, she heard his weight shift.

Vladamir was silent for a moment. He raised his hand to cup the bottom of her chin from behind. Moving his free arm about her waist, he pulled her backside tautly against his bulging erection and held her tight. Eden gasped, panted and moaned at the hard strength she felt in him and her eyes fluttered closed. She was helpless as she stood captive in his steadfast embrace.

"I'll give you your one secret, m'lady, and I'll have the answer to my one question." He pressed scorching wet kisses below her ear and onto her proffered neck. His parted lips skimmed lightly over the pulse beat he discovered and his hips rocked into her, sparking the now-familiar response in her body. "I desire you very much."

Though it wasn't the secret Eden wished to hear, the confession made her quiver with pleasure. She let him explore her neck with his feverish lips. His teeth ravished her delicate flesh and his tongue soothed the aching fire his teeth unleashed. Eden moaned, tilting her head back to rest on his chest. The forearm around her waist pulled tight in violent passion so that she imagined he might strangle the life from her body with the force of it.

Her hand moved to his head of its own accord. As her fingers dipped into his soft hair she couldn't resist him. Monster, devil, beast, whatever he was, whatever he would be, she couldn't resist. He had her completely under his spell and she didn't want to escape from it.

"And I desire for you to get on your knees and wrap your sweet lips around my cock." He paused, grabbing her jaw and forcing a finger between her lips. "I want to watch you suck on me between your teeth."

She sucked lightly on his finger before he withdrew it. The idea of taking him into her mouth excited her, as did the prospect of seeing his cock.

"Should we go back to the bedchamber, m'lord?" Eden froze at the prospect of being discovered by one of the servants. "I wouldn't want to be seen in such a precarious position. It wouldn't be proper."

"Nay," he said in barbaric denial. Vladamir moved the hand on her neck to delve into the tight bodice of her gown. He grabbed the first tender breast his hand came upon and squeezed the mound in a passionate massage. He ran his fingers over her nipple and teased a cry from her lips. As he pinched her nipple between two fingers, she thought she'd explode. A torrent released itself between her legs, making cream drip down her thighs in anticipation.

"But, the servants," Eden protested halfheartedly. The duke ground his hips into her backside. The stiffened length of his shaft pressed into her, confusing her with its mystery. She bit her lips, stifling another moan. "What if they happen by?"

"They wouldn't dare." Vladamir lightly nipped the tip of her ear with his teeth. He withdrew his hand from her strained bodice and in a deft movement grabbed the hindering material at the back of her neck. With a zealous tear, he ripped through her clothing. The jagged edges fell open to expose the long line of her spine. Instantly, his hands found her skin and caressed in long circles. The movement pushed the material from her shoulders to allow him better access to her chest.

Eden inhaled with a rush and arched her chest forward at the thrill of his desire. His hands caressed her naked back in long kneading strokes that sent flames to her core. As his fingers trailed lower to her butt, she groaned, overwhelmed at the flow of turbulent emotions that blazed in the wake of his fingers.

She leaned her head on his shoulder and reached her arms over her head to touch his hair. Vladamir gently rubbed the flesh of her sides as his roaming took him over her slender hips and to her stomach. The light scrape of his nails glided over her and she pulled his head closer to her neck, encouraging him in his savagery. She tried not to think of her lingering fears as she didn't move to stop him.

"Take off your gown," Vladamir commanded harshly with a growl. "I want you naked when you suck me."

He didn't wait for her to comply. With precise force, he ripped the clothing further from her slender shoulders, tearing it most of the way down to the floor. The material slid over her body to crash onto the dark stone and she stood naked before him.

Vladamir growled and in that moment she knew she was completely his. He sought her skin with his lips, kissing and licking down her spine, stopping to nip playfully at her ass. It was too much. She tensed, too afraid to move, too scared he would stop. Her body was a frenzy of sensations—his hands, his mouth. Before she knew it, he was kneeling before, his face pressed into her naked stomach.

The Duke kissed her hip. Taking a finger, he thrust it into her wet slit, sliding in the cream he found there and stroked her clit in small circles, caressing her with his hands. She moaned, her body awakening to him. The sound became uninhibited and throaty as it escaped her parted lips.

She was ready, more than ready. Her back arched slightly and she trembled, dousing his hand with her desire. The action pushed her sex closer to his mouth and he licked her clit, parting her folds. He allowed her one small climax before drawing his fingers away. They glistened as he drew them to his mouth to taste her.

"Exquisite," he said. With a mischievous leer lining his mouth, he stood. Her eyes stayed with him.

His gaze traveled over her lithe form and he seemed pleased that she didn't try to hide herself from him. Her breasts strained for his touch—the large mounds aching for him. The duke cupped the firm globes until his fingers overflowed with their softness. He took in her every breath, her every shudder.

"Don't think, just feel," he ordered. Leaning forward, he kissed her, rubbing her own taste over her lips. She moaned, prompting him to do the same. "I'll try to take it slow, but I wish to fuck you. I'm going to fuck you. I have to have you."

Eden gasped in pleasure as he lifted her breast and tweaked the sensitive peak with his callused thumb. The taste on his lips was strange, but addictive. She wanted more of it. She saw the black intensity of his gaze as he watched her reaction. His fingers moved lightly over her stomach, just above the throbbing center of her hips.

"Now it's your turn," he urged, reaching for his braes. He loosened the ties, freeing his cock to her. "Get on your knees. I want to feel your lips."

Eden obeyed, kneeling before him. She looked up his tight body, still covered with his tunic shirt. Reaching forward, she pulled it up. His hard shaft sprung forward, standing tall in a bed of dark hair.

Slowly, she opened her mouth. The duke groaned, thrusting his cock forward to her lips. It brushed along the seam. The firm skin was like nothing she'd ever felt before and she couldn't stop herself from licking it. He moaned in approval and she began licking at the entire long shaft, moving along the sides only to continue past the base to the soft globes hidden underneath.

"Argh!" His whole body tensed as she did it. She again licked at his balls and again he squirmed. "Suck me. Now!"

Eden pulled a globe into her mouth, sucking on the ball.

"I meant my cock… *By all the gods, don't stop!*"

Eden touched his shaft as she rolled his ball in her mouth. Feeling adventurous, she took the second globe in as well. Vladamir's hand wrapped around hers, showing her how to stroke his cock. He squeezed her tight.

"Ah," he growled. "My cock, now."

Understanding, she moved to take his cock between her lips. He thrust forward, burying himself deep in her throat. She nearly gagged, but the taste and smell of him made her crave more. She sucked him hard. The duke took her head in his hands and bobbed her face up and down, showing her how to do it.

"Harder," he urged, "suck harder. Take my sac in your hands."

Eden cupped his balls, obeying. She liked kneeling naked before him, giving him such obvious pleasure. Her thighs were so wet and she parted them, letting the air cool her.

"That's it," he grunted. "I'm going to give you some of my seed and I want you to drink it all down like a good little maiden. Don't worry, I'll hold back enough to pleasure you as well. You're going to drink what I give you, aren't you? You're going to lick up every last drop and you're going to like it, aren't you?"

She moaned in agreement, sucking harder, wanting to taste this seed he spoke of.

"That's right." His body tensed and he grunted. "*Oh, yea!*"

Salty liquid filled her mouth as he came. His body shook and she followed his command, swallowing his seed. When she'd finished, Vladamir pulled his hands away from her face and swept her up into his embrace. His grip tightened possessively on her tender flesh and he leered wickedly at her before dipping his mouth to lick her exposed nipple. Eden shrieked at the sensations his plundering mouth brought forth. The heat of his forearm pressed near her naked thighs.

Vladamir tightened his grasp on her as she spasmed and bucked in pleasure. Moving his mouth to claim hers, he pried her lips apart and delved his tongue roughly inside, probing and claiming the depths as his own.

His embrace was insistent and though it wasn't tender, he didn't hurt her either. With determination, he moved to an empty chamber. Kicking the door, he knocked the wooden obstacle open with his boot, not bothering to shut it behind them.

The chamber was one that Eden had yet to order cleaned. It looked much like the prison he'd kept her in while she recovered from Luther's beating. The dirty surroundings made her heart pound faster. Confusion and fear twirled in her head to mix with immense excitement and tremendous longing. Emotions that she couldn't comprehend overwhelmed her senses until she could do nothing but let Vladamir control her. She didn't fight his touch and didn't run from him.

Eden wrapped her hands around his neck. She quivered at the passion she felt in him. In a moment of modesty, she tried in vain to cover herself, pressing her chest to his, hiding her naked breasts in the hard fold of his war-hardened muscles. Vladamir growled a beastly sound in the barren chamber when she rubbed against him. In the back of her mind the lingering fear she'd tried to suppress grew, but his lips wouldn't stop long enough to let her dwell on the sentiment.

Vladamir's lips left her mouth to taste the tender stretch of her neck. As he carried her, his arm slipped closer to her wet slit. Her body flamed under his instruction. The fire built within her until she could no longer feel anything but the power of his touch. His smell consumed her and his hard body bewildered her resistance. Her breath escaped in heavy, needing pants. The unknown pleasures of his touch built with each haggard breath until she was forced to cry out with the strength of them.

Vladamir carried her to the old dusty bed that adorned the forsaken chamber. He tore his kiss away with the growl of a wild animal and tossed her flailing body onto the bed. She bounced on the straw mattress with a gasp of surprise.

Eden watched with wide-eyed fascination as he knelt on the bed. Her mouth opened to speak but only let out a ragged puff of air. He caressed her flushed cheek, the touch both ferocious and tender at the same time and she could only stare. His shortened overtunic didn't hide his protruding arousal from her, his cock huge with veins straining along the firm shaft. Of course she'd seen men. A woman couldn't live in a castle without seeing them nude, but he was by far the biggest. His shaft resembled a battering ram, so thick it could surely break down any defense she might put in its way.

He leaned over her, taking the back of his hand and running it over her flesh. The caress started at her chin and moved in a swipe down her throat, in the valley of her breasts, to her navel just above her slick opening. Eden's head fell helplessly back.

"Part your thighs," he ordered. "Let me see your pussy."

Instinctively her legs parted as the backs of his fingers drew near the fire churning within her thighs. He turned to cup her gently. His finger found the wetness of her opening and toyed mercilessly with her clit. Eden moaned and curved her back in surprise. Vladamir growled at her response. He grabbed her fiercely as a finger moved to part her moist folds.

Eden fell back onto the mattress and moved her hands to grip his tunic. Feeble from her passion she tried to pull at the black linen, wanting to see him. Her hips lifted into his caressing hand, begging for the unknown pleasure he promised her.

"Come here," he ordered her, his voice hoarse. "Come before me."

Eden pushed up, confused. Wasn't she before him? He stared at her mouth in a way that made her weak. Taking her by the back of her head, he pulled her to him. He kissed her hard before releasing her.

Forcefully, the duke grabbed her hips and flipped her onto her stomach, causing Eden to gasp in astonishment. His movements were stealthy and sure and he moved her as if she were no heavier than a strand of hair. With one hand on her abdomen and one on the small of her back, he pulled her hips toward him until she was kneeling before him.

She felt his feverish movements as his grip found her waist. His heat burnt into her thighs. He forced her to spread her legs from behind by nestling his knees between her own. Her breasts scraped along the dirty coverlet, bringing up a swift cloud of dust. The coverlet's fur tickled the peaks of her nipples. The sensation was oddly delightful and she moaned as his adjusting movements made her do it again.

Vladamir's nostrils flared. Greedily, he stared at the fine curve of her ass and the smoothness of her hips. He ached at the sight of her beautiful form. Her skin was fresh and perfect, save for a few scars that lined it in places but the scars were hardly noticeable, especially after the ones he carried.

He smelled her desire for him and lurched in excitement and he could hold back no longer. Her lips around him had been too much. It had been so hard not to ram himself into her throat as he watched her suck him in. He'd waited too long to bed her.

Vladamir pulled her exposed backside closer so that she crouched defenselessly before him. With the powerful push of his massive thigh muscles, he inched his body closer to hers while keeping her from closing herself to him. The soft hairs on his legs grazed the back of her sensitive thighs. He grabbed onto her hips holding her steadfast.

The animal inside him took over. His nostrils flared. Without further testing the wetness of her resolve, Vladamir thrust his rigid shaft into her awaiting sex. He slid roughly inside of her, stopping as he felt the boundary of her purity. The border only excited him more and he pushed deeper into her tightness to break through it. He let loose a primal yell of victory as he conquered her with his full length.

Vladamir tensed, shivering in victorious delight, immersed in her feel, in her soft womanly smell. He held still inside of her, enjoying the feel of her flexing muscles as she formed around him, accepting him, molding her tightened silk depths to fit only him.

He felt her stretching muscles ease to accept him. Slowly, he growled as he moved behind her. Tensing, he forced control to his rampant desires but when he pulled out of her, his hips flexed of their own accord and he slammed into her once more. Vladamir roared the violent call of an insatiable beast. Eden shuddered and let out a delicate cry of her own.

Passion overwhelmed Vladamir's control. He wanted her more than he ever wanted any other. Without thought,

Vladamir captured her hips and rode her hard as wildly as he would an untamed stallion he was trying to break. His fingers tangled in the long locks of her hair, pulling slightly back to better control her. He delved his shaft back and forth swiftly in her moistened passageway, pounding roughly against her soft unresisting flesh—fast and deep and conquering.

Eden groaned at the violent entry. Her eyes rounded and moistened with astonished tears when he completely imbedded within her. Her fingers clutched at the fur coverlet and she managed a deeply ragged breath. Biting back her tears, she suppressed her moan as the pain of his passion tried to diminish, leaving in its stead a building sense of profound longing.

She gripped the coverlet tighter and tried to relax. The burning pain lessened enough so when he withdrew to again thrust eagerly into her, she felt a semblance of the first awakenings of her body. Tension built where he plunged. Friction heated her innermost core.

Eden called out in the gratification she felt building once more inside her. This was so much better than his hand on her sex, though he did touch her with his hand as well. Vladamir quickened the ferocity of his pace. She saw her own breasts thrust forward, bobbing wantonly with each virile thrust of his shaft. Her hardened nipples peaked and strained as they grazed against the bed. A strange, albeit pleasurable, ache stirred in her midsection. She gripped her fingers into the dirty fur coverlet. His hands commanded her and his body controlled her. She was his slave but didn't care, liking the idea of being a prisoner to his body's whims.

Vladamir's powerful body pushed her onward to an unknown destiny. The beat of her heart pounded against the wall of her chest, echoing in the deaf caverns of her ears. She knew she should be scared, but she couldn't think to tell him to stop. Her body hummed as the blood rushed violently in her head.

A finger slipped along the cleft of her ass, rimming her intimately. His hips ground naughtily against her backside. He continued to ride her, pushing her higher and higher until she thought she might explode with the agony of her unfulfilled longing.

Suddenly, Vladamir grunted and her sex spasmed along his turgid flesh. Tensing, he jabbed himself one last hard time into her. She trembled and screamed her release to echo the bare walls of the chamber. Her vision grew dark, her lids fluttered lazily over them and she was unable to see from the gratification her body experienced. Their combined pants for air echoed strenuously in the soundless chamber and for a moment they were frozen as two reckless statues.

As the spasms slowly subsided, Eden noticed how cold and dirty the bedchamber was. The dust from the bed settled around her, making her cough lightly as she breathed it in. Her body shivered again, only this time from the cold. Vladamir released her hair and her head fell forward. Then as he pulled himself gradually from her, she felt the hard sting of their lovemaking deep within her belly.

The duke tentatively rested his head on the small of her back. Gently, he stroked her soft skin before standing. He completely relinquished his hold on her. Eden let her body fall to the bed and rested on her stomach, insecurely refusing to look at him. She knew a blush covered her face, could feel its heat. When she didn't hear him move, she turned her head slightly to find him under the bend of her arm. She studied him from the corner of her lowered lashes. The narrowing of his piercing gaze was the only expression he allowed. He did up his loincloth and pulled his braes to hang loosely at his waist.

Eden waited for a long breathless moment for him to say something to her. When he didn't, she lifted her head to look at him. She did her best to turn, so that her nakedness wasn't so obviously displayed.

He too noticed their surroundings and frowned as he looked her over. Eden smiled shyly as she reached her hand to rest on the fine linen tunic that covered his sweaty chest. She ducked her face into his side as she curled up next to him. Despite the cold chamber, his body felt as if it were on fire.

"M'lord?"

"Yea, m'lady," he replied hoarsely but didn't wait for her to speak as he stood.

Eden motioned helplessly, not knowing what to say at such a moment. Sitting, she drew her legs up to hide her nakedness and licked the corner of her mouth. Without another word he stalked from the room.

Eden felt her heart drop as he left her and she drew a painful breath. An ache so intense unravelled in her stomach, overbearing the duller throb of her sex. Her eyes brimmed with unshed tears. Shivering she stood only to freeze as she saw him reenter with her torn gown. He handed it to her.

"Is everything all right?" Eden asked as she took the gown, daring a glance at him though her lashes. She quickly turned away when she found him studying her and pulled the torn garment over her nakedness to shield her body from his emotionless eyes. However, the gown was too damaged to provide her with adequate coverage. When she finished dressing Vladamir's hand was held out for her to take.

She couldn't force herself to touch him. "I'm tainted, that is why—"

Vladamir looked at her sharply, cutting off her words. "Nay, you are, *were* a maiden."

"Then?" Eden shivered, relieved to hear it from him. She held the torn gown to her breast to keep it from falling and sniffed. Her eyes pleaded with him to comfort her. Vladamir's frown deepened. Slowly, she reached out to take his offered hand in hers.

"M'lady deserves a better bed than this." He glanced at her shaking palm cradled inside of his. His fingers trailed lightly over her hand to her wrist. Her hands were still a bit red from scrubbing his hall floor. A frown once again marred his brow as he let go of her. A wall once more went up between them. Eden blinked back her emotions and Vladamir didn't look at her face.

Without further comment the duke turned on his heels to walk stiffly in front of her, out of the musty chamber. She silently followed behind, letting him lead her through the turns of the darkened passageways. Following the movements of his feet with her eyes until they finally he stopped before their shared bedchamber, she waited as he silently opened the door for her.

Eden stepped past him at the soundless bidding only to turn and find him gone. He left her alone in the room. She peered down the hall as her hand strayed to close the chamber door behind him and she couldn't help but wonder what it was she'd done to anger him this time.

Chapter Ten

ဢ

Two fortnights passed with the rising and falling of a calm summer sun and Lakeshire Castle fell into a stagnant routine. Even-tempered breezes filled the days and stillness wafted the nights. The air was neither too hot, nor too cold. The servants continued to clean, the soldiers continued to practice and the evening bonfires continued to burn outside the walls and Vladamir continued to ignore his wife.

After their hasty lovemaking, he felt so remorseful that he hadn't been able to face her. He couldn't. The very touch of her innocent fingers had reminded him of his dastardly treatment of her.

Vladamir berated himself for taking her, his wife and a lady at that, like a paid whore in a dirty chamber. He'd waited for her accosting glare or vehement reproach. His insides shook with self-reproach. It mixed with his sated passions.

When he closed his eyes, he saw her virtuous form curled on the dingy bed. The supple waves of her disheveled hair fell over her shoulders to cover her perfect breasts. Her long arms gracefully encircled her legs as she pulled them into her stomach. The backs of her thighs were smooth and creamy white. She'd crossed her ankles to hide her sex from view, but he still saw the smudge of blood on her skin.

The duke shook his head with self-loathing and couldn't help but wonder if she was frightened of him. He couldn't blame her, especially now after his inexcusable behavior.

After he led her to his chamber and left her there alone, he didn't go back to her in the many nights to follow. He chose instead to help man the bailey walls. His days were filled wishing that Luther would dare to attack so that he might release his pent-up rage and frustration on someone but Luther and his armies stayed quiet. He spent his nights against the hard black stone of the wall as the smell of burning wood drifted about him, scarcely sleeping and eating even less. He found comfort in nothing, forcing himself to endure the torment of his body and soul as a punishment.

His mood was blacker than ever, due to his unappeasable desire for his wife. After his one taste of her, he was like a drunkard craving mead and because he couldn't have his blessed addiction his body ached and his mind turned sour.

Sometimes from high on the wall he would spy Eden in the bailey. She would be instructing the servants, laughing with the soldiers, gazing far off into the distance with a look of intense longing. He wondered if she dreamed of leaving him, all the time knowing she wouldn't. Her pride and honor would keep her loyal. It amazed Vladamir to think his wife had more integrity and honor inside her slender body than was common in the whole lot of the fairer sex.

The few times that he accidentally crossed paths with her, their conversations had been abrupt and he quickly left her side. When she did speak, her words were timid and she held back from him. How could he blame her? He'd treated her like a whore. The sound of her soft sweet voice reminded him of his transgression against her chastity and his deeply rooted guilt wouldn't allow him to stay near her.

Besides, I'm the lesser evil for her, naught else. She wouldn't have had me if it had been her choice to freely make. The consummation is done. That was her reason for seeking me out.

His wife didn't purposefully seek him out again and he never caught her eyes straining for him. Her gaze never lifted and her smile never lingered toward the wall. She hadn't sent word to him, not even a small message through the soldiers she laughed with.

Though she talks with them oft enough.

Jealousy burned in his chest each time he saw her with the other men. He couldn't recall her ever looking so kindly to him.

The day was still young and Vladamir had only slept a few hours that morning while on the wall. He rubbed his eyes as he looked over the bailey. He hated to admit that he was growing fond of the place, his little dukedom. As the days passed by, he grew less fond of his castle in Northumbria. It was the home he had with his first wife. He thought oft of selling it to King Guthrum so he would never have to think about it again, though such an occurrence was highly unusual.

The only thing he missed about the Northumbrian castle was his daughter. But that too would soon be reconciled. He sent word to have her delivered to him the same night of his marriage. Then, after the siege, he sent another missive telling those who delivered her to let her be carted in as a peasant. He wished for her to be kept safe. If the earl got wind that Gwendolyn was in the area, Vladamir didn't doubt that he would steal the child away from him and hold her in ransom of Eden. So he told none that she was coming save a select few and he didn't dare go after her himself for fear of drawing attention to her.

Luther, out of fear of King Alfred, had been letting the peasants who came to the duke's castle pass into his gates unharmed and those trapped within the walls hadn't been made to starve. But in case of a longer direr siege Vladamir ordered some of the animals out in the pasture brought in within the walls. The order made for a slightly louder, more crowded keep. He also ordered that the food be rationed until the danger passed. There would be no feasting at Lakeshire until the siege was over.

Vladamir narrowed his eyes as he saw his wife walk toward Raulf. Out of all the men he noticed that she spent most of her time with the young robust Saxon. A wave of jealousy entered his chest as Eden's laughter filled the air. His hand tightened on his sword as her fingers lightly brushed the handsome man's sleeve. It was just the offense his rage had been waiting for to justify itself into manifesting.

The morning breeze was pleasant as the sun shone on the horizon line. Vladamir squinted, his eyes tired, straining to keep his gaze pinned on his wife. Raulf escorted her to the stone bench in the garden. The man stood above her, his hands on his hips as they talked.

M'lady doesn't know she is being watched. Lest she wouldn't dare act so bold!

Unable to control his rage the duke stormed the length of the wall rudely knocking the posted soldier without comment. The men didn't pay heed, having grown used to the raging figure on the wall. Making his way to the ladder Vladamir climbed only a few rungs, choosing instead to jump down most of the distance. He landed firmly on the ground like a skulking beast.

He moved with swift and deadly purpose to the dark castle only to make his way to the side garden where his wife flirted dangerously with her favorite knight. Tensing, he stopped, his hands balled into fists as he listened.

"Raulf, I cannot," he heard his wife's delicate voice protest. "What would my husband do if he found out? I cannot…help you with this. At least not now."

That damned wench! Talking of cuckolding me as if 'twas nothing!

Vladamir fumed as he crept closer to listen more intently. His nostrils flared and his fists clenched at his side.

She is just like Lurlina!

"But, m'lady, I need you," Raulf persisted in a hushed tone. The desperate entreaty of his words was unmistakable.

That is it!

Vladamir growled in outrage. His body shook, begging for a fight—any fight. Hearing no more of their words through his mindless fury, he swept down upon them.

Raulf, you're a dead man!

* * * * *

Eden smiled pleasantly at the young knight. He seemed so full of hope—hope in her power over her husband. Only, Eden hated to tell him she'd barcly seen or talked to her husband nigh the last two fortnights. If not for the reports of a few servants, she would've thought he disappeared completely from the castle. He didn't even join her in the main hall to dine. She wondered where he ate and made sure the servants sent a bundle to him, though she'd never been so bold to ask where they took it.

She knew from a few discerning comments made by Raulf that her husband spent a lot of his time manning the wall. The siege was of great concern to his dukedom, but she thought his dedication a bit obsessed considering there had been no aggressions made from the surrounding army. However Eden knew she wasn't well versed in the rules of war and it wasn't her place to question Vladamir's leadership, especially not to his knights.

"Raulf, I cannot help you." Eden shook her head in denial. "The duke won't be swayed by my opinion. You must talk with him yourself."

"But, m'lady, please," Raulf ran his hand through his short hair in frustration. His eyes pleaded with her for help. "Then you must help us to marry in secret. You could write to the priest under the Lakeshire seal. I must have Lizbeth. I love her so much. You cannot know what 'tis like to love someone so profoundly and not be able to have them."

Eden sorrowfully thought of her husband and bit her lip to keep from crying. The physical ache in her stomach subsided enough to be replaced with an ache in her heart. His possessive touches, rough and unbridled as they were, only left her longing for more. She wanted to feel him against her again, wanted to hear his voice, wanted to look at him, to smell him, to have him kiss her.

"M'lady?" Raulf inquired insistently at her silence. "Will you help us marry?"

"Raulf, I cannot," Eden protested against the pain in his voice. She desperately wanted to help the young couple. She'd grown fond of them both. "What would my husband do if he found out? I cannot...help you with this. At least not now."

"But, m'lady, I need you," Raulf insisted in a hushed tone.

"Raulf, I—" Her heart stopped in her chest as Vladamir rounded the corner. She felt the color drain from her cheeks. Blinking heavily, she recovered from the threat of a swoon.

Though she'd looked for Vladamir, she hadn't glimpsed him for days. Circles darkened the duke's eyes and lines of stress edged their corners. His lips were set firmly in place to curl in a rigid path of anger and his tunic was crumpled and dirty. The long waves of his black hair were disheveled. Eden thought him the most beautiful of creatures. She drank in the sight of him and tried to smile her welcome, but she couldn't force the motion to her lips.

His gazed turned deadly as it alighted on her, swirling the depths into a black abyss. Eden held back from him in fear. He looked ready to kill and he was heading for Raulf.

"What—?" Raulf began in agitation only to stop at the look of anguish on her face. He turned around just in time for Vladamir's fist to meet his jaw. The younger man sprawled back onto the ground in confusion, taken off guard by the unsuspected blow. Pushing himself up, he wiped the blood from the corner of his mouth.

Eden jumped up from the bench as the man-at-arms went sprawling. She moved to stand defiantly in between her husband and her friend. "What are you doing? Are you mad? What has happened to you?"

Vladamir turned his cold stare to her at the sound of her voice, narrowing his lids over the demon black of his eyes as he folded his fingers once more into hard fists. His chest rose and fell with deepened breath and his accented voice crackled as he ordered, "Move."

Eden trembled at the frightening command but didn't obey. Bravely she held up her hand, desperate to calm him. She knew by the bloodthirsty light in his eyes that she risked much standing before him but she couldn't back down.

"Yea, m'lady, move. Don't protect me," Raulf said softly from behind. He'd managed to stand and now faced the angered man before him. Walking around Eden's protective shield, he placed her behind his back. Eden frowned and stepped once more into view. Her hand strayed to Raulf's sleeve as she passed him. Vladamir narrowed his eyes into slits as he watched. "M'lord, what is it I have done?"

"You dare to ask?" Vladamir raged. "I have eyes, I can see. I have ears. I know what you're about."

"M'lord, please don't be angered. Raulf only does what he does for love. Surely you can—" Eden stopped at his heated laughter. She took a step back as his face contorted to that of a monster. His eyes narrowed dangerously, his lips curled into a savage snarl.

"Love?" Vladamir spat. "Woman's nonsense! What of honor? What of respect? *What of loyalty?*"

She felt as if her heart was being slowly ripped from her chest at his offhanded dismissal of love. It was obvious her husband thought little of the emotion—so little it seemed that he didn't believe in it, was in fact incapable of feeling it. She'd been foolish enough to believe that Vladamir had mayhap been avoiding her because he was struggling with the emotions he was feeling for her, but that obviously wasn't the case.

"What of them? I don't see how this concerns your honor, nor any respect due you. At least not in any large magnitude," Eden argued. Her heart was breaking into painful tiny pieces and she was hard-pressed to hide it. If he'd been struggling with his feelings for her, she could've waited a lifetime for him to come to terms but this indifference was intolerable. Pain tore through her chest, worse than any physical injury Luther had given her.

Vladamir growled and grabbed her by the arm, throwing her aside. "I'll deal with you later, deceitful wench!"

Eden stumbled and fell into the stone bench. Her leg bounced off it as she toppled to the ground, rolling into the soft cushion of herbs. She shook as she pushed herself to her knees. Looking to her husband, she saw that his hands were wrapped around Raulf's throat. He was strangling the young knight.

"Nay!" Eden yelled, coming to her feet only to hurry forward. "Vladamir stop! You're killing him!"

Raulf's face turned blue and he lost some of his fight. His legs gave under his deadening weight and a trail of spit ran down his cheek as his throat gurgled.

"Vladamir," Eden breathed as she reached the two men. She put her body between the two men, placing her shaking fingers to her husband's face. His eyes were coldly blank and monstrous in their rage and his skin flushed red with his anger. She yelled again, but his ears were deaf to her pleas — until she touched him.

Eden rested her hand on Vladamir's cheek to get his attention and the duke let go of his prey. Raulf fell to the ground, gasping for breath. The young man's hands went to his throat to protect the forming bruise. He looked warily around as he was unable to push himself from the ground.

Eden heard the bustle of people gather and some of them went to collect the fallen man. She kept her eyes trained on Vladamir and didn't move her hand from his face. Tears brimmed her eyes, but didn't spill over. The heat from his body enticed her closer. She'd missed him terribly.

The gathering throng grew quiet, watching as the duke and duchess stood transfixed.

"I told you, he is a monster," several of the servants exclaimed such comments in excited whispers. "M'lord is a beast!"

"Look at how m'lady tames him. She stopped him with her touch." Eden recognized Haldana's voice in the back of the crowd. The sound shook her from her trance.

Taking a deep breath, Eden didn't move her eyes as she commanded the crowd, "Begone!"

The servants hurriedly obeyed, whispering anxiously among themselves about the power of their new duchess. Eden waited for their footfalls to lighten. She didn't watch the servants leave, choosing to keep her eyes trained steadily on her husband. The redness faded from his face and his dark eyes appeared to lighten and clear. Despite the fear she felt at what she'd seen him do, it felt so good to touch him again. His whisker-stubbled skin was warm under her palm, almost fiery.

"M'lord?" Eden questioned warily as she dropped her hand from his cheek. He didn't look well.

As soon as her touch left him, Vladamir came out of his trance and scowled at her in anger. His voice was a demonic yell as he demanded, "You dare protect him?"

Eden stumbled away from him. Moisture gathered in her eyes and she didn't bother to wipe it away.

Is this because of Lizbeth? You'd kill him because he dares to love her? Because he wants to marry her and treat her honestly for the rest of their days? Oh if I was given such a marriage! But, nay! My husband doesn't believe in love. Or does he? Oh, Blessed Virgin! My husband is in love with Lizbeth. That is why he doesn't want Raulf to have her!

Eden felt a hot tear stream down her face at the thought. She'd suspected once that Lizbeth was his lover. It made sense for Lizbeth was ravishing and graceful in her willowy beauty. Many men of nobility would love such a mistress.

That is why you haven't sought me out. You were with her.

Eden felt nausea rise in her throat. Lizbeth hadn't let on.

"You monster." It was the only insult that came readily to mind. Shaking her head, she backed away from him. She ignored the pain in his eyes, no longer believing it to be real. Her heart beat in dull aches as she spat, "You almost killed Raulf. And for what? Your own misguided sense of honor and pride. Why can't you allow someone else happiness? Just because we are condemned to a life of misery, doesn't mean you have to torture others!"

Vladamir studied her through veiled eyes, not moving to comfort her but something in his eyes made her feel like he wanted to. With a stalking rage, he followed her retreat across the bailey. She didn't turn her back to him.

Eden opened her mouth as if to yell at him, but her words died before they were spoken. She turned her head sharply to the side as they heard the gate being raised. They hadn't given the order to have it lifted. She momentarily forgot her anger as she turned a frightened eye to Vladamir. Her words were spoken through a breathless calm as she stated, "You're giving me back. You're going against your word."

Vladamir frowned at his wife's accusations, but didn't answer. He pushed past her to go to the gate. Several of the men eyed him cautiously as he approached, Eden close behind him. She knew the men all liked Raulf and probably didn't understand their master's sudden anger.

Eden naturally drew closer to the duke's back, panicking when she saw Luther ride under the gate. Behind him was a farmer's cart filled with hay, pulled by a large horse and led by an old peasant. Eden ignored the rickety cart, knowing it was a delivery of straw for the stables.

Luther never dared to come to the castle before, even to escort the farmers. His doing so now could only have been a bad omen. Eden shivered as she watched the knight's advance. She had a small glimmer of hope that he was only communicating a threatening message to her husband but that hoped died as she caught the possessive look on his face. His eyes traveled over her and he smiled.

"I don't care what you say. I'm not going with you!" Eden yelled as the man swung down from his horse. She couldn't stop the words from leaving her mouth. Her limbs trembled in anger, thinking Vladamir might actually try to send her back. "So turn back around and go home. Begone, Luther!"

"Careful," Luther warned in smooth confidence as he moved toward her. Pulling lightly at his leather gloves, he freed his fingers. When he saw that Vladamir did nothing, he grew bold. "Your father is not here to protect you, m'lady."

"You're lower than a pig!" Eden flung out in a disagreeable tone. Her eyes flashed with hatred. "Nay, lower than pig dung!"

"I'll remember that when you belong to me," Luther laughed. He reached his hand to her cheek and pinched the flesh hard. Eden jerked her face away from him but held her ground boldly. "And then we will see who is beneath pig dung. Have a care or I'll make you sleep in it for a sennight— with the pigs for company. You may even have to dine from their trough."

Eden swatted his hand and took a step toward Vladamir. "I'll kill myself afore I belong to you. You and your disgusting friends will never touch me again."

"See what a viperous tongue she has? Methinks I'd cut it from her if I were you," Luther recommended to Vladamir, keeping his eyes on Eden. "Are you sure you still want her? I'll take her now and mayhap the king will spare you his wrath. Other than the girl, I have no quarrel with you."

Vladamir didn't answer. Eden feared it was because he considered Luther's offer. Shivering, she studied the snide older man. Luther's lanky form towered possessively over her.

"Did this whore tell you what she did?" Luther continued, taking advantage of the earl's absence and his growing audience. "She came to me and my fellow knights during a hunt. She begged us to take her like a dog in the forest, only when she saw her father's servant watching did she change her mind. She tried to scream like she was being defiled. Damned wench ran off into the forest afore we could catch her. Methought to see her back at her father's castle—pouting."

"That isn't what happened and you know it," Eden said in shock. She looked to the growing crowd in horror.

"Whatever happened to that poor servant girl, m'lady?" Luther asked, empowered by Vladamir's continued silence. Eden stumbled away from them. Luther followed her retreat. "Methinks you had her killed for her interference."

"You know that is not what happened." She pushed her fists over her chest as Luther leered at her. Turning her pleading gaze to Vladamir, she protested his silence, "He is lying!"

Luther smirked, leaning in so only Eden could hear him. "Mayhap. But 'twas your protesting that got her killed. You were quite the passionless wench. Tell me, has the monster been able to light a fire in those frigid loins?"

Eden gasped in revulsion. The pain in her heart expanded tenfold as she looked at Vladamir. She knew that there was something wrong with her "performance" in the marriage bed—so much so that it sent her husband running. He would rather spend his nights in discomfort on a black wall than spend them next to her.

Luther came forward to stand between Eden and the duke. She looked about for help but none came forward. The men looked to Vladamir for guidance and the duke wasn't moving. Taking another step from the men as Luther continued to hiss, she made ready to run.

"All you had to do was die. Then your father would have blamed him," Luther tossed his head over his shoulder without looking back to the duke.

"You brought me here?" She wasn't surprised. "How? Why?"

"Why else?" Luther gave her a smug grin. "He's a foreigner. He's Vladamir of Kessen, Monster of Lakeshire Castle. Just look at him. He's not one of us. He doesn't belong in Wessex. By hell's fire, he doesn't even belong in the civilized world. He's a monster. Really Eden, how could you have taken him to your bed willingly? Any respectable maid would have killed herself first."

Eden glanced over Luther's shoulder and frowned. Vladamir drew closer. He did indeed look different than the Saxons she knew but she didn't care. It was why she liked him.

"I cannot believe you preferred bedding that monster to me." Luther shivered in disgust as he continued in his hushed tone. "Think of it. He kidnapped you. He ravished you and murdered you. We found the crest torn from your cloak as proof. Your father hates him anyway. Clifton talks too much when he is far into his cups and it didn't take much to learn that he hates Vladamir and hates that the monster was given land so close to his. The king would have readily believed the duke capable of such atrocities for he is after all a foreign monster."

"But then you wouldn't have had your alliance with my father. You would lose your precious title and land." Eden smiled triumphantly, though her victory felt weak and hollow. "And now you shall never have it."

"Nay, it would've gone to me. Your father is too old to have heirs and I would be his son-by-law by right, for I'd avenge you against Vladamir," Luther said softly, clearly proud with his well-thought-out scheme. "Besides you soon forget, your father needs my money."

"And you soon forget that you're speaking to my wife," Vladamir stated from behind Luther, his expression was deadly in its brutality. His cold hard accent fell over the hushed onlookers. The serving girls who lingered nearby backed away. The pages ducked behind the knights. Eden knew that the duke had heard every word the man said and was glad for it.

Luther jumped at the sound of the duke's voice. It was obvious he thought the man was still far away, ignoring his taunts. He turned to Vladamir sharply. "Give her to me. You cannot still want her. Surely you have had your fill of her—"

"But I do want her. You said it yourself, there is much hatred between Clifton and me," Vladamir snarled. "Mayhap I'll kill his daughter but then I'd be his rightful heir and you wouldn't set foot on my land."

"You wouldn't dare. King Alfred would hang you." Luther shook his head doubtfully at Vladamir's claim. "You don't have the guts to kill her."

"Mayhap he would hang me—if he knew of it. But if 'twas an accident…" Vladamir's let his words trail off coldly in mid-sentence. The implication was enough to cause Eden alarm.

A chill raced through her veins as the men calmly discussed her demise. Backing away from them slowly, she noticed that they no longer paid attention to her. She was just a pawn to them. Seeing Lizbeth crouching over the quickly recovering Raulf by the castle wall, she turned her back to the quarreling men. Defiantly, she stormed away from them.

"I'll kill you for saying such things. King Alfred will no doubt pardon me for taking what is mine," Luther stated smartly. "I'll have Lady Eden, tainted or no. 'Tis of no consequence to me."

"There's only one problem with all of your scheming." Vladamir smiled with calculation as he raised his hand to gently scratch his chin.

"And what is that?" Luther asked through clenched teeth. His small eyes narrowed resistively and his hands balled into fists as he stared down at Vladamir from his taller height.

"They all involve killing me," Vladamir answered with a tilt of his brow. He drew his broadsword from his side in one swift motion and turned to challenge the man. "So quit talking and kill."

Luther drew his sword with confidence. He pointed it at the duke as he asked, "Do you not wish hear what price I offer for her afore I run you through? 'Tis a good sum."

"I want nothing you have to give," Vladamir said as Luther circled around him. He turned to follow the man.

Luther thrust his weapon with a vicious growl, beginning the assault. His small Saxon sword was dismissed easily with a clang of the broadsword. He held his head confidently as he silently backed away and assessed his opponent. Continuing to circle, Vladamir narrowed his eyes.

Eden jumped at the sound of clashing metal, still backing toward Lizbeth and Raulf. Fear gripped her heart as she saw her former intended lunge toward her husband. In disbelief, she watched Vladamir deflect the blow. She quickly continued walking until she reached Raulf and Lizbeth. Turning to them she rushed, "Raulf, are you all right?"

Lizbeth had tears in her eyes. Eden couldn't bring herself to look at her husband's mistress. The maidservant flinched as another loud clang echoed the bailey.

Eden turned in horror to the men. A scream sat silent on the edge of her lips. A chill worked its way over her body as Luther's attacks grew bolder and her husband's defense appeared to weaken. They thrust toward each other with more and more vigor. Eden's hand fluttered to her mouth in horror. The knight's movements became bolder as they tested the other's limits. Sweat lined their brows and their chests heaved with the excursion.

"Why, m'lady? Why has the monster done this?" the maidservant demanded.

"Lizbeth," Eden began. She stopped when she saw Luther raise his sword high above his head. The duke kicked his attacker swiftly in the gut and sent him sprawling to the ground on his back. Eden jolted in alarm. The fallen man struck Vladamir with his foot as the duke descended on him, moving to strike at him as he lay on the ground. Vladamir stumbled backward but didn't fall. Eden sighed in temporary relief to see her husband right himself unscathed.

With Vladamir safe for the moment, Eden turned back to Raulf and hastened, "I'm so sorry. I'll find a way to help you. I didn't know my husband cared for Lizbeth so much. No wonder you didn't want to speak with him."

She heard another grunt and clang of the swords. Eden turned back to the men with a jolt of alarm. Raulf spoke, but his voice was hoarse and the words were lost on her as she was drawn toward the fight. Luther had her husband cornered against the wall, a foolish smile on his face.

"Nay, Luther, don't!" Eden screamed, forgetting her resolve against her husband. Her feet propelled her body forward. The beat of her heart echoed in the caverns of her ears. The duke didn't hear her plea or if he did he didn't show it. She was about to scream again but stopped, her jaw slack, when she saw Vladamir's face. The duke toyed with the other man. His eyes were the same devilish black they had been when he was strangling Raulf. He was full of confidence but it was a dangerous game he played.

"See how he taunts him," she heard a soldier near her say, confirming her suspicion. She turned to stare at the knight in disbelief. He was a scruffy man, with too long a beard and not enough hair on his head. His rounded belly jiggled as he yelled his support of her husband.

Eden turned back to the fight, her breath caught in her tightening throat. Her husband should've been on the losing side. Luther was taller and he had the duke backed into a corner.

Eden rushed forward once more. She glared at the men, intending on stopping their battle over her. Her hand fisted over her pounding heart as Luther lifted his elbow back to give Vladamir one final thrust. Her husband was bloodied with several superficial cuts and his eyes were narrowed and drooped as if defeated.

"Nay!" Eden shrieked, lifting her hand as if to pluck the image of Luther's sword from the air. Running full tilt, she tripped on a mongrel dog and landed on her stomach. The fall didn't stop her as she surged once more to her feet. She desperately wanted to save her husband. Her heart leapt in her chest as Luther swung. She stiffened with trepidation, her world crumbling all around her.

Then in a deft movement it was over. Eden gasped as Vladamir rose from his position and severed Luther's head from his body, knocking the Saxon sword aside with the same sweeping blow. Her feet froze, her lips trembling and she forced a shaking breath of air into her lungs. The head slowly fell to the ground.

Suddenly, the cheers of the watching knights broke into her head. They yelled praises at the victory. Eden blocked their shouts from her mind. Her limbs were numbed as she watched the headless Luther still standing before her husband.

As the severed head rolled across the dirt, Luther's lifeless body finally crumpled to the ground in listless spasms, blood squirting up like a fountain from his neck to splatter the ground. Eden eyed the head in horror as it rolled and bounced to the rickety cart that followed Luther inside. Beside the cart stood a short figure clothed in a black tunic gown and covered from head to foot in a matching black veil. She looked like a caller of death.

The small person held still as the head hit the tip of a boot and rolled back. The veil moved. It appeared as if the child looked up to the man who delivered the fatal blow. Eden followed the child's gaze. Vladamir no longer looked proud of his deed. Blood spotted his dark skin and marred his heathenish brow. His eyes narrowed in sorrow and regret, but he remained motionless.

The child slowly reached up her small hand and pulled back the veil to reveal a small black overtunic, with no decoration. Her hair was lighter blonde, her skin pale and drawn against her emotionless face and from that face stared two very familiar eyes.

"Gwendolyn," Vladamir whispered. He moved toward the child, a look of intense happiness on his face only he stopped when he saw the girl's expression of horror at his approach.

Gwendolyn? His daughter?

Eden gasped in alarm as she looked once more to the head. Luther's lifeless eyes stared up at the child, keeping her immobile within their deadened gaze. The child's eyes met hers, pleading with her from their cold depths for help. Eden understood and rushed forward. She ignored Vladamir's frown as she held her hand out to the girl.

"Come. I'm your new mother," Eden said so only the girl could hear. She didn't smile as she skirted past the head. Kicking Luther's head to the side with the heel of her foot so his eyes turned to the ground, she heard the men snicker.

"Load him in the cart and deliver him to his camp. Tell them to await the earl and then they are to leave my land forever. There is no more for them here," she heard her husband order. Eden ignored him.

"Then I'm your daughter," the child answered politely back. She gave a small curtsey. Her small hand fit nicely into Eden's, though it was cold. Gwendolyn's fingers didn't move, not even to shake over what she witnessed. She gave the child an encouraged pull to follow her inside.

Gwendolyn took one last look at her father before settling the veil back over her head. She let her new mother lead her away. There were no more words needed between the two. They both understood the other's place for they both understood they possessed an unwanted affection for a man— one for a father, the other for a husband.

* * * * *

'Tis truly eerie. She looks just like…

Eden shook her head in awe as she looked at Gwendolyn's steadfast gaze and quiet face. She swallowed nervously as she reached up to take the girl's veil from her head. The child sat on her bed with practiced indifference.

According to Vladamir, the child was no more than six years in age, yet she watched Eden through eyes that seemed much older, the expression just like the duke's. She had the exact same scar on her jawbone as Vladamir carried, only to a lesser degree but that is where the resemblance to the duke ended.

They were in the bedchamber Eden ordered prepared for her new daughter. She'd been excited to have the girl come and wanted to make her feel welcomed and at home. But now as she looked at the girl she wasn't sure that was possible.

"You look just like me," the girl stated flatly as if reading Eden's mind, "only older and your hair is redder."

Eden nodded. The girl's brown eyes sent a chill through her. They were her eyes, Clifton's eyes and they were staring back at her.

"What does this mean?" Gwendolyn asked. "Are you truly my mother? I was told she died in the fire trying to rescue me but you don't look scarred and you certainly are not dead."

"Nay, I'm your mother only by marriage," Eden answered, keeping her voice from cracking as she sat on the bed next to the child. "I only wed with your father a few fortnights past."

Gwendolyn nodded her head in thought. "Then...?"

"I don't know." Eden couldn't take her eyes away from Gwendolyn's eerily familiar gaze. "I don't understand it myself."

The girl picked up the veil and placed it back on her head. "I lost my wimple on the journey here. It blew away while I slept."

"I'll get you another one but I don't believe you need to wear the veil here especially over your face like that. Your father never makes me cover myself. In truth ever since I left my father's home I haven't worn one. Well, I did to my wedding, but that was it."

"That's because you don't need the veil. I do," Gwendolyn said matter-of-factly. She pulled the dark material over her head to settle over the scars.

"Who told you that nonsense?"

"Sister Mary Elizabeth," Gwendolyn folded her hands piously in her lap. "She said 'twas so that none would stare at me on this journey and that the outside world wouldn't understand—"

"Methinks wearing naught but black and hiding so much from sight draws more attention to you, but mayhap she was right." Eden pretended to concentrate on her words, prudently tilting her head.

Gwendolyn sadly nodded.

"You're too beautiful for just anyone to look at," Eden declared with a small smile. She noted how the girl's face lit up under the lace with tentative pleasure. "Methinks your father was too fearful that you'd get assaulted with suitors so early."

Gwendolyn giggled as she pulled up the veil. "Do you really think so?"

"Yea, I do," Eden said in all seriousness.

"I don't want suitors. I don't like boys," Gwendolyn confided with another laugh. "They're too mean and they put frogs in my hair. They're worthless."

"I quite agree," Eden laughed in approval of the candid confession and for the first time in days she felt real pleasure.

"But you love him don't you. Father, I mean." Gwendolyn's eyes shone with childish wisdom and her small mouth curled into a thoughtful smile. "I saw how you yelled for him and tried to save him. Though you must never have seen him fight. He never needs help. He's always the victor."

Did Vladamir kill a lot of men in front of his daughter?

"I..." Eden was unsure of her feelings for the duke.

"'Tis all right. I understand. Father doesn't love me either, not like I love him. Mayhap, he cares for us a bit but I don't think he loves." Gwendolyn glanced at her hands folded in her lap. "Not since my mother at least that is what Haldana used to say."

"Nonsense," Eden tried to protest, but couldn't. The girl's honesty tore at her heart. Already the child could see the rift between her father and her new mother-by-marriage. She gazed mournfully at the girl as she wrapped her arm about her shoulders. "Will you be all right?"

"I have seen dead men afore. I'll be fine." Gwendolyn lost a bit of her girlhood innocence at the statement. She stiffened in Eden's embrace until the woman was forced to let go of her.

"Shall I leave you to rest?" Eden wondered briefly what other scars the girl carried since the fire. She often wondered if Vladamir carried more than just his outer scars. She had a strange feeling that he bore a lot of wounds the world couldn't see. It would explain why he acted as he did.

The girl nodded with a tired yawn.

"I'll check on you in a couple of hours. I shall try to find you something besides black to wear." Eden stood. Taking the veil with her, she laid it on a small trunk. "Are these your things? Did you send them ahead?"

"Nay," Gwendolyn shook her head. "That was in here when we arrived."

Eden lifted the lid to the trunk. Inside were little tunic gowns of many colors. She held one of the dresses up and laughed.

"Methinks they might be a little too small," Eden said, examining the fine material. She felt a pang of jealousy, knowing her husband had given the girl the gowns. Yet she, his wife and a lady, was dressed as a servant.

Though, 'tis just as well. Methinks it would be too costly to give me any gowns of value, not if my husband insists on ripping them off of me.

Eden thought in dismay of the beautiful wedding gown that her husband tore to shreds to make his flag of truce. Then the gown her father helped her tear when he hit her. And, finally, the gown of somewhat better quality she received from the servants, which the duke tore from her back in a moment of passion. She blushed at the memory.

Eden didn't let her envy over the beautiful gown show to the girl. Gwendolyn had enough on her mind not to have to deal with her new mother's pettiness. The tunic was about a year too small causing the child to giggle. Eden folded the gown and put it back into the trunk.

Closing the lid, Eden stood and dusted her hands on her skirt. "I'll leave you for now. If you need aught, go belowstairs the way we came and ask the first person you see to come and get me. I'm easy enough to find."

"Thank you," the girl mumbled. She closed her eyes as she lay on the bed.

Eden swallowed hard as she gazed at the child. Taking a spare coverlet from a nearby chair, she laid it over the little form. The girl acted so mature but as she lay on the bed she was so small. It was like looking at a younger version of herself. The thought sent chills down her.

What can it mean?

Chapter Eleven

 හ

"*M'lord!*" Eden jogged the last few steps it took to reach her husband, as he walked along the top of the bailey wall. The thick linen of her skirts flung about in the air as she moved. She couldn't keep the fiery look of anger from her cheeks or the harsh bitterness from her tone as she glared up at him. "I would speak to you."

Vladamir nodded down to her and motioned his hand toward the gate where they were supervising Luther's men as they carted the nobleman's body from the castle. She took a deep breath, waiting for them to finish.

Once the gates were again lowered to lock the men outside she charged forward, yelling loudly in her ire. "I would speak to you, m'lord!"

Eden grabbed her overtunic so the linen wouldn't drag in the dirt as Vladamir stood silently on the wall, waiting for her to come to him. A smile threatened the sides of his mouth as he watched the swaying of her hips under the servant's gown. Even through her anger, seeing the duke's attention caused her to shiver with anticipation. It had been so long since they'd come together in the dirty chamber. Each night, she waited for him, longing for him, touching herself as she thought about him. She'd learned a lot about her body in that time.

Sunlight framed his head as he looked down at her from the height of the wall. His fingers curled lightly over the dark stone, holding his weight as he leaned forward. For a moment, her heart quickened, but she ignored the feelings of shy arousal and kept her eyes boldly on him. There was much her husband needed to explain. She couldn't forget the look in his face as he strangled Raulf and slew Luther—not that she was upset by the untimely demise of Lord Luther of Drakeshore.

I'm in love with a monster, she thought with a heavy heart.

Gwendolyn's words about caring for a man who didn't return their love echoed in her mind. The child was so young and had only been at the keep for an instant before she understood that fact. Eden hid her emotions as she had since that night they'd come together.

Shading her eyes, she stared up at him. A smirk lined his masculine features, as he leisurely leaned further over the edge. Peering down at her, he acted as if he hadn't a care in the world. He eyed her curiously.

"I need to speak with you, m'lord," Eden said when he didn't answer her summons. His handsome features shifted to a devilish grin and she swore he was trying to glance down the top of her tunic.

Standing, he moved toward the ladder, making his way along the walkway. Eden followed him, nearly tripping over the uneven ground in her effort to keep up with his longer stride. Reaching the ladder, Vladamir idly climbed down to face her.

When he neared the bottom, Eden said, "I'd have some answers and I'd have them now."

Vladamir raised a cool eyebrow. He jumped off the ladder and turned to her in one smooth movement. A lazy, practiced smile lingered on his tense face as if he committed no offense. He leaned his elbow on the ladder's rung. "Gwendolyn?"

Gwendolyn? We don't speak for a week, he almost kills Raulf and that's all he has to say to me?

"Yea, Gwendolyn." Eden stared at him as if he were daft. Brushing the tangle of hair from her eyes, she crossed her arms defiantly over her chest.

"How is she?" Vladamir asked, the parental concern apparent in the tired edges of his expression.

Good! Let him think about what he has done.

"She just saw her father slay a man," Eden raged in her most menacing tone. She put her hands on her hips as she'd seen her husband do. Taking a step forward, she tried to intimidate him. "How do you think she is, m'lord?"

"Eden," Vladamir began in warning. He obviously wasn't frightened. In fact he looked a little amused.

"Nay," Eden broke in, angry. "Don't take that tone with me, m'lord. She is an innocent young girl and you have her wrapped up like the dead in that—that death shroud. Telling her that she should hide her face! How dare you? She is beautifully charming—a delightful child. She should never be made to feel otherwise and so long as I'm around she'll be treated as if she were the most beautiful girl in the world. A little spoiling won't harm the poor dear one bit."

"Eden," Vladamir warned, trying to interrupt. "I never said for her to be—"

"Do not!" Eden held up her hand, unmindful of the few men who were listening above them. The knights brazenly leaned over the side of the wall, hoping to get another show. She heard their snickering and looked up at them from the ground. The men looked shamelessly to the sky and one even whistled. She ignored them, not caring about their blatant insolence at the moment. Seeing the duke also look up, she grabbed his jaw and forced his eyes back around to meet hers. "I'm not finished yet."

"You're for now, m'lady!" Vladamir said under his breath. He shook his jaw from her grasp with one hard jerk. Grabbing her arm, he led her to the side of the castle and into the kitchen garden, dragging her past the chamomile, which was still crumpled from when he'd flung her away from him to attack Raulf. He forced her to the large tree that grew by the wall only to stop. They were alone.

Eden pulled her arm angrily out of his grasp and continued as if they hadn't moved, "And about that, what is going on? Why does she look like me? Did you think we wouldn't notice the resemblance? Who is her mother? For I

241

have no older sister, only brothers and they were all dead at birth. I know she is not mine. Or did I have an older sister or an aunt? Did you marry a sister to my mother? Is that why she looks like me?"

"Eden," Vladamir stated calmly. His words were low and composed compared to the torrent of hers. He smiled, a faint gesture as he studied her. "May I speak?"

"Finally," Eden spat with a huff. She put her hand on her hips and turned to face him expectantly. "Only you had better say something of worth, lest I strangle you worse than you did Raulf. And about that—"

Vladamir forcefully pulled his angry wife into his arms with a growl. Eden gasped as he pressed his lips firmly to hers, cutting off her incensed words. She tried to pull away, but his arms were too strong as they wound passionately about her back. Leaning her head away from him, she felt his tongue flick across her bottom lip. It was too much. She couldn't help but give in as her fiery protest turned into a soft moan. He massaged her mouth into opening and kissed her deeply before loosening his grip enough for her to breathe.

"But, I wasn't..." Eden complained in breathlessness against his mouth. Her words were a useless entreaty compared to his onslaught. Unable to resist, she flung her arms about his neck and ran her fingers into the long black waves of his hair. Her eyelids fluttered closed. She'd longed desperately for him to hold her like this.

Vladamir chuckled at her eager response.

"...finished," Eden breathed at last, completing her thoughts. She pulled slightly away from him, filled with longing. "What is going on? Why did you stay away for so long?"

"Does m'lady always fall so eagerly into the arms of monsters?" Vladamir said as if he couldn't help the snide remark.

"Don't bait me with your ill humor. It won't work this time." She shook her head in sad denial before pressing her body more firmly against his solid length, refusing to let him go. "Would appear, m'lord, that there is only one monster who captures me so."

Vladamir laughed, looking surprised but stopped when she glanced sadly away.

"Why did you do it?" Eden let her hands fall from his head to his shoulders. "Why did you have to act so cruelly?"

"Methought you wanted Luther punished," Vladamir withdrew slightly, moving his hands from her back to her waist. "Dead, he can cause us no more problems."

Eden held him tighter, afraid he might try to pull away again. She didn't want him to go, not yet. The hard texture of his body felt too good. Twirling her fingers into the tie that bound his overtunic together at the neckline, she said, "Nay, Luther challenged you. I know you had a right to fight him, though methinks your hasty actions will bring the king down harder on you. It won't help your cause."

"Do you not mean our cause?" Vladamir frowned.

"Naturally." Matching his growing scowl with a playful one of her own, she dropped her hands to his chest, rubbing lightly. "I had meant—why did you try to kill Raulf? Methought he was your friend."

"Friend?" Vladamir's brows shot up in surprise. "Why would you think he was a friend? I'm his master. He's a hired soldier sent here by King Alfred. There is no friendship to be had in such an arrangement."

"Is that all these people mean to you? They are all merely servants and soldiers sent here for your pleasure by a king who imprisons you?" Her eyes teared. "I have truly married a cruel monster for 'tis what you are if that is how you feel. Have you no compassion?"

Her words were not accusing, nor were they fearful. They merely stated what she was slowly coming to believe as fact.

She looked mournfully to the chamomile. It reminded her of his hard marriage proposal.

"You dare to cry for him?" Vladamir spat as he let her go, forcing her to take a hasty step back from his anger.

"I cry for everyone here under your command. I cry for myself and your daughter. I mourn for us."

"Will you try to get out of this marriage? With Luther gone..." Vladamir's eyes narrowed in fury and he didn't bother to finish the thought.

"Nay, you'll have to send me away. I have given my word. The people need me here, if only to protect them from you. Your daughter needs me."

"*Eden the nun*, trying to save the world," he taunted with a short sneer, taking an aggressive step toward her as he silently dared her to back down. She didn't. "Mayhap I was mistaken about your temperament."

"Nay, I'm just trying to save your dukedom, *monster*," Eden scoffed back, unflinching. "And as my first order of business—"

"You dare to dictate to me?" he interrupted with an incredulous laugh.

"As my first order, you'll let Lizbeth and Raulf wed. I don't expect you to apologize to the man for your wrongful actions but this deed you'll permit them will have to suffice."

"Why do you care if they marry?"

"I don't, but 'tis what they wish and is what they shall have. Now, I understand that you wanted to keep Lizbeth for yourself, but she is no longer yours to have. You'll just have to make due with me until you find another concubine."

A curious look passed over his features. "Are you jealous, wife?"

"Don't ask such things of me for you haven't the right. My feelings are my own." Eden frowned and turned away from him. Staring into the distance at a passing soldier, she continued, "As my second order, your daughter is in need of new gowns and underclothing. So am I. I know that we don't have the gold for aught grand but I'll need something more befitting my station—something you won't tear to shreds. I have already decided that there is enough material left from the wedding gown to sew a tunic or two for the child."

"Gwendolyn has gowns," Vladamir answered, moving closer to her back. She felt his heat and the memory of how he tore her garment from her willing body only made her all the more hot. She ached, growing wet and needy between the thighs. Her hands felt nothing like his against her sex and no matter how she thrust, her fingers couldn't make her fell as full.

"If you mean that trunk that is in her chamber..." Eden pulled her shoulder away from his hot breath and stepped further away from him, trying to be strong against his sensual pull.

"Chamber? What chamber?" Vladamir asked, sounding confused. She felt him pursuing her as she again tried to step away. Something brushed against her hips and she stiffened, wondering if he touched her. She waited for him to do it again but felt nothing. Swallowing, she thought of how easy it would be for him to lift his skirt like he did on the wall, touching the bare flesh underneath. She started to sweat and her breathing deepened. It took all her willpower to concentrate on the conversation.

"Yea, the chamber I ordered readied for her," Eden said, forcing an exasperated sigh. "If you hadn't tried so hard these past fortnights to hide from me, I would've told you of it."

"I wasn't hiding," Vladamir interjected, touching her shoulder.

"'Tis of no concern to me," Eden jerked from him once more. "The gowns in the trunk are too small. If you didn't take notice, your daughter has grown some. They won't do. However I'll salvage what material I can from them."

"Fine." Vladamir lightly skimmed his finger over her flesh just below her ear. She shivered and her pulse beat quickened. "Gwendolyn shall have gowns."

"And what about me?" Eden asked, hesitant.

"You shall oversee sewing them or you can do it yourself." His lingering finger moved down over her neck in slow circles and he drew closer to her. "If you're in need of gold, you have but to ask. 'Tis your fault you have no gowns. I bid you to sew the clothing or have it overseen. 'Tis part of our arrangement afore the marriage."

"Then you don't mind?"

"Nay, I don't have time to oversee woman's work. If m'lady wishes this castle and herself to be presentable, m'lady will have to tend to it. Otherwise let it fall back into ruin. I care not." The duke continued the circles down to her collarbone and across her quivering throat. He dipped his head to whisper against her throat, "And 'tis not necessary for m'lady to try and command such things of me, if you're in need of something all you have to do is ask."

Eden felt like a dolt for not remembering. Her breaths deepened to silently urge his fingers lower. She'd thought Vladamir was just being insensitive. She forced herself not to give him the pleasure of seeing what he did to her insides. They were melting as was her resolve against him.

"What about Raulf?" she questioned timidly.

"Is his marriage what you were discussing with him?"

Eden shivered as his lips moved blithely over her skin. "Yea."

"Then he shall wed with Lizbeth," he answered.

She leaned her head back against his chest and let her body fall into his for support. Her eyes fluttered closed, blocking out the sun as its rays brimmed over the black stone of their home. The thoughts that swam jealously in her head came unbidden to her mouth, "And you won't take Lizbeth to your bed again?"

Vladamir chuckled as he drew his hands to her waist. He nuzzled a piece of her hair aside with his nose. "Nay, I'll not take Lizbeth to my —"

Eden cut off his words, turning frantically in his arms. Weaving her fingers into his hair, she pressed her fevered mouth to his for his kiss. She thrust her breasts forward against his tunic as she moved to undo the lacing at his neck. Pushing the black material aside she ran her fingers onto his hot chest and back.

"Why do you wear all these garments?" Eden asked in a rush as she moved her hands downward to pull up his tunic. She forgot her purpose in being mad at him. His nearness was driving her crazy with need. Since he didn't wear two tunics, it was easy for her to find the flesh at his muscular waist. She wanted him inside her, wanted to feel his body, see it. Her fingers trembled as she was allowed the feel of his finely tuned body for the first time. He hadn't allowed for exploring during their first coupling.

Vladamir groaned at her touch and glanced over her head to the bailey wall. Grimacing, he pulled her hand out from under his tunic only to clasp them together in front of him to hold her still.

"I," Eden began in a fluster. She tried to pull away from him, confused and a little hurt. Then she saw him peering past her. In bafflement, she turned to where he stared. Soldiers watched them from the wall. Vladamir lifted his arm in a long sweep to command the onlookers away. As the men trailed off laughing, the couple turned to each other. Eden bit her lip as she backed away from him.

"You once asked why this place was called Lakeshire when 'tis not by a lake," Vladamir said quietly. "Would you still like to know?"

Eden nodded her head, unable to speak. She wondered what possible significance the statement had. Had they not been in pursuit of more passionate aim? And a moment before that had they not been quarreling?

Vladamir smiled as he held out his hand. She glanced at it hesitantly before accepting it, wary of his changed mood. He seemed almost lighthearted.

"Come." He led her to the large oak tree. The branches swept down low against the outstretched bailey wall. Eden knew that beyond the wall was nothing but untamed forest. She'd seen it from one of the higher windows.

Vladamir walked around the tree, leading her deeper into its branches. It grew shadowy as he pushed forward to the backside of the large trunk. Eden ran her fingers lightly over the rough bark. She hesitated as Vladamir tried to pull her behind it with him.

"I don't see," Eden began, but quieted as he dropped her hand to reach behind his waist. Curiosity made her step closer to watch. Pulling out the small pouch, he undid the laces to it and produced an iron key from within the leather.

Only then did Eden notice the small door hidden within the castle's black wall. The door was old and made of thick, black iron. It blended into the wall, so that at a casual glance it would be overlooked. The old metal latch in the iron made no noise as the duke turned the key in the lock and neither did the hinges creak as he slowly pushed it open.

Vladamir had to duck his head under the low archway to fit under the small frame. Once through and able to stand, he held his hand out from the darkness for Eden to join him. Her insides bunched into knots as she took his offered hand. Her fingers touched of his scars.

"What is this place?" she asked as she ducked under the low arch. "Why haven't I been told of it?"

"Because only a few here know of its existence," Vladamir answered under his breath. "And they were instructed to tell no one. King Alfred showed me when he bestowed the castle on me. I too asked why it was called Lakeshire."

"Is this a passageway?" Eden narrowed her eyes to adjust them to the dim light. As her vision focused, she saw nothing but a long passage of dark stone. The stone molded with the blackness until she couldn't distinguish were the hall led.

"Yea," Vladamir answered. Eden stepped into the passageway. The door swung noiselessly shut behind her, blinding them with darkness. As he pulled her forward, he added, "Watch your step. Some of the stones are loose."

Eden smirked at the thoughtful advice. She felt as if they were entering a place where their outside concerns didn't matter. Following him slowly, she ran her hand over the cold damp stone of the wall. Suddenly, in the darkness, her fingers ran over what appeared to be another iron door.

"M'lord, methinks I found what you're looking for." Even though she spoke in low tones the sound rang ominous in the dank passageway. Her own voice echoed back to her. She quieted to a hush. "'Tis a door."

"Nay, that leads under the castle." Vladamir stopped to place his hand over hers on the cool metal entryway. "That isn't the door I was seeking."

Eden could hear the frown in his voice. "Dungeons?"

"Yea, m'lady," he said by way of confirmation.

"Are there prisoners there?" she questioned, straining to hear beyond the iron.

"Nay, m'lady." Vladamir chuckled. "I'm the only prisoner at Lakeshire."

His fingers searched her hand in the darkness, running along her fingers as they pressed against the door. Her ears continued to strain, trying to detect any sound of prisoners beyond the barred entryway. She struggled to keep her voice from wavering as she inquired with a squeak, "M'lord?"

"You asked for a secret, to be trusted." His voice was loud in the cold passageway. Eden shivered, her brave smile lost in the darkness. He laid his hand flat over hers, his warm palm against the back of her fingers as they pressed her into the chilled iron door.

"Yea, I did." It seemed like ages since she'd made the request, yet standing with him it was as if no time had passed between them. The hardship of the last fortnight fell from her mind.

"Then I shall grant your wish." He moved closer to her. "Though I believe you'll have to answer two questions."

Eden naturally drew closer to the heat of his chest. Her mouth angled up, longing for his kiss. "What is your first question?"

"Nay, not yet." Vladamir dropped his hand from hers. She heard him moving about before he continued, "I'll tell you what secret is underneath the castle. 'Tis not prisoners, but my personal treasury, holding within it all of my great fortune. Or should I say our fortune?"

"But, m'lord, we have no great fortune save the beating of our hearts." Eden gave a small laugh. She took her free hand and laid it on his chest so that she may feel the steady beat of his heart under her palm. "What does that have to do with Lakeshire's name?"

"Naught, only you found the door," Vladamir kept his hand over hers on the iron, running his other hand deftly down her arm. Reaching her fingers, he searched her in the shadows. His voice was almost a lost whisper as he stated, "You still wear that ring."

She felt him turn from her in the darkness after delivering the nonchalant statement. He let her hand fall from the door so she could continue to run it over the wall. She wondered what else she might find hidden under the castle. Without warning the passageway turned sharply to the left and Eden felt as if they were going down a steep incline. They traveled lower until she'd no idea how far they had gone. Vladamir didn't speak. She grew fearful.

Suddenly, Vladamir stopped. Eden stumbled into his back and gasped in panic.

"Where are we?" She hesitated as she righted herself. "Where are we going?"

"Are you afraid?" he asked in his low, thick accent. His voice mocked as he leaned into her. His hair fell over his shoulder to brush her face. She couldn't see him in the darkness but could feel the hot breath of his mouth against her skin. His scent overwhelmed her and the power of his heated body engulfed her senses. Eden lifted her hand, accidentally smoothing the lock back across his forehead with shaking fingers.

"Is that one of your questions?" she shot back with a shiver, wishing she could see his face. Her heart nearly stopped, catching in her throat at the words.

"Nay." Vladamir touched the hand near his face and pulled it into his palm away from the scars on his jaw. He wrapped his fingers around her wrist, holding her prisoner with a tightened squeeze. Her pulse beat wildly. "Are you?"

"A little," she admitted, gravitating toward him. She was drawn to the fear he produced within her, liking the dangerous quality to his words. They were alone, deep beneath the castle. What would he do to her? Would he take her again in his rough passion? She didn't know if he was her protector or someone she should wish to be protected against. Her heart beat that it was both. The air felt thin and she became lightheaded. Frightened by the darkness and feeling as if she descended into the depths of a tomb, she asked again, "Where are we going?"

"To the monster's lair." The duke let go of her hand.

Eden gasped at the demonic growl to his words. She backed away from him but it was too late to run. His hand caught up her wrist and he didn't let her go.

"P-please." Eden heard his key once again being fitted into an iron lock. She pulled at her captured hand, his grip only tightened. The passageway grew hot and the air suddenly felt damp. "Are you going to keep me prisoner? What are you doing?"

A door creaked open on its hinges and she noted how this door hadn't been well oiled like the outer door. Her mind raced in apprehension.

Mayhap, because none can hear this door. None can hear me if I were to scream. How far underground did we wander?

Eden swayed uncontrollably as Vladamir started forward. Her eyes rolled back in her head and her eyelids fluttered. She let the darkness consume her, having no choice to fight it.

Chapter Twelve

ഇ

"Your Majesty."

Clifton strode into the king's tent and bowed. Blinking slowly, he held his position until the king bid him to rise with a distracted wave of his hand. The earl stood and waited for the king's permission to speak.

King Alfred and his men had been camped on the outer border of Wessex, near Mercia overseeing the construction of one of his defensive burghs. The earl had been forced to reside there for about a sennight and a half. Only with Clifton's insistent pleading did the king agree to leave his project and ride to Lakeshire to resolve the problem of his daughter's marriage.

"Yea? What is it?" Alfred barked gruffly with a glance to the earl. Sighing, he turned his full attention from the page he was translating from Latin into English. The earl was interrupting the only leisure time he'd been afforded on the journey. Pouring sand onto the parchment to help dry the ink, he then motioned to his servant, ordering him to leave. The man nodded and ducked out of the tent flap, closing it behind him.

Clifton's face was red with anger as he waited for the servant to exit. At the excruciatingly slow rate the king's party was traveling, they were just under a quarter day's ride from Lakeshire. He'd sent dispatch to Luther that morning to tell him of their progress. A dispatch rider could make the castle gates with an hour of hard riding. And the earl just received a dire message in return.

"My liege," Clifton stated without preamble. "I just received word that Lord Luther has been murdered by that barbarian, Vladamir."

"Vladamir of Kessen rode into Luther's encampment and murdered him? In front of his men?" the king asked with disbelief. He'd met the duke and didn't see him acting so foolishly.

"Nay, Majesty. Luther was within Lakeshire's walls."

"Methought you said Luther would stay out of the castle gates," the king broke in with a furious hiss. He slashed his hand through the air. "You gave me your word that he wouldn't provoke an incident."

"And so he didn't," Clifton rushed when Alfred paused for air. A gleam of anticipation lighted in his eyes. "My dispatcher informs me that Lord Luther was personally escorting a package that arrived for the duke. They say the monster cut his head off in daylight for all to see."

Alfred held up his hand for silence and stood up from his writing table. He frowned in displeasure, not liking Clifton's use of the word monster. Thoughtfully rubbing his ink-stained fingers on a rag of fine gray wool, he moved to the corner of the large tent to take up his sword. He tied it at his waist before turning once more to the earl.

"Have you met with Lord Kessen afore he took your daughter? His land is near your own. 'Tis possible your paths have crossed." King Alfred studied the earl quietly. When Clifton had no ready answer, he continued, "For I have met Lord Kessen with a cool head and have found him to be more than what others think of him."

"Nay, majesty." The earl put his hands on his waist. "I know not why he would commit this offense on my house, but I'd have justice for it. I want him brought up on charges afore the Witan. I want him judged."

"There is more to consider here than one nobleman's life. Lord Kessen is my prisoner and not only that—he is the son-by-marriage of King Guthrum. If we charge Lakeshire and slay a duke who is under my protection it could start a war." The king held up his hand before the earl could protest. "I will send a dispatch to Guthrum alerting him as to the situation."

"So I'm to go unavenged?" Clifton's voice rang out harshly. "Majesty, I have been a loyal subject. And if there is to be another war against the Vikings I know our country can once again defeat them!"

Alfred motioned to silence the angered man. He peered down at the nobleman from the advantage of his height. Nodding sternly at the earl's patriotic decree, he knew that Clifton would be hard-pressed to join in much of the fighting. "We will ride at daybreak. I'll speak with Lord Kessen and will make my decision then. As to Lord Luther, we will investigate that also."

"But—?" the earl tried to protest, his mouth working in outrage. His hand gripped instinctively an imaginary sword, but he was stopped by the king's authoritative glare.

"I have spoken on the matter. If there is to be justice delivered I'll deliver it but not without the facts!" Alfred fumed. Taking a deep breath, he regained his calm.

The king beckoned the man to leave his tent. The earl nodded stiffly and backed away. Shaking his head to clear the ache he was beginning to feel, Alfred looked longingly at his drying pages before bundling them into a rolled leather scabbard. He wanted to finish the passage he was working on, but knew that he would have to make it wait.

* * * * *

"Eden."

Eden moaned, nuzzling her cheek into Vladamir's hand. She didn't want to wake up, though the voice was insistent. In her dream, the duke was with her, thrusting into her from behind in the dirty chamber. His hard cock was prying her open to him as his fingers explored the cleft of her ass.

"Eden." It was Vladamir's voice. She moaned, finally forcing her head from the fog of her dreams.

Blinking several times, she suppressed a delicate yawn as she saw Vladamir leaning over her. His face was so close to hers and she heard his soft breathing as it fanned her temple. The fine lines at the corners of his firm mouth twitched up into a lazy smile, causing her heart to skip. His hair fell downward over his shoulders, framing them in a dark cocoon. Vladamir's thigh brushed her leg. He knelt beside her, his upper body coming over her, supported by his muscled arms.

"Yea?" she asked, stretching as she raised her hands above her head with another delicate, closed-mouth yawn. Grass tickled her fingers and she realized they were outside.

Unable to resist the duke's appeal, she lifted her hand to his cheek to caress him as he had her. The back of her knuckles grazed his heated skin, over the rough pull of an afternoon beard. She ached for him to kiss her, though her mind was still hazy as to where she was and why. Her lips parted eagerly as she watched his gaze flicker to them. Running her fingers over his stubbled cheek, she moved her hand over his ear to his hair. Her fingers curled at the nape of his neck, delicately entwining in the long black waves.

"You fainted," Vladamir said as if reading her unasked question.

"Fainted?" Eden furrowed her brow in confusion as his words finally penetrated her brain and then she recalled her fear of him. It leapt back into her heart with an unsteady quickness to capture her breath. She moved her hand to push at his chest and shot him an accusing glare. "You said you were going to bring me to your lair."

"And so I have." He smiled, letting her push him away. His movements were controlled as he leaned back, moving more of his free will than her insistent shove. He studied her through narrowed eyes.

As his hair moved from her view, it was as if a curtain was being lifted from her vision. She watched him as he silently crouched back and away. A gasp caught in her throat as she looked up into the gently swaying trees of a forest. The leaves were green and bright as they danced guilelessly in the breeze. Their crashing motion filled the air with a gentle song that sounded like falling rain. It fell over them with a soothing brilliance. The sun peeked through the branches, making just enough speckled light to see.

She sat slowly up, not bothering to look at the duke. Her awed gaze was transfixed on their surroundings. Around them grew soft beds of grass, mixed with areas of dirt, littered by fallen leaves. She even thought to smell the light scent of flowers on the air.

"Where are we?" She noticed a door that matched the iron one inside the castle wall. It was edged with stone and overgrown with vining plants and moss. It was as if they traveled through time to a magical land. She turned her eyes finally to her husband. "Where have you taken us?"

"You wanted to know why our home was called Lakeshire," he said simply. Then, moving to pull a stray piece of grass from her hair, he waited for her nod.

"Yea, but..." Eden's words faltered as she was now transfixed by him. The peacefulness of the outdoors faded next to the inky blackness of his eyes. Her body reached to hold him with every fiber, sending a chill over her goose-fleshed skin. Her eyes dipped listlessly to his parted lips, wanting to taste them.

"Then turn," the duke commanded lightly as he looked over her head.

Eden did as he ordered her, fairly gushing with excitement. A few feet behind her lay a small pond. Its water was clear and clean and beautifully undisturbed. The liquid shimmered in the shadowy light, its surface placid. A few boulders were around the pond, ideal for sitting and watching the peaceful water.

"Where are we? Are we still in Wessex? Where have you taken us?"

"Yea, we are in Wessex," Vladamir answered with a gruff laugh. He shifted to his hands and knees and crawled toward her. Then, when he'd drawn close, he flipped onto his back to stare at the ceiling of tree limbs. "'Tis where I was trying to take you. The king brought me here. As I said afore I also asked why the castle was named Lakeshire. He said because 'tis a shire to a little personal lake and because Pondshire wasn't as impressive a name."

Eden chuckled and glanced down at his whimsical face as he spoke. He almost seemed transformed, boyish. She seated herself opposite to him but beside him. Looking out past his head and over the pond, she felt the privilege of such a secret—as if she was one of the rare few given the advantage of such a place.

"We're surrounded by a castle wall, so it's very private. If you were to walk in any direction you would run into the wall. Water from a creek along the outside feeds the pond and the only way out is beneath the water's surface. Even then it is a tight fit and hard to find. Those outside the castle wall think they've run into the castle and don't notice this small alcove, and since the forest is dense the wall can barely be seen for the shrubs and water. The tree limbs keep the area from being noticed from the castle windows and you already saw the door leading from the garden. Beside me, only the king, his dead brother and a few masons who rebuilt the castle know of it and now you."

"So we're alone?" she asked, wondering why he would bring her here.

"Yea," he answered, nodding. "And that will be three questions you must answer."

"What is your first question, m'lord?" she asked, unable to take her eyes off of him as he spoke. He seemed so relaxed in the secret alcove and when she gazed at him, the beauty of the surroundings paled in comparison to looking at his dark features.

"Nay," he shot back in denial. His eyes were blank, his gaze steady. "Not yet."

Eden tried to force herself to remember all that he'd done. But try as she might, she couldn't stop the overwhelming feeling of love that blossomed in her chest—love for her disturbingly emotionless husband. She didn't want to love him, didn't want to feel as if her whole being was made only to serve him but she did.

Her heart beat a path to her lips, urging them to take his firm mouth to hers. Closing her eyes, she forced the urge down into the pit of her stomach. Even as her heart filled and brimmed with love for him, it also throbbed and ached for he was incapable of loving her back.

"Tell me," Eden said, no longer able to keep her questions from him. In the sanctuary of his lair she felt a freedom she couldn't in the castle. She lowered her chin and looked shyly to a blade of grass that grew next to her. Plucking it from the ground, she pretended to study the dark veins that ran through it.

Vladamir closed his eyes and she stared at his handsome, unmoving face. When she didn't continue, he gave her a sidelong glance. "What is it, Eden?"

Eden blushed as he said her name, the sound so soft and gentle on his foreign tongue. "What did I do wrong?"

"When?" he asked without moving.

"There are so many times," Eden began weakly and then shook her head to clear her thoughts. Tracing her finger over the blade of grass, she gestured weakly. "Never mind, 'tis stupid."

"Ask me." Vladamir turned on his side and reached a tentative hand to her leg, resting it gently on her. Eden exhaled a soft moan, trying not to concentrate on the warmth that spread through her like an arrow of fire from his touch.

Michelle M. Pillow

"'Tis only that..." She took a deep breath. "All right. 'Tis only that night when we...consummated, you didn't like it."

Eden groaned with embarrassment as words failed her. She peered to the pond for guidance and then back to the grass blade. Her husband was handsome in that moment and she grew afraid, not because she thought him a monster but because she didn't think him one at all. To her he was a man, a man incapable of returning the love that grew with every insistent beat of her heart. Inside her body was melting for him, dying to be with him, to please him. Her stomach curled with nervous excitement whenever she thought of him and her loins heated with desire, so wet she could barely think straight.

"You didn't like me. How I was." Eden grew flustered but forced herself to go on. She had to know. Not being with him was agony. "And methought that if you were to tell me where I went wrong then I could please you and you wouldn't banish me from your bed, like you have. If I were not banished from your bed, the king would see that we were not estranged and would be likely to keep the marriage and in fact I might give you an heir so that the king would..."

"Be likely to keep the marriage," Vladamir finished as he watched her timid face. His low harsh accent echoed gently in the private haven.

"Yea," Eden admitted with a troubled pout. She rubbed her lips thoughtfully with the tip of her finger to get rid of their insistent stinging.

"Is it because you fear your father that you don't wish to go back?"

"Yea," Eden admitted, though that was only part of her reason—a very small, insignificant part. "I'm married to you and 'tis easier to stay with you then to bother with another husband. For believe me when I say my father's list is long when it comes to finding a rich man to marry me off to. I find you handsome enough and you seem not terribly displeased with my appearance and though I still have not been told why, there is the revenge for you. I'll make you a good and loyal

260

wife. I know that is what you want from me. I won't give you cause for displeasure if I can help it."

He said nothing.

"And I suppose you wouldn't like to have to find another wife. For who would be as loyal to you as I will for I have much reason to be and there is always the fact that I..." She paused, taking a deep breath. "The facts that I'm young and healthy and can most likely give you heirs without the use of herbs. At least, that is what Haldana told me. All men desire heirs and you're a man. Methinks I remember you admitting as much when you proposed we marry."

He grinned. The look tore at her heart. She wanted to touch him, hold him, kiss him. If only he would give her more encouragement, if only he would say he wanted her too.

Nay, forget what I said. The truth is I love you and cannot bear to be parted from you. Love me, m'lord. Please, just love me. That's all I want from you. Just love me...

How can you know what I want?

Vladamir's chest pounded strangely at her words. He knew that she spoke logic but he hated it anyway. He'd been watching her pink lips as she talked, wanting desperately to feel them. His fingers itched to grab the full globes of her chest in his palms. Seeing the half-truth in her eyes, he knew there was more she wasn't telling him. She seemed so fragile, so hurt. He hadn't thought he'd hurt her by avoiding her, he thought he did her a favor for after the way he bedded her like a beast she surely wasn't asking him to do it again but she was. He'd missed holding her and had thought of it often as he manned the wall.

Two fortnights was too long a time to go without the sweet caress of her body. He wondered how he managed so long. The only answer that he could claim was that he'd spent years perfecting the art of self-deprivation.

The duke rested his hand on her leg, all too aware of her body and her heat. Her skin was as soft as fresh cream and just as white. He was surprised that she'd actually fallen into a faint in the passageway as he'd merely been playing with her a bit, teasing her for her fear. Had he known she would've taken his dark accent so seriously, he would've lightened up a bit — or at least he liked to think he might have. Vladamir had plucked her from the passage and carried her to his private haven, laying her on a soft bed of grass. He couldn't help smiling as she continued talking, babbling nervously.

"And I'm smart, if you'd but teach me." Her voice cracked. "So tell me, m'lord, what did I do wrong?"

After that earnest speech, Vladamir was dumbfounded. "You did naught—"

"I know you don't want to look at me," Eden interrupted. "I understand. I seem to be bruised quite a bit of late and I look like a maidservant and not a wife. Lizbeth told me Raulf faces her and you didn't wish to look at me and that is all right because we can lie in the dark and—"

"You seem to have talked quite a bit to the servants," Vladamir broke into her guilelessness confession with a smile. Lazily, he lifted his hand and moved his finger on her leg in slow caressing circles. He felt her stiffen beneath the subtle gesture. She was stirring to him, her chest deepening with her breaths. Keeping his voice soft, he asked, "What else did they tell you?"

"That I should learn my body so that I can please you with it."

Vladamir suppressed a groan. Her big, innocent eyes almost made him come in his braes. Just thinking about her discovering the passions in her body caused his cock to lift a full size. He wondered if she would be willing to show him these self-pleasuring lessons she'd been giving herself in his absence. Grunting, he asked, "What else did they tell you?"

"Naught about you m'lord, I swear. Haldana told me the day my father was here that fourteen times is unusual and I got the impression that I had done something else wrong that day but she wouldn't say what. And Lizbeth, oh you won't be angry with her for bedding Raulf, will you? I know you like her."

"Shhh," Vladamir shook his head. He couldn't bear the raw hurt in her eyes as she said the words. "Enough of that. I don't want Lizbeth. The king sent her here to be my bedservant and I sent her away the first night. We were never together."

"Oh." Eden blushed. She bit her lip and looked away.

Now, about these lessons of yours...

"Did the servants tell you anything else? Did they tell you how to pleasure yourself to please me?"

Eden shook her head in denial and Vladamir wanted to scream in frustration. So much for getting her to talk dirty to him, not that he needed the mental stimulation.

Vladamir kept himself on the ground, moving his hand from her leg to place it behind his head as a pillow. He looked up into the trees. All this talk of coupling was making him hot and he couldn't keep his eyes from straying to her full, quivering lips, remembering how good they'd felt wrapped around his shaft. "There are many ways for a man to be with a woman. The way we were together was one."

"And?" She looked way too eager, her big eyes staring at him.

"And the way Lizbeth explained was another." The duke lowered his lashes to hide the roaming intent of his gaze as he stared at the gentle rise and fall of her generous breasts. Damn, but they'd felt nice and soft against his hand.

"And when I took you in my mouth, that was another," she offered.

Vladamir's cock throbbed painfully at the reminder. "Yea and beyond that there are many others but they are hard to explain without demonstration."

"Then fourteen is a reasonable number?" Eden concluded.

Vladamir tried not to smile. He rolled his eyes inwardly and swallowed back his uneasiness with an internal groan. If he were not careful his pretty little wife would be asking him to teach her that trick next. May the gods help him, he'd be willing to try it. "Mayhap on a very good night."

"So what do you think?" Eden's eyes shone brightly with a shy hopefulness. "Do you think 'tis a good idea?"

Vladamir smiled at her unable to remember what her "good idea" was. She'd said so much and he really didn't know what she was asking of him. But when she looked at him expectantly, he nodded his head. At that moment, he would've granted those chestnut eyes anything.

"Kiss me," he commanded huskily.

"Oh." Eden gasped, smiling with pleasure. "You mean to start the lessons now."

Eden moved to her hands and knees, seemingly unmindful of their surroundings as she looked at him. Tentatively, she crawled forward, putting her hand lightly on his chest. That touch was all it took. She fell onto him, her mouth eagerly seeking his.

When their lips touched, the resulting moans escaped their heated bodies in a loud testament of mutual need. Eden fell to the ground. His hand shot like a striking serpent from behind his head, to wrap around her. Vladamir took over the kiss as he rolled her to her back, making sure to cradle her head as he did so.

He urged her pliant mouth to open with the tip of his tongue. Her legs parted naturally to allow for his weight. The movement caused his thighs to pull her tunic tight against her legs. The material trapped her to him.

Placing his hands on either side of her head, he kept his mouth against hers. He kissed her passionately, tearing at her with his teeth, deepening the caress when it could get no deeper. His length pressed her into the soft ground. Her breasts peaked and strained against the imprisoning garment she wore.

The heaviness in his arousal pushed for release and he ground his hips to hers. Her hands ventured over his shoulders to find the heat of his taut back. Eden moaned. He pressed his hips harder into her.

"Kiss me," he groaned, pulling away.

"But...?" She blinked. "Aren't I?"

"Kiss me as you did in the hall. I've longed to feel your mouth wrapped around my cock."

Eden smiled, pushing him onto his back. She explored his hard chest, running her hands over his tunic as she worked her way down to his waist. Vladamir was already pulling the braes free by the time she straddled his legs. He pulled out his cock, stroking it, putting it to her mouth.

Parting her lips, she kissed his shaft. It was a small kiss, a chaste kiss. Vladamir moaned to see it. Every fiber in his being strained to unleash on her mouth, fucking it hard until he gagged her with his cock. He wanted to cram his dick into every hole she had, marking it, filling it with his hot come.

"Suck me," he urged. "Take me deep into your mouth."

He fitted his hands against the back of her head. When she moved to kiss him again, he pushed down while thrusting upward, slipping his arousal between her lips. Groaning loudly, he pulled her up by her hair. From his position on the ground, he got a perfect view of her mouth taking him in. The erotic show was almost as good as the feel of her lips rolling along his tip. She kissed his cock head, teasing it with her perfect mouth.

"You taste good," she said, almost shyly as she pulled him in deeper. Vladamir resisted the urge to again force her head down his shaft.

"Ah, by all that is hallowed, take me deeper," he commanded.

Eden obeyed and sucked him deeper, nearly gagging herself on his cock. The large shaft hit the back of her throat a few times and still didn't fit in halfway. Her teeth grazed the sides as she pulled up.

Suddenly, he stopped her, knowing if he didn't he'd come down her throat. As much as he wanted to watch her swallow his seed, he wanted to hold off his desire even more. This time, he wouldn't be selfish. This time, he wouldn't act the complete beast.

"What?" Eden gasped in puzzlement. Tears of uncertainty welled in her eyes and she tried to move away. He grabbed her, keeping her from getting up. "I have blundered already. I can be quiet. I swear to it. I didn't mean to moan like that."

Vladamir brought his fingers to stop her flow of words, taking harsh, deep breaths. He couldn't bear to see her so dejected. However he didn't know what to say to ease her concern. The sounds she made were innocent and fearless at the same time. She returned his kisses with untried fervor and obeyed his orders without question. So instead of trying to explain that he only stopped because he realized he was about to treat her like a whore, he stood, pulling her up with him. In one swift movement he cradled her up into his arms and walked with her to the pond.

"Where...?" She settled her hands about his neck, shyly kissing the flesh she found by his jaw. With her free hand, she touched his scars.

"I'm in need of a bath," he said simply.

I'm in need of cooling off.

"But our clothes," Eden protested as he neared the water. "You only have the one pair of shoes and I don't think we can afford more."

Vladamir didn't show his delight at the wifely concern. He had many pairs of shoes but didn't wear them, as he liked the worn comfort of his old ones. Obligingly, he set her on the ground, letting her body slide suggestively next to his as he did so.

She took a step away from him and gestured to a nearby tree. "Should I, ah, wait over there while you bathe?"

Vladamir chuckled, the noise low and seductive like the laugh of a wild animal. "Nay, m'lady, you're in need of a bath also."

"Oh," Eden gasped. Turning slightly, she sniffed to see if she was unpleasant. He pretended not to notice.

The duke pulled off his shoes, throwing them carelessly into the softened dirt. All the time he kept his eyes trained on her, waiting for her to disrobe for him. His stockings, which got caked with the mud, were soon to follow his shoes. Settling his bare feet into the muddy shore, he turned to her expectantly. His chin turned with a natural elegance to proudly tilt in the air and his eyes glowed with an unearthly light.

He smiled as she stood still, watching him. The smell of flowers was stronger by the water, encompassing them with their heady scent. The sound of the crashing leaves grew louder as a stout wind blew overhead.

"Come," he ordered.

She shook her head, backing away. Vladamir's face darkened when she didn't obey him. Intent on following her and dragging her back to him if needs be, he moved after her, but the same time he was hurt by her standoffishness. "Let me help you."

Eden had watched him in fascination, wishing he would continue disrobing. Her midsection curled with dangerous sensations as it longed to have his cock back inside her mouth, inside her pussy.

She trembled at the promise in his eyes as he stalked toward her. His hands lifted as if to rip her tunic from her willing body. Protectively crossing her arms over her chest, she took a quick step out of his reach, moving onto the drier shore. She shook her head, denying him. "Nay!"

"Come here, Eden."

"Nay, you cannot tear this gown." She took another step away from him. Vladamir stopped and placed his hands on his lean hips. He looked so handsome in his dark tunic and bare feet. "'Tis the only gown I have left. If you tear it I'll be left naked."

Vladamir's frown turned into a provocative smile.

"Then take off your clothes," he answered, keeping his eyes steadily on her.

"Go over there," Eden shooed him modestly. It was one thing to rip them off in passion, another entirely to strip as he watched from a distance—able to see *everything*.

When the duke grudgingly obeyed by walking back to the water's edge, he turned his back to her. Eden quickly slipped out of her gown, careful to keep an eye on him to make sure he didn't try to peek. Gingerly, she lifted her thin chemise over her shoulders.

Vladamir's hands lay boldly on his hips, just above the firm line of his butt. The black linen hugged his masculine body so that Eden could see the defined lines of his spine. His laces were loose and the braes would be easy to pull off his legs.

She dropped the chemise to the ground. Then as the air hit her naked body, she took off running for the water. Her feet splashed carelessly at the pond's edge and she quickly dove under the cool liquid. The glistening water slithered over her body with reckless abandon before she surfaced to turn back to her husband on the shore. Treading water with her limbs for it was too deep to touch, she smiled triumphantly back at him. Not bothering to remove his clothes, he stalked after her into the water. Diving under the surface, he met her in two bold strokes.

Eden gasped in pleasure. She felt his hands on her body before he came up for air. His strong fingers went straight to her waist, gliding with the aid of the water over her flushed skin. Her hands found his wet overtunic as he surfaced. The water trickled down his wet hair in rivulets, beading to glisten on his wet skin peeking from his neckline. She wound her fingers into his long locks, drawing him immediately to her lips. His kiss impatiently greeted hers.

Eden opened her mouth without prompting, daring to touch her tongue to his lips first. Vladamir groaned and pulled her more fully to him. Her naked body pressed tightly to his wet tunic. The material tickled her skin and the hardened length of his cock pushed at her from its watery vault.

"I want to feel you," she whispered, unsure how he would take her words.

"How do you want to feel me?" he demanded against her lips, his voice louder than hers, more confident.

"I want your cock inside me. I want you to take me like you did in the dusty bedchamber." As she fiercely returned his kiss, Vladamir drew back in surprise. Eden let him breathe, only because it allowed her to further her cause. Her long hair floated about them, mixing with the ends of his. As his lips parted for a ragged breath of air, she pulled at his tunic, struggling with the wet weight of it and unable to get grounding with her feet. Her head went under water as she pulled up.

Surfacing quickly, she swam backward pulling him with her by a fistful of tunic. Vladamir didn't protest as she led him to more stable ground. When she had her footing, she went to him and once again set to work on disrobing him.

"I want to see you." Though she was excited, her body trembled with nervous fear. Beads of water gathered on her lashes and she blinked them off. Her naked breasts bobbed on the surface hardening her nipples, the cool liquid making waves in their valley. When he didn't answer, she slowly reached her naked arms to his shoulder.

Vladamir hesitated but as her hands slid over his muscled chest, he didn't stop her. She kept her eyes steadily on him, glancing shyly at his lips. The duke grabbed his own tunic with an animalistic growl and yanked it over his head. Flinging it to shore, he turned back to her and let her keep the lead.

Eden was instantly in his arms, pressing herself to his nakedness. She gasped in pleasure at the feel of him but she didn't kiss him. Instead she allowed her hands to run a course through the ridges of his toned flesh as she explored his body freely for the first time. Her nipples peaked into hard points as they rubbed against his manly ones. She didn't think of his scars as she touched him, though her fingers ran lightly over them. He was gorgeous—so hard and hot, his body molded as if from stone. The blood in her veins quickened and raced through her with a feverish yearning. He held her fast in his grip as she moved to explore his neck with her lips.

"You taste so good." Eden groaned. She ran her fingers over his naked shoulders, his back, his neck with a burning need to consume him. "And you're so hot."

Vladamir moaned, throwing his head back with abandon. She held only a desire for him, no rejection, no fear, no accusations—just budding desire. Trailing her lips over his brawny chest, she licked him only to moan in pleasure. She ached everywhere for him but no place as much as between her thighs. Squirming to get her hips closer, she couldn't feel enough of him.

"Please," she begged, knowing what was to happen as she tried to free his cock once more. The material of his braes was much easier to push off and she slid it easily over his hips.

Cautious, she moved to feel the taut flesh of his hard butt, working her hands over the tight flesh, pulling apart his cheeks.

"Now you," she urged. Pulling his hips closer to her wet slit, she threw her head back and moaned. His hands explored her firm butt as she lifted up to grind against him. "Tell me what you like, what you want."

"I want you." He took her hand in his, teaching her how to stroke him, urging her to run her delicate hands over his shaft. The water made them glide together. When she'd the rhythm and pressure just right, he let go and slipped his finger into her slit. "I want to fuck you here." She jerked as he parted the slick folds of her body, finding her clit. He slipped a finger up into her, stretching her as he rolled it in small circles. She bucked against him and tried to ride his hand. Vladamir groaned, pulling back. Then, sliding back to her ass, he said, "And I want to fuck you here."

Eden was stunned by his admission but as he rimmed the tight rosette she couldn't think of a single reason why she should deny him. His finger slipped inside her ass and she tensed.

"Oh, yea," he groaned. "Your ass is so tight. I've imagined it around my cock so many times."

He probed deeper, rimming the hole in widening circles. Eden bucked, wiggling before him in the water.

"Yea," she moaned, giving into him.

"Ah, that's it, try to relax. Take my finger, oh yea, just a little deeper. I'm going to leave it inside you as you take my cock."

Eden shouted in surprise as he slid the finger deep. Then, urging her up, he angled her sex to his cock. In one solid thrust, he entered her ready body, His claiming didn't hurt her as it had the first time and she automatically wrapped her legs around his hips to spur him on. The tight muscles of her passage stretched to accept him, holding him deep. The finger slipped almost completely out of her ass at the position. He moved slowly in her, thrusting powerfully up after pulling to the entrance of her sex. Then, keeping himself deep inside of her, he moved himself in small strokes near her core. She jolted in pleasure and rotated her hips.

Eden explored her body on her own, touching herself as he'd touched her but it wasn't the same. It had taught her something about her passions, but though she could find pleasure with her own hand it was nothing like the pleasure she felt with him inside her. She wiggled around, keeping him deep, wishing his finger was back inside her ass.

Her wet hair stuck to her back. The heavy weight pulled her head so her breasts thrust forward toward his face. Vladamir caught a ripened nipple between his teeth as he continued to slide within her. His hands guided her by the small of her back, lifting in agonizing slowness only to plunge within her again and again, hard and deep, confident and strong.

"Please." Eden writhed and moaned against the onslaught of his passionate mouth. She bucked her hips brazenly against him, wanting him deeper, wanting his thrusts to become faster. "I want more."

Vladamir growled in response to her pleading. Again, he licked her nipple, taking a large part of the engorged breast into his mouth to suckle. With his shaft still embedded inside her, he walked them toward the shore. He knelt down by the water's edge, laying her gently on the yielding soil. Her back sank into the damp earth as his weight pressed into her. Their legs still trailed in the water. He let her breast escape his mouth so that he could press his lips to hers.

"Ah, yea, this is better," she said, spreading her legs.

The duke took her moans and pants into himself as he moved his shaft once again in the slickness of her body. Eden jolted and thrashed against him in a mindless web of ecstasy, her center hot for him as he pushed deeper into her core. He pulled back, lifting his weight with his arms. His hands sank into the mud before he reached to pull Eden from the shore to straddle his lap.

Mud caked her back and hair, causing her to moan in the exotic pleasure of it. Vladamir's hands ran over her body, trailing the mud over her pale neck and breasts, over her erect nipples. He crushed her muddied body to his, letting the moistened earth glide between them as she rode him in hard strokes.

She thought her body would explode with the intensity of it. Then she did explode, yelling the pinnacle of her desires as her body racked above him in waves of pleasure. Vladamir's grunt soon joined hers, his face tightening as he reached around his thighs to her ass. Somehow, he stopped himself from releasing with her.

"Ah, that's it," he told her. "Come for me good."

The shivers continued for what seemed like an eternity. She gasped for breath. "What about you?"

"I told you." He grinned, a truly wicked look. He pulled her off of him. "I want to fuck your tight ass."

Eden was too overtaken with the aftermath of her pleasure to protest.

"On your hands and knees."

"Should we wash off first?"

"Mm, nay, I want you just like this." He maneuvered her body around until she was on her hands and knees before him. Water splashed as he rubbed the dirt from her ass cheeks, cleaning her somewhat. Then she felt the probe of his hard cock head moving up and down along the sensitive cleft. "Try to relax for me. Oh, yea, you're so beautiful like this. I'm just going to ease it in. That's right, take me."

Eden relaxed her muscles, curious about what he wanted to do to her. She'd never heard of anything like this but as his cock slipped past the boundary, dipping around the edge of the rosette, she didn't care. Sinful or not, she was going to let him have his way with her.

Vladamir groaned in pleasure, letting her hear how much he liked it. His cock pried her open, slipping deeper with each pass. Reaching around, he stimulated her clit, rubbing it in small circles.

"By all the gods, you're tight." Groaning, he thrust all the way in, seating himself to the balls. Eden gasped, torn between surprise and passion. He moved slowly, taking shallow thrusts as he stayed deep. "That's it. Just like that. Oh, yea, come for me again. I can't hold back much longer."

They came in unison, both trembling and panting wildly. Vladamir pulled out and she felt hot semen pouring over her ass cheeks. He rubbed it into her, groaning as he continued to spurt the hot come. She'd never felt so alive and so drained at the same time. Her limbs sung with the sweet, melodious tingling of her body and she fell forward to rest on her stomach. She never wanted this day to end.

As he withdrew from her, her lips parted as if to speak, but no words came out. She turned to look at him, silently begging for his approval, a tender word. Her body was covered with wet, clinging earth.

"We should rinse, m'lady. I'd see my daughter this day," Vladamir said quietly. Somehow she knew he couldn't comfort her the way she wanted him to, that he didn't know how to form the words she needed to hear. He set her on the ground and took her hand to lead her back into the deeper water.

Eden followed him, longing to say what she felt in her heart but his eyes had been cautiously devoid of emotion. She watched the rippling muscles of his back with longing as he moved away from her to sink under the water. As he swam, she quickly rinsed the mud from her body. Then, when she turned and didn't see him, she ran ashore and quickly drew on her chemise and tunic gown. Pulling her hair from the back of her tunic, she watched him come from the water.

She felt a curling sensation in her lower stomach. Soft, black hair curled over his healthy legs. His chest sparkled with the droplets of water that beaded on his skin. Her eyes drew to his member of their own accord. It lay limp, nestled in the soft hair between his legs. Eden gasped and hurriedly turned from him.

Behind her, Vladamir chuckled softly. She glanced once over her shoulder, seeing that he quickly pulled on his clothing. When she heard him move, she finally turned. His feet were bare and he carried his muddied shoes.

"Ready?" he inquired.

She nodded her head. "Yea. Gwendolyn is sleeping. She was really quite tired from her journey. Methinks you shouldn't wake her yet."

Vladamir nodded his agreement.

Eden frowned when she saw that the duke had laced his tunic again to his neck. Without thought, she reached up to tug delicately at the laces. A smile passed over her lips as she said, "You look so severe when you do that."

Vladamir let her attend to his garment, watching her carefully. Pulling the laces out of their top holes, she let the neck of his tunic fall open. Then smoothing the damp material over his chest with a pat of her fingers, she said, "There, 'tis better. You're so handsome, you shouldn't hide…"

Eden's cheeks flushed in embarrassment, realizing all that she revealed. Vladamir shaded his gaze from her by lowering his lashes, revealing nothing as he studied her face. Thus far theirs wasn't a relationship of such candid honesty when it came to emotions. With a small sound of diversion in the back of her throat, she sighed and turned her face from him. There was nothing else so she could say to him without him speaking first. Slowly, she began walking to the door. Finding that it was still open she moved inside, not knowing whether he followed.

Vladamir watched Eden walk away. He supposed being a woman she knew more about children than he did. Vladamir wanted to see his daughter but would wait until the child rested. He'd missed his daughter and regretted the welcome he'd given her. But Gwendolyn was tough and would be all right.

Eden didn't turn to look at him but Vladamir watched her every move until she disappeared into the tunnel leading back to the courtyard. His wife was a very beautiful woman. The long length of her athletic legs, the smooth skin of her perfect ass, her slender hips and waist, they all drove him mad with need. He was grateful the cool water had held back his desire just enough to slow him, lest he again act the monster when he took her.

It amazed him that Eden could act so passionately in his arms with such instinctive purity — letting him do things most Saxons thought a sin. Suppressing a groan, he thought the Saxons foolish. If he denied himself her tight ass, it would be agony. His eyes strayed down to his cock. He would definitely be doing that again. Good thing she seemed willing to have him in her bed. He wasn't sure he could control himself anymore around her — not after sampling all her body had to offer.

The duke wondered if he would ever get his fill of her. Moving to follow Eden from the secret alcove, he sighed not wanting to go back to reality. If he had his say, he'd spend the afternoon in her arms, thinking of nothing, talking of nothing and doing many sordid things.

Chapter Thirteen

ഔ

The bailey was abnormally quiet as the penned animals lounged lazily in the warmth of the afternoon. Even the dogs appeared to yawn, basking in idle contentment. The sun was directly overhead in the clear blue sky and a lone knight marched the wall, stopping to watch the camped army in the distance before continuing along the battlement to his post.

The hours had passed slowly since their lovemaking, but Eden's body still sang with the excitement of her husband's touch. Shivering anew, she hadn't begun to comprehend how much she'd missed his touch until finally she was in his arms. Although she realized that the duke artfully avoided answering many of her questions.

Stretching her arms above her head, she sighed. Her gown had finally dried, but she still felt the lake's dampness in her hair. Every time a strong breeze blew, she trembled at the coolness of it. After leaving Vladamir alone at the lake, she'd gone to his chamber to straighten her clothing and prepare for the rest of the day. She was glad she did so, for a telltale trail of dirt smudged across her face.

She looked at the castle gate and took a deep breath, smelling the smoke from the bonfires of the surrounding soldiers. Gwendolyn slept abovestairs, not surprisingly since the child had been through a good deal. Eden had checked in on the girl.

Out of the corner of her eye, she saw Lizbeth coming from the entrance to the main hall. The tingling drained from her limbs to be replaced by concern. Her stomach ached as she witnessed the maid's tightly drawn face. The servant spotted her immediately and hurried her approach. Eden ignored the main gate as she walked to meet the serving woman.

"Raulf?" Eden asked when she was within speaking distance.

Tears streamed down the woman's face. "That monster tried to kill him. Why, m'lady?"

"Lizbeth, I know not why." Eden took the servant girl under her arm and led her back toward the manor. "Tell me, how is Raulf?"

"He'll live but I'm afraid he'll do something stupid. Raulf is very furious. I have never seen him so angry."

"Lizbeth, listen to me," Eden said, dropping her arm. Her heart went first to her husband in worry although she'd seen his guilt firsthand. "You must convince Raulf not to do aught to the duke. It won't end well for him. The duke is a very powerful man."

"You mean monster," Lizbeth interjected. "How can you now deny that he is aught but? How can you after what you have seen?"

"Because, I must have hope that he is an ordinary man," Eden said quietly. "For me you must try and believe it also."

"But why, m'lady? Why would you defend him even now?" Lizbeth looked at her in wonder before shaking her head in awe. "You have no reason…"

Eden couldn't answer as she looked at the serving woman with all the tortured love in her heart. Lizbeth sensed the answer immediately, appearing horrified.

"When?" Lizbeth asked in pity. "How long have you known?"

"Part of me has always loved him, Lizbeth, even when I'm frightened by him." Eden sighed. She tried to smile bravely but faltered. Then, taking the woman by the hand, she once again turned to the main hall. "Speak with Raulf as my friend. Do it for me."

Lizbeth didn't answer as a fresh wave of tears assaulted her. Eden knew she understood well the pain the heart could bring but unlike her mistress Lizbeth's love was returned freely. Finally, as they approached the shadowed black wall of the castle, the maidservant nodded in agreement.

"Thank you." Eden breathed a sigh of relief. It was up to them as women to keep their men safe, even if that meant keeping them safe from themselves. "I want you to go tell Raulf that his lordship has all but admitted he's regretful over what has transpired between them this day in the garden and though we don't know the true reason for it, methinks the duke made a mis — mistake."

Eden gasped, breathing hard as an unexpected cramp tightened her midsection. The dull pain worked through her stomach and down her leg.

"M'lady, what is it?" Lizbeth asked with a puzzled frown. She led the noblewoman to the stone wall of the castle.

"'Tis naught." Eden took several deep breaths. "Methinks I need rest. It has been a long day and I've been overtired as of late. There has just been too much to think about."

"M'lady, you don't look well. Mayhap, I should get someone. Haldana?" Lizbeth urged Eden inside to a bench as she spoke.

"Yea, mayhap you should," Eden agreed. Another peculiar pain entered her side. This one wasn't as bad as the first, but did cause her discomfort. Worried, she looked at Lizbeth. "I may be a bit ill. I haven't been sleeping well."

The woman gave a nod of concern and was off. Instead of sitting, Eden made her way to the stairs. She wanted the comfort of her own bed and wondered if somehow Vladamir's rough lovemaking had anything to do with the cramps.

Nay, something so pleasurable couldn't do this.

She made her way abovestairs to her bedchamber. "I don't have time for illness now."

* * * * *

"You're with child," the stout midwife announced, wiping her bony hands on her apron and turned to Lady Eden. Lizbeth sat by the duchess, dabbing her forehead with a cool cloth.

Both women gasped in unison at the discovery staring first at each other and then at the midwife. Eden jerked up from the bed. Lizbeth dropped the cloth. They were the only three in the chamber. Haldana had been there moments before but left to get Eden some broth.

"With child? You're certain?" Eden questioned in amazement. A slow smile crept into her features at the thought.

A baby! My prayers have been answered! Now, his majesty cannot annul the marriage. He'll have to let it stand and father won't want to be a grandfather to a bastard. With Luther dead, there is no one else to have me. We have done it!

"Yea, m'lady," the midwife answered with a curt nod. She busied herself putting her herbs and cloths into a basket. "Very certain."

Eden's heart pounded as her mind tried to accept the news. She looked about the bedchamber in a daze.

"M'lady," Lizbeth leaned over to whisper in Eden's ear. "You're free of him."

"What?" Eden gasped in shock. When she moved, some of her hair fell over her face. Lizbeth gently pushed the locks back. "Free?"

"Yea, m'lady," Lizbeth replied. "Now that you carry his babe you can convince him to leave you be. Most noblemen don't couple with their wives when they are with child and after you can claim any number of illnesses. You never have to touch him again. You'll be free of him."

Eden felt her smile slip from her features.

Never touch him again? Never feel the taut play of his skin? Never smell his smell? But why would I want that?

"You cannot tell so early," Eden protested weakly to the midwife. She raised her voice so that the elderly woman was once again forced into conversation.

"M'lady, I can tell. These hands have birthed nigh a thousand children." To prove her point she raised her thin wrinkled hands. "'Tis early in yer time, but 'tis yer time. The babe will come with the spring."

Eden turned to Lizbeth and asked, "But what if he beds me anyway? Will it hurt the babe?"

"Nay, but if he beds you anyway then you'll know that he is a monster." Lizbeth lowered her voice to an ominous hush and shook her head. "Then yer heart will be yer own again. The spell will be broken."

But I don't want my heart back. It would be dead to come back to me now.

Eden shook at the venom in the servant's words but even so a sweet hesitant relief overcame her.

Then he won't know about the child. We won't tell him. Not yet. There is no need for him to know. I just want a little time with him.

"I don't want anyone knowing about the babe," Eden said with a pointed look to the midwife. "I won't chance someone harming Lord Kessen by hurting the child I carry. No one will know until the siege is over and then only when I make the announcement. Are we clear?"

The midwife shrugged her shoulder, showing no interest in the statement. Lizbeth's mouth dropped open to protest.

Eden held up her hand with a confidence she didn't feel. "I have a stomach illness that is all. That is what you'll tell anyone who asks, even his lordship. Am I understood?"

"But," Lizbeth tried again. Her brow marred with a confused frown.

"Nay, I'm afraid what his lordship will do if he hears of it from any but me. I'm afraid he'll harm not only me but the messenger as well. We have seen what he's capable of." Eden ignored the pang of guilt as she once again used her husband's reputation to get her own way. She made a silent vow to never do so again.

"Yea," Lizbeth said, not liking the decree and definitely not understanding the reasoning for it.

Eden turned to the midwife who reluctantly nodded. Eden was sure that the woman didn't care when she told the world of her condition. The world would see it for itself soon enough. The midwife gathered her basket in the crook of her arm and curtsied halfheartedly before leaving the chamber.

When she was gone, Eden turned seriously to Lizbeth. "I have your promise?"

"Yea," Lizbeth consented. "I'll tell no one."

"Good," Eden said and then she smiled. "I do know of something you can tell everyone."

"M'lady?"

"His lordship has agreed to let you and Raulf marry. 'Tis what Raulf and I were discussing when his lordship... Well, the fact is that his lordship was regretful for what happened and has agreed. So make your plans."

Lizbeth's face transformed from her skeptical expression into one of pure joy. "M'lady, 'tis true? Lord Kessen has granted us —?"

"Yea, Lizbeth, 'tis very true. That is why you must keep Raulf from searching out his lordship. He's to be a husband now and you his wife."

Lizbeth hopped from the bed and ran from the chamber only to stop and rush back to her mistress. She took up Eden's hand in her own, her face shining with joy. "Thank you, m'lady. I'll keep yer secret as long as you wish and any other you might have without question! I'm forever yer loyal servant."

Eden nodded as she mustered a sad smile. The girl bolted from the chamber, undoubtedly in search of Raulf. When she was alone, Eden leaned back on the bed and felt her stomach. It didn't feel any different. Finally, after giving Lizbeth plenty of time to reach the main hall, she stood. As she made her way slowly to the chamber door, she had no doubt her secret was safe with the two women.

* * * * *

"M'lord?" Eden called to the duke's turned back. She glanced over the distance from the wall. During the day, the fires were kept low so only the tents showed over the distance of the countryside.

Vladamir was talking with Ulric about the wall's defenses. It appeared to Eden that he wasn't too worried about the surrounding army attacking until the earl returned. But then the earl would most likely bring either the king or one of his ambassadors and hopefully that would halt any excuse for a fight.

The duke turned at request for his attention, a slight smile on his lips as he glanced over her form. She was still dressed as a servant and still wore the bent wedding band on her finger. He didn't seem to notice.

"Ulric," Eden acknowledged, glancing to the seneschal. She smiled at him with a nod of her head.

"M'lady," Ulric said politely in turn.

"Ulric." Vladamir didn't turn back to the man but kept his eyes trained on his wife's face. "That will be all for now. Please see to it."

"Yea, m'lord." Ulric nodded with a swipe of his sweaty brow. He left, walking along the black bailey wall.

"M'lady?" Vladamir inquired with much formality. It didn't show in his lighthearted smile. His eyebrow raised in masculine question. Her heart soared to see the look on his face for it gave her hope. Maybe she'd been wrong. Maybe he could feel something for her.

"So proper," Eden said as she turned away. She looked to the horizon, silently praying that he wouldn't learn the truth of her condition from her own nervous tongue.

"M'lady started it," Vladamir teased. Eden wondered at his playful mood. His eyes held a wonderfully provocative light to them. He brushed a piece of hair from her cheek, before leaning over to lightly kiss her neck, letting his teeth nibble her sensitive throat. A soft sound escaped him as he nuzzled her cheek.

"Vladamir," Eden said softly as she looked at him. She licked her lips and was lost in his mysterious black orbs for a moment.

"Yea, Eden, what is it?"

"May we speak?" Eden cleared her throat. "What I mean is may we speak privately?"

Vladamir glanced around the empty wall. There was no one nearby. Turning to her, he smiled and consented with a nod and held out his arm for her to take.

She shivered as the heat from his body soaked through the tunic to her hand. Even after their earlier session, her body was ready for more. Taking a deepened breath, she forced herself to concentrate. She couldn't allow him to distract her thoughts as quickly as he had earlier in the day.

The duke led her to the ladder in silence, allowing her to go first down the wall. Watching the exposed curves of her breast as she descended, he smiled wickedly. Eden felt her face heat at the attention. Then as she waited below for him, she unashamedly checked out his tight butt. Taking her arm, he led her to the stone bench in the garden.

"'Tis a pleasant eve," Eden offered, wondering if he might be able to read the thoughts that swam around in her head. She tried to push the baby from her mind, just in case.

"How is my daughter?" Vladamir asked instead of acknowledging her statement.

"She still sleeps. Methinks the journey was an arduous one for her." Eden took a seat on the bench, mindful not to let her thoughts stray to the secret door behind the large oak. Vladamir looked at her expectantly. She didn't know where to begin. There were so many unanswered questions lingering between them.

Eden moved to the side to give him space next to her. As he sat, she turned to him. His eyes still gleamed with a pleasant light.

"May I ask you something?" Eden hesitated as her hand strayed to rest on his knee. Peeking up at him through the long length of her black lashes, she hid the full force of her gaze from him. Lightly caressing him in an absent stroke, she asked, "Without you getting angry?"

Vladamir nodded, still smiling. He leaned back against the bench and set his arm over her back. Resting it lightly over her shoulders, he took a deep breath. They could hear the slight song of birds as a peaceful breeze swept over the serene yard. Eden's eyes rested on his chiseled face. He was so handsome to her that she had to glance away. She hoped that she wouldn't upset him with her probing, but she had to know the truth.

Turning her eyes to him once more, she gazed at him delicately. She kept her expression guarded. "Who was Gwendolyn's mother? Can you tell me about her?"

"She was my wife," Vladamir stated, losing some of his good humor.

"I know that." Hiding her frustration, she took a deep breath. She hated that her words were the reason for his scowl. "Who was she? Was she related to me?"

"Nay. Her name was Lurlina. She was the daughter of King Guthrum and one of his favorite mistresses. The king couldn't wed the woman but he did provide for his child by her and legally claimed Lurlina as his own."

"That would make you royalty," Eden gasped at the thought. No wonder her husband appeared to be such a powerful man.

"Nay, not quite, only related to." Vladamir chuckled in amusement.

Eden took heart at his lightheartedness and persisted, "But why would the king send you here, if you're relation? Gwendolyn is his granddaughter."

"Yea, she is," Vladamir stated. "But my being here is politics. The king needs me here to ensure his peace."

"I know all about that." Eden dismissed his excuse. "But why you? Did you do something to his daughter? Did you—?"

"Did I kill her?" Vladamir scowled, losing his calm. "Is that what you want to know?"

"Nay, I know you didn't kill her. I don't know how I know it but I do." Eden didn't back down. For the first time since the midwife's visit, she forgot completely about her condition. "I only meant to imply that mayhap the king blamed you wrongly for the death or perchance was distraught over it and banished you because you reminded him of the daughter he'd lost."

Vladamir laughed softly at her woman's logic and his anger faded. He caressed her cheek with the backs of his hand, having trimmed his fingernails after their lovemaking session by the secret lake. He didn't know why, but only that he thought it might please her.

Eden stiffened at his laughter. "What?"

"You're a romantic," Vladamir said, feeling almost carefree, despite the talk of his late wife.

"Don't make light of me," she fumed, "and don't dismiss my questions. Your distractions might have worked earlier, but now I'd have my answers."

That comment gave him a few ideas. Grinning, he dropped his hand to her shoulder, skimming his fingers lightly over the side of her breast. She shivered at the caress. "Are you sure you won't be distracted?"

"M'lord, please!"

"Eden, don't be so quick to temper," Vladamir soothed, calmly stroking her hair as he would a wild mare he was going to tame.

"You're one to talk," she returned. Her eyes begged for him to tell her the truth. "Now quit changing the topic. How did Lurlina die?"

"In a fire," Vladamir answered with little thought of censure. Eden's hair wrapped around his fingers in a silent caress. He loved her hair, could study the color of it for hours.

"The same fire that scarred you and your daughter? How?"

Mayhap 'tis time I told you the truth.

Taking a deep breath and a leap of faith, Vladamir dropped his hand from her face. His expression turned cautiously blank. "Lurlina was a vain and selfish woman. She wasn't happy being a mother or a wife. One night, soon after Gwendolyn was born, I had just gotten back from visiting King Guthrum. The nursemaid told me she couldn't find the baby. When I went to Gwendolyn's cradle, she was gone. In my daughter's place was a draught the midwife had given Lurlina after she birthed our daughter. 'Twas to help her with the pain."

Eden didn't say a word so he continued.

"Methought Lurlina had given the draught to Gwendolyn and carried her off to bury her. I went in search of them only to find my wife in her chamber. She was swaying from the effects of the draught and Gwendolyn was lying on the bed crying.

Lurlina had set the bed afire and by the time I arrived black smoke had started to curl in the air. I tried to stop her but 'twas too late. Lurlina grabbed Gwendolyn and threatened to kill her if I came near. When I tried to stop her she jumped into the fire holding the baby. I was able to save Gwendolyn and myself but it was too late for Lurlina. She was already dead."

Eden's hand tightened on his thigh.

"The scars we carry are from that day. Methought I was going to lose Gwendolyn but we lay together in a bed and healed. I refused to let her from my sight. She was a tough child. She still is."

"I'm so sorry. I promise I'll never betray you like that." Eden kissed him.

He let her briefly, drawing comfort from her, before pulling her away. "That's not all."

"Nay," Eden shook her head. Her lips trembled with the force of her unshed tears. "I don't want to hear any more today. Tell me the rest later."

Vladamir nodded, reluctantly giving his consent and said no more. He wasn't sure his wife would like to hear the rest of it anyway. He turned to watch the setting sun.

A silence passed between them, carrying on as the sun set behind the bailey wall. Soft orange light still shone and she wasn't sure if it was from the bonfires beyond the castle wall or from the setting sun. As she sat, one thought rolled in Eden's head, gripping her heart.

You love Lurlina still. That is why you cannot love me.

As he'd spoken, his words had grown softer. Eden could feel the raw pain the memory caused him as if it happened only a moment ago, though his voice didn't quiver and his words were calmly set forth. She saw that for him the pain was still fresh. He hadn't let the past go and it was killing his soul.

She shivered as she thought of the little life that formed within her body. She laid her hand near her stomach. Already she felt protective of the baby. Already she loved the part of her husband that grew inside her. Tears streamed down her cheeks as she reached up to touch Vladamir's forlorn face.

"I heard the midwife came to visit you," Vladamir said, changing the subject. "Are you ill?"

"Nay," Eden said with a dismissing wave of her hand. "Not really."

"What did she say?"

"Not much, she's a woman of little words." Eden wondered at his interest. She tried to assure herself that in truth she wasn't lying to him. She was only answering his inquiry with as few words as possible.

Vladamir nodded. A soft scowl lined his face before he once again smiled at her but the smile didn't reach into the blackened depths of his eyes as it did before.

Eden toyed with the band on her finger. She heard the shout of soldiers in the distance. The softened glow of the bonfires as they were lit by her father's men could be seen on the edge of the wall. Shivering, she realized the besieging knights had moved the fires closer to the castle.

"Do you think my father will come soon?" Eden asked. "Do you think he'll bring King Alfred?"

"Yea." Vladamir turned his hard face to follow her gaze to the bailey wall. A soldier walked along the black stone, his silhouette outlined in the ghostly orange light. Eden shivered anew. Vladamir remained emotionless. "Since I'm a hostage and your father is a nobleman of Wessex, he'll come. 'Tis better for us if he does. Alfred is of sound character. His ambassadors are not always thus."

"Do you think he'll let the marriage stand?" Eden asked, revealing her deepest fear. Her hand moved from his knee to rest on the protective strength of his chest.

"I know not," Vladamir frowned. He didn't look at her as he took his arm off of her shoulders.

"Mayhap with Luther gone, my father won't protest so much." Eden tried to force a hopeful expression to her features. "What's done is done, mayhap he'll see that."

"Nay, the hate between your father and me runs deep. He won't agree to it unless the king makes him." Vladamir stood and moved away from her.

"Do you think you'll be sent back to Northumbria for slaying Luther?" Eden asked, standing next to him. She knew if he were, she would go with him and willingly. She would miss her homeland, but without Vladamir by her side she couldn't be happy. When she put a hand on his shoulder, he didn't move at her touch, giving her no encouragement.

"I know not." The duke moved from her, he lifted his black tunic and pulled at the pouch hanging from his belt.

Taking out an object, he abruptly handed it to her. It was a gold band encased around a perfect oval ruby. Eden took the ring and looked up to him in surprise. She was about to say something when he interrupted her.

"Methought you were right. The king would be more believing of this marriage if you had a ring. This one is better than the pitiful band you now wear." Vladamir's face was emotionless. He took up her hand and pulled the ring from her finger a little too roughly before throwing it to the ground. As she looked at his eyes, he was gone, left behind was the familiar emotionless monster. Eden slid the more expensive jewel onto her ring finger and he continued in the same dead tone. "I also sent a new gown to my chamber. I suggest you see to any adjustments that needs be done to it. The king will be here on the morrow."

"But how do you know?" Eden rushed to his departing back. She wanted to reach out and touch him, but he effectively pulled away from her.

"I saw his banner from the wall. He'll rest and be here on the morrow." His accent became more pronounced in his ire. "See to your alterations, m'lady. I have much work to do."

Eden watched Vladamir depart with a sense of alarm before rushing back to pick up the old ring he discarded. Foolish as it seemed to her, she couldn't part with it. Her face was pale as she glanced around the empty bailey. Feeling alone and abandoned, she trembled in apprehension. Indeed there was much to be done and not enough time to get it done.

Chapter Fourteen

Eden straightened her shoulders until it felt as if an iron rod had been shoved alongside her spine. She stood, donned in the gown Vladamir laid out for her. It wasn't as lavish as the wedding tunic, but still of very rich quality. Only this one was of a completely different color. The brownish-red overtunic hugged her body tightly, just like the wedding gown had and the rounded neckline was cut high, opening just at the neck. If she hadn't known better, she would've thought the gown was trying to strangle her. The sleeves were lined at the elbows with delicately embroidered roses of gold thread. Under the shortened sleeves was a gauzy fabric that flowed out over her hands and fluttered as she walked. Not having a wimple and veil to match, Eden pulled her hair back to rest in soft curls over the crown of her head.

Next to her was Gwendolyn in blue linen. The gown was less lavish than her mother-by-marriage's as it had been one of the smaller gowns. Eden had ordered it let out to fit the child. There had been no time for anything else. The child slept the entire day of her arrival and through most of the night. It made little time for Eden to talk with her new daughter. Not that it mattered. There was a silent bond of compassion that ran between them that needed no words.

Eden spent the night alone, not sleeping as she waited for Vladamir to come to her. She wanted him to hold her, to make love to her. She wanted him to tell her it was all right and that they would be together always but he didn't come to her in the night. Only very early that morning did she see him slip into their shared chamber. He washed briefly in the tepid water basin and changed his clothes and not once did he try to wake her as she pretended to sleep only a few inches away.

Soon after he left, Eden quickly dressed and went to prepare Gwendolyn for their visitor. She found the child already clothed in the blue tunic she'd set aside. Eden learned from the girl that Vladamir visited his daughter soon after leaving their chamber. She quickly arranged the child's hair, pulling it back with a light blue ribbon. Then, borrowing a ribbon out of Gwendolyn's trunk, she tied it to her own hair to adorn her upswept curls.

Eden felt her stomach flutter in nervousness as she directed the servants. She had Haldana start the preparations for a large eve meal in anticipation of the king's visit. She ordered the bedchambers abovestairs readied, in case the king wished to stay. Eden wanted to make sure there would be nary a thing that would displease his Majesty.

"Yea, Lizbeth, pour that over the rushes but do it gently as not to stir too much dust," Eden instructed when she saw the servant woman come from the kitchen. Lizbeth carried a sack of scented powder, which she poured to scent the rushes. The servant frowned as she tended her task. Raulf was still in bed recovering from Vladamir's attack the previous morning.

Eden ignored the grumpy maidservant as she turned to Gwendolyn. The child watched the preparations quietly. "Shall we sit?"

"Yea," Gwendolyn consented with a tilt of her chin. The action would rival the most proper of queens.

She carries herself just like her father.

Eden watched the child walk. The girl didn't even seem to notice the stares she received all morning. Eden silently shook her finger at several of the maids when the girl wasn't looking.

"Gwendolyn," Eden said as they climbed the platform to the high table. "I should tell you what is happening today."

"Father already told me this morning. He said the king was coming to see whether or not you were able to stay married to him. He told me not to worry that the king would most likely give his blessing, eat all of our food and then leave."

"He said that?" Eden gasped. Surely the duke was just trying to calm the child of any fears.

"Yea," Gwendolyn admitted, demurely sitting on the chair meant for her father. The child smiled sweetly up at Eden as she did so.

"Did he say aught else?" Eden asked, taking a seat next to the composed girl.

"Yea. He told me that the earl was the reason the marriage was in dispute. Father said I wasn't to discuss it with you as you'd only get upset but methinks that you can handle knowing. Methinks you're not so weak as he would believe you to be."

Why would Vladamir think to warn Gwendolyn not to speak of my father's anger? I already know the situation well and I'm already most unsettled by it.

Eden gave Gwendolyn a quizzical expression, urging the child on.

"Knowing of what?" Eden prompted. Her heart caught in her throat as she saw the duke enter from the bailey. She'd never seen him as such. He was handsomely dressed as a nobleman, in a lavish black overtunic lined with silver threading. The neck of his tunic revealed an undertunic of fine black linen. His clothing looked new, though they were of the same color. On his feet were new leather shoes, a pair Eden had never seen.

Standing at the sight of her father, Gwendolyn answered, "Methinks that Father thought you'd not understand, for he's not my real father."

"What?" Eden stood. Turning, she then knelt by the child and pretended to fuss with the girl's dress. She ran the back of her hand over the skirt, smoothing it of any wrinkles. Glancing at Vladamir in his slow approach, she silently urged the girl to hurry.

Gwendolyn nodded to her father and gave him a small smile. Keeping her face piously intact, she tried to clarify, "Lord Kessen is my real father, but not my birth one. The earl is my birth father. That is why he has come to dispute the marriage. Methinks he wants to make sure I have a good mother. That is why he comes to inspect you. So don't worry, I'll tell the king I'm happy and you'll stay. Please, 'tis a secret so you must not tell my real father, the duke, that I told you."

Eden felt the color drain from her face. What could she say to that?

Of course, that is why you look like me. You're my sister. It would make sense. Father was in Northumbria several times around the year you'd have been conceived and visited many times the following year.

Eden's mind railed at the thoughts that swam in her head and turned to Vladamir as he approached.

"Eden, don't tell," Gwendolyn insisted with a tug of her mother-by-marriage's gown. She looked incredibly vulnerable as she peered up.

Numb, Eden nodded in agreement. She tried to give the girl a reassuring smile as she patted the child's hair. Vladamir came closer. With a motherly pinch to Gwendolyn's cheek, Eden winked at the girl. Vladamir's eyes were on her and she couldn't focus her thoughts away from him.

"'Tis time," he said. "The king arrives."

"Please, m'lord." Eden needed to tell him about the baby, needed to talk to him alone. Suddenly, she felt like a fool for not telling him of her pregnancy when she had the chance. Guilt choked her as she looked at his handsome, emotionless face. One minute was all she needed to clear up all that was between them. "We must speak."

"Nay, there is no time for that," Vladamir answered softly. He took her arm and led her down the platform. He motioned Gwendolyn to go ahead of them. "He rides this moment."

"But there are things we need to say," Eden said under her breath out of fear. She clutched nervously at his arm.

"Yea, I know," he returned in his usual terseness, forcing her fingers to relax. She saw the unyielding light in his eyes. "You wish to know where I got the gown and the ring."

"Well, yea, among other things," admitted Eden in confusion.

You know that isn't what I'm saying!

"I am rich. The door you felt in the secret passage, all my gold is there along with yards of fabric, gold, jewels, clothing," the duke said without remorse. "Your wedding tunic and the gown you now wear were of the few I had stored there."

"But," Eden said pulling him to a stop. At first she thought he was joking until she saw the truth in his eyes. "Why?"

"I have had no need for riches here. I prefer to live simply." Vladamir frowned at her eager face. He narrowed his eyes and leaned toward her. "If I'd known m'lady had such a need of finery, I would've gladly locked her in with it."

"Nay," Eden protested in mounting annoyance. "I care naught about finery. I have told you that. However you could've told me, you could've trusted me."

"Because you always tell me the truth?" Vladamir yanked her arm as he stalked out of the main hall.

Eden's feet dragged behind him in silent protest. She didn't want to see her father or King Alfred. She wanted to go back, wanted to start over, beginning with the moment she saw her husband in the darkened hallway and he'd kissed her for the first time. Eden trembled at the memory as she stumbled behind him. Tears of hopelessness welled within her. He quickened his pace, leading her harshly by her arm.

"Vladamir, stop. Please. We need…" Eden's words trailed off as she desperately tried to get his attention but it was too late. The main gate was already being raised. Its screeching echoed the bailey like a summons.

Vladamir didn't turn to her as he kept a steady eye on the gate. Gwendolyn was at her side and the child tentatively put her little hand in hers, leaning into Eden's side. Eden squeezed Gwendolyn's hand in automatic reassurance, keeping her eyes steadily on her husband, waiting for him to turn to her, to give her a brief smile. She was disappointed.

The inharmonious clank of the gate stopped overhead and was replaced by the slow-moving hoofbeats of horses as the mounted knights crossed the earthen threshold. Eden turned to the gate in despair. Her heart choked any last words of protest she might have managed to pass through her throat.

Eden recognized her father first. The earl rode his stallion proudly, though his face was marred with the tired lines of days without rest. He grimly refused to look at his daughter as he entered the bailey beside the king. King Alfred was donned in a tunic of royal blue, the rich material rivaling any in Wessex in expense and make. He looked regally majestic as he swung from his horse.

Giving Gwendolyn a reassuring smile, Eden nodded to the girl. The child watched the men approach with open interest. Eden bowed her head, but curiously kept a close eye on the king from beneath lowered lashes.

The few guards who entered with Alfred also dismounted. They wore the armor of soldiers with the banner of the king set firmly above them on a pole. The king's men stayed close to his side as he approached. From the stress on their carefully guarded faces, it was clear they expected there to be trouble from the foreigner.

Holding up his hands, Alfred let the man to his side pull off his riding gloves and ordered them to stay back with a singular motion of the hand. Then somberly coming forward, he stopped in front of the duke. Vladamir knelt before the king, prompting Eden in her dazed state to curtsy belatedly.

"Get up," the king ordered quietly. He took Vladamir's hand briefly as he stood. Looking around the bailey, he said,

"Methought this place would be in ruins from what I have been told of its upkeep."

Vladamir smiled politely, obviously not at all surprised the king had set spies on him. "I owe that to my wife. The cleanliness is her doing."

With that the king sighed. Turning his attention to Eden, he smiled kindly. "Lady Eden, I presume?"

"Your Majesty." Eden presented her hand as she once again curtsied. She lowered her eyes briefly. The king raised her fingers to his lips and gave her a light kiss.

"What things you have been up to child," the king stated with a half-hearted chuckle as he gave a short nod of his head.

"Yea, majesty." Eden agreed. Her cheeks pinkened at the man's attention.

"Shall we go in?" Vladamir motioned toward the main hall. "I can have food set out."

"Nay, I have dined already once this morning. No need to do it again." King Alfred glanced at Gwendolyn for a moment. As he cleared his throat, he paid the child little heed. Eden was glad he refused to dine. She didn't think she could force food down her throat, for her stomach churned too badly as it was. The king motioned the earl forward. The man had been waiting impatiently by his horse and as he approached his feet stamped loudly on the earthen ground. "Come Clifton, let us settle this business."

Eden met her father's eyes for the first time that morning—the same eyes that she and Gwendolyn both carried. She wanted to yell at him and beat his chest for what he'd done but refrained. Her father was the first to look away.

Without further comment, Vladamir led King Alfred and the earl into the main hall. A small sense of pride overwhelmed him at the cleanliness of the castle and the fresh smell of the rushes. He narrowed his eyes and glanced blankly at his wife. She'd gone pale, her hand clutching nervously at his arm. Next to her was Gwendolyn, the girl's hand wrapped around that of his wife. His daughter gave him a shy smile, which he returned with a quick wink. Gwendolyn blushed and grew giddy at the attention.

Allowing Alfred to be the first to move up the platform to the head table, Vladamir watched as the king took his usual seat of honor. The earl sat next to Alfred. Then leading his wife up, the duke sat on the other side of the king. Gwendolyn looked nervously about as Eden sat next to her father. There were no more chairs. Eden grabbed the child and sat her on her lap. Gwendolyn smiled up at her and leaned naturally into her arms. Vladamir felt his heart lurch as Eden whispered into the child's ear eliciting a giggle from the girl.

Soon after, the knights entered and were allowed to stay to bear witness to the proceedings. They seated themselves quietly amongst the benches of the lower dining tables. The servants brought in pitchers of mead at Eden's quick prompting. Then as the last of the goblets were filled and pitchers were set at the tables, the servants were excused from the main hall.

Vladamir stood and led his wife and daughter back down the platform steps. Eden trembled next to him. They had been sitting in torturous silence for so long that she felt she might not be able to speak. As they alighted on the hall floor Alfred, who had been whispering to the earl, motioned Clifton down the platform to also stand before him.

Eden leaned down to Gwendolyn. "Just listen, unless the king asks you a question directly. Then answer as best you can."

Gwendolyn nodded, her eyes brimming with anxiety.

"Your Majesty," the earl said. Eden stood and hugged the child to her waist, putting her arm protectively on her thin shoulders. Gwendolyn buried her face in Eden's skirt. Vladamir had to force his eyes off them. Clifton moved to the foot of the platform in front of the king. "I must insist we convene the Witan. I demand justice."

"Not yet," the king answered with a lift of his hand. His voice was loud and clear as he spoke, but he could've whispered and one would've been able to hear him in the quiet hall. "My lord earl, you have served my late brother well. That won't be forgotten. But 'tis a delicate matter we have afore us and I won't have a public trial made of it. I'd rather see this handled as quietly and quickly as possible. I'm sure for the interest of continued peace between the Danes and Wessex you'd agree."

"Yea, Your Majesty." Clifton clenched his teeth, but kept his mouth shut as Alfred continued.

"I have heard your side. I'd hear the rest from Lord Kessen." The king silently looked to the angry men for many moments before inquiring. Vladamir proudly lifted his chin. "Lord Kessen, did you kidnap Lady Eden with the intent to marry her and deprive the earl of his alliance with Lord Luther?"

"Nay, Your Majesty," Vladamir answered coolly. His accented voice sent chills over his wife. Eden trembled at his side as she leaned into him and stiffly took his arm.

"Then how is it you're here, Lady Eden?" the king asked, confused. His brow rose as he awaited an answer.

"I was brought here." Eden's voice cracked under the stress and she cleared her throat.

"Explain," the king commanded.

Eden glanced to her father and then to her husband. Vladamir turned to her giving her a firm nod. She shivered uncontrollably. He wanted to comfort her but couldn't for he didn't know what to say.

"Lord Luther was my intended, 'tis true. He tried to consummate the marriage afore 'twas done." Eden took a heartening breath and looked to the floor in embarrassment.

"Lies!" Clifton shouted, raising his hand as if to slap his daughter, but stopped when he caught the eye of the king. "He makes her speak lies! She is afraid of him."

As her father lowered his hand, she said to him, "'Tis not a lie. 'Tis the truth. Luther bid me to meet you in a hunting party. He said you wished for me to join."

"Lies. I haven't hunted since your mother was alive," Clifton said.

"That is what I told him but Luther was insistent." At her words, a murmur rose over the hall. Turning an apologetic expression to the king, she proceeded, "Luther wished me to bed him and his friends on the forest floor. I refused. He beat me senseless, killed my maidservant Lynne and left me afore Lakeshire Castle for dead. I later learned, *from Luther*, that he wished my husband the duke to be blamed for my death so he could still get my father's land and title. If not for the kind attentions of Lord Kessen and his servants I'd have surely died. I owe Lord Kessen my life."

"Lynne ran away from service. There has been no body found," Clifton offered the listeners weakly, swiping the side of his mouth with his fist.

"She is dead," Eden said confidently. "I saw it. No one would think to look for a body lying beneath the earth and if you were to look for her would you not send Luther and his men?"

Clifton glared at his daughter. "That doesn't excuse your actions in defying me. Luther was your intended. 'Tis his right by law as your husband to do what he wanted with you."

"He wasn't my husband yet," Eden answered definitely in return.

"According to the law he was as good as." Clifton dared her to disagree with the hard stare of his eye.

"Nay, according to God's law, Lord Kessen is my husband," Eden argued. "And none can deny that!"

"Not without my blessing! I won't give it. You have been living in sin," Clifton bellowed, his tone rising with each breath. "You're a whor —"

"You don't have to give your blessing, 'tis done!" Eden broke in before her father could say the word. "It cannot be undone!"

"And why not?" raged Clifton. "If I so wish it?"

"Because I'm with child!" Eden shouted at the top of her lungs for all to hear. Vladamir stiffened under her hand. The nearby soldiers gasped and muttered once more amongst themselves. Just as suddenly, the noise stopped. The hall sat in stunned silence, awaiting the next surprise.

Vladamir felt his heart stop at her loud confession, remembering the day he found out about Lurlina's condition. He'd barely touched his first wife in months when she became with child. He was afraid that Eden would tell him the child wasn't his and that she didn't wish to be a mother. Just like Lurlina hadn't wanted to carry Gwendolyn. Vladamir swallowed over the knot in his throat. His stomach tightened as he thought of his wife's past deception. Now wasn't the time to speak of it.

"But he is a murderer! He murdered Luther to keep you from marrying him," Clifton finally managed after a long pause. "Methinks he has cluttered your head with nonsense. You're not with child! 'Tis not possible! I won't have it!"

"Nay! It wasn't murder," Eden said. "And whether you will it or not I'm with child. The midwife discovered it just yestereve. The babe will come with the spring."

Vladamir kept his mouth shut and his eyes cautiously blank as his wife silently pleaded with him through her long lashes. His heart twitched in his chest as a tear lined her lower lid but didn't fall. He'd been waiting for the mention of Luther's death but he knew that the king liked to begin at the beginning and ascertain as many of the facts as he could before making a judgment.

Eden turned to the king. "'Twas not murder. Luther started the quarrel."

The King held up his hands. He watched the heated battle between daughter and father in silence. Looking about the hall at the captured eyes of the fighting men, the king frowned slightly. Finally he stood and stepped down from the platform. Holding out his arm to Eden, he said, "Come m'lady, walk with me."

Eden's panicked eyes traveled to his and the duke begrudgingly let her go with the king.

"Eden?" Gwendolyn whispered. The small sound tore at his already aching heart. "What's happening?"

Eden dropped her hand from Gwendolyn, giving the child a reassuring smile. Touching the girl's face, she said, "Stay with your father. Everything is going to be just fine."

Vladamir nodded stiffly as his daughter glanced at him for confirmation. She nodded, moving closer to his side. Awkwardly, he patted her shoulder, resting his hand for a brief moment. The slight contact brought a small smile to his wife's and daughter's faces. Eden took a deep breath as she placed her hand on the king's arm.

The duke could but watch as King Alfred led his wife away. Every muscle in his body bunched with the desire to go after her, to protect. A murmur rose over the crowd. The king took her to the curtained area where the soldiers slept. Stopping, he turned to the two nobles and ordered, "There will be no fighting while I speak with Lady Eden in private."

Eden's heart fluttered nervously as the king led her toward the knights' pallets, guiding her behind a hanging curtain and then another, until they were far from the dining area. Catching a glimpse of a straw mat on the floor she shied away from the man. "I'm true to my husband, Your Majesty, I cannot lay with you."

Alfred chucked at that and glanced at the pallet, a smile lining his lips. "I'm glad to hear it, m'lady."

Eden relaxed as the king didn't move to follow her small retreat from him.

"You're with child?" His kind eyes smiled at her. He was a young king, boyishly handsome and fit, yet his bearing was such that he looked older.

"Yea, majesty," Eden answered dutifully. "I am."

"I knew Luther. I believe what you say about him for I have heard well the tales that surrounded the man," Alfred said after some thought. "How did you decide to marry Vladamir? He doesn't appear to be such a choice for someone like you."

"Like me?" Eden gasped in offense.

"Nay, I didn't mean to insult you, m'lady. I'm merely trying to ascertain what happened." The king smiled politely. "I have no wish to embarrass you in front of the knights for if you stay here as duchess you'll still have to command their respect. I won't have you humiliated beyond good reason and things were starting to be said of a most personal nature."

"Your Majesty, my husband is an honorable and noble man and he has treated me kindly." Eden relaxed, appreciating Alfred's thoughtfulness.

"To hear your father tell it, he viciously ravished your maidenhead. Are you sure you're not just vulnerable to his...*charms*?" Alfred scratched his bearded face and gave her a skeptical look.

"Nay, majesty," Eden denied with a small laugh. "As you might imagine, the duke's charms are quite unique. Methinks that they are not such that could persuade a woman against her very nature."

"Well put." King Alfred nodded. "So he has treated you well?"

"He has been gentle with me, majesty. He didn't bed me until after the vows were spoken." Eden blushed, knowing that the king wouldn't stop questioning her until he'd the whole truth. She held his gaze bravely. "And he gave me the choice to marry him. He didn't force me in any way. All he did was ask me what I wanted. I decided to marry Lord Kessen by my own free will."

"I see." Alfred nodded his head thoughtfully. "Then he is a kind lover?"

"Yea," she answered, embarrassed. Heat flamed her cheeks and she was forced to turn her eyes downward. She wrung her hands nervously.

"I don't mean to be personal and embarrass you with such things m'lady. You must understand that there is a lot at stake and I must make the best decision. This is not only between two households. This is between two kingdoms."

"I understand." Eden nodded, still refusing to look at him in her discomfiture. "I'll do my best by my husband and country."

"I'm glad to hear it," he said gallantly. "Now, has Vladamir ever treated you unkindly? In any way?"

Eden swallowed, unsure as how to answer. Sure, her husband had been prone to his moments. "He hasn't been unjust in his treatment of me or the people here and though his emotions are well hidden, a quality very becoming of a leader, he has treated everyone within his power with fairness if not kindness."

"They think he is a monster," the king insisted. "Do you not agree?"

"Nay, majesty." Eden's eyes shot up in defense. "I won't deny that those of a superstitious mind tend to believe the worst in him but he's not a monster. He's a man—a good, loyal, honorable man—and he has only acted justly both toward me and you, majesty."

"What of the blood on the bridal linen? 'Tis said there was an ungodly amount." The king watched her carefully and she knew he was waiting to see if she would lie about it to him.

"Because Lord Luther had beaten me senseless, methought that he might have violated me in other ways.

Without being sure Vladamir gave me a vial of blood so that if I wasn't a maiden no one would know of it." Eden swallowed nervously. "M'lord was sweet enough to let me sleep that first night without pushing himself on me. The next morning, I spilled the vial on the bridal linens so my father wouldn't take me away. I'm afraid I didn't know what I was about and must have done it wrong."

"But the marriage is now consummated."

Eden nodded.

"And as to your maiden status?"

"Intact, my liege. At least it was."

Alfred nodded again in thoughtful contemplation of her answers. "Continue with your story then. How did you decide to wed Vladamir? Had you met him afore your visit here?"

"Nay, I heard tales of him, 'tis true, but I had never met him. I couldn't wed such a man as Luther. He would share me with others. When I met Vladamir, he was so kind and so handsome."

The king chuckled but said nothing.

Eden demurely bowed her head, ignoring the king's skepticism. "When he asked me to marry him, I agreed. It seemed a good decision at the time and methinks 'tis still a wise decision."

The king still said nothing.

"Majesty, if I may?" Eden questioned, moving her gaze boldly to him.

"Please," Alfred said.

"This is a good alliance between two noble households and what better way to ensure peace than to align two prominent families together. Surely you know of the ties my husband has with King Guthrum's family. Vladamir's daughter is King Guthrum's own grandchild. What better reason for a marriage is there? Luther is gone and his money lost to my father. Vladamir is titled higher than Luther and I'll wager he is just as wealthy. Besides, I already carry his heir. Would you see me shunned and my child called bastard to assuage the anger of one man?"

"You speak wisely for one so young," the king said quietly.

"Then why not choose the side of wisdom," Eden persisted. "You have the power to make my father see his error. My father is a good man and he is loyal to Wessex. If you decree it, he'll obey."

"That you love him there is no doubt. It is truly an extraordinary, albeit strange, match. But why is there so much hatred between the two men?" King Alfred slowly held his hand to her. "For I feel there is more here that I'm not being told."

Taking a deep breath of air, she held back the tears that entered her eyes. With much hesitation, Eden said, "'Tis because of his daughter, Lady Gwendolyn."

* * * * *

Vladamir waited with Clifton in charged silence. The warring nobles refused to acknowledge the other. The hall was quiet except for the occasional whispers of the men. He wondered what was taking so long. He trusted the king to be honorable, but for the first time he doubted his instincts. Jealousy ignited in his chest as he imagined the king taking royal advantage of his wife. Just as he was sure he could wait no longer and was going to storm the curtains to rescue her, he heard their footsteps approaching.

Eden's face was pale and drawn. By the king's urging, she walked silently to her husband. Vladamir searched her face for a sign of what transpired. He read nothing there. She moved to her place between her father and husband. She quietly took Vladamir's arm with her hand and squeezed nervously.

"I have not made a decision," the king announced solemnly. "I desire time to reflect on what I have learned. I'll also need to question a few people afore I make my judgment."

"My castle is yours, majesty," Vladamir stated.

The king smiled briefly at the irony of the statement and nodded. "I wish to speak with Lizbeth. I understand she was present when m'lady learned she was with child. Also, I'd see the midwife."

Vladamir nodded. Eden loosened her hold on her husband's arm. She motioned to a nearby soldier to go and retrieve the servants.

"I'd also speak with your man Raulf," the king stated simply. "I have questions for him also. Methinks he would be of great assistance to me."

"Yea," Vladamir agreed a bit hoarsely. Eden closed her eyes.

"My lord earl, ride back to your camp and await me there. Today the gates to the castle will remain open. There will be no aggression on either part." The king stepped up on the platform and took his seat. Taking a drink of mead, he announced, "I'll give you my decision tonight. That is all."

* * * * *

The king wished to question the servants and soldiers alone, so they left him in the hall. Eden followed behind her husband silently. Her eyes strayed lovingly to the dark stone walls of their home. She wanted to live forever at Lakeshire with her husband. She knew the king listened to her, but he didn't give away what he thought his decision might be. She knew Raulf was still in bed and was just now beginning to get his voice back. When she'd dared a brief visit to him, but he'd been asleep so they hadn't spoken.

Raulf, the king sent you here. Please be evenhanded in your discourse with him.

Vladamir sent Gwendolyn to her chamber to relax and ordered that Haldana attend her. As he escorted Eden abovestairs, they heard the child telling the servant everything that had happened in the hall. Her childish voice filled with excitement as she could be heard bouncing about her chamber. She didn't miss a single detail.

When they reached their bedchamber, the duke silently shut the door behind them. He turned to her, his dark eyes disclosing nothing. "Did the king hurt you?"

"Nay, he only wanted to ask me some questions." Moving to the bed, Eden sat down. "I hate this thing. I cannot breathe. Methinks I'd much prefer to be a servant right now. Everything is so much easier when you're a servant."

Vladamir sighed in understanding. He went to the bed and leaned against the poster. He too pulled at his overtunic's neckline. "What did he ask that couldn't be said in the hall?"

"My father said that you ravished me. Methinks the king thought I was being persuaded or threatened by you." Eden looked up into Vladamir's hard face. "But I told him you were kind and gentle with me and that we didn't lie together until after the marriage. Methinks he wanted to be sure I wasn't forced to wed with you. I said I wedded you by my own free will and that I'd stay married to you by the same."

"What of the babe? Why did you not tell me of it yesterday in the garden?"

"I…" Eden stood and moved timidly away from him.

"I have the first of my three questions. I expect you to be honest. Why did you lie to me?" he persisted, not going after her. "Did you think the midwife wouldn't tell me of it when I questioned her? Did you not think she would tell me what was ailing you?"

"You knew?" Eden gasped, spinning around. "Why didn't you mention it to me?"

"I was waiting for you to tell me of it but you didn't. Not even after I entrusted you with the truth of Lurlina's death. Why?"

"I was afraid." Eden's eyes welled with tears. "I was afraid you wouldn't want me anymore and you didn't. Lizbeth said noblemen didn't like to touch their pregnant wives and that you would no longer have a use to bed me. And she was right."

Eden spun away from him in embarrassment. Her thin shoulders shook. Vladamir went to her in two long strides. Taking her by her frail arms, he turned her gently to his chest. Wrapping her in his strong embrace, he pulled her close to his heart and held her tightly. He rested his chin on the top of her perfectly coiffured hair.

"I hate when you bind up your hair like this," he said softly, tugging at the ribbon. Eden sighed, but didn't answer as her tears wetted his tunic. It felt so good to be held by him. The heavy length loosened about her shoulders. Vladamir caressed her back in loving strokes as he pressed her to him. "M'lady, you really need to stop receiving advice from the servants. They fill your head with such nonsense."

"But you didn't come to me last eve and I waited all night. This morning you didn't even try to wake me." Eden sobbed into his chest.

"I didn't come last night because I knew you were not being honest with me. If you'd have told me the truth I'd have carried you to bed myself."

"But," she lifted her head to look at him, searching his face. "I'm with child now. You'll get your male heir."

"Mayhap it will be a girl." Vladamir smiled, trying to make her laugh. She weakly hit his arm at the attempt and he moved to wipe her tears. "Begetting heirs is too noble a reason to bed you. I wish you understood, wife, I'm not so noble."

"Then you won't cast me aside?" Eden asked, brightening. "You won't replace me with another?"

"Nay, I could never cast you aside." Vladamir laughed with a mischievous glint to his eyes. "Besides in several months you'll be too big to cast anywhere."

"And the child? You're pleased?"

"Yea, m'lady." Vladamir sighed as he ran his hands over her arms. Lightly, he touched her flat stomach. "Greatly."

Eden grinned. Running her hands over his chest to his neck, she peeked demurely up at him. "What will we do about the king?"

"We will await his decision." He moved to sit on the bed, taking his wife with him. Tugging at the laces hidden on her shoulder that bound her tunic together, he set about undressing her.

"I told him the truth. I told him that it would be in the best interest of Wessex and peace if he let the marriage stand. Methinks he'll make my father agree to it." Eden closed her eyes before looking longingly at him. "But I have to confess something. I don't want you to be mad at me or at Gwendolyn. She truly didn't mean harm."

"What?" Vladamir questioned warily, only pausing fleetingly in his task.

"I know that she is my sister. I haven't told her nor did I tell her of her mother's deceit. She believes her mother died trying to save her. Methinks 'tis best if she continues to believe it." Eden sighed but rushed on before Vladamir could speak.

Vladamir listened to her words but wasn't deterred from his purpose as he discovered another knotted lace and set to work.

"The king wished to know why there was bad blood between you and my father. I had to tell him. How could I not?" She hoped he understood. "He won't say a thing. I made him understand that Gwendolyn is your daughter, our daughter and the granddaughter to a king. I told him Guthrum wouldn't want the news of Lurlina's transgression about the countryside. Methinks the knowledge is best kept hidden."

Vladamir nodded his head. "You did right. I was trying to tell you last night. King Guthrum is the only other person, save

311

Haldana and Ulric, who know of Gwendolyn's real parentage. He wished to save the embarrassment of Lurlina's unfaithfulness becoming known. 'Tis part of the reason I was chosen to come here and given the title of duke. He wished me gone but he also wished for his granddaughter's lineage to be secured. We made an agreement."

"But I wanted to hear no more of it yestereve," Eden finished for him. "That is why you didn't tell me."

"Yea," he admitted.

"I'm glad he sent you here to me for you have saved me."

Reaching up to cup her husband's handsome face, Eden moved her fingers into his hair. Pulling him to her, she whispered, "Kiss me."

Vladamir was already intent on doing just that. He stroked her cheek before pulling her softly to his lips. He swung her into his arms and laid her tenderly on her back, pressing her into the soft mattress with his weight. There were no more words between them on what was happening. There was no need. The future was uncertain, but promising. The past was over. There was only the present and presently Vladamir was intent on making love to her.

His lips captured hers for a long time, kissing her slowly. She savored each sensation, loving the way his tight body molded to hers. Moaning softly, she ran her hands through his long hair, caressing his face and neck.

Vladamir pulled back, gazing deeply into her eyes. "You're so beautiful."

"And I think you're the most handsome man I've ever seen." She smiled, running her hands over his face as she gazed at him. It wasn't a lie. Eden didn't care about a few scars. "Make love to me. Please, Vladamir."

He grinned, the devilishly handsome look that made her body shake with lust. His tongue flicked over her mouth, licking along the seam, teasing her as he adjusted his body. "Mm, there is one thing I've been longing to do."

Eden's eyes widened in surprise. She thought of his cock in her mouth, her pussy, her ass. What else was there? "More than we have?"

"Oh, yea, much more," he nodded. "I want to taste you as you come against my mouth, but first let's get you out of these clothes."

Eden squirmed as Vladamir insisted on undressing her. She tried to help, but he shooed her hands away. He took his time, lightly kissing almost every inch of flesh as he exposed it—working up her legs, her hips, her breasts. By the time she was laying naked before him on the bed, her sex was so wet and hot she thought she would die from it.

"Now you," she urged, again trying to reach for him despite his order to hold still and let him have his way with her. With a wicked look, he pulled off his belt. Her eyes watched his hands, eager to see his beautiful cock. Eden parted her thighs, so ready for him. Instead of continuing to undress, he took the belt and fingered it.

Straddling her legs, he ordered, "Give me your wrists."

She hesitated, eyeing the belt. What was he doing?

"Trust me," he said, smiling. "Now, give me your wrists."

Crossing them, she held them out. Vladamir wrapped the belt around them and then tied her to the bed. When her hands were trapped, he grinned.

"Much better," he said, nodding at his handiwork. "Now I can have my way with you."

"Take off your clothes," she urged him, wanting to see his body caressed by the orange of the firelight. "Let me see you."

Vladamir obeyed, standing by the edge of the bed. His muscles folded and flexed with each movement as he stripped. Eden groaned, wiggling against the bed as she pulled at her wrists to be free. Why did she ever let him tie her up? If she was free, she'd be tearing the clothes from his body. If she was free, she'd be on her knees, licking his cock into submission, drinking down his salty come.

"Untie me," she demanded, licking her lips.

"Not on your life." He chuckled. His chest was bare and he set to work on his braes, kicking his shoes off. "I might just leave you like that, tied naked to the bed, your thighs parted and ready for me, your wet pussy glistening and hot."

Eden worked her feet against the mattress, but nothing she did seemed to give her aching sex any release. "Mm, please."

Vladamir pushed the material from his hips. His cock sprung free and she groaned. As she watched, he took the large shaft in hand and stroked it. It only seemed to grow bigger. Cream dripped from her sex, wetting the cleft of her ass with her desire. His fist swallowed up the thick head and he groaned.

"Please," she begged, her knees flailing back and forth.

"I like to hear you beg for me."

"Please," she said again, drawing the word out and thrusting her hard nipples up into the air. "Please."

Vladamir groaned, crawling back onto the bed. He settled between her thighs, kissing her breasts as he massaged them in his palms. Wondrous sensations shot through her at his touch. She thrust her hips, trying to rub against him, but he pulled back.

Licking a hot trail down her sensitive stomach, he rimmed her navel. Then working lower he finally kissed the top arch of her pussy. Eden jerked, gasping for breath.

"You taste better than I remembered," he groaned, vibrating her with the low animalistic sound.

He twirled his tongue around her clit, thoroughly torturing the bud with the light strokes. She threw a leg over his shoulder, pulling at her wrists to be free, as she tried to force him more fully to her. The duke was too strong and continued to tease her.

"Oh, please," she begged, unable to think of anything else. Every nerve focused on his mouth and hands.

His fingers dug into her thighs, keeping her where he wanted her. Gradually he increased the pressure of his mouth, working his tongue up and down her slit. With each pass, he probed up into her channel, lapping up her cream and moaning in delight.

"So good," he moaned. "I want you to come for me."

Eden was beyond words. Vladamir thrust a finger up inside her, wiggling it around. She gasped. This is what she wanted. Her cream helped him slide easily as he continued to suck her clit, nibbling and licking in turn. Then, taking his wet finger, he slid it to her ass and slipped it inside the tight rosette. She jerked, instinctively tightening. Her body let loose more cream and she couldn't hide how she enjoyed his wicked probing.

"Ah, you like that, don't you?" Vladamir growled. He slipped a finger back into her pussy, probing both holes at the same time. "Oh, yea. I can see how you like this."

His mouth became more aggressive as he fucked her with his fingers. It was too much. Her clit throbbed and her body jerked, tensing as an orgasm racked her body. Eden cried out, not caring who heard her. Let all the king's men know what they did, let the whole world know.

As the tremors subsided, she fell limp against the bed. A light sheen of sweat coated her body. Eden moaned, unable to speak in the aftermath of such pleasure. Vladamir crawled over her, his thighs pushing hers apart. His hard cock slipped along her folds, her sex still wet from her incredible release.

The duke kissed her and she tasted herself on his lips. With a confident push, he thrust into her, filling her pussy to the brink. Working his hips in shallow circles, he pushed up. She watched his glorious body, dying to touch it but unable to with her wrists bound. Vladamir stared at her breasts, watching them bob up and down as he began to thrust in earnest. He pulled out, only to boldly thrust in, hitting her hard.

"Oh," Eden gasped, feeling the need return. The tension built once more. "Oh."

"You're so hot," he growled. "I want to fuck you so hard."

"Mm, I love hearing your voice." Eden met his thrusts, encouraging his roughness with her own.

Vladamir growled, pounding his hips as he continued to say wickedly delightful things — some of which she couldn't possibly understand but was more than willing to listen to. His hard cock jabbed into her, cramming her full. He closed his eyes, his tight body gorgeous as it worked above hers. Suddenly, she came again, the strength of it taking her by surprise.

Vladamir grunted a primal sound, tensing and shaking as he emptied himself inside her. Eden had never felt more fulfilled or more complete. Still buried deep, he collapsed on top of her, stopping to kiss her softly before untying her hands.

"Mm, I want to do that again," Eden said, smiling tiredly.

Vladamir laughed. "Yea, I know, fourteen times in one night. Just give me a moment to recover first, my insatiable wife."

Eden ran her hands over his shoulders, not caring that she was hot or that his weight was crushing her. Giggling, she teased, "All right, I suppose I can give you a few moments."

Groaning, he kissed her again.

Chapter Fifteen

ಐ

King Alfred stood solemnly before the gathered bailey. His royal cloak of purple stood out in a sea of the drabber colors worn by the men-at-arms. The knights respectfully waited in anticipation of the king's decision. Their low murmurs and speculations could be heard as they whispered amongst themselves.

The darkening sky was as foreboding as the mood of Lakeshire's inhabitants. Lightning flashed, contrasting the expression on Clifton's arrogant face. King Alfred ignored them all as he gazed quietly in reflective consideration at the evening sun. His face was devoid of emotion save for the thin line that edged his stoic lips.

For the first time since the siege had began, there were no bonfires burning in the distance. The king ordered the assault stopped. Though it had yet to fall the evening wind carried in it the threat of rain. Vladamir narrowed his gaze as he looked to the sky, remembering it had been such a day that brought his wife to him. He wondered if this day would be taking her away.

I'll fight to the death for her.

The duke was unable to fathom the idea of her leaving him. The image of Clifton taking Eden from him clouded his thoughts. He looked at the earl, his eyes hard as a falcon as he silently dared the man to try.

Vladamir stood with his arms around Eden and his daughter. For the first time since arriving in Wessex, he didn't bother with his well-cultivated persona of a beast. Too much was at stake in this moment for him to care. He was beginning to remember what it felt like to be happy.

Gwendolyn smiled confidently at her father as he squeezed her shoulder. Never one to lie to her, Vladamir had told his daughter the truth of Eden's relation to her but following Eden's advice hadn't disclosed the true depths of Lurlina's betrayal. The child couldn't have been more pleased with the news. Now she'd a sister and a mother and, with the announcement of Lady Eden's condition, she'd soon have a baby to spoil.

Eden tried to ignore the angry stare of her father. A part of her ached deeply that they could no longer talk civilly for he was her father, faults or no. As he stood before her as proud and overbearing as he'd always been, Eden sighed for he also looked so worn, so old. She wondered if it was only their time apart that aged the man so readily, or if the absence only cleared her vision of him.

Lightning again streaked the heavens, this time drawing closer. The onlookers waited for the king to begin but the man only continued to stare at the sky in thought.

Eden spent the afternoon wrapped contentedly in Vladamir's embrace. After he released her from her binds, he made love slowly, in a way she hadn't thought possible. When they both found their sweet release in unison, he held her naked body in his arms while they slept. Then he awakened her with his gentle kisses to take her as his own once again. Eden wanted to tell him of the love that was in her heart but there had been no time for such words. Too much had been said already—it was just too much of the wrong thing. Besides she didn't want to put a hex upon the king's judgment.

"After much contemplation I have made my decision," the king began solemnly. For a moment he still looked to the gathering storm. The contemplation brought no peace to his face. Tired yet ever regal, he rubbed the bridge of his nose. "'Tis my belief that Lady Eden is indeed with child."

Eden clutched hopefully at her husband's arm. She glanced quickly at him as a small smile of exhilaration threatened her mouth and held her breath.

"'Tis also my belief that that child is Lord Kessen's." King Alfred turned his head thoughtfully to Clifton. He took a firm stance as he addressed the earl. "Lord Kessen is a duke. He is wealthy and he is titled. His marriage to a noblewoman of Saxon descent is good for peace. Since Lord Luther can no longer claim Lady Eden's hand, 'tis my decision for the best interest of the unborn child and of peace that the marriage stands."

Eden gasped in happiness. She yelped and jumped into Vladamir's arms. Pressing her lips in a most unladylike fashion to his, she nearly knocked him down with her excitement. His arms wrapped about her without hesitation to receive her thrilled kisses as she splayed them across his face. She heard her father's grunt of disapproval and didn't care. Behind them the victorious cheers of Vladamir's men rang out over the bailey.

"Bless the saints!" Haldana cried, clapping her hands in excitement as she smiled at the embracing couple. Ulric grinned his agreement next to her.

Beaming up at her husband, Eden pulled her lips away, knowing neither one of them cared who watched. The duke nodded slightly at Eden and squeezed her tightly to his chest. A smile of contentment shone on his proud face.

The king ignored the mayhem as his gaze momentarily turned to the ground. He crossed his hands behind his back as he waited for the excitement to die down bringing his head up when the earl started to protest.

"Nay, I demand justice!" the earl yelled when the crowd finally quieted enough for him to be heard. His own men frowned menacingly and growled behind him. At Clifton's yell, they demanded justice. Their hands strayed to their swords, drawing them partly from their scabbards.

Encouraged by their unwavering support, Clifton hollered, "I want to challenge Lord —!"

"Wait. I'm not finished." The king held up his hands for silence. Glaring at the earl's defiant men, he commanded loudly, "Put down your arms. There will be no bloodshed today!"

The gathering instantly obeyed the king's motion for silence and a stunned hush fell over the bailey. Clifton turned and he nodded to his men to obey. The men relaxed their arms but not their guard. The soldiers, who made up the majority of the gathering, jockeyed for position to better hear. Some of the men still rested their hands on the hilts of their swords anticipating a bloody fight.

"Your Majesty," Eden began in a loud clear voice. She directed an obedient curtsey to the king. Alfred granted her the permission to speak with a stiff nod. Eden couldn't keep the happiness from her words as she said, "If 'tis compensation my sire desires, he can have the inheritance I'm to receive from my mother's estate and I'm sure my husband and I can provide whatever else you see fit to give him. We are a family and 'tis our intent to act as such."

"Those are noble words, Lady Eden, but I'm afraid they are not necessary." The king took a deep breath as he hardened his face. The burden of his position etched itself in the fine lines to the side of his eyes. He rubbed his nose. Lightning flashed, carrying with it an apprehension of misfortune. Eden grew cold at the king's expression. "The marriage will stand as is but as I can find no evidence that Luther wasn't slain, I have to consider that he was unjustly done to death."

An undertone washed like a tempest over the listeners. Eden felt her limbs grow numb. Shaking her head, she looked up to Vladamir in confusion.

"Nay!" Eden protested, breaking through the throng's whispering with the cry. She braced herself to Vladamir, gripping his arm to her side. The duke stood motionless, his eyes steadily on the king.

Gwendolyn looked at her father, tears of panic welled up in her eyes in the confusion. Haldana rushed forward to her but stopped as the duke pulled the child to him. Vladamir hugged Gwendolyn to his leg.

"'Twas not murder!" Eden began, but was cut off by her husband's gentle squeeze. He shook his head as if to say, *Nay, m'lady, 'tis not the time for battle.*

Clifton grinned deviously to the crowd. His hands settled on his hips as he turned to stare at Vladamir and Eden. He rubbed his hands in pleasure as the king's voice steadily boomed over the yard.

"Vladamir of Kessen, Duke of Lakeshire, 'tis my decision and judgment that you're guilty of the murder of your noble peer, Lord Luther of Drakeshore and unless evidence can be produced otherwise, you shall be put to death. Hanging to be carried out on the morrow."

Eden glanced about in disbelief as she hugged Vladamir's chest. Her ears rang in violent protest. Her sight dimmed in agony. The bailey was silent save for the continued words of the king. Finally, her eyes landed on her father, beseeching with him silently to reconsider, to stop Alfred's decision.

"Lady Eden, you will retain the title of Duchess of Lakeshire Castle and the lands adjoining that title. As long as my blood is on the throne, they won't be taken from you or your family—on this you have my royal oath. Clifton, you and yours will have no claim to the title or the lands. You'll be paid a hefty *handgeld* for the loss of your daughter and whatever else she wishes to bestow you."

"That is outrageous!" Clifton yelled. "She is a woman! She cannot manage—"

"That is my ruling," the king said softly, though he was well heard over the silence. "Woman or no, this land will be hers alone. No other will have a claim."

The earl snapped his mouth shut. His jaw clenched with anger and his eyes narrowed in defeat as he turned them to Eden. She refused to return his stare as her eyes focused dazedly on the king.

King Alfred looked to the guard at his side and nodded his head. The man moved cautiously forward and took Vladamir by the arm. Eden pushed violently at the poor red-haired knight, who tried to pry her hands from her husband, but the duke didn't resist as they led him away.

"You cannot do this!" Eden protested through her tears. She turned her pleading eyes to the king as the soldiers dragged her husband into the main hall. Rushing to Alfred, she asked, "Where are they taking him?"

"Abovestairs," the king answered, the concern for her shone in his sorrowful expression. He didn't like the work he'd to do this day. "You'll be permitted to stay with him tonight if that is your wish."

Eden nodded barely able to hear his words through the blood rushing in her ears. A fog built in her brain and she forced her mind to clear. She would have to think if she was to save her husband.

"Please, he didn't murder Luther. I'll swear my life on it." Eden took a calming breath as she heard the fading steps of the men who led her husband away. She wasn't helping matters by feeling sorry for herself. "Luther challenged him, baited him to fight. Please, there must be a way to prove it."

"I wish that were so. But the men who are loyal to the duke claim he is innocent, the men in the encampment say he is guilty and they both agree that 'twas by Vladamir's hand that Luther is dead." The king shook his head in helplessness. His hand rose as if to touch her arm only to fall back to his side. "Your husband is a foreigner to this land. If I don't have the word of someone other than his contingency of men, I have naught. The nobles of Wessex will go after my throne if I don't act justly. One of their own is dead. If I were to pardon Vladamir, they would call me weak. I must have proof of his innocence. If the nobles attack the throne, this land will be torn apart. If not by our people, then it will be ravished by the Viking armies under Guthrum. They will know the land of Wessex is weakened. I cannot, I *won't* let my people die for the life of one man. I'm sorry, m'lady. I like your husband but I love my people and my country."

Eden understood well the king's logic and deep down she knew her husband would agree with it. If Vladamir caused no argument over the king's judgment, King Guthrum wouldn't attack Wessex. "Is there naught I can do?"

"I have tried to figure out another way all day m'lady. I cannot," the king sadly shook his head. "I'm sorry."

Eden watched the king walk away from her to her father. The earl's face was lit with a grim sense of superiority. As Clifton caught her eye, she held his stare in steady defiance. She narrowed her gaze and shook her head in disgust. The earl didn't smile. Instead he turned his face away from her.

"Gwendolyn?" Eden asked, dazed. She knew that Vladamir would want her to look after the child. Her hand shook as she moved blindly to find the girl.

"Yea," the child answered from directly behind her. Eden didn't know how long the girl had been standing beside her. She looked at the solemn eyes that reflected her own sorrow. Taking the child by the hand, she turned back to her father. Clifton gave a questioning glance at Gwendolyn. As the color drained from his face, his sunken eyes shot up to Eden in shock. It was clear he'd ignored the child in his anger. In that instant, Eden knew her father had no prior knowledge of the girl.

She nodded her head with a grim look of disdain and pushed insistently on Gwendolyn's shoulder to hide her from the earl's view. Hurriedly, she led the child away.

* * * * *

"Vladamir," Eden whispered, coming into their bedchamber. The king's men brought the duke to there and shackled him to the bed like the prisoner he was. Nevertheless, Eden was grateful that the king didn't throw him into the dungeon. Her eyes brimmed with tears as she looked at his beautiful form on the bed. His position reminded her of their earlier lovemaking—only their positions were reversed and these binds were for real.

At the sound of her voice, he opened his eyes and pulled up to sit on the bed. His strong arms lounged back behind him and his legs stretched out over the mattress. There was no fire in the cool chamber only a torch that sputtered dimly in its sconce.

Eden ran to him, throwing her arms around his neck as she planted fervent kisses on his forehead, chin and lips. She pulled him to her. Feeling him in her arms, she finally breathed.

As Vladamir lifted his hands to hold her, the chain that bound him to the bed clanked. Eden pulled back to study his shackled wrist in anguish. She let him scoot back from her so that his arms would reach fully around her.

"They didn't have to bind you." She endeavored to hide her tears so that he wouldn't see them. She tried to be brave for him, but her anguish reflected from her moist round eyes. "I'll tell them to unchain—"

"Yea, they did," Vladamir broke in with a soothing whisper. He nuzzled his head against her hair. "I'm a foreigner. To them I have little keeping me here."

"They're fools." Eden sighed as she pressed her trembling lips to his scarred chin. "I defy all of them."

"They are afraid I might try to escape," Vladamir answered, his soft accent music to her heartsick soul.

"And we shall," Eden said, smiling with a spark of hope through her grief. "I'll bite through these chains if I have to. We will run away, all three of us. Give me the key to the secret passageway. I'll take as many gold pieces as I can carry and give them to Ulric. He can meet us outside the castle wall. If we ride all night through the forest we can be free of this place. The king will never find us and in ten years when the winds of politics have again changed we might venture back. But if I never see my homeland again that is fine too for you'll be with me."

Vladamir closed his eyes at her words and shook his head. "I cannot ask you to live as a pauper in some foreign land for make no mistake we would be poor."

"I don't care. If we have to live in the trees like squirrels, I don't care! So long as we are together." Taking his bold face in her hands, she pleaded with him. "I don't care."

"Nay, even if I were to agree it would never work. Your father guards the castle and would never let Ulric pass. The gates will have been closed until the morrow." Vladamir ran his hands over her face, to the back of her hair. She'd bound it back once more to stand before the king. Again he pulled it free. Unraveling the waves with one hand, he pulled the silken strands to fall all around her face. He smiled sadly as he looked at her.

"Then we break down the wall around the secret lake. We will climb over it if we must." Eden tried, nonplused by his objections. "And then we will run away on foot."

"Nay, wife. I wish that it could be so." He gently touched her stomach, massaging it with his strong hand. "But don't think of us. Think of Gwendolyn and of our child you carry. Would you raise the children in poverty? Would you have them think their father a coward?"

"Yea, I'd live in poverty if it meant we lived as a family and the children would never believe their father a coward. I'll tell them of your bravery."

"Fleeing is not honorable. My life is not worth that of my family. You haven't lived in the world without privilege of station. At Lakeshire, you'll have a home. You'll have money—more money than you and the children could spend in thirty lifetimes." The duke smoothed back her hair and a sad smile of finality crossed over his face. "And don't forget. I'm a hostage here for King Guthrum. If I were to escape the peace treaty would be broken. Many would die."

"The king said that many would die in Wessex also if he didn't punish you. But 'tis not fair! Wouldn't King Guthrum be angry at Alfred for hanging you? If we had more time, I could petition King Guthrum for asylum. We could go to Northumbria, to your castle there. We—"

"Nay, I know King Guthrum well. He won't interfere," Vladamir broke in with a sad shake of his head. "What else did the king say?"

"He said that we only had to find one worthy man of Wessex to clear your name. Your men say you're innocent. Those of my father's men who were questioned say you're not. But I could find such a man. I will find such a man."

"Who? The earl is a respected nobleman and his men are loyal. You'll find no one. If there were any here to clear my name it would have been done already."

"I must try. I cannot let you give up. You must live."

"I have lived, darling wife, for the first time in my life—with you." He leaned against the head of the bed, a soft smile came to his face as he said, "I'm still owed two questions."

Eden nodded, knowing her husband too noble a man to run from his fate. She hated that he wasn't even willing to try an escape but that stubbornness was one of the very reasons she loved him—his honor, his stubborn pride, his loyalty, his fierce passions.

"Ask." She couldn't stop the tears that welled up in her eyes as she nodded her head, looking at his chest.

"Do you love me?" Cupping her chin in his hand he lifted her eyes to his. His black gaze captured her with its gentleness. "If you do not, don't lie about it. Do you love me? Or are you just scared that you'll be left to face your father's wrath alone?"

"How can you not know? I care naught for my father's wrath. I care naught for the will of a king. I care only for you. I love you. I have always loved you, only I have been too foolish or too afraid to tell you. And I know that you'll never care for me half as much as I do you. I know that you have no reason to trust me or believe me. But I love you. I love you. I love you." Eden shook him hysterically by the shoulders. "And because I love you, you mustn't die. You cannot. I won't let you!"

She let her love shine from her face, no longer hiding it. Grabbing the back of her head, he drew her to his eager lips, kissing the breath from her lungs with his desire. The chains rattled, but she didn't care.

"I love you, Eden. I always have. I always will."

Eden felt as if her heart would explode at the admission. Pulling her face away to study him, she nodded blindly through her tears. "What is your third question? You may ask anything of me."

"Nay, I have no need to ask it of you. Naught else but your love matters." Vladamir sighed against her trembling mouth. Their breath mingled as they silently gazed into each other's eyes. "It will give me the courage I need on the morrow."

"Yea, husband. You save your question. I expect you to ask me it on the morrow and everyday following."

"And if not on the morrow," Vladamir put forth gently, "then in the afterworld where you'll someday come to meet me. I'll wait for you if it comes to that."

"Nay," Eden sobbed, pulling him once more to her embrace. She shook her head against his shoulder in painful denial. The agonizing heartache that filled her overwhelmed her soul. She couldn't lose him, not now. They hadn't been given enough time together. "I won't hear it!"

Vladamir said no more as he held his wife in his arms. For the moment, he was content doing that. The feel of her would keep him strong for what he must face and the memory of her would sustain him in the afterlife. Her tear moistened his hand as it fell from her closed eyes. Vladamir sighed, pulling her closer. Whatever happened, in this moment, he had everything.

He pulled her mouth to his, passionately kissing her. Even if he lived for a hundred years he'd never get enough of her. She was his everything and he poured his soul into her. Vladamir didn't want to die. He didn't want to leave her behind. She was his soul, his life and he would carry her into his death.

A silent need passed between them as Eden straddled his waist. Her hand worked the laces at his hips, freeing his body. His chained wrists made it hard to move, but he managed to inch up her skirt. When she'd freed his cock, she lifted her knees, helping him to lift her skirts. Without bothering to remove their clothing, or part from the kiss, she rose above him.

His body was hard for her, always hard, and he was sure that being inside her was as close to heaven as anything on Earth could be. The first touch of her slick flesh made him groan. She seated herself on him, embedding him deep. Pulling back, she looked into his eyes as her body kept him in.

"I love you," she whispered, making his heart soar. Keeping him deep, she made shallow thrusts, riding him.

"And I love you." He breathed deeply, savoring the soft feel of her body holding his tight. Tears streamed down her face and he hated to see her sad but there was nothing he could say. If all they had was this one night together, then he would make the most of it. As their bodies climaxed, shaking with the bittersweet pleasure of release, he whispered, "I'll love you for an eternity, Eden."

Chapter Sixteen

හ

The dining tables were set up and the castle dined on the great feast Eden arranged for the king's visit, though none in the hall looked to be enjoying the banquet of food when she came to the main hall. She wrinkled her nose at the smell of roasted pigs. It wasn't the celebration she had in mind when she ordered the meal prepared.

Vladamir was spending time with his daughter. The child was having a hard time of it. Gwendolyn didn't understand why her family was once again being torn apart. Eden smiled sadly at the thought. The girl didn't cry over her fate, both father and daughter were strong that way.

The hall was eerily quiet. Many of the duke's knights looked solemnly to their trenchers when she entered. A few glanced wearily at her. One, a short balding man with missing front teeth, even dared to approach.

"M'lady, the men would speak with you. We have a plan," the knight said under his breath. "We will fight the earl's soldiers tomorrow if they try to take our lord. We will lock the king out and all die within the walls if need be."

Eden eyed the man gratefully. He had never dared to speak to her before. As she looked over to the long tables filled with Lakeshire knights, she saw his determination was shared by all. The men nodded grimly at her before turning back to their barely consumed meal and menacing whispers. She laid a hand on the burly man's arm. "I have spoken with my husband. He doesn't wish bloodshed on either side. His order would be to stand down. He'll act honorably and won't run from death."

"And you, m'lady?" the man spoke insistently. His gaze narrowed, awaiting her command. "What is yer order fer us?"

Eden hesitated. It would be so easy to goad the men into battle for she saw the ready light in their eyes. Closing her lids for a moment to block her tears, she breathed slowly. Then, directing a calm stare forward, she spat, "I care not what blood sheds on my father's side. I'd take up arms with you if I could."

The man nodded in approval of her heated words. A bloodthirsty glint entered his gaze as he glared to the platform where the king sat alone. Eden knew the man was one that hailed with her husband from Northumbria. The Saxons didn't dare to show such open disapproval of King Alfred.

"But as I wouldn't lose my husband by the noose," she looked steadily to the man, "I wouldn't lose him by dishonoring him. Stand down."

The man didn't like her order but agreed with a curt nod. He turned to leave, clearly intent on telling the men her decision but his frown turned to a grim smile as she whispered sharply, "For now."

The men listened intently as the messenger repeated her words. She didn't wait to see the men's reaction to her orders, knowing they were ready to fight and that she was ready to join them.

Spying the king sitting alone at the head table, she walked toward him, her face set with a determined frown. However, she couldn't make it to him before being halted again, this time by Lizbeth. Eden fairly glowered in frustration as the maidservant beckoned to her, "M'lady."

"Yea?" Eden stopped briefly at Lizbeth's soft voice. She didn't care to dine and she didn't care to direct the servants, having only come to the main hall to greet the king as their guest and to once more plead her husband's case.

"Are you al—?" Lizbeth began as she studied her mistress with concern. Eden shot her a hard look, not having time for such conversation. She had to save her husband.

"Not now, Lizbeth," Eden broke in, hissing through clenched teeth. Her eyes were hard as she turned them briefly to the stunned girl. Seeing her distress, Eden gave the servant a disheartened smile before she continued walking.

"Your Majesty." Eden's voice was strained. She halted at the bottom of the platform, curtseying. Her eyes met those of Alfred. His brown gaze shone with sorrow as he motioned her forward.

He sat alone in the main hall and didn't seem to mind it. Eden took her place in a chair next to him. He offered her a goblet of mead and she shook her head in polite refusal. She couldn't drink.

"How is he, m'lady?" the king asked, picking up his own goblet to take a leisurely drink. His motions were relaxed but they belied the turmoil in his eyes.

"Better than I, Your Majesty," Eden admitted. She looked demurely to her lap. The king nodded sadly and Eden noticed that his trencher of meat hadn't been touched. Looking for some time at the royal seal that encrusted the ring on his finger, she watched as he again raised his goblet to his lips. When he finished his drink, she said, "Majesty?"

"Yea, m'lady?" Alfred turned his full attention to her. He placed the goblet on the table and leaned to a pitcher to refill his own drink.

"May I speak plainly?" Eden asked in a blunt tone. She dared a direct look at him and didn't take her gaze away.

"Please." Alfred smiled slightly. He wasn't offended by her directness and didn't pretend to be.

"My husband is a rich man."

"M'lady, don't think it. I cannot change my mind for money." The king shook his head in denial and gently took her hand in his. Her fingers were cold but didn't shake. "There is not enough coin in the realm for such a decision."

"Then what will change it? Me?" Eden bowed her head. She tried in vain to hide her desperation. Her hand trembled in his.

"Methought m'lady would lie with no one but her husband." The king didn't release her hand but squeezed it gently.

"I'd lie with anyone that methought could save him," Eden said boldly. "Though I somehow knew you'd not be bribed, you understand that I had to try."

"And what would your husband say to that?" the king asked with a disapproving scowl. "Do you think that is the way he would have it?"

"I care not what he would have," Eden declared so none would hear but the king. She refused to think of Vladamir's first wife and the betrayal the woman put him through.

Besides, 'tis not the same thing. I do this to save him! I love him. I have to do something. I cannot lose him. He is everything to me.

"I'd have him alive. I could spend the rest of my life making him forget it," she said. "No matter how distasteful the act might be to me."

"There are some things in this world that men cannot forget or forgive," Alfred answered, still not bothering to pretend her words offended him. He patted her hand and let it go. "I much admire your courage, m'lady. You'll need it."

"If there is naught I can say to you to change your mind I should go to my m'lord husband," Eden returned, not acknowledging his compliment. She stood on her unsteady feet. The King nodded in agreement.

Eden strode away from the head table and the hall with a solemn dignity, holding her chin up high and not letting her distress show to the people who watched. They would be looking to her on how to act and she couldn't disappoint or dishonor her husband. But as she neared the stairs, she narrowed her eyes to keep them from tearing over with despair. She was running out of options. King Alfred was as honorable as her husband was. Although she respected that honor, she also cursed it.

* * * * *

"What are you doing here, my lord?" Eden spat. Her eyes rounded in anger as she saw the earl by her husband's door. Glaring at him, she spoke through clenched teeth. "You're not welcome in my home. You're not welcome in my sight. Begone!"

"Eden." Her father rolled his broad shoulders as he took a step for her. Eden stood about an inch above him, so he only had to tilt his head slightly to talk to her.

"Nay, sir," Eden argued before he could even state his purpose. She placed her hands boldly on her hips, daring him to try and lay a hand on her. "I'm a duchess. You'll address me as such. I'm no longer your daughter. You have ruined my life."

"So you did marry him to spite me," the earl concluded, though the bitterness had disappeared from his words. "Methought as much."

"Nay, I married him to be free of Luther. I married him because I love him." Eden skirted to the side in an effort to move past him. The earl's hefty weight blocked her way. Coldly, she said over his shoulder, "An emotion you know little of."

"Don't speak to me about love!" Clifton said, raising his voice slightly. He poked his finger in the air as he spoke. "I buried twelve sons afore they even took a breath. I buried a wife."

"That is not love, that is loss," Eden claimed, shaking her head. Again she tried unsuccessfully to move past him. He placed his hand on her husband's door to stop her from leaving.

"Yea, I lost them but loss is part of love. 'Tis the way of the world." The earl's eyes cut into slits and his face turned red. "Did I not show you love?"

"Nay, you sold me to the highest bidder." Eden lifted her skirt and tried to move around him in the other direction. "You showed me I was a bartered bride."

"I did what was best for you." The earl once again shifted his weight so she couldn't pass. His eyes were wide, gleaming with the conviction of his words. "What was best for Hawks' Nest and her people!"

"Nay, if you wanted what is best for me, you'd have left me be." Eden chopped her wrist angrily against his hand causing it to fall from the heavy oak door with a thud. Pushing her way past him, she laid her hand on the latch to open the door. She would have left him in the passageway but was stopped by his next words.

"Regardless of what you think of me, I didn't know she was married," the earl said quietly. Eden shivered at the raw emotion in his words, fingering the latch but not pushing the door open. She waited for him to continue. The earl stepped closer to her. "And I never knew she carried my child."

"What do you want?" Eden refused to look at him. Her body was drained from all the fight. She was tired of arguing with the earl and wanted only to lie for an eternity in her husband's arms.

"I want to make it right. I want to talk to the duke."

Eden could feel her father move to the back of her. She felt his hand lay carefully on her shoulder. Finally, after a moment of silence, she said, "Be quick. I won't have you upsetting him. If he tells you to begone, I'll throw you out myself."

With that, Eden quietly pushed open the door. She led her father into the chamber. Moving to her husband's side, she stood before the bed where he sat with Gwendolyn. He looked up in surprise to see her enter without knocking. Then his eyes fell on Clifton. His face stiffened and he pushed Gwendolyn behind him, blocking her from the earl's view.

"What is he doing here, Eden?" Vladamir turned his hard stare to the earl. "Why did the guard let you pass?"

"There was no guard." She hadn't noticed before because she'd been focusing on her father. Eden looked at her father. The silence strained between them until she thought she might scream to break the deafening quiet. "What are you up to?"

"I sent the guard away. I told him that he was needed at the camp." The earl turned his broad form and shut the door behind him. "Most of the men are leaving today for Hawks' Nest. I'm sending them away."

Eden gripped Vladamir's elbow tightly, looking up at his handsome face, unable to help the pang of anguish that coursed through her. The duke glanced at her nervous grip and his eyes stared out at her in reassurance.

He said nothing as the older man spoke, but his eyes traveled over the man as he laid a protective hand on his wife's shoulder. The chains on his wrist clanked, giving a grave reminder of their predicament. Eden's frown deepened and she curled her lip into a sneer, refusing to speak.

"There will be no guard at the door tonight." Clifton couldn't meet their eyes. "And nary a man in the south forest. If you leave at dusk you could be well away from here. I'd send you money —"

"Why are you doing this?" Vladamir kept Gwendolyn behind him, trying to shield her from the man.

The earl didn't answer.

"There will be no need for that," Eden said. "My husband is too honorable a man to run away from fate."

Vladamir looked at his wife in surprise. She smiled mournfully back as if to say, *I understand and I love you for it.*

"I figured as much." Clifton turned his eyes away from the lovers' look. "But it never hurt to try."

"Why do you try to help us now?" Eden didn't bother to keep the fire from her tone. Suspicion lined her every movement. "'Tis your doing that we are now here. What do you have to gain?"

"Does the child know?" the earl asked with a slight tremor in his voice. He leaned to look around the duke, ignoring his daughter's accusing tone.

Vladamir nodded once.

"I didn't know Lurlina was married when I took up with her," Clifton said. "I knew none of the other men would touch her but I knew not why. Methought her dark and mysterious. I was going to ask her to wed me. After we had been together for less than a sennight I found out about you. I was jealous of you because you had her. Methinks my pride kept me angry all these years. When I saw her nearly a half year later, she was large with child. Methought 'twas your child. 'Tis what she told me. She also said that you ravished her like a beast and that you bewitched her into marrying you. There was naught I could do for I was an ambassador of King Aethelred in a foreign land. I couldn't break up the marriage of King Guthrum's claimed daughter. Methought your anger was born out of vanity. Methought that vanity killed Lurlina. I swear I never knew the truth of her deceit until…"

Eden watched her father's eyes swarm with the emotions of a broken heart. She'd never seen him cry. Her hatred of him faded.

"I later heard the rumors of her death. I heard how you killed her with fire while she slept with your child. I heard how your seed was spared but how you both were marked by hell for the deed. I hated you even more for the treachery." The earl rubbed his brow in anguish. "God help me, I loved her. I love her still. She haunts my dreams."

Vladamir relaxed next to her. She looked up into his handsome face, scarred from the fires of the past. She loved his face. She loved him.

The earl glanced at his daughter. "Not until this day when I saw the child standing next to you Eden did I know. She looks just as you did when you were a wee girl. Only her hair…"

Eden nodded. Her heart went out to her father. She'd never known he loved another. He never hinted such to her before.

"And then I knew the reason for your anger, m'lord. I knew that Lurlina's deceit wasn't yours. No matter how much I wished to think you dishonorable, you have shown yourself to be very much a nobleman." Taking a hesitant step forward, he looked Vladamir in the eye. "When I saw the blood on the head of my daughter's marriage linen, methought you acted the beast yet again. Methought the monster bewitched my daughter with his black arts just as you had with Lurlina. Methought you sought revenge because I had Lurlina's love. Now I know she didn't love me. She couldn't have."

Vladamir nodded. His hatred for the earl abated, until he realized he hadn't been angry about Lurlina's unfaithful deceit since he met Eden. He only held on to the past out of habit. He didn't love Lurlina, had never loved her. Not like he did Eden.

"She killed herself, didn't she?" the earl asked.

Vladamir froze. He glanced back to see Gwendolyn's white face. Her round eyes filled with tears. The child listened intently to every word. He gave her a wary smile. The girl didn't seem to notice.

"Yea," Vladamir answered softly, turning back to the earl. His heart broke as he heard his daughter sniff behind him. "She did."

"And you saved the girl from her treachery," Clifton concluded. "May I see the child?"

Vladamir nodded, still unable to say a word as he detected the light scent of his wife's hair under his chin. Hugging Eden to his side, he was content to let the past die, for it was finally over. His heart was free, lightened and at the same time saddened for it was too late to change his future. He wasn't foolish enough to hope that he had a chance to live. What was done would remain done. The king knew the earl wasn't there when Luther challenged him and wouldn't change his judgment on the word of Clifton. No, it had grown bigger than the petty jealousy and anger of two men. It had grown into a political trial and Luther's death had become a political event.

The duke rested his hand on Gwendolyn's head. "This is Gwendolyn."

Vladamir presented his daughter to Clifton. The earl nodded, studying the beautiful face of the young girl.

"Gwendolyn," Vladamir said with a calm loud voice. "This is your grandfather."

All knew the child heard the whole tale but Gwendolyn just smiled and accepted the change in her life as she had all others. Taking a step forward, she curtsied for the old man as her little voice sang out sweetly, "Grandfather."

Tears of appreciation came to the earl's face and he nodded his head in acceptance of his role in the child's life. He smiled gratefully at Vladamir and Eden. Kneeling, he studied the child's face before holding out his arms to hug her. The child walked toward him, letting him pull her tenderly to his chest.

Eden cried. She turned to Vladamir and buried her face into his chest. Outside, beyond the narrow slit of the window, it started to rain.

None of them moved for a long time. The earl pulled back to study his granddaughter's face before tugging her once more to his chest. None dared to break the tentative silence and outside the drumming rainfall only beat harder.

* * * * *

The pluvial dawn came too quickly. Eden and Vladamir didn't sleep. They made love all through the night—tender and slow. His eyes had stared boldly into hers as he moved within her. She refused to miss one detail of his pleasure-laden face as their bodies found a heartfelt release. Then afterwards, she lay quietly in his arms, whispering of her love for him and hearing of his.

As the sun peeked over the horizon, Eden felt her heart sink farther into her chest until it hardly beat. Vladamir's hand rested on her flat stomach and she knew he regretted the fact that he'd never see his child born. The duke had made amends with her father but it had come too late.

Looking up into the smoldering eyes of her husband, Eden squeezed him to her body. Her chest lurched as a pounding knock invaded their sanctuary. The king's man was signaling that it was time to go. Gazing at him through her tears, she kissed him, pouring her heart and soul into the embrace.

"I won't go. I cannot." Eden choked back her sobs. Shaking her head in denial of the future, she declared, "I cannot watch you die."

"You must," Vladamir said. "I cannot bear it if you're not there with me. I must see you. I must be able to see your eyes. I'd take the vision of your beauty with me."

"But," Eden tried in vain to protest. Her deadened heart ached as it thudded in her breast. Grabbing his tunic by the fistful she tugged violently at him. He moved to stand by the bed. "I want to die, too. I cannot live in our home without you. I cannot live at all. My heart won't beat without you here."

"Then I shall build us a castle amongst the heavens and await you there. Look to the clouds and you'll see it."

"Await." Eden shook, helpless. "Await my love. For life will be naught more than painful breath until we meet again."

"I need you to be strong." His face became a mask of stone as the door to the chamber opened. The young guard refused to look at him as he unlocked the duke's chains. Vladamir ignored the knight as he hushed to Eden, "I need you to be strong for the children. Promise me."

"Yea." Eden nodded. The knight pulled Vladamir toward the door. Her heart was pulled with him. She took a deep breath but didn't feel the air.

"Go to Gwendolyn." Vladamir flashed her a handsome smile. Eden's heart fluttered in her chest at the sight. Never had he looked more handsome or brave. She would keep that smile in her heart for always. "I'll see you belowstairs, lady wife."

* * * * *

Rain pelted the ground as it had all night. The sky was dismal and bleak. Lightning crashed in the distance, chased by a blast of thunder and more streaks of light. Sometime during the night hours a makeshift noose had been constructed right outside the castle wall. It hung from a thick tree branch with the free end tied to the saddle of a large stallion. Eden watched the wet noose swing gently in the softly falling rain.

Puddles of mud formed in the soggy earth. They soiled the hem of Eden's reddish-brown tunic gown and soaked her feet through her thin shoes. She hadn't changed her clothes nor had she bound back her hair. She let it hang free and wild about her shoulders as she knew her husband to like it.

She'd gone to Gwendolyn as her husband requested. He'd already told her in the night hours that he didn't want the child to see his death. Haldana refused to come out, so Eden had left her to attend their daughter.

"Eden."

The earl placed his hand at her elbow and she heard his voice through the numbness in her brain. She refused to look at him. Instead her eyes found Vladamir already standing by the noose. His long hair blew about his shoulders. Her heart thudded painfully at the sight of him and her eyes etched the memory of him on her mind. She wanted to always remember him as he looked now — so proud and strong and brave.

Eden knew that she had to be the same for her husband needed her strength just as she needed his. Ignoring the hand of her father even though she had forgiven him, she didn't want to face him right now. How could she? Clifton claimed he had tried to sway the mind of the king, but as they predicted it did no good. Luther's death held too much importance now.

Rushing forward through the silent gathering of men, she pushed past them until the crowd willingly parted to let her by. The men-at-arms watched her courage with awe. Sometime during her stay, the men had grown to respect and trust their lord. No longer were they suspicious of him. No longer was he called a monster behind his back. He was a man. He was a lord. He was their leader. And with one word from him they would turn and fight to free him. That order would never come.

Eden went to her husband and threw her arms about his neck. He leaned into her, unable to return her embrace. The guard had bound his hands behind his back. She soaked in the feel of Vladamir's body, trying to remember every curve, every detail. Her memory of him would have to sustain her for the rest of her life for she knew she would never love again.

Flattening her mouth against his, she refused to close her eyes. She wanted to see his face, his haunting gaze. Over his shoulder she spotted the king and knew she had no more words to offer Alfred only the silent defense of her eyes. He was unable to meet her mournful expression and had to turn away.

"You're my heart," Vladamir whispered in her ear. "You're my life."

"Wait for me in our castle," Eden softly answered. She grabbed his face in her hands and smiled bravely into his eyes. "For I'll wait for you."

Vladamir groaned. Tears formed in his eyes for the first time since the king's decree. Only Eden could see them as the rain slanted across his face. Soldiers tried to pull him away from her but she refused to let him go.

"Nay," she groaned. Her heart pounded in wretched torment. "Nay!"

Clifton grabbed her and pulled her back, forcing her to let go of her husband. Her weakened limbs couldn't ward off the insistent draw of her father and the soldiers.

Some of Lakeshire's knights swiped their eyes at her wretched screams, sure that the sound of her voice would forever haunt them and the surrounding countryside. Eden shook her head and held out her arms to once more hold him but it was too late. The guards walked the duke backward toward the noose. Vladamir refused to turn from her, keeping his eyes steadily on her face.

Eden caught his stare and forced herself to hold still. A knight offered the duke a cover for his head but he refused. Lifting her chin into the air, she was proud to be married to such a man. A slight smile curved her face. Defiant, she shrugged off her father's hand and stood tall.

"I love you," she mouthed. The men slipped the noose around her husband's beautiful neck.

Eden heard her own breath coming in loud pants of air. It was the only sound in her ears. She didn't take her eyes away, unable to believe that it was really happening. She saw the priest utter words of prayer over the crowd. It was the same man who'd married them. She couldn't hear his words, drawing no comfort from the man. In her breast was still the small flicker of hope that the duke would be saved. Then like a thundering strike across the rainy sky, the hangman smacked the backside of the horse.

Eden's heart stopped beating the moment Vladamir's body swung into the air. She felt the pull of deafening silence as the sound of her breathing stopped. The hands of her father slipped from her shoulders as she tore from his grasp. Running to stand beneath her husband, she reached her arms up into the darkened sky. The red depths of the ruby wedding band on her finger glinted far into the distance like a beacon. It was too late. He was too high to touch. The pain that flooded her limbs was worse than she could've ever imagined. She was dying too.

* * * * *

Vladamir closed his eyes for a moment as the rope went past his gaze. When he could again see her, the side of his mouth twitched up in a sorrowful smile. Everyone faded from his view as he focused on her. Her exquisite face shone with love, the long tresses of her hair blew heavy from the rain about her shoulders like an angel. Vladamir was sorrier for the pain his death would cause her, than the ending of his own life. He lived long enough to experience her love. He would die content in that.

His eyes clasped shut, the image of his wife with her mournful chestnut eyes and her wild-flowing hair recorded permanently in his mind. He heard Eden scream as the noose fitted itself tightly around his neck. The rope suspended him in the air, squeezing out the life from his body. His legs struggled to gain footing in the unforgiving wind. Lightheaded darkness consumed him and the blood rushed numbly from his head. In that moment, he knew that this was it. He was dying. And then his world went black.

Chapter Seventeen

ഔ

Eden couldn't move as Vladamir's body lost its fight. His legs stopped kicking in the air and his head fell to the side, no longer straining against the noose. She stood transfixed in an eternity of wretchedness and heartache, even though only a mere faltering second passed. The falling rain pelted the body of her husband as he swung motionless above her and still she heard nothing through the silence but the overpowering breaking of her heart.

Thunder crashed, lightning struck. The priest signed the cross over his breast and turned away. The men turned their heads from their leader's body, unable to watch its lifeless swinging but Eden held still and faced her fate bravely, handling the death better than any around her did. Her gaze stayed with her dead husband and her heart didn't beat again. A throbbing pain replaced the beating, it was a pain she knew would last all of her life.

Just as the reality of lost hope assaulted her and she was about to scream with the agony of it, Vladamir's body came crashing down from the gray sky. Her hands were still outstretched above her head. The duke's listless form fell to his feet, tumbling forward to land on his wife.

Eden gasped and clasped him to her chest, refusing to give up his weight to the many hands that rushed forward in confusion to help her. His unmoving form pressed her into the muddy earth, soiling the back of her gown, as his large size pushed her deeper. The breath squeezed from her lungs but she didn't care as she hugged him to her breast. She wanted him to crush her. Tears welled in her eyes. She wanted to die too.

And then through the wet black waves of Vladamir's hair, she saw Raulf standing above her. The bruise given him from her husband was still fresh on his neck. He was talking to her but she couldn't hear what he was saying. His lips moved more urgently as she held tighter to Vladamir, fighting the insistent pull of the hands.

Eden struggled to keep her husband to her. Raulf motioned some of the men to remove the duke from her body. As Vladamir was finally wrestled from her desperate grasp, she looked about in desperation. Her father was at her side, helping her to her feet but she fought his hands and those of others that only sought to help.

Eden stumbled to gain footing in the mud, lurching about like a lost child. Only when she was finally able to stand did she hear the excited murmurs of the crowd. Gradually, she noticed the rope to the noose had been severed and a guard chased after the runaway horse. The end of the sliced rope hung from the stallion's saddle as he galloped away.

"Back away!" Raulf yelled, breaking completely through her silence. The knight kneeled by Vladamir's side. "Back away! He is an innocent man!"

Through her bewildered haze she saw the king moving toward her fallen husband. Bitterly, she glared at him. Flinging her dirty hands in the air, she tried to work her way to where Vladamir's body lay. The heaviness of her wet tunic gown made it hard to walk. She fell to the ground, forced to crawl along the wet earth to her fallen love.

Getting closer, she stood and pushed a knight out of her way and into the mud. The man landed with a grunt and slid over the damp earth, knocking over several others in his glide. Eden didn't care as she pushed another man to the ground the same way. It seemed like an eternity before she was able to stand over the lifeless form of the duke.

She blocked the rain from his face with her soiled body, ready to fight anyone who dared to take him from her again. Leaning over him, she reached out. Suddenly, she stopped in astonishment, perceiving his eyes to flutter open. Skeptical of her own vision, she wiped her eyes with a fist and fell to her knees to look closer. She put a hand on his scarred jaw and he coughed. Eden gasped, finally able to breathe as sweet relief flooded her.

It cannot be!

Was she insane? She welcomed insanity if it brought with it her husband.

You were dead.

"He lives!" Raulf announced to the crowd.

Eden jolted back to reality at his words. Scooping Vladamir's dazed head into her arms, she hovered protectively over him. She would kill any if they dared to try and take him from her. The pain of losing him had been more excruciating than she could have ever imagined. She couldn't live through it again.

"Raulf?" breathed Eden, looking over the duke's chest to him. "Is it true? Am I dreaming?"

"'Tis true, m'lady," Raulf said heavily in relief. Then turning to the hovering crowd, he yelled, "Back away!"

"Please, Raulf, you have to help me get him out of here. Tell the men to fight. I order it to be so. To arms!" Eden hissed when Raulf turned back to her. "The king—"

"All is well, m'lady," Raulf broke into her panicked insistence. He directed her attention to Alfred with a toss of his head. "He'll live."

Eden looked over to the king who yelled, "Bring the royal surgeons!"

Under her palm she felt the steady rise and fall of Vladamir's chest. She couldn't believe that he was alive and once again in her arms. Looking to the sky, she let the rain mingle with her tears of joy. The grip over her heart lightened.

"'Tis sorry I am that I'm late," Raulf said at last.

"Raulf," Eden asked moving her loving gaze to Vladamir's peaceful but very living face. He was out cold but his color was fast returning to his flesh. Bruises formed on his neck where the noose held his life in its grip. "What is happening? I don't understand."

"The king is my cousin many times removed, but related nonetheless. He sent me here to keep an eye on Lord Vladamir and report back to him about his doings. I told him that I saw Luther challenge Lord Kessen," Raulf answered. He scratched his neck where the lightening bruise matched the duke's dark one.

Eden was stunned. Raulf was related to King Alfred? Overwhelmed, she tenderly stroked Vladamir's face. Her whole body flooded with relief. "But why would the king listen to you now? He didn't afore."

"The king didn't speak to me afore. Lizbeth told him I died from the pox," Raulf admitted.

Eden glanced up at him from her place in the mud. She stroked her hand over Vladamir's warm cheek.

"But why would she lie? I told her that my husband didn't mean to harm to you. He thought that we were lovers." Eden was angry. If Lizbeth had been there she would've killed the maid. She'd come dangerously close to losing everything. "She almost killed him with her stupidity."

"Nay, m'lady," Raulf answered protectively. "Don't blame her. She said that she tried to speak with you, but that you were not—available. She thought the king meant to hang Vladamir this eve. She thought we had time."

"More time for what? Tormenting us?" Eden spat in disbelief. "I'll never forgive such a sick and selfish game. He is my life. She might as well have strangled the spirit from me if she was to let him die."

"Nay, not torment, m'lady. More time for us to marry." Raulf defended Lizbeth stubbornly, all the time understanding the noblewoman's anger. He looked regretfully to the duke.

"What?!" King Alfred bellowed over them.

Eden and Raulf looked to the king in shock. They hadn't realized that he listened, that in fact the entire gathered crowd listened.

"Raulf?" Alfred inquired with a red face. "What have you done?"

"I'm married, cousin," Raulf answered with a boyish grin. He turned to impishly wink at Eden.

Eden stared back at him in stunned silence. Raulf was trying to look innocent and failing miserably as he nodded at his father in earnest candor. "You bid me to be under the duke's command, to listen to him and to learn from him. He gave his permission. Besides, you have many other men to form your alliances, my marriage is hardly of consequence to you."

Eden shook her head as she glanced up at the men. "I don't care to hear any more, Raulf, not until I know my husband is forever safe in my arms."

Raulf nodded in agreement. "Yea, Your Majesty. Let your men move him to his wife's bed. Methinks that would be the best place for him to recover."

The king waved his men forward but his face was set into a mask of stone as he watched his cousin. Eden ignored their silent quarrel. She saw the relieved face of her father in the crowd, nodding at her in relieved approval. His thin lips moved silently in a prayer of thanks. Eden waved him to her and he graciously complied. She leaned on her father's arm for support as the men lifted Vladamir and carried him under Lakeshire's gates.

As the excited throng moved back into the bailey spreading the news of the Lakeshire miracle, Eden heard the king exclaim behind them, "You married a servant!"

Nothing could've wiped the smile from her face as she walked behind the motionless body of her husband. He was safe and he was hers.

* * * * *

"Shoo! Go!" Eden ordered, excited. She waved the servants from the bedchamber with a frantic sweep of her hands. Her heart fluttered with giddy excitement and she nearly slammed the doors on the ogling girls before they were completely clear of the heavy wood. Sighing as she turned to the bed, Eden beamed. They were finally alone. Her lips trembled and her eyes brimmed with tears of joy.

Vladamir had been brought to their chamber as commanded by the king. A very relieved Gwendolyn was in the hands of her new grandfather and an extremely nervous, albeit happy, Lizbeth was being introduced to her new father-by-marriage. The king had only been partly upset by her lie and was mostly relieved that his son hadn't in fact died from the pox.

The king's personal surgeons looked the duke over and declared he would recover quickly, though he would need much rest. Although he'd only wavered in and out of awareness since his hanging, they were certain he would completely regain his wits by the nightfall. They also determined that he hadn't been without air long enough to do damage to his head.

Nearly leaping her way across the bedchamber to her prone husband in her happiness, Eden sat on the edge of the bed to watch over him not caring how long he rested. She smiled through her tired yawn, not willing to sleep until he looked at her and said her name. Only then would she relax her watchful guard.

The duke needed his rest but she couldn't help her delight. She'd informed the king that she would be indisposed — intent of spending every moment of her patient's recovery by his side. Leaving Haldana in charge of the kitchen and Raulf in charge of the soldiers, she made sure that their guests' every comfort would be met while she tended her beloved.

Everyone had been so relieved that he lived that they hadn't thought to worry about an illness. The king declared that it was nothing short of divine intervention and soon after the servants whispered that the hanging killed the monster that had overtaken Vladamir's body, freeing the real man trapped inside. Eden laughed as Ulric confessed their gossip. The old servant only smirked, saying one maid had even gone so far as to claim she'd seen the monstrous spirit leaving the duke's body.

Eden brushed back the tangled waves of Vladamir's hair from his face. He was caked with mud, his skin marred and darkened by the grimy earth. She had quickly washed the dirt from her own skin and donned a fresh servant's tunic while the surgeons examined her husband.

Running the back of her hand over his dirty face, across his bruised neck and down the front of his wet overtunic, she frowned. It was quite possible Vladamir could still die from a lung sickness if she weren't careful. Taking a clean coverlet that had been left by the bed, Eden unfolded it and laid it next to her husband's cold body. She pulled off his shoes and wet stockings, discarding them on the floor. Then crawling over him to the waistband of his braes, she lifted his tunic to expose the navel carved into his flat stomach. She tugged at the laces that bound his braes together.

Suddenly, she stopped when the exposed muscles of his stomach vibrated. Her breath caught in pleasure as a powerful thigh came up between her legs.

"I didn't molest you, m'lady, while you were helpless and within my grasp." Vladamir's voice was hoarse and low as his accent washed over her.

Eden grinned up at him, her breath catching on a relieved sigh. She let all her love for him shine on her face. With either hand along the side of his waist, she felt him suggestively push up at her sex with his thigh. Pleasure and desire washed over her, making her instantly wet to accept him.

"I don't know that for sure," she said lightly before moaning in arousal.

"And you never will. After all monsters cannot be trusted." He coughed at the obvious effort it took to speak but didn't stop smiling.

Eden grinned mischievously. "And neither can innocent maidens."

Vladamir chuckled at that only to wince at the effort. When he was finished, he wiped a drop of moisture from his eye and asked, "What happened?"

"You nearly died," Eden whispered with a painful lump forming in her throat. Her body quivered at the remembrance and she couldn't take her eyes from him. Part of her was still afraid that this was a dream and she would wake up to find he was really gone.

"That much I remember," Vladamir said. "For methinks I'm dead and you're my angel and we are in our castle above the Earth."

"Nay, m'lord, you're very much alive. But methinks we do float above the Earth and I don't ever want to come down." Eden braced herself as his leg once again pushed lightly at her sex. She moaned seductively as a spasm of gratification made its delighted way up her body.

"How is it so?" His lips curled into a provocative half smile and he flicked his tongue over the corner of his mouth as his eyes strayed to her breasts. Eden blushed. Vladamir growled. "Did you attack the king's army, lady wife? Are we at war even now?"

"Raulf." Eden sighed as Vladamir once again caressed her with his thigh. A deep fire raged through her blood at his nearness. Her heart pounded and her skin became flushed with arousal. She wanted to press herself to him, but held back, fearful of his health. "You had better stop that. You're in no condition to finish this."

"Nay?" Vladamir's devilish smirk widened. "Methinks my body says otherwise."

Eden glanced down at his prompting. Beneath her his engorged cock pushed against his unlaced braes. She gasped in amazement. "Just an hour ago you were dead."

"'Tis a wonder what an hour will do, m'lady." Vladamir reached his tapered fingers to her chin. Neither one of them noticed nor cared about the scars that marred his hand. "How is it that I'm here?"

"Raulf told the king that you were innocent. He was late because he had to marry Lizbeth first." Eden smiled when Vladamir suddenly stopped moving and frowned. She rushed to explain, "Raulf is the cousin of King Alfred. The king sent him here to spy on you. Raulf knew that if the king discovered his plans to marry Lizbeth he would never agree, so he married her in secret this morning. Since you gave them your blessing the king's priest didn't try to stop them. When the king tried to find Raulf last eve, Lizbeth told him Raulf died from the pox. Raulf was actually just hiding from his cousin until the wedding was done only Lizbeth got the time wrong and thought the execution was set for tonight. When Raulf learned that it was actually this morning, he left his bride at the altar and rode straight to the rope and cut you free."

Vladamir listened intently, pressing his thigh into her body as he tried to caress her.

"If he would've been a moment later you'd be lost to me." Tears streamed down her cheeks at the thought and she leaned down to rest her forehead on his stomach. His arousal pressed near the peak of her breast. She sighed in longing, trying to force back her desire so he could recover.

"Methinks this is fate, you and I," Vladamir whispered to her, stroking her damp hair. "'Tis beyond us to control."

Eden crawled up to him, moving to lie against his side, nestling into his arms. "I'm waiting for your last question, m'lord, for it will be your last. After this there need not be any more bargains between us."

Vladamir tilted his head in thought before whispering, "Would you promise to love me forever, lady wife?"

"Don't you know? I already have." Eden tilted her head to receive his tender kiss. His body turned so that he inched slightly above her. His lips moved over hers slowly. She sighed dreamily, knowing they had all the time in the world.

"Eden?" Vladamir moaned playfully against her mouth after a long moment.

"Yea, Vladamir?" Eden ran her fingers into his muddied hair. Her smile was brilliant as she gazed at his dirt-smudged face. Her heart poured out her love for him.

"What were you doing to me while I fainted?" the monster asked the woman he held captive beneath him.

The maiden just laughed bewitchingly as she pulled him back into her embrace. Her lips touched his and she kissed him, intent on never letting him go again.

Epilogue

ଚେ

Eden's body was sore from giving birth to her son two days earlier, but as she looked into his dark, already devilishly handsome face, she didn't care. The pain had been worth it. The baby had his father's looks, down to his sinfully dark eyes and hair until there was absolutely no mistaking who he would take after. Even his temperament was like that of his father—slightly incorrigible, incredibly demanding and ever sweet and loveable.

Vladamir held the baby in his arms as he walked around their bedchamber, rocking the boy gently. He smiled proudly, cooing to the babe and unmindful that he sounded like fool. The baby's fist pounded his father's scarred wrist. The duke laughed, looking at his wife. "Did you see that? He's not afraid of anything. He's ready to take on his sire already." Then to the child, he said, "You're going to be a great knight, aren't you Vlad? Yea, you are. Yea, you are."

Eden laughed, turning to Gwendolyn at her side to roll her eyes heavenward. Her daughter giggled as they secretly poked fun at Vladamir.

"I saw that!" the duke growled, turning to playfully grimace at them. Eden and Gwendolyn rolled with laughter as the duke charged forward, mindful of the delicate bundle he carried. Sitting on the bed next to his daughter, he kissed her lovingly on the head. The girl instantly reached for the baby, gently wrestling it away from her father. Eden giggled, watching them fight over who got to hold the baby yet again. Finally Vladamir relented and Gwendolyn took her brother to the end of the bed and laid him down to play with him.

Coming to his wife's side, Vladamir pulled her to his chest. "How are you feeling, my love? Better?"

"Mm, I am now," she answered, snuggling into his chest. Closing her eyes, she knew that this moment was perfect—just one of many perfect moments to come in her life.

"I love you, Eden," Vladamir said. "And I thank you for a fine son."

Eden laughed and returned wryly, "Yea, don't think you can sweet-talk me, monster. Haldana already told me you want twelve more from me and you can just forget it."

"But—"

"Nay," Eden growled, tightening her arms around his chest in a loving embrace. She giggled, not opening her eyes. "And I love you too."

"Fine, maiden," Vladamir said, kissing the top of her head. Gwendolyn's giggle sounded as she talked to baby Vlad. Eden sighed happily, almost asleep as she heard her husband whisper, "I'll just have to settle for eleven."

The End

Why an electronic book?

We live in the Information Age—an exciting time in the history of human civilization, in which technology rules supreme and continues to progress in leaps and bounds every minute of every day. For a multitude of reasons, more and more avid literary fans are opting to purchase e-books instead of paper books. The question from those not yet initiated into the world of electronic reading is simply: *Why?*

1. *Price.* An electronic title at Ellora's Cave Publishing and Cerridwen Press runs anywhere from 40% to 75% less than the cover price of the exact same title in paperback format. Why? Basic mathematics and cost. It is less expensive to publish an e-book (no paper and printing, no warehousing and shipping) than it is to publish a paperback, so the savings are passed along to the consumer.

2. *Space.* Running out of room in your house for your books? That is one worry you will never have with electronic books. For a low one-time cost, you can purchase a handheld device specifically designed for e-reading. Many e-readers have large, convenient screens for viewing. Better yet, hundreds of titles can be stored within your new library—on a single microchip. There are a variety of e-readers from different manufacturers. You can also read e-books on your PC or laptop computer. (Please note that Ellora's Cave does not endorse any specific brands.

You can check our websites at www.ellorascave.com or www.cerridwenpress.com for information we make available to new consumers.)

3. *Mobility.* Because your new e-library consists of only a microchip within a small, easily transportable e-reader, your entire cache of books can be taken with you wherever you go.

4. *Personal Viewing Preferences.* Are the words you are currently reading too small? Too large? Too... ANNOYING? Paperback books cannot be modified according to personal preferences, but e-books can.

5. *Instant Gratification.* Is it the middle of the night and all the bookstores near you are closed? Are you tired of waiting days, sometimes weeks, for bookstores to ship the novels you bought? Ellora's Cave Publishing sells instantaneous downloads twenty-four hours a day, seven days a week, every day of the year. Our webstore is never closed. Our e-book delivery system is 100% automated, meaning your order is filled as soon as you pay for it.

Those are a few of the top reasons why electronic books are replacing paperbacks for many avid readers.

As always, Ellora's Cave and Cerridwen Press welcome your questions and comments. We invite you to email us at Comments@ellorascave.com or write to us directly at Ellora's Cave Publishing Inc., 1056 Home Avenue, Akron, OH 44310-3502.

THE
✝ ELLORA'S CAVE ✝
LIBRARY

Stay up to date with Ellora's Cave Titles in
Print with our Quarterly Catalog.

TO RECIEVE A CATALOG,
SEND AN EMAIL WITH YOUR NAME
AND MAILING ADDRESS TO:

CATALOG@ELLORASCAVE.COM

OR SEND A LETTER OR POSTCARD
WITH YOUR MAILING ADDRESS TO:

CATALOG REQUEST
C/O ELLORA'S CAVE PUBLISHING, INC.
1056 HOME AVENUE
AKRON, OHIO 44310-3502

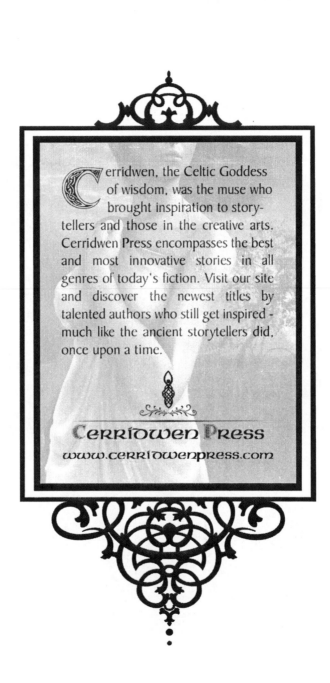

erridwen, the Celtic Goddess of wisdom, was the muse who brought inspiration to storytellers and those in the creative arts. Cerridwen Press encompasses the best and most innovative stories in all genres of today's fiction. Visit our site and discover the newest titles by talented authors who still get inspired - much like the ancient storytellers did, once upon a time.

Cerridwen Press

www.cerridwenpress.com